Beatrix Potter
The V&A Collection

The
Rain
It
Raineth
Every Day—

Beatrix Potter

The V&A Collection

THE LESLIE LINDER BEQUEST OF BEATRIX POTTER MATERIAL

watercolours, drawings, manuscripts, books, photographs and memorabilia

Catalogue compiled by
ANNE STEVENSON HOBBS & JOYCE IRENE WHALLEY
with the assistance of Emma Stone & Celia O'Malley

Under the general editorship of Joyce Irene Whalley

THE VICTORIA AND ALBERT MUSEUM and FREDERICK WARNE
London 1985

Published jointly by
THE VICTORIA AND ALBERT MUSEUM
and FREDERICK WARNE

Penguin Books Ltd,
    Harmondsworth, Middlesex, England
Viking Penguin Inc.,
    40 West 23d Street, New York, New York 10010, U.S.A.
Penguin Books Australia Ltd,
    Ringwood, Victoria, Australia
Penguin Books Canada Ltd,
    2801 John Street, Markham, Ontario, Canada L3R 1B4
Penguin Books (N.Z.) Ltd,
    182–190 Wairau Road, Auckland 10, New Zealand

First published in 1985

ISBN 0–7232–3260–1

Filmset in Great Britain by
Tradespools Limited, Frome, Somerset

Printed and bound in Great Britain by
William Clowes Limited, Beccles and London

British Library Cataloguing in Publication Data available.

Library of Congress CIP Data available

Half-title: PLATE I
Border of snowdrops, for photograph mount (cat.991)

Frontispiece: PLATE II
'Fishes come bite!' a frog fishing (cat.709)

Endpapers:
Endpaper designs No. 5 and No. 4 (cat. 949,948)

Front of case:
From *Peter Rabbit's Painting Book* (cat. 1885)

IMPORTANT NOTE

Availability of the Collection

Much of the material in the Linder Bequest is both valuable
and fragile and cannot be made generally available. Anyone
undertaking serious research on any aspect of the collection
should write to: The Chief Librarian, The National Art
Library, Victoria and Albert Museum, London SW7 2RL.
The researcher should state which items he or she wishes to
consult (quoting the reference numbers from the Catalogue
of the V&A Collection) and the date of the proposed visit
to the Library. Written permission is necessary before any
item can be issued to a reader, and the Library staff have
been advised accordingly. Unmounted items may not be
issued. This regulation has been made in accordance with
Museum practice and with the wishes of the donor, Leslie
Linder, to ensure the conservation of the Bequest.

General enquiries concerning Beatrix Potter should be
addressed to the Linder Collection, at present at the
National Book League, where a representative selection
is held for the benefit of the general public.

Other Potter material in
the National Art Library

The V&A Library houses a small collection of Potter
material independent of the Linder Bequest. This consists
mainly of books, but a picture letter dated 1911 was donated
by Mrs Fellowes in 1981 and a collection of photographs was
donated by Mrs Joan Duke in 1983.

CONTENTS

LIST OF COLOUR PLATES

*The page numbers given are those opposite the colour plates, or,
in the case of a double-page spread, those either side of the plate*

INTRODUCTION

The Beatrix Potter Collection came to the Library of the Victoria and Albert Museum on the death of Mr Leslie Linder in 1973. It consists of over 2000 items, and includes watercolours, sketches, manuscripts, first editions, photographs and various other memorabilia relating to Beatrix Potter and members of her family. Much of the collection had already been sorted and catalogued by Leslie Linder, and his own manuscript catalogue came with the Bequest, as well as the transcripts of letters, etc., made by his sister Miss Enid Linder. However a considerable amount of material remained unsorted, its provenance and documentation known only to Leslie Linder and so lost with his death.

The Linder Collection had been meticulously mounted and labelled, and housed in fireproof safes in a shelving system of Linder's own devising. Anyone who has worked on Beatrix Potter, as author or artist, admits the debt owed to Leslie Linder. He knew his collection intimately and had acquired much detailed information on all aspects of Beatrix Potter's life and career. His publication *The History of the Writings of Beatrix Potter* (Warne, 1971) is a model work.

When the Bequest was acquired by the V&A two particular aspects of the collection still needed attention, for Leslie Linder was neither an art-historian nor a specialist in children's books, and so no attempt had been made to place the material in the context of these two important areas. But the first task was to sort through the mass of material, both the catalogued and the uncatalogued. The Library was fortunate in obtaining the services of art-historian Emma Stone, who for nearly two years went carefully through the material item by item – some of them no more than rough scraps of paper – listing, numbering, locating and identifying the various pieces. Using Linder's own manuscript catalogue as a basis for at least half the collection, she gradually welded the whole into a usable form. Linder's method had been to group comparable items together, but basically they were distinguished by their location – in other words he had produced a finding list (albeit a detailed one) rather than a catalogue. The next task was to put the complete catalogue into a form most likely to assist the researcher wishing to consult the original material. Experience had shown that most enquiries came in subject form, and so a careful survey was made of the scope of the collection before deciding on a practical list of subject headings for the catalogue. The list of headings or sub-divisions of the material, as printed here, has proved its suitability over years of use in manuscript form.

Emma Stone's trained eye was particularly good at remembering and linking widely separated items, and identifying scenes and incidents from Beatrix Potter's œuvre; the form taken by the present catalogue is based on her work. The sorting and cataloguing of the material took nearly two years – and then the money ran out. The Museum entered upon a long period of stringent economy and the publication of the catalogue was one of many projects that had to be postponed. In the meantime interest in Beatrix Potter showed no signs of diminishing and the inaccessibility of the Collection, owing to the lack of a proper catalogue, was a source of great concern. The Library could have continued to use the (now well-worn) handwritten catalogue until times improved, but decided instead to publish the work, with all its possible inaccuracies and inconsistencies, in order to facilitate further study. The typing of the complicated entries was carried out by various helpers both inside and outside the Museum, the initial identification of the photographs was made by David Wright, and much of the preliminary checking and editing was done by Celia O'Malley with the general assistance of the Curator responsible for the collection, Joyce Irene Whalley.

The catalogue brings together for the first time the full range of Beatrix Potter's work. Tentative drafts and sketches, childhood letters and letters to publishers, first hints of well-known stories, and ideas which never came to fruition – these are recorded in all their complexity and detail. The editors have tried to achieve consistency in the arrangement and listing, but, as will be obvious to anyone reading through the catalogue, a mass of miscellaneous material such as the Leslie Linder Bequest did not readily lend itself to any kind of uniformity. Since additional information will undoubtedly come to light, a catalogue of this kind can never be deemed complete.

Joyce Irene Whalley
August 1980

Postscript

On the death of Miss Enid Linder in 1980, further material was added to the original Bequest (see Addenda section), as well as the mass of Linder papers (The Linder Archive – as yet uncatalogued) relating to work by both brother and sister in the field of Beatrix Potter studies. Their achievements are fittingly commemorated in the annual Linder Memorial Lecture organised by the Beatrix Potter Society. The delay in publication of the catalogue, during which time the Victoria and Albert Museum itself decided to undertake responsibility for its production, has provided the opportunity for extensive editing and revision and has made possible the compilation of a list of holiday dates and a comprehensive index. This work has been carried out by Anne Hobbs, who assumed responsibility for the Collection and the progress of the catalogue through the press on the retirement of the previous curator, Joyce Irene Whalley. The editors are greatly indebted to the designer Gail Engert, who has also assisted with editorial work.

J. I. W.
August 1983

The Catalogue

List of abbreviations

See also Appendix: Holiday Dates (abbreviations, p.225)

The Art	*The Art of Beatrix Potter* (rev. ed.) 1972
BM	British Museum (Natural History)
HBP	Helen Beatrix Potter (her earlier form of signature)
HBH	Helen Beatrix Heelis (her later form of signature)
Hist., H	*A History of the Writings of Beatrix Potter*, Leslie Linder, 1971
Journal, J	*The Journal of Beatrix Potter*, 1881–1897, 1966
LL	Leslie Linder; information supplied by Leslie Linder
LL Cat.	Information from Leslie Linder's manuscript catalogue (cat. 2149–50)
NBL	The Linder Collection, National Book League
RP	Rupert Potter
VAL	Victoria & Albert Museum Library (National Art Library)

L; R	left; right
MS	manuscript
n.d.	no date
w/c	watercolour
w/m	watermark

Location marks

F.	Folder (as S.14.F.A)
P.C.	Plan Chest (as P.C.45)
S.	Shelf (as S.14.F.A)
T.	Tray (as T.23.R)

PART I

Watercolours, drawings and other graphic work

EARLY WORK

Beatrix Potter was a very precocious artist. The Linder Bequest includes two early sketch books, done when she was aged 8 and 9 (cat. 1090 and 1091), which already show her interest in natural history and her obvious desire to draw all the objects or scenes which she saw in her daily life, or in her own imagination. Her father's sketch book (cat. 1121) suggests that she probably had his example before her, while her mother too produced more than competent watercolours. This group of material includes her work up to the age of 16 in 1882, with the exception of the early sketch books, which will be found in a later section of the catalogue. Inevitably much of the work is childish and unformed, and a certain amount of schoolroom work and copying is included. Nevertheless, as she reached her middle teens her work was showing great technical ability and artistic skill.

This section of the catalogue offers a curiously mixed selection of her work, but in view of its early date it seemed more appropriate to place it together; by the time Beatrix Potter had moved into her late teens, her work showed such maturity that it could stand comparison with the rest of her œuvre, and it is accordingly so placed in this catalogue.

Animals

1 A dead deer, with rough sketches of the same animal above and below.
Inscribed (above the lower drawing): July 24th 1880.
Inscribed (verso): At Dalguise (LL).
Pencil and wash. 25.5 x 17.5
BP.889   P.C.24

2 Dachshund.
Inscribed (verso): Cannot place this? We *never* had a dachs. H.B.P; also: About 1880? (LL).
Pencil. 15.5 x 23 (with shaped corners)
BP.890   P.C.24

3 Study of a donkey in harness.
Inscribed (verso): August 21 1880.
Pencil. 13 x 17
BP.1467   P.C.14

4 Study of a rabbit.
Believed to be a painting of Benjamin Bunny.
Inscribed (L): 1880.
W/c. 18 x 25
BP.272   S.5.F.B   (*see* PLATE III)

5 A recumbent rabbit.
Inscribed (on transparent cover): Peter, about 1880 (LL).
W/c. 17.5 x 25
BP.893   P.C.24

Birds

6 A canary and a green budgerigar.
Pencil and w/c. 26 x 17.5
BP.748   T.40.R

7 Green budgerigar.
Pencil and w/c. 26 x 17.5
BP.749   T.40.R

8 Sketch of a budgerigar, with two more flying in a
hilly landscape.
Inscribed: By Beatrix Potter (LL).
Pencil, on card. 16 x 25.5
BP.1200   P.C.18

9 Budgerigar with one wing spread.
Verso: Light pencil sketch of drapery (?).
W/c. 17 x 17, narrowing to 4.5 at top
BP.1195   P.C.18

10 Three blue-fronted Amazon parrots on a perch.
W/c, heightened with white. 15 x 18
Information from the Natural History Museum,
London.
BP.1197   P.C.8

11 Dead chaffinch.
Inscribed: Chaffinch August [1]9/79.
Drawn at Dalguise, Perthshire.
Verso: Part of a cupboard.
Pencil. 14 x 22
BP.274   S.5.F.B

12 Dead siskin, drawn at top of sheet.
Inscribed: Siskin, who died August 20th 1879
at Dalguise.
Pencil. 24 x 13
BP.275   S.5.F.B

13 Front and profile view of a dead yellowhammer.
Inscribed: September 3rd 1880.
W/c, on card. 14 x 18.5
BP.277   S.5.F.B

14 *Unused.*

15 *Unused.*

Buildings

16 Bolton Gardens. View through trees of roof-tops,
with a tower in the centre.
Believed to be Bolton Gardens, but failed to
identify tower (LL Cat.) [Tower is that of Natural
History Museum.]
W/c. 21.5 x 24
Verso: Part of a study of wallflowers.
Inscribed: June 1882.
Pencil and w/c.
BP.301   S.7.F.A   (*see* PLATE IV)

17 Bolton Gardens. Roof-top view with trees.
Verso: Cowslips in a vase.
Inscribed: June 1882.
W/c. 16 x 25
BP.302   S.7.F.A

18 Bolton Gardens. The back garden at 2 Bolton
Gardens (LL Cat.) showing part of the lawn, path
and wall.
W/c. 29.5 x 23
BP.303   S.7.F.A

19 A ruined tower on a cliff, with sailing boats in the
background.
Inscribed: February 1882.
Near Tenby? (LL Cat.)
Sepia wash with some pencil. 25.5 x 18.5
BP.283   S.5.F.C

20 Unfinished painting of a church steeple through
trees (R). Enlarged version of the steeple (L).
Inscribed: July 82.
W/c and pencil. 35 x 25
Verso: Unfinished painting of a ruined tower by the
sea, with a few experimental brushstrokes at the
bottom of the sheet. Near Tenby?
Pencil and sepia wash.
BP.885   P.C.35

21 Study of a barn with an open door.
Inscribed: 1882.
Verso: Similar study of the barn, but less complete.
Pencil and sepia wash. 25.5 x 33
BP.886   P.C.35

22 Camfield Place? Part of a country estate showing a
roadway with buildings and a well.
Inscribed (on folder): Camfield Place (LL).
Verso: Sketches of dogs.
Pencil. 8.5 x 6.5
BP.1035   P.C.21

23 Signalman's house (?) by a railway line; houses and
hills in the background.
Inscribed (verso): (See *The Art*. . . p. 33) October,
1877 (LL).
Pencil. 17.5 x 25.5
BP.898   P.C.24

Flowers

24 Bluebell.
Inscribed: Helen Beatrix Potter. July 5th 1877.
Pencil and w/c, on blue-grey paper. 18 x 11
BP.766   T.40.R

25 Yellow broom in flower.
Inscribed (verso): H.B. Potter July 5th 1877.
Pencil and w/c, on blue-grey paper. 18 x 11
BP.764   T.40.R

26 Three buttercup flowers and leaves.
Pencil and w/c, on cream notepaper. 14 x 11
BP.762   T.40.R

27 Red and white carnation in a blue and white jug
with a leaf pattern, on an olive-green wash
background.
Inscribed (verso): About 1880 (LL).
W/c. 21 x 16
BP.897   P.C.24

28 Two celandine plants with roots.
W/c, on cream notepaper. 8 x 9
BP.760   T.40.R

29 Various studies of cornflowers
(two are unfinished).
Verso: Study of geranium.
W/c, on torn sheet. 21 x 13
BP.904   P.C.46

30 Two cornflowers and two daisies.
Inscribed (verso): June 81.
Pencil and w/c, on cartridge paper. 23 x 21
BP.1163   P.C.46

31 Cowslips.
Pencil and w/c. 26 x 17.5
BP.747   T.40.R

32 Cranberries: berries and leaves.
Pencil and w/c. 17.5 x 14
BP.949   P.C.47

33 Forsythia.
Pencil and w/c, on blue-grey paper. 25.5 x 17.5
BP.757   T.40.R

34 Grasses: four different types (by R. Potter?).
Pen and sepia ink. 18.5 x 10
BP.774   T.40.R

35 Harebells and marguerites (above).
Light w/c sketch of purple heather (below).
Verso: Marguerites.
Inscribed (verso): July 5th 1880.
W/c. 34 x 21
BP.267   S.5.F.A   (*see* PLATE V)

36 Honeysuckle in full flower, with roughly painted
leaves.
W/c. 20.5 x 27.5
Verso: Rough study of broom flowers, the stem and
leaves indicated only.
W/c and pencil.
BP.946   P.C.47

37 Sketch of a blue hyacinth with leaves.
Verso: Pink hyacinth.
Pencil and w/c, on white cartridge paper.
26 x 17.5
BP.746   T.40.R

38 Drawing of a hyacinth in a pot.
Pencil. 12.5 x 8.5
BP.942   P.C.47   (*illustration overleaf*)

39 Iris flowers and bud with leaves.
Pencil and w/c, on blue-grey paper. 25.5 x 17.5
BP.758   T.40.R

38

44

40 Irises and other flowers in a vase.
    About 1876 (LL Cat.)
    Pen-and-ink. 24.5 x 16.5
    BP.772   T.40.R

41 Ivy leaves on a green wash background.
    Verso: Ivy leaves with tendrils.
    Inscribed: About 1880 (LL).
    W/c, on card. 11 x 21.5
    BP.888   P.C.24

42 Marguerite and a grass.
    Inscribed: July 5th, 1877.
    Verso: H.B. Potter.
    Pencil and w/c, on blue-grey paper. 18 x 11
    BP.763   T.40.R

43 Marguerites in a blue and white vase, with
    buttercups lying in front.
    Inscribed (verso): 1881 sum[mer].
    W/c. 22.5 x 26.5
    BP.266   S.5.F.A

44 Narcissus.
    Inscribed: 20 Nov. 1876 HBP.
    (LL Cat.): Age 10 years 4 months.
    Pencil. 25 x 18
    BP.273   S.5.F.B

45 Single narcissus stem.
    Pencil and w/c, on blue-grey paper. 25.5 x 17.5
    BP.755   T.40.R

46 Narcissus; also rough outline (unfinished) of a
    rabbit on right of sheet.
    Inscribed (L): Helen Beatrix Potter, March 1876.
    Pencil. 17.5 x 25
    BP.717   P.C.26

47 Three orchids of different types.
    Inscribed (verso): H.B. Potter July 5th 1877.
    Pencil and w/c, on blue-grey paper. 18 x 11
    BP.765   T.40.R

48 Two single pansies and a white dog-rose.
    Pencil and w/c, on brown paper. 16.5 x 26
    BP.744   T.40.R

49 Rough sketch of pansies and a fern in a green vase.
    Pencil and w/c. 25.5 x 17.5
    BP.751(b)   T.40.R

50 Four pansy flowers.
    Inscribed (R): H.B. Potter; and: HBP.
    Inscribed (verso): July 16 1879.
    W/c. 19 x 15.5
    BP.771   T.40.R

51 Study of four pansy heads (two yellow and
    two violet).
    Pencil and w/c. 23 x 17
    BP.903   P.C.46

52 Study of three pansy heads.
    W/c. 16 x 29
    Verso: Unfinished drawing including a wooden
    panel and other pencil lines.
    BP.909   P.C.46

53 Red petunia (?) and yellow daisy (?).
    Inscribed: June [crossed out] May 80.
    Verso: Purple vetch and partial w/c of yellow
    petals.
    W/c. 23.5 x 31.5
    BP.276   S.5.F.B

54 Primrose flowers and leaves.
    Inscribed: HBP.
    Pencil and w/c. 21 x 14
    Verso: Faint sketch of a primrose.
    Pencil.
    BP.911(vi)   P.C.45

55 Rhododendron bloom and leaves.
    W/c, on brown paper. 17.5 x 15
    BP.745   T.40.R

56 A single rhododendron bloom.
    W/c, on blue-grey paper. 18 x 17.5
    BP.754   T.40.R

57 Study of roses, carnations etc. in a vase
    (unfinished) with a brown background.
    W/c. 25 x 35
    BP.221   S.I.F.A

58 Bowl of roses and a group of plums, on a brown
    surface against a brown background (unfinished).
    W/c. 23 x 29.5
    BP.224   S.I.F.A

59 Painting of dog-roses.
    Inscribed: July 26th 1880.
    Verso: Unfinished sketch of a pink rose (?).
    Pencil and w/c. 20 x 25.5
    BP.265   S.5.F.A

60 Rose-hips.
    W/c. 18 x 17
    Verso: Pencil drawings of a tree.
    1878 or 1879. See similar painting at
    NBL (LL Cat.)
    BP.268   S.5.F.A

61 Two sprays of rose leaves, one unfinished.
    Inscribed (L): June 1880.
    Pencil and w/c. 31.5 x 23.5
    Verso: A tulip flower in red wash (unfinished).
    BP.895   P.C.24

62 Study of two roses, one pink and one red;
    also sketch of a small pink flower.
    Verso: Drawing of a yellow rose.
    Pencil and w/c. 27.5 x 20.5
    BP.906   P.C.46

63 Snowdrops in a blue glass vase.
    Pencil and w/c, on blue-grey paper. 18 x 12
    BP.753   T.40.R

64 Snowdrops in a vase.
    Pencil, on folded sheet. 17.5 x 11
    BP.941   P.C.47

65 Tiger lily with a fern in a green vase.
    Pencil and w/c. 25 x 17
    BP.751(a)   T.40.R

66 Violet plant.
    W/c, on blue-grey paper. 11 x 8
    BP.761   T.40.R

67 Bunch of wallflowers and a branch of almond
    blossom(?).
    Pencil and w/c, on cartridge paper. 25 x 17.5
    BP.905   P.C.46

68 Study of wallflowers.
Pencil and w/c. 29 x 14
BP.951   P.C.47

69 Pink vetch-like plant with leaves.
Pencil and w/c, on blue-grey paper. 25.5 x 17.5
BP.756   T.40.R

70 Two white daffodil flowers.
Pencil and w/c, on blue-grey paper. 17.5 x 25.5
BP.759   T.40.R

71 Pink thistle-like blooms.
Belongs to the same series as BP.763–66; cat.42,
25, 47, 24, but not inscribed.
Pencil and w/c, on blue-grey paper. 18 x 11
BP.767   T.40.R

72 Two partly finished paintings of flowers (one red
and green, the other yellow and green: fuchsia);
faint outlines of other stems.
Pencil and w/c, on two folded sheets. 22 x 18
BP.768 (a, b)   T.40.R

73 Yellow buttercup-like flower.
Verso: Violet (unfinished),
Pencil and w/c. 18 x 11
BP.770   T.40.R

Imaginary happenings

74 Study of a crane-like bird in a jungle.
Possibly copied from a book illustration.
About 1876 (LL Cat.)
Pen-and-ink. 23 x 16.5
BP.773   T.40.R

75 Heraldic figure of unicorn on an ornamental plinth
topping a column.
Inscribed (verso): Dalguise, about 1879 (LL).
Note by D.C. Duncan: This was the original
Mercat Cross of Dunkeld. It can still be seen in the
grounds of Dalguise House.
See also photographs of Lady Millais, BP.1275,
1284; cat.1993, 2007.
Pencil. 31 x 18.5
BP.892   P.C.24

76 African scene, showing animals by a river;
included are zebra, ostriches etc.
Inscribed (verso): Nov. 1876. (See Sketch book,
age 10) [i.e. BP.743; cat.1093] (LL).
Possibly copied from a book illustration?
Pencil, on card. 26.5 x 36.5
BP.900   P.C.26

77 Jungle scene, showing a snake coiled round a
branch which overhangs a pool; approaching the
snake on the same branch is a jaguar.
Below, two tortoises; above, monkeys in the trees.
Inscribed (verso): Nov. 1876. (See Sketch book,
age 10) [i.e. BP.743; cat.1093] (LL).
Possibly copied from a book illustration?
Pencil, on card. 26.5 x 36.5
BP.899   P.C.26

Interiors

78 Wray Castle library.
Inscribed (verso): Wray Castle July 1882.
W/c. 35 x 25
BP.231   S.2.F.A

79 View of a spiral staircase in a church.
Believed to be at St Mary's Tower, Birnam, the
home of Henry J.B. Manners. This staircase was
used by Millais as background for 'The Grey Lady'.
More likely to be near Tenby? (LL Cat.)
Inscribed (verso): 1882.
Sepia wash with pencil. 25.5 x 18
BP.287   S.6.F.A

Landscape

80 Rowing boat on the shore.
Inscribed (L): Sept. 6th 1879 Dalguise.
Pencil. 17.5 x 25.5
BP.894   P.C.24

Portraits and people

81 Various studies of Bertram Potter: four heads, one
head and shoulders, one hand, two figures – front
and back.
Inscribed (L): '82.
Verso: Study of Bertram at a table reading a book.
Pencil. 17.5 x 14.5
BP.530   S.20.F.C

PLATE III (left)
'Benjamin Bunny'
1880 (4)

PLATE IV (below)
View from 2 Bolton
Gardens (16)

PLATE V (right) Harebells and marguerites 1880 (35)

PLATE VI (below) Caterpillars, drawn at the age of 8 (1090)

PLATE VII Grapes and peaches 1883 (**90**)

PLATE VIII (left) Bat 1887 (**109**)

PLATE IX (below) Dead thrush, Woodcote 1902 (**118**)

82 Eight studies of the head of Bertram Potter.
Believed to have been drawn in 1882 when
Bertram was ten (LL Cat.)
See also BP.530; cat.81.
Pencil. 16 x 18.5
BP.529   S.20.F.C

83 Woman washing, with farm buildings and a chalet-
like house behind.
Possibly not by BP?
Inscribed (verso): July 1882.
W/c. 35 x 16.5
BP.887   P.C.35

School work

84 Seven lines of Latin text, copied from Virgil's
Aeneid, Book I, on strip torn from exercise book.
Ink; scansion marks inserted in pencil. 8 x 16
BP.562   T.23.L

85 Page torn from exercise book, with the first twenty-
two lines of Virgil's *Aeneid*, Book I (in Latin) and
a rough pen-and-ink sketch of bird in margin.
Ink. 17 x 17.5
Verso: List of picture titles scribbled down, and
faint sketch of a face.
Pencil.
BP.563   T.23.L

86 Map of Ascension Island.
Inscribed: H.B. Potter July 2nd 1880.
Pencil. 13 x 18 (lower edge torn)
BP.769   T.40.R

87 Map of England with coloured ink outlines
of counties.
30 x 24
BP.219   S.I.F.A

Still life

88 Detail of a frieze.
Inscribed: June '82.
Age 15 (LL Cat.)
Sepia wash with light pencil outline. 13 x 35,
on sheet 25 x 35
BP.222   S.I.F.A

89 Five green apples.
W/c. 23.5 x 31.5
Verso: Pencil drawing of the coat-of-arms of
Stewart of Dalguise.
Inscribed: October 1880.
BP.223   S.I.F.A

90 Grapes and peaches.
Inscribed: Woodfield Oct. 83.
Age 17 (LL Cat.)
W/c. 23 x 29.5
BP.220   S.I.F.A   (*see* PLATE VII)

91 Study of sea shells, antlers and Japanese calendar.
W/c. 25.5 x 32
BP.1159   P.C.2

92 Brown and fawn jug standing on a blue-grey
surface.
Inscribed (verso): About 1880 (LL).
W/c. 31.5 x 23.5
BP.896   P.C.24

Trees

93 Painting of leaves: silver birch(?).
Pencil and w/c. 34.5 x 24
BP.884   P.C.35

94 Study of a pollarded(?) willow.
Inscribed: May 82.
BP.225; cat.95 is of the same tree.
On high quality hand-made drawing paper, which
has been attached to a board by drawing pins.
W/c. 34 x 25.5
BP.226   S.I.F.B

95 Study of a pollarded(?) willow.
Inscribed: Feb. 82–.
Unlikely to be done in Feb – more likely May – as
in BP.226; cat.94 (LL Cat.)
W/c. 34 x 27
BP.225   S.I.F.B

96 Study of a tree.
Inscribed: Spring '82.
Verso: Partly finished study of the same tree.
Pencil and w/c. 35.5 x 26
BP.227   S.I.F.B

97 Study of trees (two trees growing close together).
W/c, on hand-made drawing paper. 33 x 25.5
BP.228   S.I.F.B

98 Study of trees.
Inscribed (verso): June 25th 1879.
Black crayon. 37.5 x 27
BP.229   S.I.F.B

99 Weeping willow tree.
Inscribed (verso): June 1879, from a drawing.
Pencil. 20 x 23
BP.891   P.C.24

Miscellaneous: lino cuts

100 Two ducks.
6.5 x 3.5
BP.561(b)   T.23.L

101 A stork standing by some reeds.
Made on shiny backed paper (LL Cat.)
6 x 3.5
BP.561(c)   T.23.L

102 Horse feeding.
Made on part of an envelope.
7 x 16
BP.561(d)   T.23.L

Another copy. 3 x 3.5
BP.561(a)   T.23.L

103 Several studies of the nose of a rat(?).
Inscribed (verso): 2 Bolton Gardens.
Made on part of a torn envelope.
8 x 6 (approx.)
BP.561(e)   T.23.L

Miscellaneous: transfer prints

104 Mother rabbit and five babies.
Inscribed: H.B.P. 1880.
Violet ink. W/m: Wood paper/mmond/ware Road.
11.5 x 18
BP.560(a)   T.23.L

Another copy. 11.5 x 15
BP.560(b)   T.23.L

106

105 A horse's head in harness.
Violet ink. W/m: Wood paper/ammond/eware
Road. 18 x 11
BP.557   T.23.L

106 Original transfer print of a dormouse.
Inscribed: H.B.P. 1880.
Violet ink. 10 x 14.5
BP.558(a)   T.23.L

Duplicate print. Very faint impression.
11.5 x 18
BP.558(b)   T.23.L

107 Original transfer print of a Lhasa terrier (Tibetan
Apso) and the head of another dog, with mouse in
foreground.
Inscribed: HBP. 1880.
The print was probably made by putting the
original, while still wet, face down on a gelatine
film so that some of the ink was transferred to the
gelatine. The original was removed and the
gelatine film used as a printing surface. The heavy
inking of BP.559(a) would indicate an original
impression.
Violet ink. 11 x 14.5
BP.559(a)   T.23.L

Duplicate prints. Impressions vary in degrees
of faintness.
11 x 18
BP.559(b–g)   T.23.L

NATURAL HISTORY

Natural history was obviously one of the greatest interests in the life of Beatrix Potter from her earliest childhood, and it permeated all her subsequent work. Behind each of her children's books, with its rabbits, mice, frogs, gardens, fields or lakes, lay long and detailed studies of the actual creatures or scenes. Her animals are *real*, and even in her most imaginative stories she sees them without sentiment – they remain creatures apart, in a world of their own. It is these basic studies of the natural world that will be found here. The works cover the whole of Beatrix Potter's life (apart from her early years) and the range is considerable. Obviously this section includes only the material that has come to rest in the Linder Bequest – there is more elsewhere, testifying to her immense interest and output. The scientific accuracy of her work is most impressive, and her paintings of fungi have long been famous. Even in her sketches of a humble beetle or fly, Beatrix Potter was able to capture not only the physical exactness but also the sheer beauty of its detail.

Many of the drawings and paintings were to be used later in her books; where such related sketches can be positively identified they will be found in the section headed 'Backgrounds for Books'. Here are listed only the more straightforward natural history drawings and watercolours.

Badgers

108 Studies of badgers and foxes.
Possibly in preparation for *The Tale of Mr Tod*.
Pencil. 16.5 x 19
BP.1135(b)   P.C.38

Bats

109 Two studies of bats within pencil-drawn circles; two drawings of a bat's skull, viewed from above and below; also a drawing of a complete bat skeleton; in addition, one pencil circle left empty.
Inscribed (verso): April 8th '87.
W/c and pen-and-ink, on card. 27 x 36.5
BP.250   S.3.F.C   (*see* PLATE VIII)

110 Front view of a bat with wings outstretched.
Inscribed: Jan 31 '84.
W/c. 10 x 20.5
BP.397(a)   S.12.F.B

111 Bat viewed from above, with wings outstretched, flying over an insect.
Inscribed: Jan 31 '84 (LL); and (in Capt Duke's writing): Aged 17.
W/c. 10 x 18
BP.397(b)   S.12.F.B

112 Side view of a bat with wings folded.
Inscribed (verso): December '85.
W/c. 11.5 x 12
BP.398(a)   S.12.F.B

113 Side view of a bat with wings folded (part of one leg is unfinished).
W/c, pen-and-ink and pencil, on card. 9 x 11
BP.398(b)   S.12.F.B

114 Side view of a bat with wings folded.
W/c, on card. 9 x 11
BP.398(c)   S.12.F.B

115 Side view of a bat with wings folded.
Inscribed (verso): Camfield Sept. '86.
W/c, on card. 9 x 11
BP.399   S.12.F.B

116 Front view of a bat (unfinished).
Verso: Unfinished study of the gardener's cottage at
Camfield Place.
Identified by Camfield gardener (LL Cat.)
W/c and pencil. 7.5 x 11.5
BP.400(a,b)   S.12.F.B

Bears

117 Rough studies of a bear walking, and standing on
its hind legs begging.
Verso: Similar studies of bears.
Pencil. 25 x 17.5
BP.1468   P.C.14

Birds

118 Studies of a dead thrush in various positions.
Inscribed: Woodcote 1902 picked up dead in
the snow.
Inscribed (verso): Studies of a dead thrush –
rabbits, from life. H B Potter.
Woodcote in Surrey was the home of her uncle,
Sir Henry Roscoe.
Pen-and-ink and w/c. 22.5 x 29
BP.418   S.13.F.B   (*see* PLATE IX)

119 Studies of a dead finch(?); also pencil studies of cats
and rabbits.
Verso: Study of a rabbit lying down.
W/c and pencil. 17.5 x 25.5
BP.1013   P.C.12

120 Studies of birds' heads and claws.
Pencil. 26.5 x 21
BP.1202   P.C.14

121 Study of a dead bird: robin redbreast; and two
sketches of a cat's head.
W/c and pencil. 17 x 19
BP.1141   P.C.16

122 Studies of heads, wings and claw of rooks (*Corvus
frugilegus*).
Information from the Natural History Museum,
London.
Possibly by Bertram or Rupert Potter.
W/c and pencil. 25 x 18
BP.1198(a)   P.C.18

123 Study of a rook (*Corvus frugilegus*), and an
unfinished sketch of a baby rook(?).
Possibly by Bertram or Rupert Potter.
W/c. 14 x 18
BP.1198(b)   P.C.18

124 Study of an owl.
W/c and pencil. 25 x 35.5
BP.1210   P.C.19

125 Three rough sketches of owls.
Verso: More owl studies.
Possibly studies for Old Brown in *The Tale of
Squirrel Nutkin*.
Black crayon, on torn sheet. 19 x 19
BP.1212   P.C.19

125 (*detail*)

126 Rough studies of owls.
Verso: Studies of owls (including several studies of
an owl's head).
Possibly studies for Old Brown in *The Tale of
Squirrel Nutkin*.
Pencil. 17.5 x 21
BP.1213   P.C.19

127 Four studies of an owl's head.
Possibly studies for Old Brown in *The Tale of
Squirrel Nutkin*.
Wash and pencil. W/m: Oyez Typewriting,
22 Chancery Lane W.C. 20 x 26
BP.1214   P.C.19

128 Two birds, possibly tree-creepers; a sketch possibly of a dead bird; the lightly pencilled background suggests reeds or grasses, with a lake or landscape(?) below.
Pen-and-ink and pencil, on card. 26 x 17
Verso: W/c head and wing of budgerigar, and light pencil sketches of mice, birds, interiors etc.
Inscribed (L): Sep. 83.
Inscribed (on mount): By Beatrix Potter. Sept. 1883 (at Bush Hall) (LL).
BP.1201 P.C.18

Cats

129 Studies of a cat asleep (mainly heads).
Pencil. 25.5 x 16
BP.383 S.11.F.C

130 Several rough sketches of cats.
Verso: Sketches of mice.
Pencil, on folded notepaper. 25 x 20
BP.384 S.11.F.C

131 Head and fore-paws of a sleeping cat.
Pencil, on sheet cut at angle. 8.5 x 11 (approx.)
BP.385(a) S.11.F.C

132 Sketch of a cat's face, with two faint pencil studies of the same.
W/c and pencil, on unevenly cut sheet. 10 x 23
BP.385(b) S.11.F.C

133 Studies of cats, a horse, ducks and cows.
Pencil. 25 x 18
BP.1011 P.C.12

134 Studies of a kitten sleeping.
Verso: Similar studies of cats.
Pencil. 20 x 19
BP.1016(i) P.C.12

135 Studies of a kitten's head.
Verso: Studies of a kitten washing etc.
Pencil. 26 x 16
BP.1016(ii) P.C.12

136 Studies of a kitten in various positions.
Pencil. 26 x 16
BP.1016(iii) P.C.12

137 Studies of a kitten sitting.
Pencil. W/m: Britannia. 32 x 20
BP.1016(iv) P.C.12

138

138 Studies of a kitten sitting.
Pencil, on unevenly cut card. 12 x 10 (approx.)
BP.1016(v) P.C.12

139 Studies of a kitten in various positions.
Pencil. W/m: Fine. 17 x 10
BP.1016(vi) P.C.12

140 Study of the head of a kitten.
Pencil, on unevenly cut sheet. 15 x 10
BP.1016(vii) P.C.12

141 Study of a cat: back view.
Pencil, on notepaper. 11 x 18
BP.1016(ix) P.C.12

142 Studies of a cat playing with a fish etc.
Pen-and-ink and pencil, on unevenly cut strip. 18 x 13
BP.1016(viii) P.C.12

143 Studies of a kitten sitting.
Pencil, on torn sheet. 25 x 18 (approx.)
BP.1016(x) P.C.12

143 (detail)

155 (*detail*)

144 Study of a kitten sleeping.
W/c and pencil, on unevenly cut sheet. 19 x 14
BP.1017(i)   P.C.12

145 Studies of the head of a kitten.
W/c and pencil, on unevenly cut sheet. 20 x 10
BP.1017(ii)   P.C.12

146 Studies of the head of a kitten.
W/c and pencil. 17 x 17
BP.1017(iii)   P.C.12

147 Studies of kittens.
Verso: Similar studies.
Pencil and grey wash. 20 x 13
BP.1017(iv)   P.C.12

148 Studies of a ginger cat.
Verso: Study of cat asleep.
W/c and pencil, on folded sheet. 25 x 21
BP.1017(v)   P.C.12

149 Studies of kittens.
Verso: Similar studies.
W/c and pencil. 25 x 20.5
BP.1017(vi)   P.C.12

150 Studies of cats.
W/c and pencil. 29 x 22.5
BP.1017(vii)   P.C.12

151 Study of cats.
Verso: Sketches of rabbits.
W/c and pencil, on notepaper. 20 x 13.5
BP.1143   P.C.16

Cattle

152 Studies of two heads of cows, the side view of a
cow standing, and rear view of a cow drinking
from a trough.
Verso: Faint sketches of three shrews and a
bird's head.
Pencil. 19 x 17.5
BP.392   S.12.F.A

153 Studies of a cow's head and four cows lying down.
Verso: Studies of cows and horses standing.
Top corner: BP's money calculations.
Pencil. 25 x 17.5
BP.393   S.12.F.A

154 Group of cows wading into a pond.
Inscribed (R): HBP.
Pen-and-ink. 18 x 25.5
BP.391   S.12.F.A

155 Studies of cows; also rough studies of cats, birds
and chickens.
Verso: Rough studies of a cow's leg and a cow
lying (rear view); also pen-and-ink sketches
of leaves.
Pen-and-ink and pencil. 25 x 17.5
BP.394   S.12.F.A

156 Two cows in a field with trees and a cottage in
the background.
Inscribed (L): Sidmouth.
Pencil. 17.5 x 25
BP.395   S.12.F.A

157 Studies of a bullock and foxes.
Pencil. 16 x 25.5
BP.396   S.12.F.A

158 Sketches of a cow standing and one lying down.
Inscribed: Dec 10. 86.
Verso: Cow lying down (viewed from behind).
Probably at Camfield (LL Cat.)
Pencil. 17.5 x 11
BP.642   T.29.R

159 Sketches of a cow standing.
Inscribed: Feb. 87.
Verso: Further sketches of cows.
Probably at Camfield (LL Cat.)
Pencil. 20 x 12.5
BP.641   T.29.R

160 Two unfinished studies of a cow lying down.
Verso: Rough study of a room interior.
Pen-and-ink and pencil. 25 x 17.5
BP.1450   P.C.14

161 Three studies of a cow standing.
Verso: Faint sketches of figures within a
pencil frame.
Pencil. 20 x 11
BP.1451   P.C.14

162 Studies of calves' heads and of a calf lying down.
Inscribed (verso): H.B. Potter.
Pencil. 17.5 x 25
BP.1452   P.C.14

163 Study of a bull's head and of a bull lying down.
Verso: Rough sketch of an owl.
Pencil. W/m: Towgood's Fine. 32 x 20
BP.1453   P.C.14

Chickens

164 Head of a dead hen, speckled grey in colour.
Inscribed: April 6. 1900.
Inscribed (verso): Study of head of a dead hen.
H. B. Potter.
W/c. 25.5 x 18
BP.421   S.13.F.C

165 Sketches of chicks, five of which are partly in
yellow wash.
Pencil and yellow wash. 25.5 x 18
BP.422   S.13.F.C

166 Five studies of hens' heads against grey
backgrounds.
Verso: Six studies of hens' heads.
W/c and pencil. 17.5 x 25.5
BP.423   S.13.F.C

167 Seven sketches of hens' heads.
Pencil. 22.5 x 17.5
BP.424   S.13.F.C

168 Six studies of hens' heads; four have grey
backgrounds.
Verso: Two rough sketches of hens' heads.
W/c with pencil. 18 x 25.5
BP.425   S.13.F.C

169 Several rough studies of chicks and chickens
(some partly coloured).
Pencil with wash, on folded sheet. 22.5 x 28.5
BP.426   S.13.F.C

170 Rough sketches of chickens in a field.
Pencil and pen-and-ink. 20 x 32
BP.1203   P.C.14

171 Sketches of hens and chicks.
Pencil, on notepaper. 17 x 21
BP.1208   P.C.17

Deer

172 Finished study of two roe-deer lying in the hay in
the corner of their hut.
Inscribed: H.B.P. Roedeer & fawn, at Zoological
Gardens June 91.
Pen and wash, with white highlights. 12.5 x 15.5
BP.379   S.11.F.B

173 Study of a dead fawn (coloured); also sketches of
head and legs.
W/c and pencil. 25.5 x 28
BP.381   S.11.F.B

174 Studies of a gazelle (at the Zoological Gardens?).
Pencil. 15 x 23
BP.410   S.13.F.A

172

175 Study of a young roe-deer lying on the ground.
Pencil. W/m: Holyrood. 12.5 x 20
BP.411   S.13.F.A
(Mounted with BP.412; cat.179)

176 Sketches of a dead fawn, with two studies of
its head.
Pencil. 23.5 x 16
BP.1461(a)   P.C.14

177 Sketches of a dead fawn, with two studies of its
head (heads have w/c added); also study of a newt
(in wash).
W/c and pencil. 22.5 x 21
BP.1461(b)   P.C.14

Dogs

178 Sketch of 'Kep' guarding sheep in a snow-
covered field.
Inscribed: Kep March 5 1909 Beatrix Potter.
(LL Cat.): Inscription inked over by Stephanie
Hyde-Parker, to whom this drawing was given.
Stephanie pasted it in her album. The album was
given to Rosemary when Stephanie, her mother,
died. (Stephanie born 1894, lived at Melford Hall,
Suffolk, moved to Castle Cottage on death of Mr
Heelis, died 1953.) This is one of a number of
rough w/c sketches drawn in the snow – one
duplicate of 'Kep' and all others of landscape
(about 16 in all, plus the two of Kep, drawn
between March 2 and 7, 1909 at Sawrey). Later it
was torn out of the album and offered for sale to aid
an old people's home in Rhodesia.
Pencil and w/c, on drawing paper mounted on
card: part of album, with coloured scrap still
adhering. 17.5 x 25
Verso: Carrots and turnip. W/c by Amy
Hyde-Parker.
BP.297   S.6.F.C

180

179 Study of a dog curled up asleep.
   Pencil. W/m: Britannia. 13 x 16
   BP.412   S.13.F.A

180 Study of a black and white terrier curled up on an
   orange rug.
   (LL Cat.): Believed to be 'Nip'; 'Nip' is a black and
   white bitch, a very good one. She was bred at
   Brother's Water. See *Fairy Caravan* Explanatory
   Notes – frontispiece of dogs (see p.296).
   W/c with pencil. 17.5 x 25.5
   Verso: Sketch of an arch at Hawkshead.
   (LL Cat.): Arch at Hawkshead used for *The Tale of
   Johnny Town-Mouse*.
   Pencil.
   BP.415   S.13.F.A

181 Side view of 'Kep'.
   (LL Cat.): The collie in *The Tale of Jemima
   Puddle-Duck*.
   W/c with pencil. 21 x 14
   BP.513(b)   S.19.F.C

182 Studies of the head of 'Kep'.
   W/c with pencil. 17.5 x 13
   BP.513(a)   S.19.F.C

183 Dog's head peering round sacks of flour.
   Illustration on front of an envelope addressed to BP
   at Bolton Gardens and postmarked Oct 20 1910.
   Pen-and-ink. 9 x 14.5
   BP.724   T.38.R

184 Study of a dog on its hind legs.
   Light grey wash. W/m: Willow Extra. 18 x 11.5
   BP.1252   P.C.14

185 Study of dog's head and sheep's head.
   Pencil and pen-and-ink. 17 x 11
   BP.1459   P.C.14

186 Study of a dog, a tree and a harebell.
   Verso: Faint sketches of a bee(?).
   Sepia ink. W/m: Aviemore. 26.5 x 21
   BP.1460   P.C.14

Ducks

187 Studies of a duck in various positions.
   Verso: Studies of duck (faint outline).
   Pencil and wash. 19 x 22.5
   BP.1204   P.C.17

188 Sketches of ducks' bills.
Verso: Sketches of ducks' heads and bills.
Pencil. 17.5 x 25
BP.1205   P.C.17

189 Faint outline studies of ducks.
Verso: Outline of child running.
Pencil. 22.5 x 19
BP.1206   P.C.17

190 Sketches of ducklings.
Verso: Outline sketches of ducklings.
Pencil. W/m: Towgood's Extra Fine. 20.5 x 17
BP.1207   P.C.17

191 Studies of ducks, hen coop and tree.
Pencil and sepia ink. W/m: Oceana Fine.
21 x 26.5
BP.1209   P.C.17

192 Studies of ducks and hens.
Pencil and sepia ink. W/m: Oceana Fine.
21 x 26.5
BP.1248   P.C.17

193 Study of ducks' heads.
White chalk and crayon, on brown paper.
28 x 22.5
BP.1249   P.C.17

194 Studies of ducks.
Verso: One duck study.
White chalk and crayon, on brown paper.
28 x 24.5
BP.1250   P.C.17

Fish

195 Study of a small orange fish and (beneath) a
drawing of a sea anemone.
Inscribed: Weymouth April 14th 95.
(LL Cat.): Boar fish full size, picked up on the
beach and referred to in her Journal.
W/c and pencil. 20 x 26
BP.403   S.12.F.C

196 Study of a dragonet seen from above.
Inscribed: April 23rd 96. Swanage. dragonet
callionymus lyra.
Inscribed (verso): Drawn from Nature. Beatrix
Potter.
W/c, on card. 21.5 x 28
BP.408   S.12.F.C

197 Two views of a lamprey (from above and from
the side).
Inscribed: Oct '84.
W/c. 13 x 20.5
BP.407   S.12.F.C

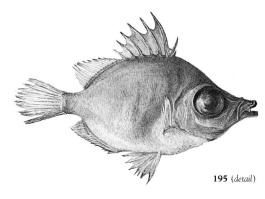

195 (detail)

Flowers

198– Various studies of wood anemones and a study of
199 a violet plant with roots.
W/c with pen-and-ink, on card. 24 x 30
BP.1180   P.C.51

200 Study of a branch of apple blossom.
W/c and pen-and-ink. 15 x 29
BP.1168   P.C.51

191 (detail)

201 Rough sketches of apple blossom and a few
polyanthus flowers.
Verso: Sketches of two violet plants, and
individual studies of single flowers and buds.
W/c with pencil. 26.5 x 21
BP.932 P.C.47

202 Branches of apple blossom.
W/c and pen-and-ink. 22.5 x 19
BP.919 P.C.47

203 Studies of carnation flowers.
Sepia ink. 29 x 22.5
BP.1167 P.C.51

204 Rough studies of chervil or parsley.
Verso: Sketch of five seeds.
Sepia ink and pencil. 31 x 25 (section of sheet
cut off)
BP.914 P.C.47

205 Studies of flowers of umbelliferous kind (chervil?),
with groups of leaves, mainly green, white and
yellow.
W/c. 29.5 x 23
BP.915 P.C.47

206 Two purple clematis flowers.
W/c. 28 x 21.5
BP.908 P.C.46

207 Leaf pattern (unfinished), possibly the basis for
wallpaper, textile or endpaper design.
Sepia ink and pencil. 23.5 x 19.5
BP.375 S.11.F.A

208 Sketch of cowslip plants growing amongst
vegetation.
W/c with pencil. 22.5 x 18.5
BP.934 P.C.47

209 Sketch of a cowslip plant growing amongst
vegetation.
Inscribed: May 7th. 04.
W/c with pencil. 18.5 x 22.5
BP.947 P.C.47

210 Sketch of cowslip plants growing amongst
vegetation.
W/c with pencil. 22.5 x 18.5
BP.935 P.C.47

211 Studies of cuckoo flowers.
W/c and pen-and-ink. 27.5 x 20
BP.911(xv) P.C.45

212 Brown vase of daffodils against mauve background.
Verso: Comments by members of the Drawing
Society to which BP belonged; also inscribed: p. 38
Vase of Daffodils. The property of Capt. Duke.
W/c. 19.5 x 17
BP.270 S.5.F.A

213 Three flowering daffodils and a bud in two pots.
W/c with pen-and-ink, on card. 30.5 x 24
BP.912(v) P.C.5

214 Partly finished study of fuchsia flowers (one flower
uncoloured), and a rough pencil sketch of a
fuchsia.
W/c. 29 x 22.5
BP.1164 P.C.51

215 Two gaillardia flowers.
Inscribed (L): June 21.
W/c, on stiff cartridge paper. 27.5 x 22
BP.902 P.C.46

216 Study of grasses with mauve heads (unidentified).
W/c and pencil. 17 x 17
BP.948 P.C.47

217 Two studies of a clump of grass growing on a
bank(?).
Pencil and sepia ink, on folded sheet. W/m:
Britannia. 32 x 20
BP.924 P.C.47

218 Different kinds of grasses, and leaves of a
water plant.
Verso: Study of tall grasses.
W/c with pencil. 21 x 19
BP.911(xii) P.C.45

219 Sketches of a clump of grass, amphibious bistort
and saxifrage(?).
W/c and pencil. W/m: Edmeston. 25 x 20
BP.911(xiii) P.C.45

220 Study of partly opened honeysuckle flower, with
stem and leaves.
W/c with pen-and-ink. 27.5 x 15.5
BP.952 P.C.47

221 Unfinished study of honeysuckle (some parts
pencilled in only).
W/c and pencil. W/m: /ue & Co. 18 x 11
BP.911(vii)   P.C.45

222 Iris seed-pods showing orange seeds inside.
Verso: Rough sketches of cats.
W/c. 18 x 12.5
BP.362   S.10.F.B

223 Group of white irises, one in flower.
Inscribed (verso): A garden flower. H.B. Potter –
/8; and (in another hand, in pencil): Your Swanley
Iris have all turned out to be this (3).
This is possibly from the sketching society.
W/c and green pen-and-ink, on card. 27 x 21
BP.912(ix)   P.C.5

224 Rough studies of iris flowers: three pencil sketches
and three w/c; also w/c of tulip heads.
W/c and pencil. 19 x 12
BP.933   P.C.47

225 Sketches of lavender.
W/c with pencil. 32.5 x 20
BP.911(xiv)   P.C.45

226 Study of a lily(?).
Inscribed (verso): Do you see in the Times that
Robert Ashton is married again.
Pencil and pen-and-ink. 15 x 9.5
BP.911(ix)   P.C.45

227 Various sketches of marsh helleborine including
coloured drawings of leaves and flowers; also two
drawings of single flowers.
Inscribed (verso): Marsh Helleborine,
Derwentwater.
W/c and pen-and-ink. 28 x 21.5
BP.356   S.10.F.A

228 Study of mint leaves and stems.
Pen-and-ink, on folded sheet. W/m: /nson/rfine.
18 x 11
BP.940   P.C.47

229 Narcissus flowers and leaves.
W/c, on a folded sheet of notepaper. 17.5 x 11
BP.911(x)   P.C.45

230 Group of narcissus.
W/c and green ink, on card. 28 x 15
BP.912(vi)   P.C.5

231 Two w/c studies of nasturtium and four pencil
sketches of individual flowers.
Verso: Rough study of a nasturtium.
W/c and pencil. 25 x 17.5
BP.950   P.C.47

232 Studies of pansy flowers (seven in colour and one in
pencil for size).
Inscribed (L): June 5. 09 from [Veitch's] Prize
English; with pencilled indications as to positions
of the various flower beds.
Verso: Eight cell colonies, highly magnified (alga,
probably *Desmococcus*).
W/c with pencil. 28 x 22
BP.361   S.10.F.B

233 Pansy plant with buds.
Inscribed (on mount): Sept 21.96.
Inscribed (verso): 'A winter evening' H.B. Potter.
Old House at Winchelsea, Sussex.
(LL Cat.): This sheet was originally used as a
mount for another painting, and was separated
in June 1958.
W/c. 28.5 x 23.5
BP.363   S.10.F.B

234 Studies of pansy flowers and leaves.
W/c and pencil. W/m: R. 21 x 13
BP.911(ii)   P.C.45

235 Nasturtium leaves and flowers.
Verso: Sketch of grasses.
Pen-and-ink with pencil, on a folded sheet. W/m:
Joynso/ 1858. 17 x 12
BP.939   P.C.47

236 Study of three nettles (one is a sepia sketch and
two are filled in with w/c).
Pencil, sepia ink and w/c. 29 x 22
BP.918   P.C.47

237 Sketches of pansy plants.
Pen-and-ink and pencil. 20 x 25
Verso: Rough sketch of a rose bush(?) and a
cow (rear view).
Pencil.
BP.931   P.C.47

238 Head of a pansy.
W/c, on card. 10 x 21.5
BP.1182   P.C.42

239 Several studies of parsley.
W/c and sepia ink. 29 x 22.5
BP.1171   P.C.51

240 Pelargonium flowers on a single stem.
Verso: Sketch of roses(?).
W/c. 25 x 17.5
BP.953   P.C.46

241 Polyanthus.
Pencil. W/m: Bold Ivory HM. 11 x 18
BP.901   P.C.46

242 Rough study of potentilla flowers, stems and leaves.
Pen-and-ink and pencil. W/m: Edmeston. 20 x 25
BP.926   P.C.47

243 Cluster of primroses with leaves and moss.
The card and w/c have been cut in half.
W/c and pencil, on card. 24 x 15.5
BP.912(vii)   P.C.5

244 Two paintings of primulas with purple flowers.
Inscribed (L): From Stromness, Orkney, July 21st
1902; and (below): Natural size – Primula Scotica,
wild auricula – hard leaf & *very* strong scent like
the garden auricula.
(LL Cat.): Apparently only found in Orkneys [sic]
(Mr. Clegg).
W/c with pen-and-ink, on card. 24 x 13
BP.359   S.10.F.A

245 Sketch of ragwort.
Sepia ink. W/m: Oceana Fine. 27 x 20
BP.921   P.C.47

246 Reeds (including bulrushes?) growing in water.
Inscribed (on folder): Swanage?
W/c with faint pencil. 23 x 19
BP.911(v)   P.C.45

247 Pink rosebud with leaves.
Inscribed (at top): Sept 25 96.
(LL Cat.): Painted at 'Lakefield', Sawrey Sept 25
1896.
W/c. 22 x 27.5 (formerly folded)
BP.360   S.10.F.B

248 Pink rose and buds.
W/c with pen-and-ink, on card. 21 x 13.5
BP.912(i)   P.C.5

249 White rose.
W/c and pencil, on card. 16.5 x 21.5
BP.912(ii)   P.C.5

250 Yellow rose and bud.
W/c, on card. 30.5 x 24
BP.912(x)   P.C.5

251 Sketches of roses, buds, flowers etc.; also rough
sketch of a dog sitting.
Pencil. 11.5 x 29
BP.911(xvi)   P.C.45

252 Rough sketches of a rosebud, carnations and a
flowering branch etc.
Pencil and sepia ink. W/m: Parsons' Line/
Holyoke Ma/. 26.5 x 21
BP.923   P.C.47

253 Study of sea holly with various umbellifera and
other flowers.
W/c and sepia ink. W/m: Edmeston. 25.5 x 20
BP.920   P.C.47

254 Sedges and bog cotton(?) and another flower.
W/c with pen-and-ink, on card. 27 x 20.5
BP.912(iii)   P.C.5

255 Three studies of a snapdragon.
Pencil and sepia ink. W/m: I & JH Kent. 29 x 22.5
BP.913   P.C.47

256 Two pink thistle plants.
Inscribed (verso): A weed. H.B. Potter.
W/c with pencil. 27 x 22.5
BP.364   S.10.F.B

257 Tiger lily stem with flowers.
Sepia ink. 29 x 22.5
BP.916   P.C.47

258 Tiger lily flowers growing from a single stem.
W/c and sepia ink. 29 x 22.5
BP.1165   P.C.51   (*see* PLATE X)

259 Tiger lily blossoms and other flowers.
Sepia ink. 29 x 22.5
BP.1166   P.C.51

260 Yellow tulips.
W/c, on card. 30 x 24
BP.912(xi)   P.C.5

261 Two pink and white tulips.
W/c with pen-and-ink, on card. 21 x 16
BP.912(iv)   P.C.5

262 Studies of tulips and primula.
Verso: Faint sketch of a rabbit.
Inscribed: 16 inches [not referring to rabbit;
meaning unclear].
Pencil and pen-and-ink. 20 x 13
BP.1172   P.C.51

263 Three tulips.
W/c with pencil, on card. 30 x 23.5
BP.907   P.C.46

264 Dahlia plant with pink and cream flowers.
Possibly from Fawe Park as background to *The Tale
of Benjamin Bunny*.
W/c and pen-and-ink. 22.5 x 19
BP.1264(viii)   P.C.40

265 Three double daisies.
Inscribed (R): Peculiar growth of a double daisy.
Inscribed (verso): H.B. Potter.
W/c with pencil, on card. 24 x 17.5
BP.271   S.5.F.A

266 Sketch of two daisy plants.
Pencil. W/m: Britannia. 16.5 x 10
BP.911(iii)   P.C.45

267 Study of two daisy plants.
Pencil. W/m: Britannia. 14.5 x 10
BP.911(iv)   P.C.45

268 Studies of seeded dandelions, poppies and
strawberry runners(?).
Verso: Studies of strawberry runners with ripening
strawberries.
Sepia ink with pencil. 26.5 x 22
BP.929   P.C.47

269 Various studies of a hart's-tongue fern with the
stems curled up.
Inscribed (verso): Beatrix Potter May 01–.
W/c with pencil. 29 x 22.5
BP.365   S.10.F.B

270 Unfinished rough study of foxgloves.
Verso: Study of a fox cub(?) curled up asleep; also
other rough studies of a guinea pig(?).
W/c and pencil. 29 x 22.5
BP.1245   P.C.31

271 Various studies of French marigold plants (mainly
in sepia ink, with two left as pencil sketches).
Sepia ink and pencil. W/m: 7 [in a cartouche].
17.5 x 26.5
BP.922   P.C.47

272 Two studies of purple vetch (unfinished) and a
dianthus.
Inscribed (verso): Dianthus deltoides, Smaillholm
[sic] Sept 25th '94; and: Burnmouth Sept 14th '94.
W/c with pencil, on card. 21.5 x 28
BP.358   S.10.F.A

273 Rough studies of violets and bluebells.
W/c with pen-and-ink, on card (partly cut away).
21.5 x 28
BP.912(viii)   P.C.5

274 Rough sketches of wallflowers.
Verso: Sketches of wallflowers.
Pencil and pen-and-ink, on a folded sheet. 28 x 23
BP.928   P.C.47

275 Waterlilies: a close-up view of leaves and flowers
amongst reeds.
Inscribed (on mount): Water lilies – Esthwaite
Water (LL).
W/c with pen-and-ink. 23 x 29
Verso: Cats' heads.
Pencil.
BP.239   S.2.F.B   (*see* PLATE XI)

266 (*detail*)

276 One finished w/c drawing of a white dead-nettle, and three pen-and-ink drawings of the same.
W/c and pen-and-ink. 27 x 22
BP.917   P.C.47

277 Sketch of a plant with long spiky seeds and small flower clusters.
Pencil and pen-and-ink. W/m: St. Neots' Mill No. 24. 16 x 20
BP.925   P.C.47

278 Unidentified flower with mauve and white striped petals and slim olive-green leaves, rather narcissus-like in shape (ipheion?).
Inscribed: April 16.08.
W/c and pencil, on a torn piece of paper.
14 x 10 (approx.)
Verso: Faint sketch of a dog ('Duchess'?).
Pencil.
BP.911(viii)   P.C.45

279 Unidentified white blossom.
W/c with pencil. 16 x 7.5
BP.936   P.C.47

280 Various studies of French marigold, flowers and leaves.
Verso: Studies of grasses(?).
Sepia ink and pencil. 20 x 25
BP.930   P.C.47

281 Freesia flowers (a few of the leaves unfinished).
Inscribed (on folder): Sept 16 1904, Newlands.
W/c with pen-and-ink, on folded sheet of notepaper. 17.5 x 11
BP.911(xi)   P.C.45

Foxes and ferrets

282 Study of a fox.
W/c. 25 x 17.5
BP.1458   P.C.14

283 Unfinished sketch of ferrets(?).
Verso: Sketches of rats' heads(?).
Pen-and-ink and pencil. W/m: Joyn/First Q/.
11.5 x 18
BP.1439   P.C.13

Frogs

284 Several studies of frogs.
Verso: Similar sketches of frogs.
Pencil. 20.5 x 16.5
BP.409   S.13.F.A

284 (detail)

285 Study of three tadpoles swimming.
Pencil. W/m: /a. 8 x 11.5
BP.1254   P.C.14

286 Study of a frog, with a rough sketch of its head.
Pencil, on very thin paper. 13 x 19
BP.1263(xviii)   P.C.36

Fungi

287 Study of orange fungi (*Aleuria aurantia*) growing amongst fallen leaves.
Inscribed: H.B.P.
Inscribed (verso): Beatrix Potter. Oct. 1893; and (in another hand): Peziza[sic] aurantia – (vide *Guide to Sowerby's Models of British Fungi* in British Museum) – The specimens painted by Miss Potter were found in the Woods of Strathallan – by the Honble Francis Drummond – Octr 1893. –
W/c. 21 x 28
BP.354   S.10.F.A

288 Bracket fungus (*Coriolus* (or *Trametes*) *versicolor*) growing amongst cherry blossom, twigs and flowers.
Inscribed: Sidbury camp Ap. 16th 98.
Inscribed (verso): Polyporus versicolor.
W/c and pen-and-ink. 24 x 30.5
BP.245   S.3.F.B

289 Group of brownish-coloured mushrooms (*Amanita aspera*).
Inscribed (verso): Top; and (on mount, now detached) in another hand: Amanita Asper.
W/c. 20 x 26
BP.355   S.10.F.A

PLATE X Tiger lily (258)

PLATE XI Waterlilies, Esthwaite (275)

290 Two photographs of polypore, on a cream mount.
Inscribed (on mount): Polyporus Melanopus.
9 inches in diameter. On elm logs Putney Park
Oct 9th 96.
Sketch of spores (on mount), inscribed: x 600
Photographs: contact bromide prints (LL Cat.)
11 x 15.5 (size of print)
BP. 357(a)
BP. 357(b) identical set of prints   S. 10. F. A

291 Birch tree fungus (*Piptoporus betulinus*) growing on
a tree trunk.
Slightly larger than life size.
W/c. 43.5 x 37
BP. 243   S. 3. F. A

292 Two examples of a Yellow grisette (*Amanita
crocea*) (L).
Inscribed: Ullock Sep 2nd '97.
Two examples of a Scarlet fly cap (*Amanita
muscaria*), with a cross-section of another (R).
Inscribed: Sept 3. 97.
Inscribed (verso) in another hand: Scarlet fly cap
Amanita muscaria; and: Yellow Grisette
Amanitopsis vaginata, variety fulva.
W/c and pen-and-ink.   31 x 43
BP. 244   S. 3. F. B   (*see* PLATE XII)

293 Bracket fungus (on one side of folded sheet);
section of oak tree polypore (*Inonotus dryadeus*) (on
other side of folded sheet).
W/c. 27 x 34 (one side of folded sheet), 27 x 24.5
(other side)
BP. 246   S. 3. F. B

Hedgehogs

294 Several studies of a hedgehog.
Pencil. 29 x 22.5
BP. 1012   P. C. 12

295 Hedgehog on the palm of a hand (sketched
outline).
W/c and pencil. 25 x 17.5
BP. 1454   P. C. 14

296 Study of a hedgehog's face.
Verso: Sketches of mice.
W/c and pencil. 18 x 11
BP. 1455   P. C. 14

297 Study of a hedgehog's face.
W/c and pencil. W/m: Fine. 20.5 x 16
BP. 1456   P. C. 14

298 Sketch of a hedgehog's snout.
Pencil. W/m: Britannia. 16 x 14
BP. 1457   P. C. 14

Horses and donkeys

299 Sketches of horses in harness eating from nosebags,
and study of heads; also sketch of hung rabbits.
Inscribed: Nov. '85.
(LL Cat.): *Journal*, p. 320.
Verso: Sketches of dogs' heads and windows.
Pen-and-ink and pencil. 17.5 x 11.5
BP. 637   T. 29. R

299 (*detail*)

300 Sketches of horses, including a horse trotting and
one standing.
Inscribed: Jan '86.
Verso: More sketches of horses.
Pen-and-ink and pencil. W/m: Jo/. 18 x 11.5
BP. 638   T. 29. R

301 Sketches of horses standing, including back and
front view.
Inscribed: Nov 23. '85.
Verso: Two detailed sketches of a horse's nose
with harness.
Pen-and-ink and pencil. W/m: & Sons. 14 x 12.5
BP. 639   T. 29. R

302 Sketches of horses' legs and heads.
Verso: Sketches of horses' legs and head.
Inscribed: May 19th '86.
Black and red pen-and-ink. W/m: Joy/. 10 x 16
BP.640   T.29.R

303 Study of a horse eating out of a nosebag.
Pencil, on notepaper. 12.5 x 14
BP.1462   P.C.14

304 Sketches of horses and sheep.
Pencil. 25.5 x 16
BP.1463   P.C.14

305 Sketches of a horse in harness and a horse eating
from a nosebag.
Verso: Sketches of a rabbit.
Pencil. 25 x 17.5
BP.1464   P.C.14

306 Sketches of a horse in harness, and of its legs.
Verso: Sketches of an owl.
Pencil. 26.5 x 20
BP.1465   P.C.14

For another drawing of a horse, see BP.959;
cat.330.

307 Sketches of a donkey (R). Sketch of garden
steps (L).
Inscribed: Garden at Tenby 1900 (LL).
Pencil, on a folded sheet. W/m: Bodleian Ivory
Wove /H M & S. 22.5 x 18
BP.1137   P.C.16

308 Sketch of a donkey in harness.
Inscribed (by BP): 60 stop first.
Pencil, on slightly torn sheet. 12.5 x 8.5
BP.1466   P.C.14

Insects (non-microscopic studies)

309 Study of nine beetles.
Identified by the Natural History Museum (for LL)
as, top (L to R): stag beetle, violet ground beetle,
rose chafer; middle: bloody-nosed beetle; bottom:
Necrodes larva, *Ontholestes tessellatus*, green tiger
beetle, house cricket, *Agonum sexpunctatus*(?).
W/c. W/m: Turkey Kent. 11.5 x 13
BP.401(a)   S.12.F.B   (*see* PLATE XIII)

310 Study of five beetles.
Identified by the Natural History Museum (for LL)
as, top to bottom (L): burying beetle, dor beetle,
Prionus coriarius; top to bottom (R): oil beetle,
Pterostichus.
W/c, on writing paper headed: Gorse Hall, Staley
Bridge. 17.5 x 11
BP.401(b)   S.12.F.B

311 Rough sketches of grasshoppers.
Possibly used in *The Tale of Mr Jeremy Fisher*.
Pencil. 22 x 16.5
BP.1470(a)   P.C.14

312 Sketches of a grasshopper (mainly pencil, but a few
studies are filled in with w/c).
W/c and pencil. 23.5 x 17.5
Verso: Rough pencil sketches of grasshoppers.
Possibly used in *The Tale of Mr Jeremy Fisher*.
BP.1470(b)   P.C.14

Mice etc

313 Study of a dormouse sleeping.
Inscribed (verso): Decem. 14. '87.
Sepia ink and pencil. 8.5 x 11.5
BP.386(b)   S.11.F.C

314 Five studies of a dormouse, one full-length and four
of heads.
Inscribed (verso): Decem. 11 '87.
(LL Cat.): 'Edible' dormouse.
Sepia ink and pencil. 17.5 x 11.5
BP.386(a)   S.11.F.C

315 Sketches of mice (mainly faint outline studies).
Verso: Rabbits (mainly faint outline studies).
Pencil. 25.5 x 16
BP.389   S.11.F.C

314 (*detail*)

316 Sketches of mice including paintings of heads and
a claw; also a sketch of a besom.
Verso (upper half): sketches of cats; (lower half):
garden path and vegetable patch.
(LL Cat.): Possibly Camfield Place?
W/c and pencil. 16 x 25.5
BP.390 S.11.F.C

317 Sketches of mice, including front and side views.
Inscribed: Thurs 2.
Pencil. 20 x 16.5
Verso: Sketches of reeds; also various sweeping
brushstrokes.
Sepia ink.
(LL Cat.): Believed to be reeds on sand-dunes
at Swanage [sic]. [Grange over Sands?]
BP.388 S.11.F.C

318 Five studies of a shrew.
Verso: Unfinished painting of fungus (*Omphalina
mutila?*) surrounded by grasses.
W/c with pencil, on card. 22 x 21
BP.416 S.13.F.A

319 Rough studies of mice.
Pencil. 29 x 22.5
Verso: Mouse studies.
Pencil and a few strokes of green wash.
BP.1015(i) P.C.12

320 Mouse studies.
Verso: Similar mouse studies.
Pencil, on thin strip of paper. 26 x 8
BP.1015(ii) P.C.12

321 Studies of a mouse: head and side views
(mainly outline).
Verso: Faint studies of a mouse.
Pencil. 14 x 12.5
BP.1015(viii) P.C.12

322 Studies of mice.
Pencil. W/m: Coat of arms [with monogram]
S & H. 12.5 x 20
BP.1015(ix) P.C.12

323 Studies of mice (mainly outline).
Pencil. W/m: St Neot. 10 x 16.5
BP.1015(x) P.C.12

324 Studies of mice (mainly outline).
Verso: Similar studies.
Pencil, on sheet with roughly scalloped edge.
10 x 12
BP.1015(xi) P.C.12

325 Studies of mice (mainly outline).
Pencil. W/m: Oceana Fine. 17.5 x 10.5
BP.1015(xii) P.C.12

325 (*detail*)

326 Outline studies of mice.
Pencil, on L-shaped sheet. 11 x 11 (approx.)
BP.1015(xiii) P.C.12

327 Studies of mice (mainly outline) and one wash
study of a rabbit.
Pencil and wash. 23 x 15
BP.1015(xiv) P.C.12

328 Studies of the head and underparts of a harvest
mouse(?).
W/c and pencil. 25 x 17.5
BP.1438 P.C.13

329 Sketches of a rat's head.
Pencil, on notepaper. 8.5 x 20.5
BP.1440 P.C.13

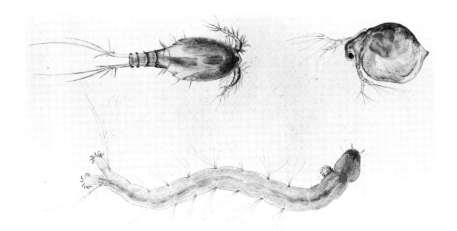

332

Horses and donkeys (addendum)

330 Xerox copy of a sketch (in pen-and-ink and pencil and inscribed by BP) of BP's pony Dolly crossing a stream.
Sent to LL in 1966 by the owner, Vera Dorothy Petersen of Portland, Oregon.
10.5 x 17.5 (size of original)
BP.959   P.C.14

Microscopic studies (including insects)

331 Study of an ant, viewed from above and below (highly magnified).
Inscribed (verso): March '86.
Yellow wash with pen-and-ink, on card. 18 x 27
BP.402   S.12.F.B

332 Three fresh-water creatures (highly magnified).
Inscribed (on mount) by LL: Cyclops (top L); Simocephalus (water-flea) (top R); Chironomus (larva of a midge) (bottom R).
c. 1887 (LL Cat.)
W/c and pen-and-ink, on card. 27 x 36.5
BP.258   S.4.F.B

333 Top: view of a ground beetle (*Carabus nemoralis*) from above and below. Inscribed: twice life size [with pencil measurement of original].
Middle: tarsus of middle leg, inscribed: B; front leg, inscribed: A [study incomplete].
Bottom: enlarged view of joint of leg within pencil frame, inscribed: C; enlarged view of joint more highly magnified, inscribed: D.
Cleaned by BM (LL Cat.) [Refers to Natural History Museum?]
W/c and pen-and-ink. 36.5 x 27
BP.257   S.4.F.B

334 Highly magnified study of a beetle (*Notiophilus biguttatus?*).
Enlarged drawing of the whole insect (L).
Enlarged w/c of head (R).
Inscribed (verso): Beatrix Potter March 4th 87.
Cleaned by BM (LL Cat.)
W/c, pen-and-ink and pencil. 27 x 36.5
BP.260   S.4.F.B

335 Studies of a brown butterfly with magnified wing scales shown on the right.
Inscribed (in ink, on paper pasted on to the card): Painted Lady Butterfly – Vanessa Cardui. Scales on lower side of wing highly magnified.
Below: orange brown butterfly with magnified wing scales (shown L).
Inscribed: Small Tortoiseshell Butterfly. Vanessa [sic] Urticae. Scales on upper side of wing highly magnified.
W/c and pen-and-ink, on card. 35 x 26.5
BP.249   S.3.F.C

336 Various studies of damselflies.
Two views of damselfly, one pen-and-ink outline and one magnified w/c (top L). Magnified view of leg and head (top R). Magnified view of gills (bottom L). Magnified view of eggs on leaf (bottom R).
c. 1887 (LL Cat.)
W/c and pen-and-ink, on card. 21.5 x 28
BP.259   S.4.F.B

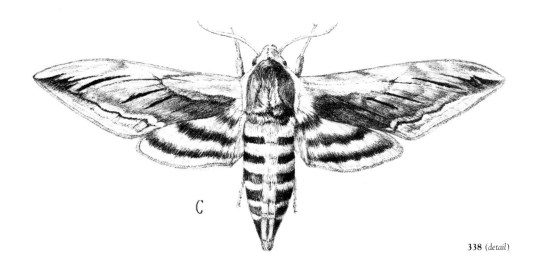

C

337 Study of a leg of a gnat (highly magnified).
Inscribed (verso, in red ink): Leg of gnat.
Feb 7th '86.
W/c with pen-and-ink. 7.5 x 10.5
BP.380 S.11.F.B

338 Lithograph of various details of a privet hawk moth
indicated with letters.
A: caterpillar. B: chrysalis. C: view from above of
the moth. D x 20, E x 20, F x 20: magnified legs.
G x 50 and L x 50: magnified wing scales. H x 600
and K x 600: details of head. I x 5: head with
proboscis.
Printed beneath: H.B. Potter ad nat. del. Sphinx
Ligustri. Copyright. West, Newman imp.
Litho, on card. 22.5 x 26.5
BP.368 S.10.F.C

339 Lithograph as BP.368, but chrysalis and hawk
moth are partly hand-coloured brown.
Litho, on card. 22.5 x 26.5
BP.369 S.10.F.C

340 Incomplete lithograph of Sphinx ligustri (privet
hawk moth).
See BP.368; cat.338 for final version.
The chrysalis is partly coloured green. All parts of
the insect are lithographed but the letters, numbers
and titles are filled in by BP in pencil.
Inscribed (in pencil): H B Potter ad nat lith
SPHINX LIGUSTRI [etc.]; and inscribed with
printer's ref. no.: 20750.
Inscribed (verso): Sphinx ligustri ← small L.
Litho, on folded sheet. 22.5 x 26.5
BP.370 S.10.F.C

341 Three studies of caterpillars, mounted on a
white sheet.
Inscribed: Poplar Hawk Moth, Puss Moth, Privet
Hawk Moth.
The sheet is mounted on yellow card inscribed:
Caterpillars, these turn into large moths.
Also mounted on yellow card is a study of a fly's
foot, inscribed (on mount): A Fly's foot, very much
magnified [etc.].
W/c. 39.5 x 27 (size of mount)
BP.248 S.3.F.C

342 Study of a spider, yellow-brown in colour.
(LL Cat.): Identified as Xysticus cristatus, male crab
spider.
W/c and pen-and-ink, on card. 27 x 36.5
BP.252 S.4.F.A

343 Study of a spider, grey-brown and white in colour.
W/c and pen-and-ink, on card. 27 x 36.5
BP.253 S.4.F.A

344 Study of a spider, grey-white in colour.
Cleaned by BM and all three re-mounted (LL Cat.)
[i.e. BP.252–254; cat. 342–344].
W/c and pen-and-ink, on card. 27 x 36.5
BP.254 S.4.F.A

345 Study of a spider, greenish-brown with a reddish
tinge.
Inscribed: July 14th 1887.
Pen-and-ink, on card. 27 x 36.5
BP.255 S.4.F.A

346 Unfinished study of a yellowish-brown spider.
W/c, pen-and-ink and pencil, on card. 36.5 x 27
BP.256 S.4.F.A

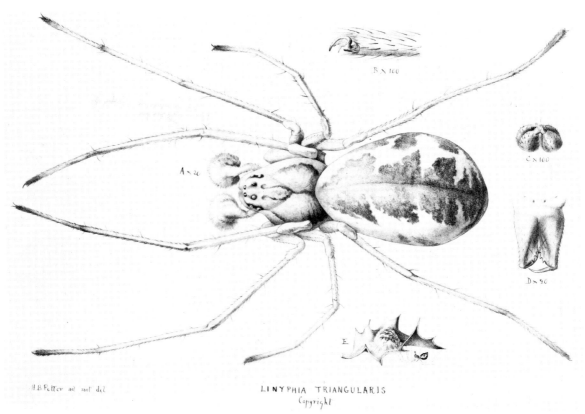

LINYPHIA TRIANGULARIS
Copyright

347

347 Lithograph of a spider (highly magnified).
Inscribed (in BP's writing): H.B. Potter ad nat del
LINYPHIA TRIANGULARIS. Copyright.
A pencil arrow points to a leg, inscribed: There is a
double line here. Could the outside line be scraped
off? Spider inscribed: A x 20.
Also four enlarged details of the spider.
Claw on leg inscribed: B x 100; cephalothorax
inscribed: C x 100; detail of mouth inscribed:
D x 20; holly leaf with nest and spider underneath
inscribed: E.
Litho, on card. 28 x 37.5
Verso. Faint pencil diagrams and inscriptions.
BP.367   S.10.F.C

Molluscs

348 Studies of snails: seven w/c and one pencil.
W/c and pencil. 20 x 12.5
BP.404(a)   S.12.F.C

349 Study of two snails.
W/c and pencil, on card. 11 x 9
BP.404(b)   S.12.F.C

Pigs

350 Three studies of a piglet (R). Gate in a wall (L).
W/c. 25 x 17.5
BP.1449   P.C.13

351 Outline sketches of pigs in various positions.
Verso: Sketches of pigs (faint outlines).
Pencil. W/m: Britannia. 15.5 x 13
BP.1138   P.C.16

Rabbits

352 Head of BP's pet rabbit 'Benjamin Bunny'
(six studies).
Inscribed (L): H.B.P. Aug 90.
Cleaned by BM (LL Cat.)
Pencil, mounted on stiffer paper. 25.5 x 16
BP.261   S.4.F.C

353 Two rabbits nibbling a turnip, watched by a bird.
Inscribed: H.B.P.
Pencil. 25 x 17.5
BP.377   S.11.F.B

354 Study of a rabbit lying down (Peter: LL Cat.);
also two sketches of its head.
Inscribed: Feb 14 99. B.P.
Pencil. 17.5 x 25.5
BP.378   S.11.F.B

355 Sketches of rabbits lying down.
Inscribed: From life H.B. Potter.
Pencil. 20.5 x 16.5
BP.382   S.11.F.B

356 Four rabbits in a burrow.
(LL Cat.): They can be assumed to be Peter,
Flopsy, Mopsy and Cottontail.
Ex Mrs Gaddum.
W/c, on stiff cartridge paper. 16.5 x 19
BP.470   S.16.F.C   (see PLATE XIV)

357 Sketch of a rabbit's head (Peter: LL Cat.)
W/c and pencil, on a sample sheet of Joynson
drawing paper. 19 x 11
BP.648   T.29.R

358 Three drawings mounted on a brown paper folder.
Sheet 1: three heads of a rabbit.
Inscribed (above head of a black rabbit): A little
wild black rabbit – accidentally killed by getting
fast in some wire netting.
Sheet 2: six heads of rabbits.
Sheet 3: head of a sheep.
Inscribed: Study of a dead sheep. Sept '04,
H.B. Potter.
W/c with pencil. 22.5 x 19 (each sheet)
BP.650   T.29.R

359 Two sketches of a rabbit (Benjamin?) by a door,
and front view of a rabbit sitting up.
Sepia ink and pencil, on folded notepaper.
W/m: /eston. 12.5 x 20
BP.649   T.29.R

360 Sketch of a crouching rabbit, and a cat.
Pencil and green-grey wash. W/m: Holyrood.
20 x 12.5
BP.1014(i)   P.C.12

361 Studies of a rabbit in different positions.
Verso: A rabbit stretching.
Pencil. 25 x 16
BP.1014(ii)   P.C.12

362 Rabbit in a box asleep, and studies of a rabbit
washing itself.
Pencil and grey wash. 27 x 12
Verso: Faint study of a rabbit.
Pencil.
BP.1014(iii)   P.C.12

363 Two studies of rabbits resting.
Pencil. 25.5 x 18
BP.1014(iv)   P.C.12

364 Partly finished study of a rabbit on its hind legs
(front view).
Pencil. 25.5 x18
BP.1014(v)   P.C.12

365 Studies of a rabbit lying down.
Verso: Similar studies.
Pencil, on long folded paper strip. 40 x 5
BP.1014(vii)   P.C.12

366 Various studies of a rabbit.
Verso: Similar studies.
Pencil, on folded sheet. 25 x 20
BP.1014(viii)   P.C.12

367 Study of a rabbit sitting, and studies of heads.
Pencil. W/m: Fine. 20 x 16.5
BP.1014(ix)   P.C.12

368 Studies of a rabbit sitting.
Verso: Study of back view of a rabbit.
Pencil. W/m: /s' Mill/24. 16.5 x 10
BP.1014(x)   P.C.12

369 Studies of a rabbit and mouse.
Verso: Similar studies.
Pencil. W/m: Fine. 16.5 x 10
BP.1014(xi)   P.C.12

370 Study of a rabbit lying down, on extreme left
corner of sheet.
Pencil. 20 x 13
BP.1014(xii)   P.C.12

371 Studies of a rabbit sitting, and washing itself.
Pencil, on unevenly cut sheet. 12.5 x 14
BP.1014(xiii)   P.C.12

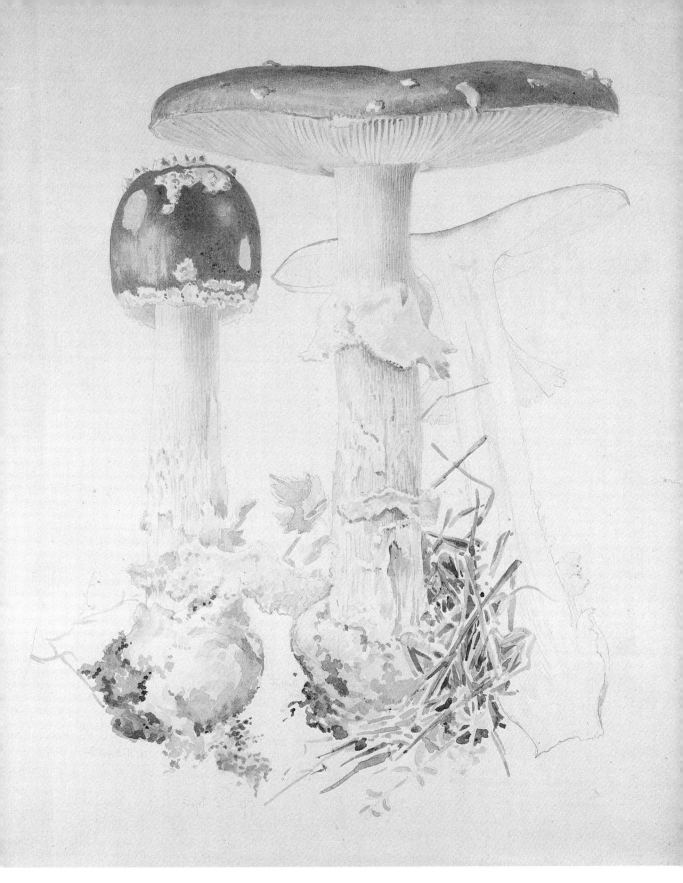

PLATE XII Scarlet fly cap 1897 (**292**)

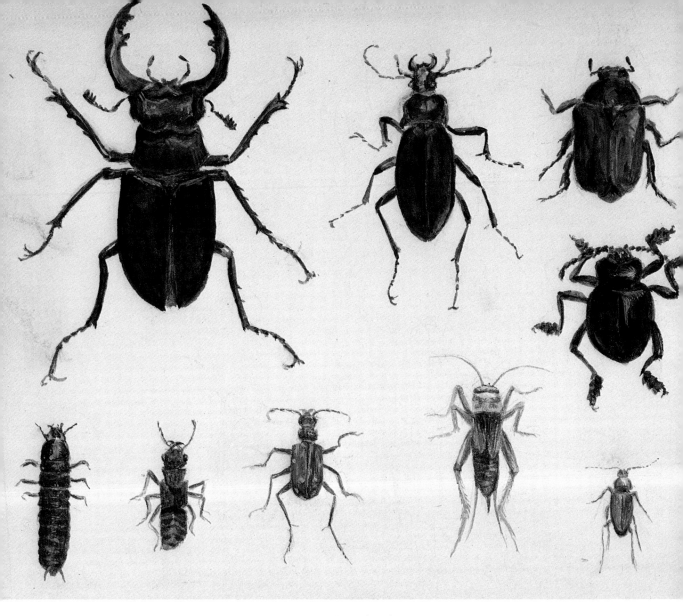

PLATE XIII Nine beetles (309)

PLATE XIV Four rabbits in a burrow (356)

PLATE XV Two squirrels on a log (396)

375

372 Study of a rabbit sitting, and studies of heads.
     Verso: Sketch of a fungus (polypore).
     Pencil. W/m: Britannia. 10.5 x 16.5
     BP.1014(xiv)   P.C.12

373 Studies of a rabbit's head, and of a rabbit washing
     its ears.
     Verso: More studies of rabbits.
     Pencil. 17.5 x 11.5
     BP.1014(xv)   P.C.12

374 Studies of the head of a rabbit, and of a rabbit
     lying down.
     Pencil, on notepaper. 16 x 10
     BP.1014(xvi)   P.C.12

375 Faint studies of rabbits.
     Pencil. W/m: Britannia. 20.5 x 20
     BP.1014(xvii)   P.C.12

376 A rabbit sitting (Peter?).
     Pen-and-ink, monochrome wash and white
     highlights. 12 x 16
     Verso: Unfinished sketch of rabbit, with leaves
     (cut off at top).
     Pen-and-ink and pencil.
     BP.1145(b)   P.C.16

377 Finished study of a rabbit sitting (Peter?), and light
     wash of a rabbit lying down.
     Pen-and-ink, monochrome wash and white
     highlights. 20 x 15.5
     BP.1145(a)   P.C.16

Reptiles

378 Study of a lizard against an unfinished background of vegetation.
Inscribed: Feb '84. Judy (the lizard) came from Ilfracombe, probably April 83, and died on Sunday 20th April 1884 when BP was staying at Minehead (LL Cat.)
W/c, pen-and-ink and pencil. 11 x 17.5
BP.405   S.12.F.C

379 Two views of a brown lizard: one side view, and one view from below.
Inscribed: 1885.
W/c. 18.5 x 12.5
BP.406   S.12.F.C

380 Snake curled around the branches of a tree.
W/c. 16 x 22
BP.417   S.13.F.A

Sheep

381 Four studies of a ram's head.
Pencil. 18 x 11.5
BP.414   S.13.F.A

382 Sketches of a sheep, horse, pig and cow.
Pencil, on folded sheet with torn edge. 30.5 x 17
BP.1441   P.C.13

383 Studies of sheep and a horse, and of clumps of grass and trees.
Inscribed (in pencil): Sept 16th '04.
Sepia ink. 22.5 x 19
BP.1442   P.C.13

384 Studies of a sheep's head.
W/c and pencil. 22.5 x 18
BP.1443   P.C.13

385 Studies of sheep heads (two are coloured with wash).
W/c with pencil. 22.5 x 19
BP.1444   P.C.13

386 Study of a sheep's head (front view).
W/c with pencil. 22.5 x 19
BP.1445   P.C.13

387 Study of the head of a lamb, and of the lamb lying down.
Verso: Studies of a lamb's head.
W/c with pencil. 20.5 x 16.5
BP.1446   P.C.13

388 Studies of sheep and three horses grazing.
Inscribed (in pencil): Sept 16th '04.
Sepia ink. 22.5 x 19
BP.1447   P.C.13

389 Sketch of a lamb, and studies of its head and legs.
Verso: More studies of a lamb.
Pencil, on card. 30 x 24
BP.1448   P.C.13

390 Three studies of a sheep's head.
White chalk and crayon, on brown paper. 28 x 24.5
BP.1469(i)   P.C.15

391 Studies of sheep huddled together in a fold.
Verso: Similar studies.
White chalk and crayon, on brown paper. 28 x 24.5
BP.1469(ii)   P.C.15

392 Two studies of a sheep's head.
Verso: Similar studies of a sheep's head.
White chalk and crayon, on brown paper. 28 x 24
BP.1469(iii)   P.C.15

393 Studies of sheep and lambs.
White chalk and crayon, on brown paper. 28 x 24.5
BP.1469(iv)   P.C.15

394 Sketches of sheep lying down, and grazing.
Pencil and pen-and-ink. 25 x 17.5
BP.1139   P.C.16

394 (detail)

403

Squirrels

395 Study of squirrels.
Probably 1903 (LL Cat.)
Verso: Sketch of fungus (*Amanita rubescens*).
Inscribed: old spec. Rubescens. Howes End Oct
2nd '97; also has indication in pencil, pointing to
the stem: Red all over.
Pencil and grey wash. 28 x 33.5 (rectangular piece
cut out of corner)
BP.247   S.3.F.B

396 Two squirrels sitting on a log.
W/c. 21 x 18
BP.376   S.11.F.B   (*see* PLATE XV)

397 Studies of ferrets and squirrels (mainly pencil, but
also two wash drawings).
Pencil and green wash. 23 x 15.5
BP.413   S.13.F.A

398 Rough sketches of squirrels.
Verso: Two outline sketches of a squirrel.
Possibly studies for *The Tale of Squirrel Nutkin*.
Pencil. 20 x 12.5
BP.1436   P.C.13

399 Several rough sketches of squirrels.
Verso: Similar sketches of squirrels.
Possibly studies for *The Tale of Squirrel Nutkin*.
Pencil. 25.5 x 16
BP.1437   P.C.13

Trees and shrubs; vegetables

400 Four studies of climbing ivy sprigs with berries and
leaves.
W/c and pen-and-ink, on card. 33 x 26
BP.1174   P.C.51

401 Ivy plant growing up the side of a building.
Probably 1885 (LL Cat.)
Pen-and-ink. 17.5 X 11
BP.374   S.11.F.A

402 Viburnum branch with leaves, fruit and flowers.
W/c with pen-and-ink. 22.5 x 19
BP.1177   P.C.51

403 Two sprays of a sweet bay tree.
Inscribed: Direct light from this side; and: Against
the light. The veins in the leaf are slightly
transparent. There has been no sunshine &
evergreen leaves show very little transparent light
without it.
Inscribed (verso): H.B. Potter. S.B. Feb. 1900.
W/c. 18 x 25.5
BP.269   S.5.F.A

404 Study of the branch of a beech tree.
Verso: Partly finished studies of grasses,
nettles etc.
W/c and pen-and-ink. 28 x 35.5
BP.957   P.C.52

405 Studies of leaves and various branches of a tree,
probably a beech; also money calculations.
Verso: Similar study of a single branch.
Pen-and-ink with pencil. W/m: 7. 21 x 26.5
BP.958(a)   P.C.52

406 Studies of the branches of a tree, probably a beech.
Verso: Similar studies.
Pen-and-ink and pencil. W/m: 7. 21 x 26.5
BP.958(b)   P.C.52

407 Branch of a flowering elder.
W/c with pen-and-ink. 22 x 27.5
BP.1173   P.C.51

408 Four studies showing hazelnuts and leaves.
Verso: Faint outline sketch of a rabbit.
W/c with pencil. 26 x 22.5
BP.1170   P.C.51

409 Unfinished sketch of a horse-chestnut tree trunk
(partly in pen-and-ink and partly outlined
in pencil).
Verso: Sketch of a horse-chestnut.
Inscribed: June 17 Camfield.
Pen-and-ink and pencil. 17.5 x 11
BP.954   P.C.45

410 Rough study of a bush growing out of a bank –
possibly an oak seedling.
Pencil. 22.5 x 19
BP.945   P.C.47

411 Three studies of the branches and leaves of a tree
in a wood – probably an oak.
W/c with pen-and-ink and pencil. 27.5 x 37.5
BP.955   P.C.52

412 Study of an oak branch with acorns and leaves.
Pen-and-ink with pencil, on sheet with folded
edge. 26.5 x 37 (excluding folded edge)
BP.956(a)   P.C.52

413 Study of an oak branch with leaves.
W/c and pen-and-ink. 26 x 37
BP.956(b)   P.C.52

414 Studies of an oak branch with acorns.
Pen-and-ink with pencil, on sheet with folded
edge. W/m: 7. 26.5 x 39 (excluding folded edge)
BP.956(c)   P.C.52

415 *(detail)*

415 Studies of oak branches with leaves and oak apples;
also studies of hazelnut clusters.
Pencil and sepia ink, on folded sheet (originally
folded into four – one part now missing). W/m:
Aviemore. 26.5 x 22 (size of one side)
BP.960   P.C.52

416 Two finished studies of oak leaves with oak apples;
also unfinished study of hazelnut clusters.
W/c and sepia ink. 17.5 x 28
BP.1169   P.C.51

417 Study of a plane tree(?) showing branches and
leaves.
Pen-and-ink and pencil. 12.5 x 10 (cut down)
Verso: Study of a man fishing (in wash) and
drawing of a fern, grasses and twigs (in pen-and-ink
and pencil).
BP.938   P.C.47

418 Study of vine leaves (unfinished).
Pen-and-ink and pencil. 14.5 x 18
Verso: Very rough sketch of the head of a bat.
Pencil.
BP.937   P.C.47

419 Sketches of yew branches with berries.
Verso: Very rough sketch of an interior.
Pencil, on folded sheet with torn edge.
27 x 20.5 (approx.)
BP.944   P.C.47

418

420 Studies of cabbage plants.
Pen-and-ink. W/m: 7. 14 x 21
BP.1175   P.C.51

421 Sketch of a marrow plant, with faint pencil
outlines to indicate the flowers and also the slate
border.
Pen-and-ink and pencil. W/m: 7. 21 x 26.5
BP.1176   P.C.51

422 Various plant studies including parsley, rhubarb
and beetroot.
Inscribed: Lingholm Sept 3 '07.
Verso: Sketches of cabbage, rhubarb, parsley etc.
W/c and pencil. W/m: Willowbrook Extra Fine.
20.5 x 33
BP.911(i)   P.C.45

423 Unidentified sprays of leaves, one showing a
seed-pod.
Inscribed (in pencil): Sept 2 '03.
W/c and sepia ink. W/m: Kent. 29 x 22.5
BP.1264(ix)   P.C.40

424 Rough sketch of unidentified twigs with small
spiky leaves.
Verso: Similar sketches.
Pencil and pen-and-ink. W/m: Towgood's Fine.
20.5 x 32
BP.927   P.C.47

425 Very rough sketch of unidentified twigs with
leaves.
Verso: Rough sketch of leaves.
Pencil. 21 x 11
BP.943   P.C.47

REPRESENTATIONAL WORKS

The heading of this section has purposely been left vague, since it was intended to cover many of the subjects which could not be allocated elsewhere. Its primary concern is with factual drawings which do not relate to natural history, the Peter Rabbit books, or other published or projected works. Beatrix Potter drew many of the buildings she knew and loved, both exteriors and interiors, even down to the chairs and fire-places. But the largest group of paintings and drawings is of landscapes, and these have been identified whenever possible, although some still await identification. Her drawings of buildings are always precise, but her landscape sketches vary from a mere hint of wash on a page to finished paintings. This section also contains representations of people – a subject field in which Beatrix Potter never excelled. If she merely attempted a rough sketch, she was often successful, but further elaboration was usually disastrous. A careful study of the various human figures represented in her books will confirm the impression which this very small selection of 'People' conveys, namely that she was not at her best or happiest in this area of her art.

Buildings

426 Roadway with a wall, barns and iron gateway; a close-up study of a gateway in the left corner.
Inscribed: 'and bars'.
Back of Bedwell Lodge Estate (LL Cat.)
Verso: Rough sketch of a mouse.
Pencil. 16 x 25.5
BP.329   S.8.F.B

427 Greenhouse and back door (?) of Bedwell Lodge, with geraniums in the foreground.
Inscribed (on folder): Bedwell Lodge 1891 (LL).
Pencil. 25 x 20
BP.1229   P.C.30

428 Front of Bedwell Lodge showing the porch and two gables (LL).
Pencil, heightened with crayon. 25.5 x 16
BP.326   S.8.F.B

429 Corner of the backyard at Bedwell Lodge, showing the back door; two peacocks on left.
Inscribed (L): Sept '91.
Inscribed (verso): Bedwell Lodge nr. Camfield.
Pencil. 16 x 25.5
BP.327   S.8.F.B

430 Various studies of windows at Bedwell Lodge.
Inscribed: Oct 4th '91.
Inscribed (on folder): Bedwell Lodge (LL).
Verso: Faint sketch of flowers.
Pencil. 24.5 x 19
BP.1219   P.C.30

431 Bolton Gardens at dusk, as seen from 2 Bolton Gardens (BP's home).
Inscribed (verso): A November day. H.B. Potter.
Mainly grey wash with pencil. Printed (on the back): Winsor & Newton's watercolour sketching boards. 27 x 18.5
BP.230   S.2.F.A   (see PLATE XVI)

432 Farmhouse at Brookthorpe (almost completed).
See BP.235(b,c,d,e); cat.433–435, 598.
Pen-and-ink with pencil. W/m: Oceana Fine.
26.5 x 20.5
BP.235(a)   S.2.F.A

433 Farmhouse at Brookthorpe.
See BP.235(a,c,d,e); cat.432, 434–435, 598.
Sepia ink with pencil. W/m: Oceana Fine. 27 x 21
BP.235(b)   S.2.F.A

434 Farmhouse at Brookthorpe.
See BP.235(a,b,d,e); cat.432–433, 435, 598.
Sepia ink with pencil. 26.5 x 21
BP.235(c)   S.2.F.A

435 Printer's proof of farmhouse (same as BP.235(b);
cat.433).
Inscribed: Use a process black. (Indian ink used.)
Proof of pen-and-ink drawing. 25.5 x 17.5
BP.235(d)   S.2.F.A

436 Bush Hall from the grounds (unfinished).
In between the red roofs, the bell tower is visible.
Inscribed (verso): Bush Hall, an old brick house
on the Lea near Hatfield. Summer of 1884.
H.B.H. 1934.
Endorsed in 1934 when BP was sorting through
portfolios (LL Cat.)
W/c and pencil. 17.5 x 25.5
BP.323   S.8.F.A

437 Two projecting gables, Bush Hall.
Drawn in the summer of 1884 (LL Cat.)
Crayon. 24 x 14.5
BP.319   S.8.F.A

438 View through trees of a roof-top with chimney and
dormer windows.
Inscribed (on mount): Bush Hall, Herts. Summer
1884 (LL).
Crayon. 29.5 x 22
BP.320   S.8.F.A

439 View of one side of Bush Hall, partly obscured by a
tree on the left. On the right, a woman is hanging
out clothes.
Inscribed: Sept 12 '84.
Crayon. 30.5 x 23.5
BP.321   S.8.F.A

440 Corner of the back-yard at Bush Hall, with a dog in
front of a long low building.
Crayon. 25 x 25
Verso: Sketches of cows in various positions.
Inscribed: October 1884.
Pencil.
BP.322   S.8.F.A

441– Melford Hall seen over the garden pool and wall,
442 with greenhouses.
(LL Cat.): The home of BP's cousin Ethel Hyde-
Parker, mother of Stephanie. This unsigned
painting belonged to Stephanie.
W/c. 18.5 x 22.5
Also loose brown paper folder inscribed: Melford
Hall Suffolk H.B. Potter, with pencil note on verso
(almost obliterated): The property of Mrs Duke,
3 Holland Park Avenue W.11.
BP.295(a,b)   S.6.F.C

443 Sketch of a chimney on a steep-pitched roof
(Bush Hall).
Pencil, on notepaper. 20 x 12.5
Verso: Sketches of chickens.
Pencil and w/c.
BP.324   S.8.F.A

444 Sketch of a mullioned window.
Verso: Sketch of similar window.
Possibly Bush Hall (LL Cat.)
Crayon. 26 x 17
BP.325   S.8.F.A

445 Hill Top by night.
The ground is covered with snow and a glow of
light shines from the porch and windows (LL Cat.)
W/c. 12 x 9.5
BP.294   S.6.F.C   (*see* PLATE XVII)

446 Sketch of an inn with horse and trap at entrance
(upper half). Part of inn with inn sign (lower half).
Inscribed (on mount): Kelso? Cross Keys Inn? (LL).
1894? (LL Cat.)
Pencil. 25 x 17.5
BP.330   S.8.F.B

447 Farm buildings with a fence in the foreground
(Gloucestershire).
Inscribed: Oct 6th '04.
Inscribed (verso): H.B. Potter.
Pencil and sepia ink, mounted on brown paper.
20.5 x 26.5, on sheet 26.5 x 32.5
BP.1155   P.C.20

448 Two sketches of Sawrey, one of yard at Hill Top.
Inscribed (verso): Earliest scribbles of Peter Rabbit,
Jeremy Fisher, Pig Robinson [no reference to
sketches on front].
Pencil. 14 x 16.5
BP.1217   P.C.30

449 Gable and roof-tops among trees.
Inscribed (on mount): A sheltered cot H.B. Potter.
[information repeated on back]
Inscribed (verso) in another hand: p.80 The
property of Capt Duke.
W/c and pen-and-ink. 13.5 x 22.5, on
card 21 x 28
BP.306   S.7.F.B

450 View through an open gate to a house: sketch of
roof and chimney (L); repeat of part of sketch (R),
with a small version of left-hand sketch.
Pencil. W/m: Parson's Linen L/Holyoke Mass.
21 x 26.5
BP.1221   P.C.30

451 Church tower and chancel (exterior view).
Inscribed (on folder): Salisbury (LL).
Pencil. 25.5 x 17.5
BP.1216   P.C.30

452 Rough sketch of cottages with dogs in front.
Verso: Various studies of dormer windows, porch,
bay windows etc.
Pencil. 11 x 17.5
BP.1218   P.C.30

453 Study of roof tiles and skylight.
Pencil. 12.5 x 17.5
BP.1220   P.C.30

454 House in a street with a Dutch gable at the back
(unfinished) and two lightly pencilled figures (R).
Pencil and pen-and-ink. 12.5 x 17.5
BP.1224   P.C.30

455 Rough sketch of a group of farm buildings, with a
horse (unfinished) in the foreground.
Pencil and wash. W/m: I & JH Kent. 15 x 23
BP.963(i)   P.C.32

456 Photograph of an etching (inscribed: H.B.P.99)
showing a group of farm buildings with a field in
front and trees behind (near Lingholm?).
10 x 14 (size of original)
BP.544   P.C.33

Gardens

457 Corner of the kitchen garden with a rose growing
against a wall and a vegetable frame in front; a
besom and a wicker basket by the frame.
Bedwell Lodge 1891 (LL Cat.)
Pencil. 25.5 x 16
BP.328   S.8.F.B

458 Sketch of a garden with cabbage plants and flower-
pots in the foreground.
Inscribed (on folder): Bedwell Lodge 1891 (LL).
Pencil. 25 x 19.5
BP.1230   P.C.30

459 Porch with trellis and faintly sketched flower-beds
in the front (Bedwell Lodge?).
Pencil. W/m: Britannia. 20 x 32.5
BP.1231   P.C.30

460 Vegetable frame with a garden wall behind it and
house beyond.
Inscribed: Sep 27 '91.
Inscribed (on mount): Bedwell Lodge (LL).
Pencil, on notepaper. 20 x 25
BP.1234   P.C.31

461 Unfinished study of a garden pump with waterbutt.
Inscribed (on transparent cover): Bedwell Lodge
1891 (LL).
W/c with pencil. 25 x 17.5
BP.1235   P.C.31

462 Sketch of a walled garden with flower-beds and
buildings (greenhouse?) in one corner; also
sketches of plants (Lingholm).
See detailed study, BP.343; cat.463.
Pencil. 15 x 19.5
BP.1226   P.C.30

463 Detailed study of garden path with geraniums
and buildings at the end.
Lingholm (LL Cat.)
See study for drawing, BP.1226; cat.462.
Blue-grey monochrome wash and pen-and-ink.
16 x 12
BP.343   S.9.F.B
(Mounted with BP.342; cat.606)

470

464 Melford Hall. View along a buttressed wall with trees in the background.
Inscribed (on folder): Melford Hall (LL).
Sepia ink and pencil. W/m: Oceana Fine.
26.5 x 20.5
BP.1030   P.C.22

465 A walled garden with mountains in the background.
Inscribed (on mount): 'Lakefield', Sawrey (LL).
Inscribed (verso): Aug. 'An English Garden' Bunny.
(LL Cat.): BP's pen-name when circulating paintings in a small Drawing Society portfolio (probably 1900).
Verso also inscribed with partly torn off comment on work: 'wanting in colour & life'.
W/c with pen-and-ink. 22.5 x 29
BP.238   S.2.F.B

466 Studies of baskets, one of which is a lobster basket, and a garden pump.
(LL Cat.): May have been drawn at Sidmouth.
Pencil. 25.5 x 18
BP.278   S.5.F.C

467 Garden with a fishpond and herbaceous border seen from a stone wall.
Inscribed: April 1900.
Inscribed (on folder): Garden at Tenby.
Verso: Comments by members of the Drawing Society when drawing was circulated in their portfolio (LL Cat.)
There appear to be some touches in oil paint on the flowers and foliage. A smaller duplicate of this picture hangs in one of the bedrooms at Hill Top, Sawrey (LL Cat.)
W/c. 23 x 29
BP.241   S.2.F.B

468 A walled garden [at Tenby] in the snow, with fruit trees and a group of birds feeding in the foreground. The snow-covered roof of a cottage can be seen behind the garden wall.
Inscribed (on mount, now detached): Feb. 01
Winter in a garden H.B. Potter.
W/c and pen-and-ink. 10.5 x 20.5
BP.298   S.7.F.B   (*see* PLATE XVIII)

469 Sketch of an opening in a wall with ferns growing on the top of a stone slab.
W/c and pencil. 17.5 x 12.5
BP.1241   P.C.31

470 Corner of garden with flower-beds and beehives.
Inscribed (verso): H.B. Potter.
Sepia ink. W/m: Aviemore. 17 x 25.5
BP.1238   P.C.31

471 Sketch of walled garden with flower-beds.
Possibly drawn at Gwaynynog as background for
The Tale of the Flopsy Bunnies.
Inscribed: Jan 22 11.
W/c and pencil. 17.5 x 12.5
BP.1242 P.C.31

472 Sketch of a cypress-lined avenue leading to a gate.
Pen-and-ink and pencil. W/m: A Pirie 190/.
17.5 X 11
BP.986 P.C.34

473 A potted fuchsia on a brick wall in garden
surroundings (unfinished).
Possibly drawn at Fawe Park as background for
The Tale of Benjamin Bunny.
W/c and pen-and-ink. 22.5 x 19
BP.1264(vii) P.C.40

474 A garden scene with carnations and antirrhinums.
Inscribed (L): July 25 '03.
Possibly drawn at Fawe Park as background for
The Tale of Benjamin Bunny.
W/c and pen-and-ink. 22.5 x 19
BP.1264(vi) P.C.40

475 Open trap-door to a cellar from a garden path.
Possibly drawn at Fawe Park as background for
The Tale of Benjamin Bunny.
W/c and pencil. 22.5 x 19
BP.1264(iv) P.C.40

Interiors

Churches (unidentified)

476 Part of perpendicular moulding from a church or
cathedral.
Pencil. 14.5 x 10
BP.595 T.25.L

477 Church interior showing a round arch.
Pencil. 25 x 17.5
Verso: Flower studies (unidentified): flower blue-
pink in colour.
BP's work?
W/c and pencil.
BP.999 P.C.11

478 Church interior showing nave built in Gothic
style.
BP's work?
Pen-and-ink and pencil. 29.5 x 21
BP.1000 P.C.11

Furniture etc.

479 Several studies of chairs.
Inscribed: Fawe Park.
(LL Cat.): The Potters spent the summer of 1903
at Fawe Park, Derwentwater.
Sepia ink with pencil. 26.5 x 21
BP.233 S.2.F.A

480 Three Staffordshire figures of women.
Inscribed: Old Staffordshire figures. Gwaynynog.
Sept 19–23rd '08.
Inscribed (verso): H.B. Potter.
W/c. 25.5 x 17.5
BP.372 S.11.F.A

481 Three sketches of a high-backed chair.
Inscribed (on folder): Chairs at Gwaynynog 1910.
Pencil, on notepaper. 16.5 x 21.5
BP.1007 P.C.10

482 Four studies of a chair (Gwaynynog?).
Pencil. W/m: St. Neots Mill No.24 Fine.
20.5 X 19
BP.997 P.C.11

483 Two studies of a high-backed chair.
Inscribed (verso): Gwaynynog May 4th to 7th '10.
Sepia ink with pencil, on notepaper. 22.5 x 21
BP.998 P.C.11

484 Study of a wicker chair from two different angles.
Verso: One wicker chair (Gwaynynog?).
Pencil. W/m: Britannia. 16.5 x 20
BP.1008(b) P.C.10

485 Three studies of a cane chair, one chair incomplete
(Gwaynynog?).
Pencil and sepia ink. W/m: Aviemore. 18.5 x 26
BP.1009 P.C.10

486 Study of a wicker chair from two different angles
(Gwaynynog?).
Pencil and pen-and-ink. W/m: Britannia. 16 x 20
BP.1008(a) P.C.10

487 Sketch of a linen chest with open lid
(Gwaynynog?).
Verso: Faint sketches of boulders and trees by
a stream.
Pencil. 17.5 x 23
BP.1002 P.C.10

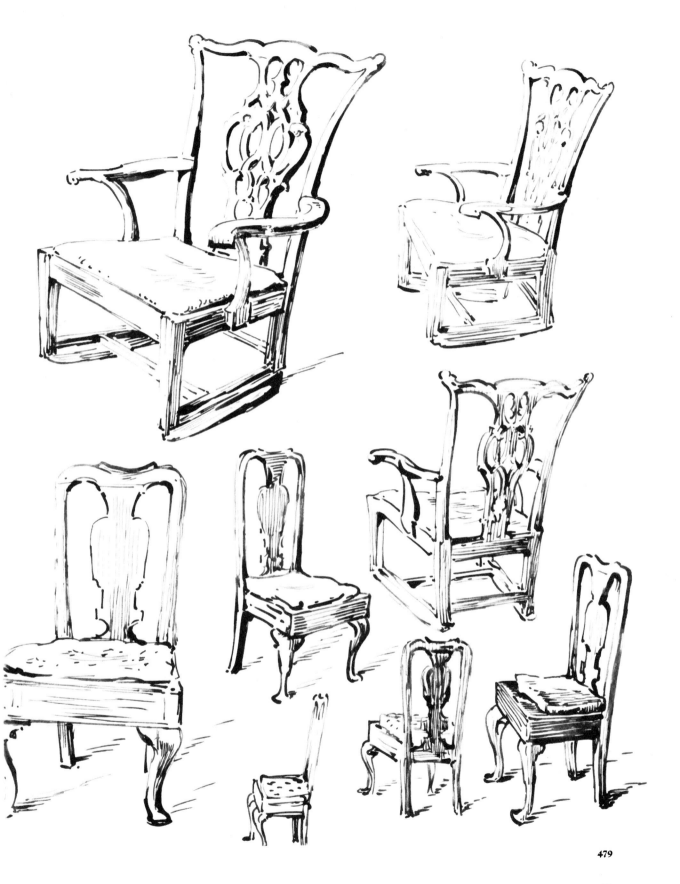

479

488 (*detail*)

488 Study of a Jacobean chair and part of a fire-place
with fire-screen (Melford Hall).
Sepia ink with pencil. W/m: Aviemore.
18.5 x 26.5
BP.1161   P.C.11

489 Writing desk and mirror (Gwaynynog?).
Sepia ink with pencil. W/m: Aviemore.
26.5 x 19.5
BP.1160   P.C.11

490 Corner of a room with a Jacobean cupboard and
open doorway.
Verso: Sketches of kitchen range, window, scales
etc. (Hill Top).
Pencil, on notepaper. 22.5 x 20
BP.989   P.C.11

Rooms (Domestic & Outhouse)

491 Dining room at Bedford Square.
Inscribed (front L): 8 Bedford Square. Nov. 1905.
Beatrix Potter.
Given to Fruing Warne; a duplicate belongs to Mr
Frederick Stephens. Painted soon after Norman
Warne died – it was his home. The cupboard on
the left was used for sweets and candies. It was a
large room and this is just the end of it (LL Cat.)
W/c. 26.5 x 21, on card 28 x 23
BP.284   S.6.F.A

493

492 Interior of a potting shed with a watering can on
the right, and gardening tools on the left.
Inscribed: Aug. 91. '40 [sic].
This is the interior of the Peter Rabbit potting shed
at Bedwell Lodge, Herts., and is also the setting for
the drawing of Peter and Benjamin potting
geraniums (LL Cat.)
See also BP.431; cat.1001.
Crayon. 23 x 16
BP.279   S.5.F.C

493 Interior of Bedwell Lodge: the back stairs viewed
from the landing above.
Inscribed (L): H.B.P. Sept 21. 91.
This was later used as the setting for 'The Mice in
their Storeroom' (LL Cat.)
See also BP.430; cat.1021.
Pencil and grey wash. 25.5 x 16
BP.286   S.6.F.A

500

494 Interior of a barn with cat and two kittens.
Inscribed (verso): Sunlight & shadow. H.B.
Potter.
Painted in September 1891 at Bedwell Lodge,
Hertfordshire. See duplicate at NBL (LL Cat.)
See also BP.1088; cat.495.
Black and grey monochrome wash with white
highlights. 25 x 17.5
BP.288   S.6.F.A   (*illustration p.53*)

495 Interior of a barn with cat and two kittens.
Inscribed (L): H.B.P. Aug '91.
Inscribed (verso): Bedwell Lodge 1891 (LL).
See BP.288; cat.494.
Black and grey monochrome wash with white
highlights (darker in tone than BP.288). 25.5 x 16
BP.1088   P.C.2

496 Bedroom interior (Bedwell Lodge) including a
towel rail in the foreground.
Inscribed: Oct 4th 91.
Pencil. 16.5 x 19.5
BP.291   S.6.F.B

497 Corner of a living room with flower-pots on the
window-sill (Bedwell Lodge, 1891).
Same curtain rods as BP.291; cat.496 (LL Cat.)
Pencil. 25 x 20
BP.292   S.6.F.B

498 A view along a panelled passage-way (Bush Hall).
Inscribed: 8/4.
Crayon. 23.5 x 17
BP.281   S.5.F.C

499 The junction of two panelled passage-ways, with a
doorway on the left side.
(LL Cat.): Bush Hall, Hertfordshire, drawn in the
summer of 1884.
Crayon. 24 x 15.5
BP.282   S.5.F.C

500 Bedroom interior with a half-tester bed.
Inscribed: Bedroom. Camfield Place. Hatfield.
Herts. 'No 4' where I always slept. After my
grandmother's death I asked for the bedstead with
green hangings. The chair, the looking-glass &
3 pictures were given me. I still have them. Also
the alabaster figure of Ariadne riding the leopard,
which was under a glass shade on the mantelpiece.
The red bed quilt also I had many years at
B. Gardens.
Pen-and-ink and pencil. 9.5 x 11.5, on
sheet 17.5 x 11.5
BP.285   S.6.F.A

501 Two views through doorways into attic rooms.
Inscribed: Eeswyke Oct 1st 1900.
Pencil and grey wash with touches of yellow wash.
22.5 x 29
BP.293   S.6.F.B

502 Attic room containing a rabbit.
Inscribed (on folder): Ees Wyke [sic] 1900 (LL).
Sepia ink with pencil. 16 x 20
BP.1003   P.C.10

503 Corner of an attic room.
Inscribed (on folder): Ees Wyke [sic] 1900 (LL).
Sepia ink with pencil. 16.5 x 20
BP.1004   P.C.10

504 Attic room with views into two rooms.
Inscribed (on folder): Ees Wyke [sic] 1900 (LL).
Sepia ink with pencil. W/m: Aviemore. 18.5 x 27
BP.994   P.C.11

505 Empty attic room with prominent beams.
Inscribed (on folder): Ees Wyke [sic] 1900 (LL).
Sepia ink with pencil. W/m: Aviemore. 26.5 x 19
BP.995   P.C.11

506 Hall or landing with a curved archway (Bedwell
Lodge).
Passage, identified by the curved oak arch timbers
(LL Cat.)
Pencil. 20 x 17
BP.290   S.6.F.B

507 Fire-place and chair (Gwaynynog?).
Sepia ink (chair) and grey wash (fire-place).
W/m: Britannia. 19 x 23
BP.1005   P.C.10

508 Part of a room with dresser and grandfather clock
(at Hill Top?).
Pencil, on card. 16.5 x 19
BP.990   P.C.11

508

509 Corner of a panelled room with a table, and a
grandfather clock in one corner.
Inscribed (on transparent cover): Gwaynynog (LL).
W/c with pencil. 25.5 x 17.5
BP.993   P.C.11

510 View of a passage and staircase.
Inscribed (on transparent cover): Hill Top (LL).
Pencil and wash. 21 x 17.5
BP.1087   P.C.2

511 Unfinished study of stairs and banister.
Inscribed (on transparent cover):
Lennel 1894 (LL).
W/c and pencil. 13 x 9
Verso: Faint pencil study of a hallway.
BP.636(a)   T.29.R

512 Sketch of a staircase.
Inscribed (on transparent cover):
Lennel 1894 (LL).
Pencil. 9 x 7
BP.636(b)   T.29.R

513 Sketch of a landing with an open doorway leading
into a bathroom.
Inscribed (on transparent cover):
Lennel 1894 (LL).
Pen-and-ink. 6.5 x 5
Verso: Section of a study of leaves (cut down).
Grey wash with pencil.
BP.636(c)   T.29.R

514 Sketch of a doorway with panels.
Inscribed (on transparent cover):
Lennel 1894 (LL).
Verso: Part of a room with a window at the end.
Pen-and-ink with pencil, on small unevenly cut sheet.
4.5 x 4
BP.636(d)   T.29.R

515 View of a passage-way (L). View of hallway and
stair-rail (R).
Inscribed (on folder): Lennel 1894 (LL).
Grey wash with pencil (L). Pencil (R). 15 x 23
BP.1001   P.C.10

516 View through an open door of a passage leading
to a room.
Inscribed (on transparent cover):
Lennel 1894 (LL).
Monochrome wash and pencil. 29 x 19
BP.992   P.C.11

517 Melford Hall: interior of room with a close-up view
of a window-seat and chair.
This picture belonged to Stephanie (LL Cat.)
Sepia ink with pencil. 26.5 x 21
BP.296   S.6.F.C

518 Sketch of a candlestick.
Part of set of drawings of interiors at Derwent
Cottage, Winchelsea, Feb 1900 (LL Cat.)
Pencil, on card. 23 x 14
BP.373   S.11.F.A

518a Corner of library, once thought to be at Wray
Castle, showing part of fire-place and open
doorway.
Inscribed (on mount) by Mrs Gaddum?: Wray
Castle; and (by LL): Location by Mrs Gaddum
[1966].
Pen-and-ink. 12 x 8.5
BP.289   S.6.F.B

518a

PLATE XVI (above) 'A November day': Bolton Gardens (**431**)

PLATE XVII (right) Hill Top on a winter night (**445**)

PLATE XVIII (top) Walled garden and birds in snow 1901 (468)

PLATE XIX (above) Harvest at Esthwaite (537)

PLATE XX 'Rain': Lingholm 1898 (555)

PLATE XXI Sawrey under snow 1909 (669)

519 View of a room through an open doorway.
Verso (upper half): mountain scene with lake;
(lower half): sketches of a pig's head and legs.
Pencil. 26.5 x 18.5
BP.988   P.C.11

520 Two studies of a window and window-seat.
Sepia ink with pencil (L). Pencil (R).
W/m: Linen Ledge/olyoke Mass 1895.
26.5 x 21
BP.1236   P.C.11

520 (*detail*)

521 Kitchen corner with fire-place and spit, and stone-
built copper.
Pencil and grey wash. 14.5 x 15
Verso: Mountain stream with stone bridge and
trees in background.
Pencil and w/c.
BP.1086   P.C.2

522 Rough sketch of a kitchen interior.
Inscribed (on folder): Probably in
Cumberland (LL).
Pencil. 22.5 x 18
BP.1006   P.C.10

523 Sketch of a kitchen showing a range and baby's cot
(probably in Cumberland).
Verso: Studies of ironwork, including a fender, arm
of a settle, details of other ironwork.
Pencil. 21 x 26.5
BP.991   P.C.11

524 Hallway and stairs.
Pencil. 7 x 6
BP.1010   P.C.10

525 Sketch showing sink below a window, with a
work-bench etc.
Inscribed (on transparent cover): Miss Hammond's
brother's studio (LL).
Pencil and wash. 13 x 18
BP.1085   P.C.2

Watermill

526 Interior of a watermill, showing mill wheel.
Inscribed (verso): October '84; also (in unknown
hand): p.64. Grinding Mill. The Property of
Capt Duke.
A Hertfordshire watermill, drawn in the summer
of 1884 when the Potters were staying at Bush
Hall (LL Cat.)
Black crayon. 28 x 23.5
BP.232   S.2.F.A

527 Interior of a watermill, showing mill wheel.
Drawn . . . at Bush Hall, Hertfordshire in the
summer of 1884 (LL Cat.)
Black crayon. 24.5 x 18
BP.280   S.5.F.C

Landscapes

Arranged alphabetically according to *place*, when
this is ascertainable.

528 Bury St. Edmunds.
Inscribed (on transparent cover): Street scene,
Bury St Edmunds (LL).
W/c. 19 x 23
BP.1080   P.C.1

529 Camfield Place. View across fields of woods and
parklands.
Inscribed (verso): View from the drawingroom
window at Camfield, Herts.
W/c. 18 x 26.5
BP.299   S.7.F.A

530 View of a misty landscape with trees, seen from the
corner of a terrace.
Inscribed (verso): Camfield. Decem 9th 1884.
Illustration surrounded by LL's instructions to
the printer in connection with *The Art of
Beatrix Potter*.
W/c, on paper mounted on card. 12.5 x 23
BP.300   S.7.F.A

531 Coniston. View across Coniston Water to the
mountains and hills.
Inscribed (on folder): Lake Coniston? (LL).
Wash and pencil. 12.5 x 17.5
BP.1076   P.C.25

532 Derwent Bay. Windswept tree by the lakeside.
Inscribed (on folder): 1903 Derwent Bay (LL).
Sepia ink and pencil. W/m: Aviemore. 21 x 27.5
BP.1026   P.C.22

533 Derwentwater. Lake scene with mountains.
Inscribed (L): Derwentwater.
Inscribed (R): H.B. Potter.
Wash. 17 x 25.5
BP.1083   P.C.1

534 View across lake to mountains, showing St
Herbert's Island.
Inscribed (on folder): Summer 1903 Derwentwater,
Herbert Island.
The island in *The Tale of Squirrel Nutkin*.
Sepia ink and pencil. W/m: Aviemore. 20 x 26
BP.1029   P.C.22

535 View across lake to mountains.
Inscribed (on transparent cover): Derwentwater
1903 (LL).
Sepia ink and pencil. 21.5 x 28.5
BP.1023   P.C.23

536 View across Derwentwater to the mountains
opposite.
Inscribed (on folder): Derwentwater (LL).
Wash. 12.5 x 17.5
BP.1075   P.C.25

537 Esthwaite Water. Painting of a harvest scene.
Inscribed (on mount): A view from Sawrey,
overlooking Esthwaite water, and Coniston Fells
in the background.
Inscribed (verso): Harvest. Bunny [i.e. BP]; also
comments from the Drawing Society members.
W/c, on cartridge paper. 25.5 x 36
BP.240   S.2.F.B   (*see* PLATE XIX)

538 View across Esthwaite Water to snow-covered hills.
Inscribed (on brown paper mount, now removed):
Esthwaite Water Dec 1913 H.B. Potter (LL).
W/c, on cartridge paper. 12.5 x 18
BP.340   S.9.F.A

539 View across the lake to wooded hills. A house can
be seen through the trees.
Inscribed (on mount): Esthwaite Water. HB Potter.
Good light, but much too spotty.
Sepia ink and pencil, mounted on brown paper.
18.5 x 26.5, on sheet 25 x 33
BP.1034   P.C.22

540 Lake scene with mountains.
Possibly Esthwaite Water?
Wash and pencil. 12.5 x 17.5
BP.969   P.C.34

541 Sketch of mountains and Coniston Water on a
misty day.
Inscribed: Nov 16 '09.
Inscribed (on folder): Nov. 16 '09. Esthwait-
water [sic] (LL).
Inscribed (verso): Monk Coniston Moor [7.00
morn.] HB Potter.
Wash and pencil. 18 x 25
BP.1057   P.C.25

542 View across Esthwaite Water to hills and
mountains.
Inscribed: Nov 21st '09.
Inscribed (on folder): Esthwaite Water 1909 (LL).
Inscribed (on verso of brown mount): HB Potter.
Esthwaite Water.
Wash, mounted on brown paper. 18 x 25.5
BP.1079   P.C.25

543 Fawe Park. Fir tree in the foreground with a view
beyond of Derwentwater and distant mountains.
Inscribed over the picture are indications of
intended colours: blue, white, dark blue, grey.
Drawn at Fawe Park, 1903, no doubt intended as
a guide for a finished w/c (LL Cat.)
Pencil. 22.5 x 19
BP.492   S.18.F.A

544 Forest scene, showing tree roots and small plants.
Inscribed (L): Sept. 22 '03.
Verso: A stepped passage (rabbit hole?) into the
trunk of a tree.
Both done while BP was at Fawe Park. Similar to
Old Brown's oak tree.
Pen and w/c, on card. 24 x 30
BP.1132(viii)   P.C.40

545 Grange over Sands.
Sand dunes with grass (upper half).
Studies of purple flowers (lower half).
Believed to be Grange over Sands, 1887.
See *Journal* (LL Cat.)
W/c with pencil. 22.5 x 19
Verso: Studies of shrimps.
Pencil.
BP.335   S.8.F.C

546 A flat, sandy beach with a pinkish sky beyond.
Believed to be drawn from Grange over Sands,
1887 (LL Cat.)
W/c with pencil. 19 x 22.5
BP.336   S.8.F.C

547 Gwaynynog. Sketch of a view from Gwaynynog of
forests and distant mountains.
Inscribed (in pencil): Gwaynynog Oct 1st 09.
W/c with pencil. 13.5 x 19.5
BP.305   S.7.F.A

548 Sketch of parkland (L). Gwaynynog? (LL Cat.)
Pathway through trees (R).
Inscribed: May 18. '12.
Pencil, on folded sheet. W/m: 7. 27 x 21.5
BP.331   S.8.F.B

549 Moorland with a line of trees on left.
Inscribed: Gwaynynog June 3 '11.
Inscribed (on folder): June 3, 1911 Gwaynynog.
Denbigh Wales (LL).
Sepia ink and pencil. 13.5 x 21
BP.1028   P.C.22

550 Woods and fields with sheep grazing and hills in
distance.
Inscribed (on folder): Gwaynynog (LL).
Wash and pencil. 18.5 x 26.5
BP.1047   P.C.25

551 Sketch of a view across a field to trees and hills;
also small, very rough sketch of man and horse.
Inscribed: May 23. '13.
Inscribed (verso): Near Denbigh N Wales
HB Potter.
Wash and pencil. 18.5 x 26.5
BP.1048   P.C.25

552 Hawkshead. Sketch of fields and a bridge leading
to houses.
Wash and pencil. 12.5 x 18
Entrance to Hawkshead, Sawrey side (LL).
Verso: Sketch of meadows and trees.
Pencil.
BP.1050   P.C.25

553 Holyhead Harbour. A view from above of a ship's
deck at the quayside.
Inscribed (verso): Holyhead. May 89/Banshee.
Leinster/Shamrock Connaught/North Wall. Lord
Spencer. Sutherland.
Pen-and-ink with pencil. 17.5 x 12.5
BP.309   S.7.F.B

554 Photograph by Rupert Potter of a similar but wider
view including quay on right-hand side and quay
alongside railway terminus.
BP drew right-hand quay only (cat.553).
BP.318   S.7.F.B

555 Keswick. Lingholm with mountains beyond
obscured by mist and rain.
Inscribed (verso): 'Rain', Aug 98 H.B. Potter.
W/c with pencil. 29 x 22.5
BP.237   S.2.F.B   (see PLATE XX)

556 Road through a forest.
Inscribed: Sept. 1903.
Near Keswick? (LL Cat.)
Grey and blue wash. 25.5 x 18
BP.344   S.9.F.B

557 River with trees and distant hills.
Inscribed: Sept 19th '04.
Inscribed (verso): The Greta, Near Portinscale,
Keswick. H.B.P.
Sepia ink with pencil. W/m: Aviemore. 20 x 26.5
BP.1149   P.C.20

558 Sketch of a forest scene with fence and gate.
Inscribed (verso): Near Keswick. H.B. Potter.
Pencil and grey wash, on cartridge paper.
25.5 x 17.5
BP.1044   P.C.3

559 Forest scene with a stony clearing in the foreground
(near Lingholm?).
Inscribed: Sept 17. '04.
Sepia ink and pencil. W/m: Aviemore. 27 x 20
BP.1031(i)   P.C.22

560 Path with boulders and flowers (near Lingholm?).
Inscribed: Sept 16th '04.
Sepia ink and pencil. W/m: Oceana Fine.
21 x 26.5
BP.1031(ix)   P.C.22

561 Part of rocky hillside with steep incline on one side
covered in bracken (near Lingholm?).
Inscribed: Sep 14. '04.
Possibly a background for *The Tale of Mrs Tiggy-
Winkle*.
Sepia ink and pencil. W/m: Aviemore. 26.5 x 21
BP.1031(viii)   P.C.22

562 Woodland scene with a wooden post near a fence
in the foreground (near Lingholm?).
Inscribed: Sept. 15. '04.
Sepia ink and pencil. W/m: Aviemore. 20 x 26.5
BP.1031(xii)   P.C.22

563 House in a steep-sided valley with winding road.
Inscribed (verso): H.B. Potter – 18.
Possibly associated with background material for
The Tale of Mrs Tiggy-Winkle.
Pencil and w/c. 25 x 17.5
BP.1129(v)   P.C.4

564 Sketch of meadows with mountain in distance
(near Lingholm?).
Inscribed: Sept 15.'04.
Pencil. W/m: Oceana Fine. 21 x 26.5
BP.1041   P.C.33

565 Gnarled tree and edge of a wall (near Lingholm?).
Inscribed: Sept 16th '04. H.B. Potter.
Inscribed (verso): 19.
Sepia ink. W/m: Oceana Fine. 21 x 26.5
BP.1237   P.C.31

566 Kirkcudbright Bay. View of a bay with purple mountains beyond. A few cows can be seen grazing on the extreme right.
(LL Cat.): Believed to be Kirkcudbright Bay, 1899.
W/c with pencil. 18 x 25.5
BP.307   S.7.F.B

567 Lennel, Coldstream. View across a meadow of the Tweed, with hills in the background.
Inscribed: A ford on the Tweed at Coldstream.
July 22nd '94.
Inscribed (verso): The Tweed near Coldstream.
Beatrix Potter.
Orange-brown wash with pencil. 25.5 x 20
BP.312   S.7.F.C

568 Sketch of the Tweed surrounded by woods with the Cheviots in the background.
Originally on mount, now detached.
Inscribed (on brown paper mount): Tweed with Cheviots.
Sepia wash and pencil. 18 x 25.5
BP.313   S.7.F.C

569 View from a hillside of the Tweed and surrounding meadows.
Inscribed: Tweed at Coldstream.
Grey wash and pencil. 26.5 x 20.5
BP.314   S.7.F.C

570 View from the bank of a bridge over the Tweed.
W/c and pencil. 25.5 x 17.5
BP.315   S.7.F.C

571 Forest scene with bracken and boulders.
Inscribed: Beatrix Potter.
(LL Cat.): Believed to be at Lennel, nr. Coldstream.
Yellow-brown wash and pencil. 20 x 26.5
BP.316   S.7.F.C

572 View along a path through a forest.
Inscribed: Sept '94.
(LL Cat.): Believed to be at Lennel, nr. Coldstream.
Grey wash and pencil. 26.5 x 20.5
BP.317   S.7.F.C

573 Sketch of a gate leading into a wood.
Inscribed (on folder): Lennel 1894? (LL).
Brown wash and pencil. 17.5 x 12
BP.1070   P.C.25

574 Long Melford. Meadow with trees in the background.
Inscribed: June 11 11.
Inscribed (on folder): Nr. Melford (LL).
Wash and pencil. 25 x 17.5
Verso: Faint outline sketch of fields.
Pencil.
BP.1046   P.C.25

575 Lyme Regis or Sidmouth. Sketch of a track through hilly country.
Inscribed (by BP?): Sidmouth or Lyme Regis.
Pencil and pen-and-ink, on cartridge paper.
14.5 x 25
BP.1045   P.C.3

576 Field with hedgerow and trees.
Inscribed: Lyme Regis?
Inscribed (on folder): April 1904. Lyme Regis (LL).
Sepia ink and pencil. 29.5 x 19
Verso: Outline sketch of a mirror.
Pencil.
BP.1024   P.C.22

577 View down a village street with an inn, and a horse and cart in front.
Inscribed: Near Lyme Regis.
Sepia ink and pencil. 20.5 x 26.5 (part cut out of sheet)
BP.1018   P.C.23

578 Merioneth. View of stooked wheat with a cottage in the middle ground and plain beyond.
Inscribed: Aug 24th '05.
Inscribed (on transparent cover): Merioneth, Wales, 1905 (LL).
Pencil and w/c. 22.5 x 19
BP.1082   P.C.1

579 Newlands. Sketch of a gateway leading from a wood into a field.
Sepia ink with pencil. W/m: Aviemore.
17.5 x 20
BP.310   S.7.F.B

580 Possibly a preliminary drawing for BP.310; cat.579.
Inscribed: Sept 17th 04.
(LL Cat.): Newlands in Cumberland.
Sepia ink. 21 x 26.5
BP.311   S.7.F.B

581 Sketch of a valley with distant mountains.
Inscribed: Sept 23.
Inscribed (on folder): Newlands and
Littletown (LL).
Pencil. W/m: Oceana Fine. 21 x 26.5
BP.1040   P.C.21

582 Sketch of a rocky slope with ferns and trees.
Inscribed (on folder): Newlands (LL).
Verso: Sketch of a steep gully.
Pencil. 26.5 x 18.5
BP.1039   P.C.21

583 Sketch of mountains from Newlands.
Inscribed: Sept 13.'04.
Inscribed (on folder): Newlands (LL).
Ex Mrs Gaddum.
Wash and pencil. 19 x 22.5
BP.1074   P.C.25

584 View from a hill across valleys.
Inscribed (on folder): Newlands? (LL).
Wash and pencil. 17.5 x 13
BP.1077   P.C.25

585 Sawrey. Sheaves of corn in a field.
Inscribed (verso, at bottom): Cut a little before
Grasmere Games – rained 15 days – Monday to
Sat. 9th Sept dry – 5 carts/some carted 9th –
rain night.
(LL Cat.): Capt Duke gave this picture to his
daughter Rosemary after BP died and inscribed it
(above): This is Redmaynes, the field next to Far
Sawrey & next to the one we had the caravan in.
You can see our barn & roof in the distance. It is
oats this year & will be cut in 10 days or so. WD.
11/8/46.
W/c with pencil. 17.5 x 25
BP.341   S.9.F.A

586 Sawrey and Esthwaite Water. Field with a wall
containing a small gap, and wood beyond.
Inscribed: Aug 29 '10.
Inscribed (verso) by Capt Duke for his daughter
Rosemary: The hole in the wall is called a Hogg
hole for letting sheep through.
W/c with pencil. 18.5 x 25.5
Verso: Three sketches of a landscape near
Esthwaite Water and also two drawings of a child.
Pencil.
BP.347   S.9.F.B

587 Hillside with five trees.
Inscribed: Aug 22 '11.
Inscribed (on transparent cover): Hill Top
Farm (LL).
Pencil and w/c. 25.5 x 18
BP.1084   P.C.1

588 View along a lane bordered by a wall and trees;
also sketches of rabbits and a boy crying
(unfinished).
Inscribed (on folder): Item 49 Stoney Lane Sawrey.
Ex Mrs Gaddum (LL Cat.)
The sketch is a more finished version of
BP.1033(b); cat.589.
Sepia ink and pencil. 29 x 22.5
BP.1033(a)   P.C.22

589 View along a lane with a wall and trees; a less
finished version of BP.1033(a); cat.588: the trees
have been only faintly sketched in.
A piece of tracing paper depicting a boy crying has
been attached.
Sepia ink and pencil. 22.5 x 29
BP.1033(b)   P.C.22

590 Sketch of stone wall, meadows and distant hills
and woods.
Inscribed (on folder): Stoney Lane Sawrey? (LL).
Wash and pencil. 17.5 x 18
Verso: Sketch of house.
Pencil.
BP.1049   P.C.25

591 Study of corn sheaves with trees behind.
Inscribed (on folder): Redmayne's Field
Sawrey (LL).
Wash and pencil. 17.5 x 12.5
BP.1052   P.C.25

592 Sketch of a meadow flanked by a line of trees.
Inscribed (on folder): Hill Top Farm – Row of trees
just by Hill Top (LL).
Wash and pencil. 22.5 x 17
BP.1053   P.C.25

593 View from a lane with trees.
Inscribed (on folder): Sawrey (LL).
Wash and pencil. 12.5 x 17.5
BP.1054   P.C.25

597

594 Sketch of a lane with wooded hills beyond.
Inscribed: Nov 15. 1909 Road to Esthwaite water
from Sawrey village.
Wash and pencil. 25 x 17.5
Verso: Rough outline sketch of mountains.
Pencil.
BP.1055   P.C.25

595 Roof-tops and wooded slope with hills beyond.
Inscribed (on folder): Probably Sawrey
hillside (LL).
Wash and pencil. 17.5 x 25
Verso: Outline sketch of Sawrey(?).
Pencil.
BP.1056   P.C.25

596 Unfinished sketch of Hill Top Farm(?) and
surroundings.
Inscribed: Sept. 3. '10.
Brown wash and pencil. 18 x 25
BP.1060   P.C.25

597 Seven Leas Lane.
Study for proof (BP.236(b); cat.598).
Sepia ink. 23.5 x 20.5
BP.236(a)   S.2.F.A

598 Seven Leas Lane and farmhouse at Brookthorpe.
Edmund Evans's proofs of two of BP's drawings
mounted together.
Inscribed (L proof): "Seven Leas Lane" Oct. 1904
[a lane with haystacks on one side].
Inscribed (R proof): Farm-house at Brookthorpe
Glos Oct 1904 [a Tudor farmhouse seen from the
front garden wall].
Inscribed (on back of mount): Printed from line
blocks from pen-and-ink HB Potter. Engraved and
printed by Edmund Evans & Co. at the Racquet
Court Press.
See also BP.235 (a–d); cat.432–436.
Proofs of pen-and-ink drawings, mounted on
brown paper. 25 x 17.5 (L); 25.5 x 17.5 (R),
on sheet 29.5 x 39.5
BP.236(b); BP.235(e)   S.2.F.A

599 Another copy of the Seven Leas Lane proof, unmounted.
25 x 17.5
BP.1152   S.2.F.A

600 Shaldon, nr. Teignmouth.
Sketch of part of the mouth of a river, with houses along a projecting spur of land on the right.
(LL Cat.): Shaldon, nr. Teignmouth.
W/c. 14 x 29
BP.332   S.8.F.C

601 Sidmouth. Sidmouth Beach, with figures on the sand in the foreground and cliffs receding into the distance behind them.
Inscribed (L): Sidmouth April [15th] 1902.
Inscribed (verso): 'like some tall cliff' Sidmouth, Devon, H.B. Potter.
W/c, mounted on drawing paper. 20 x 27 (size of sheet)
BP.242   S.2.F.B

602 Sketch of a path through trees; also cottage with trees and distant hills.
Inscribed (R): Sidmouth.
Pencil and grey wash. 15 x 19.5
BP.346   S.9.F.B

603 Sketch of a path leading to cottages surrounded by fields and woods.
Inscribed (verso): Near Sidmouth.
W/c. 19 x 22.5
BP.345   S.9.F.B

604 View of a bridge from across a river, with boat in foreground.
Inscribed (verso): Teignmouth.
W/c. 14 x 23
BP.333   S.8.F.C

605 Study of rowing boats on a beach, with river beyond.
Inscribed: Teignmouth.
W/c. 14 x 23
BP.334   S.8.F.C

Unidentified Landscapes

606 Sheep in a meadow in front of tall trees: vignetted scene.
W/c and pencil, on cartridge paper. 19 x 10
BP.342   S.9.F.B
(Mounted with BP.343; cat.463)

607 Pathway to moorland(?) passing through a stone gateway, surrounded by trees.
Pencil and w/c. 18 x 12.5
BP.1081   P.C.1

608 Mountain stream with vegetation and rocks (near Lingholm?).
W/c and sepia ink. 19 x 22.5
BP.1129(ii)   P.C.4

609 Detail of a large tree trunk in a field at the edge of a wood.
W/c. 18 x 12.5
BP.1153   P.C.20

610 Sheep grazing in a field with trees.
Inscribed: Sept 23.
Sepia ink and pencil. W/m: Oceana Fine.
20 x 26.5
BP.1151   P.C.20

611 Woodland scene with a stream and a meadow.
Sepia ink and pencil. 20.5 x 25.5
BP.1150   P.C.20

612 Beech tree in a field (near Lingholm?).
Inscribed: Sept 16 '04.
Sepia ink with pencil. W/m: Oceana Fine.
20.5 x 26
BP.1148   P.C.20

613 Two sketches of wooded landscape.
Verso: Rough sketch of trees.
Pencil. 26.5 x 18
BP.1036   P.C.21

614 Cumberland. Sketch of a small stream in a field, on right side of folded sheet.
Verso: Studies of a lane leading to a house.
Pencil. W/m: Aviemore. 20 x 26.5
BP.1037   P.C.21

615 Cumberland. Sketch of a brook flowing into a field from a wood.
Inscribed (on folder): Cumberland (LL).
Pencil. 21 x 15
BP.1038   P.C.21

616 Forest scene.
Sepia ink and pencil. W/m: Oceana Fine. 21 x 27
BP.1031(ii)   P.C.22

623

617 Forest scene with a view along a path.
Sepia ink and pencil. 26.5 x 21
BP.1031(iii)   P.C.22

618 Forest scene with a view along a path and open
foreground.
Sepia ink and pencil. 26.5 x 21
BP.1031(iv)   P.C.22

619 Field with fence and tree behind it.
Sepia ink and pencil. 21 x 28.5
BP.1031(v)   P.C.22

620 View along a path in a forest with a fence on
the left.
Sepia ink and pencil. W/m: Aviemore. 26.5 x 21
BP.1031(vi)   P.C.22

621 Detailed study of vegetation.
Sepia ink and pencil. W/m: Aviemore. 21 x 26.5
BP.1031(vii)   P.C.22

622 Detailed view of a fence, tree trunk and
vegetation.
Sepia ink and pencil. 21 x 27
BP.1031(x)   P.C.22

623 Detailed view of fence, gate and vegetation.
Sepia ink and pencil. W/m: Aviemore. 26.5 x 21
BP.1031(xi)   P.C.22

624 View along the edge of a field with a fence and
hedge.
Sepia ink and pencil. 21 x 16.5
BP.1031(xiii)   P.C.22

627

625 Corner of a field bordered by hedge, gate and
stone wall.
Sepia ink and pencil. W/m: I & JH Kent. 21 x 29
Verso: Faint beginnings of a sketch of a tree.
Pencil.
BP.1031(xiv)   P.C.22

626 View of a meadow surrounded by woods; a rabbit in
the foreground.
See also BP.1233(v); cat.636.
Sepia ink and pencil. W/m: Oceana Fine. 20 x 30
BP.1021   P.C.23

627 Field with open gate, fence and wall; wooded hills
beyond.
Sepia ink. W/m: Aviemore. 19 x 26.5
BP.1022   P.C.23

628 Rough sketch of mountains with a valley in the
foreground.
Pencil, within pencilled frame.
W/m: J. Whatman 1905. 25.5 x 22.5
Verso: Study of iris.
Pencil and w/c.
BP.1019   P.C.23

629 Sketch of sheep grazing in a field, with trees in the
background.
Wash and pencil. 11.5 x 12.5
Verso: Rough outline sketch of trees.
Pencil.
BP.1058   P.C.25

630 Unfinished sketch of meadows and a wood.
Wash and pencil. W/m: Newton Mill. 11 x 17
BP.1059   P.C.25

631 Sketch of stream running through a field.
Wash and pencil. 15.5 x 10.5
BP.1073   P.C.25

632 Sketch of a woodland scene with a path in the
foreground.
Inscribed (on folder): ex Mrs Gaddum.
Wash and pencil. 25 x 17.5
BP.1078   P.C.25

633 Unfinished study of a patch of ground with stones
and small plants.
Pen-and-ink and w/c, on card. 24 x 30.5
BP.1246   P.C.31

634 Sketch of a wood with marshes (near Lingholm?).
Inscribed: Sept 16th '04.
Sepia ink with pencil. W/m: Oceana Fine.
21 x 26.5
BP.1233(iv)   P.C.31

635 Sketch of sheep sheltering against a fence in
a wood.
Sepia ink with pencil. W/m: Aviemore.
26.5 x 21.5
BP.1233(iii)   P.C.31

636 Sketch of an open field bordered by a wood; also a
very rough pencil sketch of rabbits (L).
See also BP.1021; cat.626.
Sepia ink with pencil. 19 x 28
BP.1233(v)   P.C.31

637 View along a boulder-strewn path with a fence and
wood on one side (near Lingholm?).
Inscribed: Sept 16. '04.
Sepia ink with pencil. 21.5 x 26.5
BP.1233(ii)   P.C.31

638 Wooden stile with a view into the neighbouring
field.
Sepia ink with pencil. 13 x 21
BP.1233(i)   P.C.31

639 Shores of a lake, with trees.
Pencil. W/m: Danehurst Parchment. 20 x 25
BP.1042   P.C.33

640 Study of a hollowed-out tree trunk.
Possibly a background for *The Tale of Peter Rabbit*
or *The Tale of Squirrel Nutkin*.
W/c, pen-and-ink and pencil, on card. 24 x 30.5
BP.1253   P.C.34

641 Small unfinished study of a view, through trees,
of mountains.
Wash and pencil. W/m: /od's. 16 x 17.5
BP.987   P.C.34

642 Unfinished study of sheep grazing on the edge
of a lake.
Wash and pencil. 27 x 21
BP.985   P.C.34

643 Unfinished study of a lake with trees and a
stormy sky.
Wash and pencil. W/m: Danehurst Parchment.
16 x 20
BP.984   P.C.34

644 Detailed study of plants in faint landscape.
Pencil and sepia ink. 22.5 x 27.5
BP.1032   P.C.22

645 Study of a cliff path with ferns.
Possibly a background for *The Tale of Mrs
Tiggy-Winkle*.
Wash and pencil. 22.5 x 19
BP.983   P.C.34

646 Unfinished study of a patch of ground with stones
and clover (enlarged).
Pencil, pen-and-ink and w/c. 20.5 x 27
BP.982   P.C.34

647 Study of undergrowth with grasses, clover and a
snail (unfinished).
Pencil, pen-and-ink and w/c, on card. 20 x 21.5
BP.981   P.C.34

648 Unfinished study of a stream with waterlily leaves.
Wash and pencil, on sheet with a piece cut out at
the corner. W/m: Towgood's Extra Fine. 20 x 19.5
BP.980   P.C.34

649 Study of a stream with boulders.
Wash and pencil. 19 x 22.5
BP.979   P.C.34

650 Unfinished study of a stream running through
forest, with ferns in the foreground.
Wash and pencil. 25 x 17.5
BP.978   P.C.34

651 Rough study of a stream with stakes and boulders.
Inscribed (with an arrow): Too dark.
Wash and pencil. 19 x 22.5
BP.977   P.C.34

652 Study of undergrowth with grasses, clover etc.
Wash and pencil. 22.5 x 19
Verso: Faint outlines of leaves.
Pencil.
BP.976   P.C.34

653 Unfinished sketch of a view, through trees, of the roof of a house; also part of sketch of a horse.
Wash and pencil. 14 x 22.5
BP.975   P.C.34

654 Sketch of forest scene in autumn.
Verso: Unfinished study of a house by a lake and mountains in the snow.
Wash and pencil. 25.5 x 18
BP.974   P.C.34

655 Partly finished sketch of mountains and a line of fir trees.
Wash and pencil. 17.5 x 25
BP.973   P.C.34

656 A river traversed by stone piles forming a bridge (probably Cumberland).
Wash and pencil. 17.5 x 25
BP.972   P.C.34

657 Study of a mountain ridge, with a wood and roof-top of a house in the foreground (probably Cumberland).
Wash and pencil. 12.5 x 18
BP.971   P.C.34

658 Unfinished study of a forest dell.
Wash and pencil. 18 x 12.5
BP.970   P.C.34

659 Rough sketch of a path in a wood, in autumn.
Wash and pencil. 17.5 x 12.5
BP.968   P.C.34

660 Sketch of a lake with a line of trees on the far bank.
Wash and pencil. W/m: /edger/1895. 12 x 21
BP.967   P.C.34

661 Rough study of mountain peaks in the mist.
Wash and pencil. 12.5 x 18
BP.966(b)   P.C.34

662 A cliff walk with trees.
Inscribed (verso): Prepared by Winsor and Newton.
Inscribed (on folder) by LL: Oil painting by Beatrix Potter, for many years hanging on the wall at Castle Cottage, Sawrey.
Oil painting, on canvas stretched over wooden frame. 25 x 35
BP.1502   P.C.59

Snow Scenes

663 Snow scene of lake and mountains.
Wash and pencil. 12 x 15.5
BP.966(a)   P.C.34

664 Snow scene at Hill Top (LL Cat.) with two cows advancing down the hill; also sketches of chickens (R).
W/c, on cartridge paper. 17.5 x 25
BP.338   S.9.F.A

665 Cart track covered in snow, with fields beyond Sawrey.
Probably Jan 1913 (LL Cat.)
W/c with pencil. 25.5 x 17.5
BP.339   S.9.F.A

666 Snow scene showing a hillside with a stormy sky.
Inscribed: Jan 11. 13.
Rising ground nr. Jemima's Wood (LL Cat.)
W/c and pencil. 25.5 x 18
BP.337   S.9.F.A

667 Snow scene with fields and a line of trees.
Inscribed: March 4. '09.
Wash and pencil. 25 x 18
BP.1156   P.C.20

668 Sketch of trees on a slope under snow(?).
Wash and pencil. 14 x 12
BP.1071   P.C.25

669 Snow scene of a village.
Inscribed: March 7 '09.
Inscribed (verso): Sawrey from Tower Bank Arms.
Inscribed (on mount): This is Capt Duke's writing (LL).
W/c with pencil. 23.5 x 18
BP.1157   P.C.20   (*see* PLATE XXI)

670 Sketch of mountains and fields covered in snow.
Inscribed: Jan 11. '13.
Inscribed (on folder): Esthwaite Water (LL).
Wash and pencil. 13 x 17.5
BP.1051   P.C.25

671 Sketch of a clearing in a wood under snow.
Inscribed: Jan 31 '11.
Wash and pencil. 14 x 10.5
BP.1072   P.C.25

672 Rough study of a mountain landscape.
Inscribed (L): March 4 '09.
Inscribed (on folder): Sawrey (LL).
Wash and pencil. 18 x 25.5
BP.965(i)   P.C.27

673 Snow scene showing a farm with outbuildings, and
hillside beyond (near Sawrey).
Inscribed: March 3rd '09.
Inscribed (verso): H.B. Potter 20.
Inscribed (on folder): Sawrey (LL).
Wash and pencil. 25 x 18
BP.965(ii)   P.C.27

674 Snow scene showing trees and roofs under deep
snow (rough study).
Inscribed (R): March 4 '09.
Inscribed (on folder): Sawrey (LL).
Wash and pencil. 25.5 x 18
BP.965(iii)   P.C.27

675 Impression of a mountain scene with lake,
under snow.
Inscribed (L): March 4 09.
Inscribed (on folder): Sawrey (LL).
Wash and pencil. 18 x 25.5
BP.965(v)   P.C.27

676 Snow scene (near Sawrey) showing deep foot-
prints winding across a field enclosed by stone
walls. In the distance, a village and hills.
Inscribed: March 5th '09.
Pencil and w/c. 25 x 18
BP.1477   P.C.27

677 Snow-covered barn (near Sawrey) among snow-
laden trees set in a landscape.
Inscribed: March 7th '09.
Pencil and w/c. 25.5 x 18
BP.1478   P.C.27

678 Hillside under snow, showing sheep in the
foreground and stone walls beyond.
Inscribed (R): March 4 09.
Inscribed (on folder): Sawrey (LL).
Wash and pencil. 25.5 x 18
BP.965(iv)   P.C.27

679 Unfinished study of a group of buildings at the foot
of a hill, all under snow.
Inscribed (L): March 2 '09.
Inscribed (on folder): Sawrey (LL).
Pencil and wash. 29 x 23
BP.964(i)   P.C.29

680 Hilly scene with trees, under snow.
Inscribed (L): March 3 '09.
Inscribed (on folder): Sawrey (LL).
Pencil and wash. 25.5 x 18
BP.964(ii)   P.C.29

681 Study of a man walking down a hillside path beside
a stone wall, all under snow.
Inscribed (R): March 3 '09.
Inscribed (on folder): Sawrey (LL).
Pencil and wash. 18 x 13.5
BP.964(iii)   P.C.29

682 Mountains under snow; a snow-covered valley with
trees in the foreground.
Inscribed (L): March 4 '09.
Inscribed (on folder): Sawrey (LL).
Pencil and wash. 18 x 25.5
BP.964(iv)   P.C.29

683 Snowy landscape showing a path between fences in
a wooded area.
Inscribed (L): March 3 '09.
Inscribed (on folder): Sawrey (LL).
Pencil and wash. 25.5 x 18
BP.964(v)   P.C.29

684 Sketch of door and doorstep, with chickens lightly
sketched in (R).
Waterbutt in the snow (top L); chicken in the
snow (bottom L).
Inscribed (L): Nov 20 '10.
Inscribed (verso): Sawrey Nov 17th.
Pencil and wash. 17.5 x 25
BP.963(ii)   P.C.32

685 Snow scene (near Sawrey) with path and trees.
Inscribed (L): March 5 '09.
Pencil and wash. 25.5 x 18
BP.963(iii)   P.C.32

686 Hill-top with rocks, under snow (near Sawrey).
Inscribed (R): March 5 '09.
Pencil and wash. 18 x 25.5
BP.963(iv)   P.C.32

687 A snow scene looking across the tarn to fields and
a wooded hillside opposite.
Inscribed (on a separate piece of paper): 'We think
this is Tarn Hows'; and: Identified by Mrs Gaddum,
1967 (LL).
Pen-and-ink and w/c. 16 x 10.5
BP.1154   P.C.20

Portraits and people

688 Interior of 2 Bolton Gardens (LL Cat.) with
a lady in mediaeval attire being handed grapes by
a page.
Inscribed (verso): June 85.
(LL Cat.): See pp. 146–147 of *Journal*.
W/c with white highlights. 17.5 x 16
BP.304   S.7.F.A

689 Sketch of a woman at her spinning wheel (the head
is unfinished), and sketch of her hands.
(LL Cat.): Probably old Kitty Macdonald at
Birnam, 1892? Note: Beatrix Potter was using Kent
drawing paper in 1903 and this may mean that the
woman was not Kitty.
Pencil. W/m: I & JH Kent. 29.5 x 22.5
BP.527   S.20.F.C

690 Sketches of a little girl's head and of girl kneeling.
(LL Cat.): Lucie Carr?
Verso: Two sketches of an oak sideboard.
From Fawe Park, 1903 or from Lingholme [sic],
1904? (LL Cat.)
Pencil. 22.5 x 19
BP.531   S.20.F.C

691 Two sketches of the head of an old woman.
(LL Cat.): This may have been the Potter's
housemaid Sarah?
Pencil. 13 x 9.5
BP.528   S.20.F.C

692 Sketches of figures, a man and children, a cow,
a cart-horse and a dog.
Inscribed: C. Keene [under man in bowler hat];
and: Corbould [between cow and horse].
(LL Cat.): Impressions of a North-Country show:
probably copies. See *Journal*, p. 417.
Sepia ink and pencil. 15 x 19
BP.643   T.29.R

693 Sketches of a horse and cart and back views of men
standing.
Verso: Sketches of figures and horses' heads.
(LL Cat.): as BP.643; cat.692.
Pencil and pen-and-ink. 11 x 18.5
BP.644   T.29.R

694 Back view of two boys standing in a field with
sheep, reading a large notice board which says
'NO I WONT BRUSH MY TEETH' with the
caption below: shocking result of injudicious
admonition.
Pen-and-ink. W/m: Britannia. 20.5 x 16.5
BP.1192   P.C.44

695 Rough sketch of Stephanie Hyde-Parker lying full-
length reading a book.
A preliminary study for the leaflet (see BP.532;
cat.696).
Verso: Similar to above.
Pencil. 13 x 19.5
BP.533   S.20.F.C

696 Sketches of Stephanie Hyde-Parker lying full-
length reading a book, and also standing holding
pinafore.
(LL Cat.): Drawn when planning a trade leaflet for
Frederick Warne's 1905 season. The original
painting for this leaflet, for which Beatrix Potter
charged two guineas, belongs to Warne's.
Pencil, on folded sheet. W/m: Oceana Fine.
26 x 20.5
BP.532   S.20.F.C

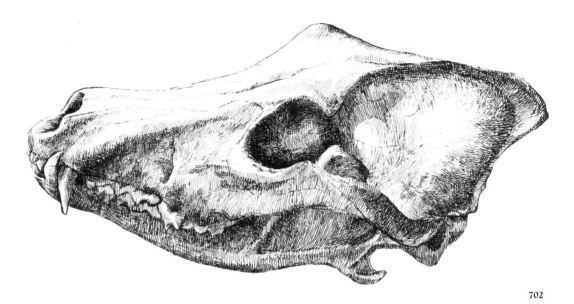

702

Miscellaneous drawings and lithos

697 Rough sketches of a mouse, cat and part of a
building which could be the stable end of Bedwell
Lodge, Hertfordshire (LL Cat.)
Formerly inserted into the working copy of
The Tailor of Gloucester.
Pencil. W/m: A Pirie & Sons 1900. 22 x 17.5
BP.594   T.25.L

698 Two identical lithographs of the following subjects:
four fungi (probably *Hygrophorus* species), leg of a
fly (highly magnified), privet hawk moth,
caterpillar and chrysalis of a hawk moth, jug, head
of a gazelle, two rabbits, parts of a moth(?)'s wing
scales.
Inscribed: HBP April [9]6.
Litho. 22.5 x 28.5
BP.366(a,b)   S.10.F.C

699 Study of two caterpillars (of a privet hawk moth,
and a puss moth), a primitive musical instrument
(probably bone pipe) and two fragments of Roman
pottery.
From archaeological excavations, London 1872?
Pencil. 25 x 19.5
BP.371   S.10.F.C

700 Sketch of a two-wheeled carriage, sledge (troika)
and saddle.
Copied from objects in the Science Museum,
London (LL Cat.)
Pencil. W/m: Gur/Ivory. 17.5 x 11
BP.646   T.29.R

701 Sketch of a shoe (18c.) with the word 'shoe'
written in reverse (shop sign?); also a spinning
wheel, a weaving loom and crest.
Copied from objects in the Science Museum,
London(?).
Pen-and-ink and pencil. W/m: /ood's Fine.
18 x 11
BP.647   T.29.R

702 Study of a horse's(?) skull.
Inscribed: January 1. 86.
Pen-and-ink. 11.5 x 22.5
BP.651   T.29.R

703 Two alternative designs for a bookplate of cats'
faces set within a lozenge frame. Beneath the page
design is a ribbon motif inscribed with the words:
a faithful friend.
Left-hand design inscribed: Best side; and
marked: 2.
Right-hand design inscribed: Squinty; and:
crooked; and marked: 3. Beneath this design is
a kitten and the inscription: Lucy Roscoe
[cancelled out].
Refers to BP's aunt.
Inscribed (verso): Book pamphlet.
Pen-and-ink with pencil. 15 x 11
BP.1194   P.C.44

BACKGROUNDS FOR BOOKS

This important section needs little explanation since the title tells all, except to say that, for convenience of reference, the various Peter Rabbit books are arranged in alphabetical order of title rather than chronologically in order of writing or publication. This section must of course be seen in conjunction with the sections on natural history, landscape etc. Whenever the relevance to a particular book was immediately obvious, the item was placed under that book title. But Beatrix Potter made many 'background' sketches of places and animals which she later used in her books, and sometimes the decision as to where to insert an item in the catalogue may seem somewhat arbitrary – however all such works should be traceable through the Index at the end of this publication.

The interesting fact is that many of the 'backgrounds' are so often immediately recognisable: the actual garden path, the waterbutt, the distant hills, the contours of the lake – all these she may have sketched with no further idea in her mind at the time, but they reappeared later, transmuted or identical, in one or other of the books. It is this charm of actuality which many people find so appealing – they can still find the scene, the building, the wall, which has been familiar to them since their childhood reading.

The Peter Rabbit books

Appley Dapply's Nursery Rhymes
1905 Book of Rhymes

704 'Come dance a jig, to my Granny's pig': drawing of a cat playing a fiddle while three hens dance and a pig and more hens look on.
This rhyme was left out in the 1917 version of the 1905 (unprinted) book.
For coloured version, see BP.523; cat.705.
Pen-and-ink. 15.5 x 18, on sheet 21 x 25
BP.1124(i)　P.C.9

705 'Come dance a jig, to my Granny's pig': a cat playing a fiddle while three hens and a pig look on.
See also BP.1124(i); cat.704.
W/c and pen-and-ink. 18.5 x 20
BP.523　S.20.F.B

706 'Come dance a jig, to my Granny's pig': a cat playing a fiddle, leading hens towards a pig in a sty.
Inscribed : H.B.P.; and: Please reduce by one third & print proofs in brown ink.
The setting combines Bedwell Lodge and Bush Hall, Herts.
Pen-and-ink. 20 x 29
BP.348　S.9.F.C

707 Proof of BP.348; cat.706, printed in sepia ink.
19 x 25
BP.349(b)　S.9.F.C

708 'Come dance a jig, to my Granny's pig': sketch of background for BP.348; cat.706, showing farmyard with a pig-sty in foreground.
Pencil. 20 x 33
BP.349(a)　S.9.F.C

716

She had so many children
She did not know what to do!

717 (detail)

PLATE XXII 'Toads' tea party' (*1905 Book of Rhymes*) (**710**)

PLATE XXIII The Amiable Guinea Pig (*Appley Dapply's Nursery Rhymes*) **(718)**

PLATE XXIV Rats dancing in the Mayor's cellar (*Tailor of Gloucester*) (**790**)

PLATE XXV Lady mouse curtseying in front of a
tea cup (*Tailor of Gloucester*) (**793**)

PLATE XXVI Gentleman mouse bowing in front of a
tea cup (*Tailor of Gloucester*) (**794**)

709 A finished picture showing a frog fishing and
inscribed: 'The rain it raineth every day'
(*Twelfth Night*, v. i.).
Illustrating the verse:

> Fishes come bite! Fishes come bite!
> I have fished all day; I will fish all night,
> I sit in the rain on my lily-leaf boat,
> But never a minnow will bob on my float.
> Fishes come bite!

Inscribed (verso): H.B. Potter.
W/c and pen-and-ink, on front of folded piece of
notepaper. 18 x 11.5
BP.506   S.19.F.A   (*see frontispiece*)

710 'The Toads' Tea Party': toads sitting on toadstools
eating cakes and drinking out of acorn cups.
Illustrating the verse:

> If acorn-cups were tea-cups, what would we have
>   to drink?
> Why! honey-dew for sugar, in a cuckoo-pint of
>   milk;
> With pats of witches' butter and a tansy cake, I
>   think,
> Laid out upon a toad-stool on a cloth of cob-web
>   silk!

For the *1905 Book of Rhymes* (LL).
W/c and pen-and-ink. 20.5 x 16
BP.518   S.20.F.A   (*see* PLATE XXII)

711 Decorative border of acorn cups and twigs.
Pencilled in lower framework are the words:
acorn cups.
Possibly one of the preliminary designs to illustrate
'If acorn-cups were tea-cups'.
See BP.518; cat.710.
Pen-and-ink. 16 x 12, on sheet 26 x 20.5
BP.1133   P.C.39

712 A mouse knitting.
Similar to BP.519(a); cat.713: the design used in
the book to illustrate the second verse of 'There
was an old woman who lived in a shoe'.
W/c and pen-and-ink. 21 x 13
BP.519(b)   S.20.F.A

713 Three sketches of a mouse knitting, for the second
verse of 'There was an old woman who lived in
a shoe'.
See also BP.519(b); cat.712.
Pencil (2) and w/c (1). 10.5 x 16.5
Verso: Pencil sketch of a mouse knitting.
BP.519(a)   S.20.F.A

714 Mice in a shoe: illustrating the first verse of 'There
was an old woman who lived in a shoe'.
Removed from the MS of the *1905 Book of
Rhymes* (LL Cat.)
Version as used in the current publication.
W/c. 9.5 x 12, on sheet 21 x 18
BP.516   S.20.F.A

715 Shrew (Billy Brown Shrew: LL Cat.) with its
children on an overgrown bank; with a pencil
border, inscribed: shrews.
The appropriate verse has not been added.
W/c. 26 x 21
BP.520   S.20.F.A

716 Study for 'There was an old woman who lived in a
shoe', illustrating the line 'And put them to bed': a
mouse with a baby on its lap sitting by a cradle
containing two other baby mice.
See BP.433; cat.1022 for an early example.
Pencil. 16 x 10
BP.621   T.28.L   (*illustration p.72*)

717 Set of five sheets, stitched with cotton, inscribed
on the first sheet: There was an old Woman who
lived in a Shoe Feb. 9[7] unfinished.
1r. Rough pencil drawing of mice in a shoe,
    endorsed as above.
1v. Pen-and-ink sketches of mouse children
    playing near the shoe, 'She had so many
    children She didn't know what to do!'.
2r. W/c of the mother mouse running with a bowl
    of broth, 'She gave them some Broth Without
    any Bread'.
2v. Blank.
3r. W/c of three mouse heads and a switch of twigs,
    'She whipped them all round'.
3v. Blank.
4r. W/c of the mother mouse with a baby on her
    lap, and two other mice asleep in a cradle beside
    her, 'And put them to Bed'.
4v. Blank.
5r. W/c of a mouse in bed (no verse).
W/c and pen-and-ink. 10.5 x 17.5
BP.620   T.28.L   (*illustration p.72*)

718 'The Amiable Guinea Pig': a guinea pig combing its hair.
A line version was used on the title page of the book; similar also to the book version illustrating the verse:

> There once was an amiable guinea pig
> Who brushed back his hair like a periwig.

W/c. 8 x 6, on card 9 x 6
BP.622   T.28.L   (*see* PLATE XXIII)

719 'Old Mister Prickly Pin': a hedgehog wearing blue shoes and sitting in some undergrowth.
This version is similar to the book version and illustrates the verse, which is slightly altered in the 1917 book:

> Old Mister Prickly Pin
>   With never a cushion to stick the pins in!
> His nose is black, and his beard is gray,
>   And he lives in an ash-stump over the way.

In the published version the name 'Mr Pricklepin' is used (LL Cat.)
W/c, mounted on board. 16 x 20
BP.517   S.20.F.A

720 Sketch of a mouse knitting, within an oval border. Believed to be a cover design drawing which was not used (LL Cat.)
Pencil. 10 x 9
BP.624   T.28.R

721 (detail)

721 Three sketches with two lines of verse beneath each, showing: (i) Appley Dapply going to a cupboard; (ii) she opens the door, and picks out a jam-pot; (iii) she runs away (verso).
Pencil, sepia ink and w/c. 15 x 9.5
BP.625   T.28.R

722 Rough design for a page of the book, showing Appley Dapply opening a cupboard.
Illustrating the verse written on the page:

> Applely [sic] Dapply
>   A little brown Mouse–
> Goes to the cupboard
>   In Somebody's house.

The whole enclosed within a frame which includes (at the bottom) a tea-pot and a candlestick.
Inscribed: July 14th 05.
Pen-and-ink, pencil and w/c. 11 x 9, on sheet 20 x 15
BP.628(a)   T.28.R

723 Rough design showing Appley Dapply running with some pies.
Illustrating the verse written on the page:

> Applely [sic] Dapply
>   has little sharp eyes,
> And Applely Dapply
>   is *so* fond of pies!

The whole enclosed within a frame which includes (at the top) decanters and dishes.
Pen-and-ink and pencil. 10 x 9, on sheet 20 x 15
BP.628(b)   T.28.R

720

724 Rough design for page 1 of the rhyme 'You know the old woman who lived in a shoe?', with a verse above, mice in a shoe below and a border of bootlaces containing more mice.
Inscribed: border bootlaces.
Pencil and sepia ink. 11 x 8, on sheet 12.5 x 20
BP.628(c)   T.28.R

725 Rough design of the last verse of 'There was an old woman who lived in a shoe', showing the mouse whipping her children. The verse is above, and there is a decorated border containing mice.
Pencil and sepia ink. 11 x 8, on sheet 19.5 x 16
BP.628(d)   T.28.R

726 Sketch for 'There was an old woman who lived in a shoe', showing a sturdy shoe with mice inside it. A different type of shoe was used in the published version.
Pencil. W/m: Gurne/. 8 x 16
BP.1132(ii)   P.C.39

727 Sketch of Cottontail looking at the basket of carrots left outside her door; also a sketch of the Little Black Rabbit across the bottom of the page.
Pencil. W/m: FH [entwined]. 20 x 16
Verso: Seven little sketches of a black and white mouse, three of which are slightly coloured.
Pencil and w/c.
BP.1132(iii)   P.C.39

728 Sketch of the Little Black Rabbit, who is shown knocking at a door, basket over arm.
Pencil. W/m: Towgood's Extra Fine. 16 x 13, on sheet 20 x 16
Verso: Two studies of clumps of grass, one in w/c.
BP.1132(v)   P.C.39

729 Rough sketch of a rabbit carrying a basket.
See also BP.1132(v); cat.728.
Pencil. W/m: Britannia. 16 x 20
Verso: Two studies of clumps of grass, one in pen-and-ink, one in w/c.
BP.1262   P.C.41

730 Three studies for Appley Dapply with her basket and key, for the verse:

> Appley Dapply, a little brown mouse,
> Goes to the cupboard in somebody's house.

This view of Appley Dapply appears in the 1905 unpublished version but not in the 1917 published book.
Verso: Appley Dapply in reverse.
Pencil, slightly foxed. 10 x 21.5
BP.1132(iv)   P.C.39

731 A mouse in an apron lifting a jar from a cupboard in the wainscot, illustrating the verse:

> Appley Dapply, a little brown mouse,
> Goes to the cupboard in somebody's house.

W/c with pen-and-ink, slightly foxed. 9 x 11.5, on sheet 11 x 14.5
BP.1132(vi)   P.C.39

732 Study for Appley Dapply with her basket and key; there are three similar drawings (with the cupboard background drawn in one sketch) on the same sheet.
Verso: Appley Dapply in reverse.
This view of Appley Dapply appears in the 1905 unpublished version but not in the 1917 published book.
See also BP.1132(iv); cat.730.
Pencil. 12 x 20
BP.1132(i)   P.C.39

Cecily Parsley's Nursery Rhymes

733 Line study for the frontispiece 'Gentlemen came every day': two rabbits smoking pipes, sitting on a settle by the fire.
See also coloured version of same 1902 sketch (BP.522; cat.744).
Pen-and-ink. 15.5 x 18, on sheet 21 x 25
BP.1124(iii)   P.C.9

734 Line study for Cecily Parsley brewing ale (or cider?), showing a rabbit tipping apples from her apron into a large bowl, in a cellar with bottles and barrels.
Pen-and-ink. 15.5 x 18, on sheet 22 x 27
BP.1124(ii)   P.C.9   (*illustration overleaf*)

734

735 Rabbits looking at a little door in the undergrowth.
The door has a 'To Let' sign.
This is an earlier sketch for the final w/c version;
the earliest record of such a doorway is in the 1897
version of the rhyme.
Sepia ink and pencil. W/m: Aviemore. 18.5 x 26.5
BP. 1124(iv)   P.C.9

736 Study for the binding and jacket design, showing
a rabbit (Cecily Parsley) running with a
wheelbarrow.
This idea was taken from the earlier sketches made
for the rhyme in 1897.
Pen-and-ink (rabbit) and pencil (rest of sketch).
15.5 x 18, on sheet 22 x 26.5
BP. 1124(v)   P.C.9

737 Study of foliage with a rabbit (Cecily Parsley)
running with a wheelbarrow into a burrow.
The foliage is drawn in an earlier style and the
rabbit was possibly added later when BP was sorting
through her portfolios to find material for the 1922
book. The original idea of a rabbit with a
wheelbarrow is shown in the 1897 version of the
rhyme (see BP. 1124(v); cat. 736).
Sepia ink (foliage) and pencil (rabbit). W/m:
Oceana Fine. 20 x 23
Verso: Line drawing of the same (a later version).
Pencil.
BP. 1124(vi)   P.C.9

738 Sketch for 'Goosey, Goosey, Gander' showing
some geese looking into a pig-sty in which a pig
is tucked up in bed.
See BP. 1142; cat. 747 for the final version.
Pencil with pen-and-ink. 16.5 x 18
BP. 1124(vii)   P.C.9

735

736

739 Study for 'How do you do, Mistress Pussy?': a cat and a dog sitting at a table having tea in the kitchen.
This may be related to a much earlier sketch (see *The Pie and the Patty-Pan*, BP.1125(iii); cat.767).
Pencil. 15.5 x 18
BP.1124(ix)   P.C.9

740 Study for *Three Blind Mice* (possibly traced?).
The w/c of the same subject is with the National Trust.
Pencil, on a thin tracing paper. 14.5 x 20
BP.1124(viii)   P.C.9

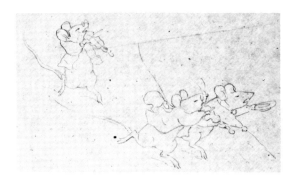

740

741 Guinea pigs gardening, with the blue-coated guinea pig looking on.
Inscribed (verso): Jan 93.
Later redrawn for the 1922 *Cecily Parsley* (LL Cat.)
Pen-and-ink and w/c. 10 x 16.5
BP.521(a)   S.20.F.B

742 Guinea pigs going to their garden, following a large guinea pig in a blue coat.
An 1893 drawing later redrawn for p.45 of *Cecily Parsley's Nursery Rhymes*, omitting the guinea pig in a blue coat with glasses, and adding some garden background (LL Cat.)
W/c and pen-and-ink. 10 x 16.5
BP.521(b)   S.20.F.B

743 Sketch for guinea pigs going to their garden (see BP.521(b); cat.742).
Verso: Sketch of the guinea pig with the blue coat.
Pencil and pen-and-ink. 10.5 x 20.5
BP.521(c)   S.20.F.B

744 'Gentlemen came every day': two rabbits smoking pipes, sitting on a settle by the fire.
Inscribed: HBP. 1902.
Original w/c drawn for Noël Moore in 1902, from which BP took her inspiration for the frontispiece of the book (it was originally intended for the 1905 *Book of Rhymes*). In the book, the second rabbit has a newspaper instead of a pipe.
Inscribed (verso) by Noël Moore: After Beatrix Potter had written to me the first Peter Rabbit letter in Sept 1893, she made me some cardboard toys to amuse me during illness. Later on (in 1902) I asked her if she would make a drawing for my album of friends' paintings and drawings. This drawing of a somewhat older Peter is the result. It was drawn for me in 1902. Noël C. Moore.
See also BP.1124(iii); cat.733.
W/c and pen-and-ink. 19.5 x 23.5
BP.522   S.20.F.B

745–746 Folded sheet showing a sketch of Cecily Parsley running with a wheelbarrow into a burrow, together with two small sketches for a pair of facing pages, one of three rabbits at the little door of Cecily Parsley's premises, looking at the 'To Let' notice, and the other of 'The Pen Inn C. Parsley' sign hanging from elder blossom.
BP has pencilled in the verse: Till Cecily Parsley ran away!
See also BP.1124(iv–vi); cat.735–737.
A similar picture of Cecily Parsley running away, dated 1896, was given to Caroline Hutton (LL Cat.)
Pencil and w/c. 20.5 x 23.5 (folded)
BP.660   T.30.R

747 Sketch for 'Goosey, Goosey, Gander' showing some geese looking into a pig-sty in which a pig is tucked up in bed.
For preliminary sketch, see BP.1124(vii); cat.738.
Pen-and-ink with white highlights. 20 x 24
BP.1142   P.C.16

748 Drawing of a forest floor showing tree trunks and ferns, with two rabbits lightly pencilled into the foreground and an indication of a rabbit coming out of a burrow.
Thought to be an unused sketch for the rhyme 'Cecily Parsley brewing cider'. This and BP.1124(iv, vi); cat.735, 737 are earlier sketches of the period c.1904.
Sepia ink with pencil. 19.5 x 25
BP.1264(v)   P.C.40

Ginger and Pickles

749 Characters from the Peter Rabbit Books are seen
making towards the shop doorway of 'Ginger and
Pickles'.
Inscribed (verso): Ginger & Pickles.
Inscribed (on transparent cover): For Music Book,
not used (LL).
Pencil. 13 x 20
BP.1089   P.C.50

The Pie and the Patty-Pan

750 Background study for Duchess reading Ribby's
invitation: a garden with flowers and a gate, with
a woman (Mrs Rogerson?) walking past along the
village street.
Inscribed (verso): Property of Capt Duke.
(LL Cat.): The house opposite is 'Ginger and
Pickles' but the shop window is not visible in the
picture.
W/c. and pen-and-ink. 21 x 23
BP.501   S.18.F.C

751 Setting for 'The Veal and Ham Pie': the door of
Sawrey Post Office with the tiger lilies from *Ginger
and Pickles* bordering the path.
Inscribed (verso): Property of Capt Duke.
The w/c is unfinished – the door and flowers are
almost complete but the figures in the doorway are
only faintly sketched in and are not associated with
this story.
See also BP.1562; cat.2135.
Pencil, pen-and-ink and w/c. 19.5 x 22
BP.502   S.18.F.C

752 Interior: study of Ribby's larder in Lakefield
Cottage, showing a corner of the larder with a
window-sill and shelves on the left.
(LL Cat.): In the book the larder is shown in
a black and white drawing.
W/c. 12.5 x 18
BP.503   S.18.F.C

753 Interior: study of Ribby's sitting room with a table
by the side of a kitchen range.
Inscribed (verso): In Mrs Lord's cottage, Lakefield
Cottages, Sawrey, used for Patty Pan.
(LL Cat.): In the finished picture, Ribby and
Duchess are having tea together.
Pencil and w/c. 22.5 x 29.5
BP.504   S.18.F.C

754 Interior: background study showing the entrance
passage of Lakefield Cottage with an open door.
Pencil and sepia ink. 21 x 20
BP.505   S.18.F.C

755 Rough sketch of Ribby sitting in front of her
kitchen range.
Inscribed: 4 x 5½ I think this looks too big for
the page.
A similar w/c sketch (at Hill Top) inserted in the
copybook containing the 1903 version of the story
is inscribed: "frontispiece". It was used, however,
as one of the book pictures (LL Cat.)
W/c with pencil. 18 x 13.5
BP.599   T.26.L

756 Sketch of Ribby and Duchess.
Pencil, on a slip of torn paper. 11.5 x 8
BP.1126(a)   P.C.6

757 Interior: study for Ribby and Duchess in the
hallway of Ribby's cottage.
Pencil. 21 x 13
BP.1126(b)   P.C.6

749

758 Sketches of Duchess (mostly in pencil, but some in ink).
A piece of the right-hand bottom corner has been cut out.
Pencil and pen-and-ink. 19 x 22.5
BP.1126(c)   P.C.6

759 Three sketches of Duchess.
Duchess was a Pomeranian dog belonging to Mrs Rogerson, an inhabitant of Sawrey; however it was Darkie, her other Pomeranian, whom BP used as a model (LL).
Pencil. 22.5 x 19
BP.1126(d)   P.C.6

760 Studies for Duchess (mostly of heads).
Verso: More studies for Duchess, one in ink (mostly heads).
Pencil and pen-and-ink, on a folded sheet.
W/m: Britannia. 20 x 32.5
BP.1126(e)   P.C.6

760 (detail)

761 Study of Duchess in the porch of Ribby's cottage, calling for tea.
Duchess is only faintly pencilled in.
This is the porch of one of the Lakefield cottages at Sawrey (LL).
1902 (LL: *History of the Writings*).
Pen-and-ink and pencil. W/m: I & JH Kent.
15.5 x 18, on sheet 22.5 x 29
BP.1126(i)   P.C.6

762 Study of Duchess in the porch of Ribby's cottage, calling for tea.
Duchess is only faintly pencilled in.
This is the porch of one of the Lakefield cottages at Sawrey (LL).
1902 (*Hist.*)
Pen-and-ink, sepia ink and pencil. W/m: Britannia. 15.5 x 18, on sheet 20 x 27
BP.1126(ii)   P.C.6

763 Study of Ribby drawing water from a spring.
Ribby is only faintly pencilled in.
1902 (*Hist.*)
Sepia ink and pencil. W/m: Aviemore. 19 x 26.5
BP.1126(iii)   P.C.6

764 Study of Duchess walking down a leafy path with a stone wall to the right.
Duchess is only faintly pencilled in.
1902 (*Hist.*)
Sepia ink and pencil. 19 x 25.5
BP.1126(iv)   P.C.6

765 Interior: study of Ribby's kitchen/sitting room, with Ribby (half-finished) standing on a rocking-chair, looking into a cupboard.
For first version of the story.
Drawn in Lakefield Cottage, Sawrey (LL).
1902 (*Hist.*)
Sepia ink with pencil. W/m: Aviemore.
20.5 x 26.5
BP.1125(i)   P.C.8

766 Interior: Ribby at the top of the stairs. Her bonnet, basket and a bunch of honesty hang on the right.
Ribby's head is finished in ink, her body is sketched in pencil.
Sepia ink with pencil. W/m: Aviemore. 19 x 24
Verso: Rough pencil drawing of Ribby and Duchess in hallway.
For first version of the story.
Drawn in Lakefield Cottage, Sawrey (LL).
1902 (*Hist.*)
BP.1125(ii)   P.C.8

766

767 Interior: study of Ribby and Duchess in the
hallway.
Inscribed: 19— H.B. Potter.

> How do you do Mrs Pussy?
> Mrs Pussy – how do you do?
> I thank you kindly little dog
>   I fare as well as you! old song.

Sepia ink with pencil. W/m: Aviemore.
18.5 x 26.5
Verso: Rough pencil sketch of Ribby and Duchess
in the sitting room with table laid for tea.
For first version of the story.
Drawn in Lakefield Cottage, Sawrey (LL).
1902 (*Hist.*)
BP. 1125(iii)　P.C. 8

768 Interior: working study of Ribby and Duchess(?)
sitting by the fire.
For first version of the story.
Drawn in Lakefield Cottage, Sawrey (LL).
1902 (*Hist.*)
Sepia ink with pencil. W/m: Aviemore. 19.5 x 26
BP. 1125(iv)　P.C. 8

769 Interior: study of Ribby in a pantry surrounded by
bottles, jars and boxes of apples.
Ribby is only faintly pencilled in.
For first version of the story.
Drawn in Lakefield Cottage, Sawrey (LL).
1902 (*Hist.*)
Sepia ink with pencil. W/m: Aviemore. 19 x 26.5
BP. 1125(v)　P.C. 8

773

770 Interior: study of Ribby standing on the sofa,
looking out of the window for the arrival of
Duchess.
For first version of the story.
Drawn in Lakefield Cottage, Sawrey (LL).
1902 (*Hist.*)
Sepia ink with pencil. W/m: Aviemore. 19 x 26.5
BP.1125(vi)   P.C.8

771 Interior: study of Ribby getting ready for the tea-
party by taking 'a black silk apron' from the drawer
of a kneehole desk.
Ribby is only partly drawn in ink.
For first version of the story.
Drawn in Lakefield Cottage, Sawrey (LL).
1902 (*Hist.*)
Sepia ink with pencil. W/m: Aviemore. 19 x 26.5
BP.1125(vii)   P.C.8

772 Interior: study of Ribby dressing, looking in an oval
wall mirror.
Ribby is only faintly pencilled in.
For first version of the story.
Drawn in Lakefield Cottage, Sawrey (LL).
1902 (*Hist.*)
Sepia ink with pencil. W/m: Aviemore. 19 x 26.5
BP.1125(viii)   P.C.8

773 Interior: study of Ribby in a pantry, with jars and
bottles.
Ribby is only faintly pencilled in.
For first version of the story.
Drawn in Lakefield Cottage, Sawrey (LL).
1902 (*Hist.*)
Sepia ink with pencil. W/m: Aviemore. 21 x 27
BP.1125(ix)   P.C.8

774 Interior: study of window with potted plants.
Drawn in Lakefield Cottage, Sawrey (LL).
1902 (*Hist.*)
Sepia ink with pencil. 19.5 x 25.5
BP.1125(x)   P.C.8

774

775 Interior: study of Ribby looking in a cupboard,
standing on a fringed stool. The scene is set in
an attic.
Ribby is only faintly pencilled in.
For first version of the story.
Drawn in Lakefield Cottage, Sawrey (LL).
1902 (*Hist.*)
See BP.996; cat.776 for a preliminary sketch.
Sepia ink with pencil. W/m: Aviemore.
19.5 x 26.5
BP.1125(xi)   P.C.8

776 Attic room showing a cupboard, chest and rabbit.
See BP.1125(xi); cat.775 for a similar study, which
includes Ribby but omits the rabbit.
Sepia ink with pencil. W/m: Aviemore. 19 x 27
BP.996   P.C.11

777 Printer's proof of a sepia drawing: Ribby sitting
beside the fire with Duchess.
Inscribed (verso): Printer's proof (LL).
14.5 x 23
BP.1158   P.C.41

The Roly-Poly Pudding

778 Study for Samuel Whiskers, Anna Maria and Tom
Kitten ('Anna Maria! Anna Maria!' squeaked the
rat): Samuel Whiskers sitting under the rafters with
Anna Maria appearing in the corner.
Tom Kitten is only faintly sketched in, and in the
book is reproduced on the opposite page.
Sepia ink and pencil. W/m: /meston. 9.5 x 15
BP.1131(a)   P.C.28

779 Interior: Hill Top front room, with Mrs Ribby
('What is all that soot in the fender?'). Mrs Ribby
pokes at the fender with her umbrella.
Pen-and-ink and pencil. 13 x 21
BP.1131(b)   P.C.28

780 Tom Kitten on the ledge inside the chimney.
Tom Kitten is worked in ink, the chimney
sketched in pencil.
Pen-and-ink and pencil. W/m: [partly
illegible] ARS/Hol/. 13 x 20.5
BP.1131(c)   P.C.28

781

781 Study for Anna Maria peeping round a window shutter with potted geraniums, on her way to steal dough.
Pen-and-ink. 13 x 20.5
BP.1131(d)   P.C.28

782 Study for Tom Kitten confronting a rat.
Inscribed (below) by BP: Same size practically.
Pen-and-ink. W/m:/ston. 12.5 x 20
BP.1131(e)   P.C.28

783 Rough sketch for Samuel Whiskers and Anna Maria.
Pencil, on a scrap of paper. 6.5 x 6.5
BP.1131(f)   P.C.28

782

784 Study for Samuel Whiskers and Anna Maria in their hole: 'Nonsense! Butter and dough', replied Anna Maria.
Sepia ink and pencil. W/m:/meston. 9.5 x 14.5
BP.1131(g)   P.C.28

785 Study for the view from the chimney top: a chimney in the foreground and a view of a stone-walled lane rising over a hill.
Pencil and w/c, badly foxed with a fold down right-hand side of sheet. 17 x 16, on sheet 26 x 31
Verso: A very rough pencil sketch of same (?).
BP.1131(h)   P.C.28

786 Sketch of Tom Kitten up the chimney.
Study for book picture.
Pencil. 3.5 x 6.5
BP.512   S.19.F.C

787 Tabitha Twitchit standing on the staircase landing.
Inscribed: By Beatrix Potter. duplicate illustration from Roly Poly Pudding.
Inscribed (verso): Mrs Tabitha Twitchit searching for her son Thomas.
(LL Cat.): The head of Mrs Tabitha Twitchit has been pasted on.
W/c, on card. 24 x 20
BP.509   S.19.F.C

788

Story of a Fierce Bad Rabbit

788 One rabbit pushing over another, having snatched
a carrot; both standing on a bench.
Inscribed: For panoramic book. Fierce bad
rabbit (LL).
Inscribed (verso): Tuppenny (endorsed by LL:
From *The Fairy Caravan*).
Pencil and pen-and-ink, on card. 13 x 12
BP.1093   P.C.50

The Tailor of Gloucester

789 Two studies of a boy posing as a tailor: (i) sewing
cross-legged and (ii) asleep in a chair; also a pencil
sketch of the boy's arm.
Inscribed (verso): from life H.B. Potter. June 1903.
Parton's little boy at Harescombe Grange, Stroud.
(Parton was the Huttons' coachman.) (LL Cat.)
Pencil and w.c. W/m: I & JH Kent. 23 x 29.5
BP.264   S.4.F.C

790 Two drawings from the privately printed edition.
Rats dancing in the Mayor's cellar (L); mice
making coats and one threading a needle (R).
Original drawings for the privately printed edition.
The first drawing was not included in Warne's
edition. The second was redrawn and only the
mouse threading the needle was included (LL Cat.)
W/c and pen-and-ink, within a square frame,
mounted on card. 10.5 x 18.5
BP.471(a,b)   S.16.F.C   (*see* PLATE XXIV)

791 Study for the lady mouse with a tea-cup.
Pencil. 12 x 13
BP.472(a)   S.16.F.C

792 Study for the gentleman mouse with a tea-cup.
Pencil. 15 x 8
BP.472(b)   S.16.F.C

789 (*detail*)

792

793 Completed illustration of lady mouse curtseying in front of a tea-cup.
Ex Nurse Edwards.
W/c. 11 x 9.5
BP.473(a) S.16.F.C (*see* PLATE XXV)
(Mounted with BP.473(b))

794 Completed illustration of gentleman mouse bowing in front of a tea-cup.
Ex Nurse Edwards.
W/c. 11 x 9.5
BP.473(b) S.16.F.C (*see* PLATE XXVI)
(Mounted with BP.473(a))

These last two mouse illustrations are not the book originals, though similar to them. Dr Renshaw exchanged them with Nurse Edwards for an oil painting. See LL Cat., p. 107, pt. 1 (BP.1557; cat.2149) for a fuller account.

795 Sketch of three mice making coats.
Pencil. 20 x 8
BP.474 S.16.F.C

The Tale of Benjamin Bunny

796 Two studies of a cat sleeping; also sketches of paws and head.
Inscribed (L): June 2nd '03.
Inscribed (verso): H.B. Potter from life.
W/c. 22.5 x 29.5
BP.479 S.17.F.B

797 Study of a lettuce bed: background study for Benjamin and Peter leaving footmarks in the bed.
Inscribed (L): Aug 29 '03.
W/c. 19 x 23
BP.480 S.17.F.B

798 Background studies for Benjamin and Peter filling their pocket handkerchief with onions: study showing onions in a vegetable patch.
W/c. 23 x 19
BP.481(a) S.17.F.B (*see* PLATE XXVII)

799 A group of three onions.
Inscribed (R): Aug. 26 '03.
Sepia ink and w/c. W/m: I & JH Kent. 21.5 x 29
BP.481(c) S.17.F.B

800 Sketches of a group of four onions, and three single onions.
Inscribed (R): Aug. 30 '03.
Sepia ink and w/c. W/m: I & JH Kent. 22 x 28
BP.481(d) S.17.F.B

801 A basket and flower-pots in a corner of a garden; the basket is the one on which the cat sat for five hours.
Inscribed (L): Sept 16 '03.
Inscribed (verso) by Capt Duke: The local name for these baskets is a 'shill' [sic, i.e. a swill].
W/c. 22.5 x 19
BP.482 S.17.F.C

802 The pear tree down which Benjamin climbed.
Inscribed (L): Sept 8th '03.
W/c. 22.5 x 19
BP.483 S.17.F.C

803 Study for the wall on which Old Mr Bunny pranced.
W/c. 22.5 x 19
BP.484 S.17.F.C

803

809

804 Background study for the walk on planks leading through a vegetable patch.
Inscribed (L): Sept 8th 03.
W/c and pencil. 22.5 x 19
BP.485   S.17.F.C

805 Background study (not used) showing a path alongside a greenhouse, probably at Fawe Park.
See also BP.1264(vii,vi,iv); cat.473–475.
W/c. 22.5 x 19
BP.486   S.17.F.C

806 Background study for the originally proposed frontispiece: carnations growing in a flower bed, subsequently used in the picture of Peter letting go of the onions for the second time.
Inscribed (R): Aug.23rd.
Pen-and-ink and w/c. W/m: I & JH Kent.
22.5 x 18.5
BP.488   S.18.F.A

807 A background study of carnations in bloom.
Pen-and-ink and w/c. 22.5 x 19
BP.489   S.18.F.A

808 Study for the frontispiece: a rough sketch of Benjamin and Peter standing underneath the carnation.
Inscribed (below): Proposed frontispiece to 'Benjamin Bunny' not used –.
Pencil with pen-and-ink. W/m: E.H. [or B.H.]
20.5 x 16
Verso: Sketch of Old Mr Bunny jumping down on to the cat (far left corner).
Pencil.
BP.490   S.18.F.A

809 Partly finished study for the original proposed frontispiece: carnation in ink and colour, the rabbits only sketched in.
This would have been one of the 'book pictures' had it been completed (LL Cat.)
Pencil, pen-and-ink and w/c. 18 x 15
BP.491(a)   S.18.F.A

810 Sketch of carnations: a study for the original proposed frontispiece.
Pencil, pen-and-ink and w/c. 22.5 x 10
BP.491(b)   S.18.F.A

811 A background study (not used) of a rose bush supported by a stake, with other roses in the background and flower-pots; the drawing only partly finished (background uncoloured).
Inscribed: August 2nd 03.
Pencil, pen-and-ink and w/c. 22.5 x 19
BP.493   S.18.F.A

812 Sketches of Old Mr Bunny smoking a pipe; also a robin, and back view of Peter and Benjamin.
The inscription on the front [P.R., i.e. Peter Rabbit] in Capt Duke's handwriting is a mistake (LL Cat.)
Pencil. 11.5 x 17.5
Verso: Outline sketch of Old Mr Bunny.
Pencil and pen-and-ink.
BP.584(3)   T.24.R

812 (detail)

813 Rough sketch of Old Mr Bunny and other rough
sketches of Peter and Benjamin.
Pencil. 11.5 x 20.5
BP.584(6)   T.24.R

814 Rough sketch for the cover picture of Benjamin in
a tam-o'-shanter.
Pencil. 20 x 11.5
BP.584(7)   T.24.R

814

815 Rough study for Peter and Benjamin on the wall.
Pencil. 13 x 10.5
BP.584(8)   T.24.R

816 Study of waterbutt, flower-pot and garden basket.
W/c. 22.5 x 19
BP.1264(i)   P.C.40   (*see* PLATE XXVIII)

817 Sketch of a garden gate by a floral border.
W/c and pencil. 22.5 x 19
BP.1264(ii)   P.C.40

818 Study showing two planks as a path between a red
brick wall and vegetation.
Inscribed (L): Aug. 29 '03.
W/c. 19 x 23.5
BP.1264(iii)   P.C.40

819 Two groups of onions.
Inscribed (R): Aug. 27 '03.
W/c. W/m: I & JH Kent. 23 x 29.5
BP.481(b)   S.17.F.B

820 Roses outside the greenhouse window
(not used: LL Cat.).
W/c. W/m: I & JH Kent. 22.5 x 19
BP.487   S.17.F.C

821 Sketch (not used) of Old Mr Bunny smoking a pipe
in an interior with rabbit tiles in the background,
subsequently modified for 'Gentlemen came every
day' in *Cecily Parsley*.
Pencil and pen-and-ink. 16 x 10
BP.584(5)   T.24.R

822 Two sketches of Mrs Rabbit nursing her children;
also sketches of Benjamin and Peter.
Verso: Sketch of a rabbit.
Pencil. 16 x 20
BP.584(4)   T.24.R

823 Rough sketches of Mrs Rabbit knitting in her
burrow, for the final frontispiece.
Pencil. W/m: Fin/. 10.5 x 17
BP.584(2)   T.24.R

824 Study for the final frontispiece, showing Mrs
Rabbit knitting, as well as other rough rabbit
sketches.
Pencil with pen-and-ink. W/m:/good. 10.5 x 17
BP.584(1)   T.24.R

See also BP.589; cat.915 for drawing of Old Mr
Bunny.

The Tale of Johnny Town-Mouse

825 Unused book picture to illustrate: 'When up the
sandy path all spick and span with a brown leather
bag came Johnny Town-Mouse!'
Unfinished w/c of Johnny Town-Mouse holding
the bag, greeting Timmy Willie surrounded by corn
sheaves etc.
Pencil, sepia ink and w/c, within black ink frame.
9 x 11
BP.525   S.20.F.B   (*see* PLATE XXIX)

PLATE XXVII (above) Study of onions
(*Benjamin Bunny*) (**798**)

PLATE XXVIII (right) Garden study with waterbutt,
Fawe Park (*Benjamin Bunny*) (**816**)

PLATE XXIX Johnny Town-Mouse greeting Timmy Willie (825)

PLATE XXX Aunt Pettitoes feeding her piglets (*Tale of Pigling Bland*) (**917**)

PLATE XXXI Squirrel in a wood near Derwentwater 1903 (*Squirrel Nutkin*) (918)

833

826 Duplicate of a book picture: Timmy Willie running
to his hole.
Inscribed: 22 [i.e. page no. of book].
W/c. 15 x 10.5
Verso: Faint pencil sketch of the carrier's cart in
a lane against a hilly background.
BP.524   S.20.F.B

827 Background study for Johnny Town-Mouse: sketch
of the arch and house at Hawkshead (LL Cat.)
Pencil. 20.5 x 12.5
BP.526   S.20.F.B

The Tale of Little Pig Robinson

828 Landscape: hillside with trees and fields, a house in
the middle distance.
Inscribed (L and R): Sidmouth.
Pencil and w/c. W/m: Britannia. 24.5 x 20.5
BP.1127(i)   P.C.7

829 Study for a stile.
Inscribed (L): Sept. 19 '04 Sidmouth.
Sepia ink and pencil. W/m: Oceana Fine.
26.5 x 17.5
BP.1127(ii)   P.C.7

830 A wooden bridge over a small stream, surrounded
by trees and bushes.
Inscribed (L): Sidmouth.
Sepia ink and pencil. W/m: 7. 26 x 17.5
BP.1127(iii)   P.C.7

831 Street scene with horse and cart.
Inscribed (L): April 1904.
Inscribed (verso): Lyme Regis.
Sepia ink and pencil. W/m: Aviemore. 26 x 20.5
BP.1127(iv)   P.C.7

832 A street of shops leading down to the sea.
Inscribed (L): Lyme Regis.
Pencil and pen-and-ink. W/m: Aviemore.
19 x 26.5
BP.1127(v)   P.C.7

833 Steep street leading down to the sea, with a horse
and cart in the middle distance.
Inscribed (L): Lyme Regis.
Sepia ink and pencil. W/m: Aviemore.
19.5 x 27.5
BP.1127(vi)   P.C.7

836

834 Street corner with cottages.
  Inscribed (verso): H.B. Potter – 14.
  Background to one of the coloured illustrations.
  Sepia ink and pencil. 20 x 26.5
  BP.1127(vii)   P.C.7

835 A cottage, with a walled garden in front, and a
  road in the foreground.
  Inscribed (verso): nr. Sidmouth I think.
  Pencil and w/c. 23 x 14
  BP.1127(viii)   P.C.7

836 Robinson and the Sailor walking on the quay,
  with the 'Pound of Candles' in the background.
  Pencil and pen-and-ink. 20 x 16.5
  BP.1128(i)   P.C.7

837 Robinson in a rowing boat, with the 'Pound of
  Candles' on the horizon.
  Pencil and pen-and-ink. 20 x 16
  BP.1128(ii)   P.C.7

838 Robinson arrives at the island with the Bong tree. Verso: Robinson rowing away from the 'Pound of Candles', seen in the middle distance.
Pencil. 20.5 x 16
BP.1128(iii)   P.C.7

The Tale of Mr Jeremy Fisher

The three following items (cat.839–841) are mounted on thin paper endorsed: H.B. Potter.

839 Jeremy Fisher sitting on a waterlily leaf, fishing, both feet on the leaf.
Pen-and-ink and w/c. 20.5 x 13
BP.508(a)   S.19.F.A

840 Jeremy Fisher sitting on a waterlily leaf, fishing, one foot in the water, with three fish lightly sketched below in the water.
Pencil and pen-and-ink. 20.5 x 12.5
BP.508(b)   S.19.F.A

841 Jeremy Fisher dining on grasshopper with Sir Isaac Newton and Mr Ptolemy Tortoise, inscribed with their names: grasshopper, newt, tortoise.
Pencil and pen-and-ink. 19 x 13
BP.508(c)   S.19.F.A

842 Large fish (trout?) about to snap at the foot of Jeremy Fisher: unused sketch?
Pencil. 19 x 13
BP.1263(i)   P.C.36

843 Jeremy Fisher sitting on a leaf sucking his sore fingers: light sketch.
Pencil, with a touch of pen-and-ink. W/m: /ston. 20.5 x 12.5
BP.1263(v)   P.C.36

844 Jeremy Fisher sitting on a waterlily leaf, fishing: rough sketch.
Pencil, on very thin paper. 18 x 18
BP.1263(vi)   P.C.36

845 Jeremy Fisher sitting on a waterlily leaf, fishing.
Pencil, on very thin paper. 13.5 x 18
BP.1263(vii)   P.C.36

846 Rough sketch of Jeremy Fisher.
Pencil, heightened with touches of pink, green and yellow w/c. 16.5 x 20
BP.1263(xi)   P.C.36

847 Sketch of Jeremy Fisher on the window-sill, reading a newspaper.
Pencil. 19 x 13
BP.1263(xii)   P.C.36

848 Jeremy Fisher receiving his friends outside his house.
Pencil. W/m: /ston. 20 x 13
BP.1263(xiv)   P.C.36

849 Jeremy Fisher receiving his friends outside his house.
Pencil and pen-and-ink, with touches of w/c. W/m: Edmes/. 20 x 13
BP.1263(xv)   P.C.36

850 The trout swallowing Jeremy Fisher.
Pencil and pen-and-ink. 13 x 13
BP.1263(xvi)   P.C.36

851 The trout spitting out Jeremy Fisher, with a few rough outlines of a fish etc. below the picture.
Pencil and pen-and-ink. 19 x 13
BP.1263(xvii)   P.C.36

851

The Tale of Mr Tod

852 Study of a stile in a stone wall with meadow and
hillside beyond.
Inscribed (by BP): Gwaynynog – used for Mr
Todd [sic].
It is used in reverse for the cover picture.
Verso: Sketch of trees (very faint).
Pencil. W/m: Aviemore. 20 x 17.5
(crease down left-hand side of page)
BP.1135(a)   P.C.38

853 Sketch of Peter and Benjamin Bunny.
See also BP.1136(b); cat.854 for similar study
including a rough background for Bull Banks.
Pencil. 11 x 9, on sheet 19 x 13
Pin holes in top right-hand corner.
BP.1136(a)   P.C.38

854 Sketch for Peter and Benjamin Bunny near the
wood at the top of Bull Banks; rocks and
background roughly sketched in.
See also BP.1136(a); cat.853 for study of the two
rabbits for same subject.
Pencil. 11.5 x 9.5, on sheet 18.5 x 13
Ripped, with two holes in top right-hand corner.
BP.1136(b)   P.C.38

855 Rough sketch for Mr Tod finding Tommy Brock in
his (Mr Tod's) kitchen.
In this sketch BP has omitted Tommy Brock.
Pencil. 11 x 9, on sheet 19 x 12.5
Pin holes in top left-hand corner.
BP.1136(c)   P.C.38

856 Sketch for Mr Tod tying the rope over Tommy
Brock, who is asleep in Mr Tod's bed.
See also a similar rougher sketch (BP.1136(e);
cat.857).
Pencil. 19 x 12
BP.1136(d)   P.C.38

857 Rough sketch for Mr Tod tying the rope over
Tommy Brock, who is asleep in Mr Tod's bed.
See also a more finished sketch of the same subject,
BP.1136(d); cat.856.
Pencil. 11 x 9.5, on sheet 19 x 12.5
BP.1136(e)   P.C.38

858 Rough sketch for Tommy Brock in Mr Tod's bed,
with the pail of water suspended over his head.
Pencil. 11.5 x 9.5, on sheet 18.5 x 12.5
Pin holes in top left-hand corner.
BP.1136(f)   P.C.38

856

859 Sketch for Mr Tod, peeping 'through the hinges of
the half-open bedroom door'.
Used for the frontispiece as well as for a half-length
black-and-white illustration in the book.
Pencil. 11 x 10, on sheet 19 x 13
BP.1136(g)   P.C.38

860 Sketch for Mr Tod, peeping 'through the hinges of
the half-open bedroom door'.
Used for the frontispiece as well as for a half-length
black-and-white illustration in the book. Slightly
heavier pencil than BP.1136(g); cat.859 (a green
ink stain on right-hand side).
Pencil. 11 x 9, on sheet 18.5 x 12
BP.1136(h)   P.C.38

861 Study of Tommy Brock climbing into Mr Tod's bed.
Done in the style of the small black-and-white
illustrations in the book, with a heavily drawn
frame.
Pencil and sepia ink. 7.5 x 9, on sheet 11 x 13
BP.1136(i)   P.C.38

860

861

862 Proof taken from printer's block, with corrections by BP inscribed: Please cut away line marked. It shows Cottontail 'sitting in her doorway, with four or five half-grown rabbits playing about'.
4 x 5.5, on sheet 6.5 x 11
BP.1136(j)   P.C.38

863 From the proofs: Black-and-white book pictures, together with colour plate of Mr Tod creeping towards the kitchen.
BP.1255(i–xix)   P.C.41
BP.1255(i) is the colour plate

The Tale of Mrs Tiggy-Winkle

864 Sketch of mountains surrounding a valley with a river running through it. Probably the Newlands valley.
W/c with pencil. 17.5 x 25.5
BP.1129(vi)   P.C.4

865 Background study: doorway into hillside, with a path leading up to it.
Inscribed: Kelbarrow, Grasmere Aug 1st '99.
Inscribed (verso): Grasmere H.B. Potter.
(LL Cat.): Assumed to be background setting for the door in the hill called Catbells?
Blue-grey wash and pencil. 23.5 x 14.5
BP.494   S.18.F.B

866 Study of two heads of a hedgehog. Assumed to be Mrs Tiggy-Winkle.
Verso: Study of one head of a hedgehog and study of a mouse.
Pencil and w/c, on a sample sheet of Joynson drawing paper. 19 x 11
BP.495   S.18.F.B

867 Six pencil studies of the head of Mrs Tiggy-Winkle and two wash drawings of her snout.
Pencil and grey wash. 22.5 x 28
Verso: Study of leaves.
W/c and sepia ink.
BP.496   S.18.F.B

868 Rough study of Lucie standing by the door in the hillside; also several sketches of her head and legs.
Pencil. W/m: Oceana Fine. 18 x 21
Verso: Pencil sketches of Lucie, and w/c and pencil sketch of Mrs Tiggy-Winkle.
BP.497   S.18.F.B

870

869 Unfinished picture of Mrs Tiggy-Winkle, partly
sketched with pencil, partly inked and coloured.
Pencil, pen-and-ink and w/c, on card. 25.5 x 22.5
BP.499   S.18.F.B

870 Unfinished w/c study of Mrs Tiggy-Winkle and
Lucie. Mrs Tiggy-Winkle, holding an iron, is
worked in pen-and-ink and w/c, but Lucie is
sketched in pencil.
Inscribed (verso): saith.
Four cut-outs have been taken from the sheet,
which may have been pasted on original drawings.
See *Hist.* (LL Cat.)
Pencil, pen-and-ink and w/c. W/m: Britannia.
20 x 18
BP.498   S.18.F.B

871 Background study: view of Newlands valley.
(LL Cat.): Believed to be as seen from
Lucie's path?
W/c. 12 x 18
BP.500   S.18.F.B

872– Mrs Tiggy-Winkle with an umbrella, looking
873 through a shop door; also rough sketches of two
figures.
Inscribed (not in BP's writing): Not used – see
rhyme on back.
The drawing is an unused book picture (LL Cat.)
Pen-and-ink with pencil. 14.5 x 21.5
Verso: Three pen-and-ink sketches of dog's head
(Duchess?).
Inscribed with the verse:

> Lily white and clean – oh!
> with [deleted] Little frills between – oh! [etc.]

One line is repeated below in code.
BP.602   T.26.L

874 Study for the spring, which Lucie found 'bubbling
out from the hill side'.
Pencil and w/c. W/m: Kent. 22.5 x 19
BP.1129(i)   P.C.4

875 Interior: study of Mrs Tiggy-Winkle's kitchen, showing dresser and beamed ceiling with washing.
W/c, pen-and-ink and pencil. 19 x 22.5
BP.1129(iv)　P.C.4

876 Woodland sketch: path to distant trees and hillside.
Inscribed (L): Near Catbells.
Pencil and grey wash. 15 x 19.5 (unfolded)
Verso: Faint pencil sketch of trees.
BP.1129(vii)　P.C.4

877 Interior: study of Lucie entering Mrs Tiggy-Winkle's kitchen.
Pencil. W/m: /a. 18 x 10
BP.1130(a)　P.C.4

878 Study of Lucie talking to Sally Henny Penny in the farmyard.
Verso: Rough sketches, three of Lucie and one of Mrs Tiggy-Winkle holding tea-pot(?).
Pencil. W/m: Fine. 16 x 12
BP.1130(b)　P.C.4

879 Study for background: part of a rocky hillside with a door leading into it.
Inscribed (on folder): Door at Catbells. 'Entrance to Tin Mine' (LL).
Pencil and sepia ink. 25 x 21
BP.1025　P.C.22

880 Interior: study for Mrs Tiggy-Winkle's kitchen, showing dresser, hanging hams, laundry basket and chest of drawers.
Sepia ink and w/c. 22.5 x 19
BP.1129(iii)　P.C.4

881 Two rough sketches of Mrs Tiggy-Winkle, in one pushing a handcart and in the other hanging up washing.
Pencil. 16 x 10
Verso: Pen-and-ink drawing of a hazel twig.
BP.1251　P.C.41

The Tale of Mrs Tittlemouse

882 Three rough sketches of Mr Jackson, and one of Mrs Tittlemouse seeing him off.
Inscribed (verso): Mr Jackson (Mrs Tittlemouse) (LL).
Pencil. 20 x 13
BP.1091(a)　P.C.50

883 Mrs Tittlemouse talking to a butterfly.
Inscribed (verso): Mrs Tittlemouse. Title page drawing (LL).
Pen-and-ink. 10.5 x 13
BP.1091(b)　P.C.50

The Tale of Peter Rabbit

884 Sketches of various scenes from *Peter Rabbit* (some unfinished).
Copy of the pictures in the Peter Rabbit story-letter. Her final file copy is at Hill Top (LL Cat.) 4ff. (in booklet form); pencil or pen-and-ink.
W/m: Silverburn Linen. 20 x 12.5
BP.881　T.11

885 Rough study for the frontispiece: Mrs Rabbit giving Peter a dose of camomile tea.
Inscribed (top R): 3.
Pencil. 20.5 x 18
BP.583(1)　T.24.R

883

886

886 Drawing for a variant of the frontispiece: Mrs
Rabbit giving Peter a dose of camomile tea.
Sepia ink with pencil. W/m: /ana/ne. 21 x 13.5
BP.583(2)   T.24.R

887 Two sketches of Peter for the title page.
Pencil and pen-and-ink. 12.5 x 20.5
Verso: Two sketches of Peter, one in pen-and-ink
and one in pencil.
BP.583(3)   T.24.R

888 Rough sketches of Mrs Rabbit with a basket; also
pencil sketches of rabbit heads and of a rabbit lying
on its back.
Pencil and pen-and-ink. 11 x 20.5
BP.583(4)   T.24.R

889 Rough sketch of Mrs Rabbit and her family.
Inscribed (R): rough sketch.
Pencil. W/m: /brook /Fine. 18 x 11.5
BP.583(5)   T.24.R

890 Rough sketch of Mrs Rabbit and her family,
including Peter with his hands in his pockets.
Pencil. 11.5 x 16
BP.583(6)   T.24.R

891 Studies for Peter Rabbit's sisters, and Peter with his
hands in his pockets.
Pencil. W/m: Britannia. 10 x 16.5
BP.583(7)   T.24.R

892 Rough sketch of Mrs Rabbit and her family,
including Peter with his hands in his pockets.
Pencil. 10.5 x 16.5
BP.583(9)   T.24.R

887 (detail)

PLATES XXXII, XXXIII The White Rabbit (*Alice's Adventures in Wonderland*) (**972, 973**)

PLATES XXXIV, XXXV *The White Cat*: kittens with game (**985** a, b)

893 Rough pencil sketch of Mrs Rabbit and her family, and pen sketch of back view of Peter.
Pencil and pen-and-ink. W/m: Cream laid. 20.5 x 16.5
Verso: Almost indecipherable light pencil sketch of a hedgehog and a squirrel by a door (?) or gate (?) or reading notice board.
BP.583(10)   T.24.R

894 Rough sketch of Mrs Rabbit buttoning up Peter's coat.
Inscribed (below): Rough copy.
Pencil and pen-and-ink. W/m: Willo/Extr/. 18 x 11.5
BP.583(11)   T.24.R

895 Rough study of Peter squeezing under the gate (inscribed: 3) and Peter eating lettuces (inscribed: 4).
Pencil. 10.5 x 16.5
BP.583(12)   T.24.R

896 Rough sketch of Peter squeezing under the gate and Peter amongst the lettuces.
A more complete sketch than BP.583(12); cat.895.
Pencil. W/m: Britannia. 10.5 x 16.5
BP.583(13)   T.24.R

897 A more finished sketch, as compared with BP.583(15, 16); cat.910, of Mr McGregor and Peter and the cucumber frame.
Pencil with pen-and-ink. W/m: Willo/Extr/. 18 x 11.5
BP.583(17)   T.24.R

898 Very rough sketch of Mr McGregor in the potting shed.
Pencil. W/m: /wbrook/a Fine. 18 x 11.5
BP.583(18)   T.24.R

899 Very rough sketch of the Peter Rabbit gate, or a later-drawn gate? (LL Cat.)
Verso: Sketch of toadstools (agarics).
Pencil, on ruled paper. 15 x 13
BP.583(19)   T.24.R

900 Background study for the Peter Rabbit gate: a garden in front, with trees in the background.
Pencil and w/c, on cartridge paper. 13 x 17.5
BP.583(20)   T.24.R

894

901 Flopsy, Mopsy and Cottontail eating blackberries, with a rough sketch (R, the other way up) of mice sewing.
Pencil and pen-and-ink. 11 x 20.5
Verso: Rough pencil sketch of rabbits, and pen-and-ink sketch (in corner) of landscape with trees and sheep.
BP.583(21)   T.24.R

902 Rough sketches of Flopsy, Mopsy and Cottontail eating blackberries; also a rough sketch of Peter squeezing under the gate, with other rabbit studies.
Pencil. 10.5 x 16.5
BP.583(23)   T.24.R

903 Rough sketch of Flopsy, Mopsy and Cottontail
eating blackberries.
Verso: Rough outline of a rabbit.
Pencil. W/m: Britannia. 10.5 x 16
BP.583(24)   T.24.R

904 Rough sketches for the privately printed *Peter
Rabbit*: two studies of a robin on a shoe.
Pencil. 16 x 9.5
BP.582(ii)   T.24.R

905 Rough sketches for the privately printed *Peter
Rabbit*: two studies of Mrs Rabbit knitting.
Pen-and-ink and pencil. W/m: Towgood's Fine.
20 x 10
Verso: Pencil studies of Mrs Rabbit knitting and
Peter running to the fir tree.
BP.582(i)   T.24.R

906 Mrs Rabbit pouring out tea for Peter while her
children look on.
Inscribed (at top) by the printer Mr Herring:
Duplicate – other design used; also (below):
– reduce together.
(LL Cat.): Must have been paired with another
drawing. Used when blocks were re-engraved in
Sept. 1907 and not replaced by the earlier drawing
until about 1911. It is finer workmanship.
Pen-and-ink and w/c, in a lightly pencilled frame.
W/m: Towgo/. 14.5 x 10
BP.468   S.16.F.C

907 Mrs McGregor presenting a pie to Mr McGregor,
though only his hands are visible holding knife and
fork on the table.
Inscribed (below, in red ink): We still do not like
the old woman's face. Will you please have another
try at this. [Norman Warne's signature.]
(LL Cat.): This is the same old woman that appears
in the privately printed *Peter Rabbit* [but not in
Warne's edition].
Pen-and-ink and w/c. W/m: St. N [illegible].
20.5 x 12
BP.469   S.16.F.C

908 Rough sketch of Mrs Rabbit and her family;
also sketches of birds.
Pencil. 10 x 16.5
BP.583(8)   T.24.R

911 (detail)

909 Rough sketches of Peter running away, chased by
Mr McGregor, and back view of Peter.
Pencil. W/m: Fin/. 16.5 x 10
BP.583(14)   T.24.R

910 Two rough sketches of Mr McGregor and Peter by
the cucumber frame.
Pencil. 10 x 17
BP.583(15,16)   T.24.R

911 Rough sketch of the three rabbit children eating
blackberries; also a sketch of Peter Rabbit
squeezing under the gate.
Pencil. 16.5 x 10.5
BP.583(22)   T.24.R

912 Preliminary layout: cover of Warne's *Peter Rabbit*.
Design shows a rabbit running.
Inscribed: PETER RABBIT. BEATRIX POTTER
[followed by the Warne imprint].
Inscribed (above the cover design): Yellowish
ground – dark brown lettering & shading on
rabbit's back? blue coat? here rough idea for cover?
would *blue* print on yellowish paper colour?
The rabbit running is picture number 17 in the
privately printed edition (LL Cat.)
Pen-and-ink and pencil, on yellow card (back of
writing block). 17.5 x 11.5
BP.590   T.25.L

913 Another preliminary design for the *Peter Rabbit* cover: probably a rough study for BP.590; cat.912, and with the same format.
Pencil. W/m: Emissary Bond. 19 x 14.5 (approx.)
BP.591   T.25.L

914 Two sketches of Peter Rabbit running away, chased by Mr McGregor, for picture 17 in the privately printed edition.
Pencil and pen-and-ink. 9 x 12.5; 9 x 8
BP.592(a,b)   T.25.L

915 Printer's proof of a pen-and-ink drawing of Old Mr Bunny.
For *The Tale of Benjamin Bunny*, see cat.796–824.
18.5 x 12.5
BP.589   T.25.L

915

916 Printer's proof of the coloured frontispiece of *Peter Rabbit*. Stamped in the centre: 13 Aug 1901. Inscribed: Miss H.B. Potter, Lingholme [sic], Keswick, Cumberland [cancelled in pencil]; also inscribed: 3 colour block & 500 copies; and: 2 Bolton Gardens, S. Kensington S.W. (blocks returned to me).
14 x 10
BP.586   T.25.L

Other copies:
BP.587(a–h) 14 x 10   T.25.L
BP.588 12.5 x 19   T.25.L

The Tale of Pigling Bland

917 Duplicate of an illustration for *Pigling Bland*: Aunt Pettitoes feeding her piglets.
Pen-and-ink and w/c. 19.5 x 16.5
BP.514   S.19.F.C   (*see* PLATE XXX)

The Tale of Squirrel Nutkin

918 Background study showing a squirrel in a wood, with a view along a leafy avenue.
Believed to be the woods by Derwentwater as drawn for *The Tale of Squirrel Nutkin*, 1903, at Fawe Park (LL Cat.)
W/c and sepia ink. 20.5 x 16
BP.475   S.17.F.A   (*see* PLATE XXXI)

919 Detailed view of part of a tree trunk. Old Brown's oak? (LL Cat.)
W/c. 22.5 x 19
BP.476   S.17.F.A

920 Unfinished sketch of Old Brown in one corner, surrounded by faint pencil sketches of squirrels.
Pencil and w/c, on Bristol board. 20.5 x 15.5
BP.477(a)   S.17.F.A

921 Sketch of an owl (Old Brown) within a pencil frame.
Pencil, on Bristol board. 20.5 x 15.5
BP.477(b)   S.17.F.A

922 Faint sketches of squirrels approaching Old Brown in front of his oak tree.
Pencil. W/m: Britannia. 19.5 x 16
BP.477(c)   S.17.F.A

923 Studies for Old Brown.
Wash with pencil. 22.5 x 29
BP.1211(a)   P.C.19

924 Studies for Old Brown.
Wash with pencil. 22.5 x 29
BP.1211(b)   P.C.19

925 Proof of colour plate (frontispiece) showing squirrels gathering nuts.
11 x 9
BP.1255(xx)   P.C.41

The Tale of the Flopsy Bunnies

926 Background study of a trellis, with an apple tree growing along it.
W/c and pencil. 17.5 x 25
BP.1244   P.C.31

927 Background study (not used) of garden beds and path, with trees in the background.
See also BP.1242; cat.471.
Pencil and w/c. 16 x 17.5
BP.1243   P.C.31

928 Background study of flower-beds and corner of a path.
W/c with pencil. 12 x 17.5
BP.1240   P.C.31

929 Background study of flower-beds surrounded by box hedges, with buildings in the background.
W/c with pencil. 11 x 17.5
BP.1239   P.C.31

930 Background study of garden with flowers and a path through trees, a barn visible behind a fence.
Inscribed (on folder): Gwaynynog (LL).
Sepia ink. 25 x 20
BP.1027   P.C.22

931 Background study of a trellis (L), and a path leading to an archway with buildings (R).
Inscribed: Gwaynynog Feb 6th to 16th '03.
Pencil, on folded sheet. 35.5 x 25
BP.1225   P.C.30

932 Background study of a walled garden.
Inscribed (on folder): Gwaynynog (LL).
Verso (upper half): mountains and wood;
(lower half): single tree.
Pencil. 18 x 26.5
BP.1228   P.C.30

933 Background study: unfinished sketch of a path leading to a gate in a garden wall.
Inscribed (on folder): Gwaynynog (LL).
Pencil and w/c. 17.5 x 25.5
BP.1232   P.C.30

934 Background study, showing a corner of a walled garden with little hedges skirting the borders.
Inscribed: Studies for backgrounds H.B. Potter.
Verso: Studies of pink phlox and blossom.
Possibly sketched in March 1909 at Gwaynynog, her Uncle's house in Denbigh, North Wales (LL).
W/c. 25 x 18
BP.1134(i)   P.C.37

935 Background study for the words: 'They watched him go into his house [etc.]', showing a garden path, edged by little hedges and deep borders, disappearing under an overgrown arch.
Inscribed: Gwaynynog June 30th to July 4th.
Inscribed (verso, in pencil): H.B. Potter An Old Garden in Wales; and (in ink): June 30th to July 4 '11.
W/c. 25 x 17.5
BP.1134(ii)   P.C.37

936 Background study, showing a deep flower-border with a rose-covered trellis-work.
Pencil notes in the sky indicate colour.
W/c. 17.5 x 25
Verso: Sketch of blossom over a fence.
Pencil.
Thought to be from her Uncle's garden at Gwaynynog, Denbigh, North Wales, where she visited in March 1909 (LL).
BP.1134(iii)   P.C.37

937 Background study of stone-built shed with slate roof, housing an iron stove with chimney.
This sketch was one of many BP prepared at her Uncle's house at Gwaynynog, Denbigh, North Wales for the background of *The Tale of the Flopsy Bunnies*.
W/c and pen-and-ink. 14 x 17.5
BP.1134(iv)   P.C.37

938 Background study of a shed, cold frames and waterbutts.
Inscribed: Directions? – Sept 23rd '07.
This sketch was one of many BP prepared at her Uncle's house at Gwaynynog, Denbigh, North Wales for the background of *The Tale of the Flopsy Bunnies*.
W/c. 18 x 25
BP.1134(v)   P.C.37

The Tale of Timmy Tiptoes

939 Sketches of a chipmunk, mainly in outline (four
have touches of colour).
Inscribed (on transparent cover): Timmy Tiptoes
sketches (LL).
Pencil and w/c. 27.5 x 25
BP.1090(a)   P.C.50

940 Sketches (some unfinished), of a chipmunk; at one
corner, a rough w/c sketch of a river scene (?).
Inscribed (on transparent cover): Timmy Tiptoes
sketches (LL).
Pencil. 25 x 17.5
BP.1090(b)   P.C.50

The Tale of Tom Kitten

941 Cover picture for Tom Kitten: Tom Kitten in a
blue suit with burst buttons.
Inscribed: "Beatrix Potter".
Inscribed (verso): Original drawing by Beatrix
Potter.
W/c and pen-and-ink. 9.5 x 7
BP.510   S.19.F.C

941

Endpaper designs for
Peter Rabbit books

942 Unfinished version of endpaper design No. 1.
The design is complete but uncoloured.
Inscribed: 3¹³⁄₁₆ [with arrows defining width]
(Mr Herring's writing: LL Cat.)
Originally an uncoloured endpaper was envisaged
(LL Cat.)
Design 1 in colour belongs to the National Trust.
Pencil and pen-and-ink. W/m: Britannia.
18 x 13.5
BP.466   S.16.F.B   *(illustration overleaf)*

943 Endpaper design No. 2. The design includes Peter
Rabbit, Squirrel Nutkin, and mice from *The Tailor
of Gloucester.*
Inscribed: Reduce to this width & deep etch as
before. (Mr Herring's writing: LL Cat.)
W/c and pen-and-ink, mounted on card. 20 x 14
BP.460   S.16.F.A

944 Endpaper design No. 3. The design includes the
Bad Mice, Mrs Tiggy-Winkle, Benjamin Bunny.
W/c and pen-and-ink, mounted on card.
19 x 13.5
BP.461   S.16.F.A

945 Unfinished version of endpaper design No. 3.
The cat is coloured but the remainder of the design
is only pencilled, except for two partly inked figures
and some partly coloured scrollwork.
Possibly indicating BP's general procedure when
preparing her endpaper drawings (LL Cat.)
Pencil, pen-and-ink and w/c. 20 x 17
BP.467   S.16.F.B

946 Endpaper design No. 4.
Inscribed: Reduce to this width and deep etch
as before.
Inscribed (verso): D 2916–1.
Similar to design No.3 except that Appley Dapply
is replaced by Jeremy Fisher.
Pen-and-ink and w/c. 20.5 x 16
BP.462   S.16.F.A

947 Endpaper design No. 5. The design includes Tom
Kitten, Peter Rabbit, Squirrel Nutkin, and mice
from *The Tailor of Gloucester.*
Inscribed: 4½ Beneath.
Pen-and-ink and w/c. W/m: Britannia. 20 x 16.5
BP.463   S.16.F.A

942

948 Endpaper for foreign translations: design No. 6 redrawn without any lettering or books. It includes Jemima Puddle-Duck, Flopsy Bunnies, Jeremy Fisher etc.
Inscribed: 3¾ inches wide *deep etched*.
(LL Cat.): Design never used.
Pen-and-ink and w/c. W/m: Parsons' Linen/ Holyoke Mas/. 26.5 x 21
BP.464   S.16.F.B   (*see endpapers*)

949 Endpaper for foreign translations: design No. 7 redrawn without any books. It includes Tom Kitten, Squirrel Nutkin, Mrs Tittlemouse.
(LL Cat.): Design never used.
Pen-and-ink and w/c. 26.5 x 21
BP.465   S.16.F.B   (*see endpapers*)

950 Pen-and-ink sketches of squirrels for an endpaper design for *Squirrel Nutkin*, in a pencil frame; also two other squirrel sketches.
(LL Cat.): Design never used.
See also BP.213; cat. 1740.
Pen-and-ink and pencil. W/m: Aviemore. 21 x 26.5
BP.478   S.17.F.A

Backgrounds for other books

The Fairy Caravan

951 Original book drawing of tail-piece, Chapter IX, on page 84, showing girls spinning outside a hillside cottage.
Inscribed: A very narrow space, but Mr M[cKay?] has marked it 'tailpiece'; also (in different writing): Not remade.
Pen-and-ink, on two pieces of paper joined together. 10.5 x 18
BP.665   T.32.R

952 Sketch of part of a house with three storeys.
Inscribed: Thimble Hall, an ancient house in Hawkshead. Beatrix Potter 1929.
Sketch used for pictures 45 and 179 in *The Fairy Caravan* (LL).
Pencil. 21.5 x 11
BP.666   T.32.R

953 Painting (unfinished) showing a cart drawn by a goat. A cat is serving from a basket on the cart. A mother cat and her two kittens appear through a gateway with a plate.
This is a variation of the illustration heading Chapter XXI of the book: '". . . the fisher-cart comes round from Flookborough on Wednesdays", purred Mary Ellen'.
See also *History of the Writings*, p.299.
Oil painting, on card. 20.5 x 40.5
BP.1265   P.C.43

Kitty-in-Boots

954 Study for the frontispiece of *Kitty-in-Boots*, within an ink frame. Kitty carries a gun and game. In the background, hills by Esthwaite Water.
Pencil, pen-and-ink and w/c, mounted on card. 15.5 x 13.5
BP.515   S.19.F.C

955 Unfinished book picture of Kitty and the fox in the woods. Kitty and the fox are only faintly sketched in.
Pen-and-ink and w/c with pencil. 15.5 x 12.5
BP.615   T.27.R

ILLUSTRATIONS
FOR BOOKS

Work by other authors, known and unknown

Perhaps Beatrix Potter's peculiar talent is nowhere better revealed than in her own illustrations for the works of well-known and much illustrated authors. Not for her the traditional interpretation of subjects but rather one which comes much nearer to her own imaginative world. This is particularly evident in her *Cinderella* sketches, although other surviving drawings such as those for *Aesop's Fables* show that she was equally adept with a wide range of literary material.

957 Study of a crow against a faintly sketched background within an oval pencil frame.
W/c with pencil, on card. 15 x 11
BP. 1140(b)   T. 30. L

958 Study of a crow with a piece of cheese in its beak, looking down at a fox from a pine tree.
A more finished version of BP. 1140(a, b); cat. 956–957.
W/c with pencil, on card. 15 x 9
BP. 1140(c)   T. 30. L

Aesop's Fables: The Fox and the Stork

In 1919 BP planned a book based on *Aesop's Fables*. She adapted several of them, but only *The Fox and the Stork* was fully illustrated. Seven of her pictures were finished (LL Cat.)

964

Work by other authors

Aesop's Fables: The Fox and the Crow

956 Two studies of a crow with a piece of cheese in its beak, against a faintly sketched background: one front view and one side view.
Probably a preliminary design for *The Fox and the Crow*.
W/c with pencil, on card. 15 x 20
BP. 1140(a)   T. 30. L

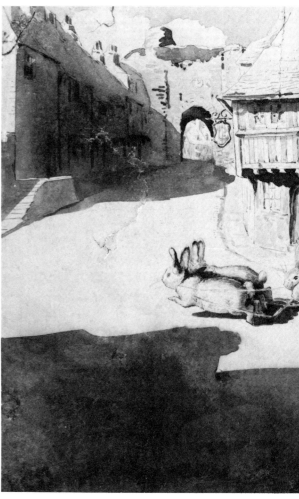

974 (*Cinderella*)

959 The fox (Mr Tod) looking across the stream at the stork (King Stork) standing by a clump of reeds in a lake.
W/c with pencil, on card. 13 x 10.5
BP.652(1)   T.30.L

960 The fox (Mr Tod) and stork (King Stork) having a meal in a room with a fire-place in the background.
W/c with pencil, on card. 16.5 x 11
BP.652(2)   T.30.L

961 The Lapwing bringing an invitation, against a mountainous background (L); and a faint pencil outline of the same (R).
W/c with pencil, on card. 15 x 20
Verso: Rough pencil sketch of a bird, and sketch of a crow with the head finished in w/c.
BP.652(3)   T.30.L

962 The fox (Mr Tod) looks up at the stork (King Stork) standing on top of the tower of an old red brick mansion (Melford Hall).
W/c with pencil, on card. 10 x 15
BP.652(4)   T.30.L

963 Mr Tod following King Stork up a corkscrew staircase.
W/c with pencil, on card. 15 x 12
BP.652(5)   T.30.L

964 King Stork feeding out of a narrow-necked jar while Mr Tod looks on; both are standing in front of a large fire-place.
W/c with pencil, on card. 15 x 11
BP.652(6)   T.30.L

965 Mr Tod taking leave of King Stork, in a panelled room.
W/c with pencil, on card. 15 x 12
BP.652(7)   T.30.L

966 Unfinished w/c sketch of Mr Tod pouring out tea into a saucer.
W/c with pencil, on card. 9 x 7, on card 13 x 13
BP.652(8)   T.30.L

967 King Stork walking with Mr Tod through a mountain glade (L); and Mr Tod looking up at two birds in the air (R).
Pencil, pen-and-ink and w/c. 15 x 19.5
BP.652(9)   T.30.L

968 Mr Tod walking through a wood.
The fox has been completed in w/c but the background is only faintly pencilled in.
Pencil and w/c, on card. 15 x 12
BP.652(10)   T.30.L

Aesop's Fables: The Hare and the Tortoise

969 Study of the Tortoise (Ptolemy Tortoise) beside some leaves.
The leaves are faintly sketched in pencil; the shell of the tortoise is a more highly finished pen-and-ink and pencil sketch.
Pencil and pen-and-ink, on card. 21 x 28
Verso: Rough sketch of a frog.
Pencil.
BP.910   T.30.L

Andersen, H.C., Little Ida's Flowers

970 Mounted illustration of a child looking through a doorway at tulips dancing. Underneath is a line of German Gothic text: "Nun tanzen sicherlich alle Blumen drinnen!", with a surround of tulips.
Inscribed (verso): Little Ida's flowers, Andersen's fairy tales. Beatrix Potter.
Pen-and-ink and w/c, mounted on card.
11.5 x 9, on card 30.5 x 24
BP.439   S.14.F.C

Carroll, Lewis, *Alice's Adventures in Wonderland*

971 Trial of the Knave of Hearts, with the White Rabbit as herald addressing the court. The illustration (in pencil) mounted and set within a frame outlined in red and black ink and bordered by a suit of Hearts playing cards.
On one of the cards is written:

> The Queen of Hearts
> She made some tarts
> All on a Summer's day,
> The Knave of Hearts
> He stole those tarts
> And took them quite away.

Inscribed (R): H.B.P. Jan '94.
Pencil, pen-and-ink and w/c. 16.5 x 10, on card 30 x 23.5
BP.454   S.15.F.B

972 The White Rabbit running along a long panelled corridor, pulling on his gloves as he runs.
W/c with pencil. 17 x 11, picture size (within pencilled frame) 9 x 7.5
BP.455(a)   S.15.F.B   (*see* PLATE XXXII)

973 Rear view of the White Rabbit running away along the corridor, having dropped his fan and kid gloves behind him.
See also BP.455(a); cat.972.
W/c with pencil. 17 x 10, picture size (within light pencilled frame) 8.5 x 7.5
BP.455(b)   S.15.F.B   (*see* PLATE XXXIII)

Finished paintings of cat.972–973 are at NBL.

Fairy Tales: Cinderella

974 Pumpkin carriage drawn by three pairs of rabbits, with mice as coachmen, passing through a medieval-looking town by moonlight. Other small animals carrying sedan-chairs and lanterns.
Inscribed (verso): Cinderella's carriage going to fetch her from the ball, intended for *moon*light. H.B. Potter.
(LL Cat.): The illustration was damaged by Mrs Gaddum's dog.
Subsequently repaired and mounted.
Grey wash with pen-and-ink. 14 x 28
BP.452   S.15.F.B   (*illustration pp. 104–5*)

971

975 Sketch for Cinderella's coach drawn by three pairs of rabbits. The coach is pumpkin-shaped and one of the rabbits is licking its paws, while a mouse-coachman adjusts the harness of another rabbit.
Ex Mrs Gaddum (LL Cat.)
Pencil and pen-and-ink. W/m: No. 24 Fine.
14 X 20.5
Verso: Very light pencil sketch of a frog holding an umbrella, leaping into a boat.
BP.456   S.15.F.B

976 Preliminary sketch for Cinderella's coach drawn by three pairs of rabbits. The coach is sedan-chair shaped and one of the rabbits is scratching itself.
Ex Mrs Gaddum (LL Cat.)
Pencil, with parts of the sketch outlined in pen-and-ink. 17.5 X 25
BP.457   S.15.F.B

Fairy Tales: The Sleeping Beauty

977 Page design of 'The doves asleep upon the house-
tops'. Small mounted illustration showing, as a
background, a street and distant church. Around
the frame is a group of roses and below right, lines
of German text in Gothic lettering, headed:
Dornröschen.
Inscribed: HBP Ap.99.
Inscribed (verso): "Sleeping Beauty" The doves
asleep upon the housetops. H.B. Potter March 99.
See also BP.438(b); cat.978.
The other drawings in this set were sold by Capt
Duke to a local dealer and are now in the
Philadelphia Free Library (LL Cat.)
Sepia wash and pen-and-ink for the drawing;
w/c, wash and pen-and-ink for the surrounding
roses on card mount. 10.5 x 8, on card 30.5 x 24
BP.438(a)   S.14.F.C

978 Rough sketch for mounted illustration of 'The
doves asleep upon the house-tops' (see BP.438(a);
cat.977).
Pencil and sepia wash. 10.5 x 8
BP.438(b)   S.14.F.C

Harris, Joel Chandler, *Uncle Remus*

979 Mounted illustration of a fox with a gun in a wood,
looking at a 'dead' rabbit beneath a tree.
Inscribed (R): H.B.P. Nov 96.
On the card mount is sketched a rabbit lying beside
a game bag, looking at it, with faint outline of a
tree and the text: Brer Fox he look at Brer Rabbit,
an' he sort of study – "Dese yer rabbits goin' ter
waste./I'll des 'bout leave my game yer', an I'll go/
back 'en git dat udder rabbit".
Inscribed (verso) by Capt Duke(?): Brer Fox goes
a-hunting, but Brer Rabbit bags the game. Drawn
by Beatrix Potter.
Details in pencil, with pen-and-ink for the border
sketch. Inset illustration 19 x 14, on card 28 x 21.5
BP.458   S.15.F.C

979

981 (spread)

980 Mounted illustration, pasted on card, of a formally-dressed rabbit entering a garden holding an empty shopping bag and umbrella, while a child looks on through a half-opened gate.
On the card is the text: "What kind of lookin' man *is dis* Mr. Billy Malone?" / "Split lip, pop eye, big y'ear an' bobtail, daddy." Also on the card (bottom R) is a drawing of the rabbit running away with cabbages from the garden.
Inscribed (R of illustration): H.B.P. Sept. '95.
Inscribed (verso) by Capt Duke(?): Brer Rabbit personates 'Mr Billy Malone' & persuades the little girl to let him into her daddy's garden. Original, drawn by Beatrix Potter.
Details in pencil, with pen-and-ink for the border sketch. 15 x 12, on card 28 x 21.5
BP.459   S.15.F.C

Lear, Edward, *The Owl and the Pussy Cat*

981 MS booklet of *The Owl and the Pussy Cat* made out of four sheets of notepaper sewn into a paper cover.
Inscribed (on cover): The Owl and the Pussy-cat 8 Drawings.
The title page (p.1.r) inscribed (in pencil): Words from Edward Lear's Nonsense Book.
The illustrations show:
p.1.r. A pot of honey and a bag of coins.
p.1.v. Text.
p.2.r. The Owl and the Pussy Cat in the sailing boat.
p.2.v. A seascape with island and a setting sun.
p.3.r. The Piggywig looking out to sea at the boat.
p.3.v. A ring (at the top) and a coin (at the bottom).
p.4.r. The Owl with a purse buying the ring from the Piggywig.
p.4.v. The Owl towing the boat containing the Pussy Cat towards the island with the Turkey on top of the hill.
Pen-and-ink, with traces of pencil under both text and illustrations. W/m: CSCSL [below a crown].
17.5 x 11
BP.619(a)   T.28.L

982 Four sheets of folded paper with five rough drawings for *The Owl and the Pussy Cat* illustrations. No text.
Pencil and pen-and-ink. W/m: Imperial Treasury de la Rue. 17.5 x 11
BP.619(b)   T.28.L

983 Four sheets of folded paper with five sketches of *The Owl and the Pussy Cat* illustrations. No text.
Pencil, with some parts completed in pen-and-ink.
W/m: CSCSL [below a crown]; and a second sheet: Imperial Treasury de la Rue. 18 x 11
BP.619(c)   T.28.L

Shakespeare, William, *A Midsummer Night's Dream*, II. i.

984 Cowslips and bluebells in a brown earthenware jug, against a dark background; set in the bottom left-hand corner of the picture, with only the top right-hand of the jug visible.
Inscribed (below the picture, in pencil) the verse:

The Cowslips tall her pensioners be:
In their gold coats spots you see:
Those be rubies, fairy favours –
Midsummer Night's Dream.

Inscribed (verso): Original, Beatrix Potter.
W/c, on card. 20.5 x 12, picture size (within frame) 11.5 x 10.5
BP.453   S.15.F.B

The White Cat

985 (a) Two tabby kittens, one wearing a green coat and game bag, shooting at birds in snow-covered fields, near a farm with mountains in the background.
(b) The kittens sitting on a farmyard fence examining the contents of the game bag.
Inscribed (verso): Subject 'The white cat' – Kittens collecting game for the White Cat's supper. HB Potter.
Intended as illustration for the fairy tale?
W/c and pen-and-ink. 17 x 10 (each sheet), on paper mount 23 x 29
BP.1473(a,b)   P.C.58   (*see* PLATES XXXIV, XXXV)

986 Two versions of the kitten in the brown coat carrying a gun and a brace of birds, in a snow-covered field with the farm in the background.
Inscribed (verso): Hertfordshire 1894.
The larger sheet inscribed (front R): H.B.P. 1894.
See also BP.1473(a,b); cat.985.
W/c and pen-and-ink. 17 x 12; 12.5 x 10
BP.1146(a,b)   P.C.58

Page designs for photograph mounts (flowers)

987 Unfinished page design: showing a rambling rose partly painted, with a blank inset for further design or illustration. *c.*1898–99.
See *The Art*, pp. 214–15, for finished designs.
W/c and pencil, on card. 24 x 30.5
BP.1190   P.C.42

988 Page design: showing a cluster of violets, with a blank inset for further design or illustration.
*c.*1898–99.
See *The Art*, etc.
W/c and pencil, on card. 30 x 24
BP.1189   P.C.42

989 Page design: showing full-blown yellow roses (one rose has been stuck on), with blank insets for further design or illustration. *c.*1898–99.
See *The Art*, etc.
W/c and pencil, on card. 30 x 24
BP.1183   P.C.42

990 Page design: showing woodland flowers, with a blank inset for further design or illustration.
*c.*1898–99.
See *The Art*, etc.
W/c and pencil, on card. 24.5 x 21.5
BP.1184   P.C.42

991 Page design: showing snowdrops, with a blank inset for further design or illustration.
Inscribed: March '98.
Inscribed (verso): HB Potter, intended for photograph mount. March 1898.
See *The Art*, etc.
W/c and pencil, on card. 23.5 x 29.5
BP.1185   P.C.42   (*see half-title*)

992 Unfinished page design: showing wild flowers, with a blank inset for further design or illustration.
*c.*1898–99.
See *The Art*, etc.
W/c and pencil, on card. 24 x 30.5
BP.1186   P.C.42

993 Page design: showing a bunch of tulips, with blank insets for further design or illustration. *c.*1898–99.
See *The Art*, etc.
W/c and pencil, on card. 30.5 x 24
BP.1187   P.C.42

994 Unfinished page design: showing globe flowers, with a blank inset for further design or illustration.
*c.*1898–99.
See *The Art*, etc.
W/c and pencil, on card. 24 x 30.5
BP.1188   P.C.42

995 Page design: showing tulips, with a blank inset for further design or illustration. *c.*1898–99.
See *The Art*, etc.
W/c and pencil, on card. 30 x 24
BP.1178   P.C.42

996 Page design: showing daffodils, with a blank inset for further design or illustration. *c.*1898–99.
See *The Art*, etc.
W/c and pencil, on card. 30 x 24
BP.1179   P.C.42

Authors unknown

997 Rough sketch for an illustration (for the Grimm's fairy tale *The Three Spinners*, or (LL Cat.) for *Snow White?*), showing a peasant girl at the door of a house talking to a little old woman holding a distaff. Frame sketched in.
Inscribed (below, in pencil): Old fairy woman is rather good. She should have an enormous foot. The girl should be *fair*, smiling & looking down at the old woman, bending forward to welcome her.
Inscribed (above the drawing, by the house): Perhaps better omit window, as it is violent perspective/white washed house/house door hangs inside the porch.
W/c with pencil. 18 x 11.5
BP.441   S.14.F.C

998 Page design: small mounted illustration showing a procession of mice carrying ears of corn into their hole. Around the scene is a border of ears of corn.
Inscribed (verso): Golden corn. Oct '99. H.B. Potter.
W/c with pencil, on card. 21.5 x 28
BP.1144   P.C.16   (*see* PLATE XXXVI)

999 Rabbit opening a door to find a basket of food, including carrots, on the doorstep.
Reproduced on the cover of *Changing Pictures: a book of transformation pictures*. Published by Nister in 1894.
A similar illustration can be found in *Appley Dapply*.
Pencil and w/c. 13.5 x 9.5
BP.1259   P.C.41

IMAGINARY HAPPENINGS & NURSERY RHYMES

This section requires little comment. Its contents vary from 'occasional pieces' involving mice to complete sets of pictures such as *The Rabbits' Christmas Party* or *A Frog he would a-fishing go*, and the exquisite version of the nursery rhyme *Three little mice sat down to spin*.

Imaginary happenings

1000 Little pig in a tub with a towel horse, water-can, soap and sponge beside it.
Inscribed: H.B.P. '99.
W/c with pen-and-ink. 23 x 29.5
BP.263   S.4.F.C   (*see* PLATE XXXVII)

1001 'The Rabbits' Potting Shed': two rabbits busy potting geraniums.
The setting is Bedwell Lodge, 1891. This later became the background for Mr McGregor's potting shed in *The Tale of Peter Rabbit* (LL Cat.)
See also BP.279; cat.492.
Grey wash with pen-and-ink and chalky highlights. 21 x 16.5
BP.431   S.14.F.B

1002 A rabbit (Peter) asleep, dreaming of himself in a four-poster bed; the 'dream' is shown framed by sketches of his different sleeping positions.
The setting is No. 4 bedroom, Camfield Place (LL Cat.)
Pen-and-ink. W/m: St. Neots Mill No. 24 Fine.
31.5 x 20.5
BP.432   S.14.F.B

1003 *The Rabbits' Christmas Party*. Five rabbits dressed in blue and carrying umbrellas, arriving at a house in the snow.
Inscribed: HBP.
One of four pictures given to Beatrix Potter's Aunt Lucy, described on p. 61 of Margaret Lane's biography *The Tale of Beatrix Potter*, 1968 (LL Cat.)
See also BP.1471(b–d); cat.1004–6.
W/c and pen-and-ink, on card. 16 x 15.5
BP.1471(a)   S.14.F.A   (*see* PLATE XXXVIII)

1004 *The Rabbits' Christmas Party*. Rabbits eating a Christmas dinner, with vegetables in the foreground.
Inscribed: H.B.P.
W/c and pen-and-ink, on card. 16 x 15.5
BP.1471(b)   S.14.F.A

1005 *The Rabbits' Christmas Party*. Rabbits around the hearth. One of the rabbits is roasting an apple.
W/c and pen-and-ink, on card. 16 x 15.5
BP.1471(c)   S.14.F.A   (*see* PLATE XXXIX)

1001

1010

1006 *The Rabbits' Christmas Party*. Rabbits saying farewell. One is opening the door and holding a candle.
W/c and pen-and-ink, on card. 16 x 15.5
BP.1471(d)   S.14.F.A

1007 A jackdaw carrying a set of sweep's brooms.
Inscribed: Drawn for Nister & Co.
Believed to be the drawing referred to on p. 242 of the *Journal*, Sat July 30, 1892 (LL Cat.)
W/c and pen-and-ink. 16.5 x 12.5
BP.428   S.14.F.B

1008 Four rabbits in the snow: one is pulling a sledge, two are pushing a log and the fourth is carrying some faggots on his back.
Inscribed: H.B.P.
W/c. 14 x 20
BP.1476   S.14.F.B

1009 Rabbits falling from their toboggan into the snow. The two rabbits are drawn in ink and painted; the snow and toboggan are only lightly sketched and the work appears half-finished.
W/c, sepia ink and pencil. 13.5 x 21
BP.1256   P.C.41

1010 A poultry shop, showing 'W. Weasel unlicensed to sell GAME' in the doorway of his shop, with dead birds, eggs, mice and rats hanging up for sale.
Inscribed: (Rough sketch – 'Sparrows are CHEAP today').
c.1891.
Pencil. 20 x 25 (paper formerly folded vertically on right-hand side, and now splitting)
BP.1193   P.C.44

1011 Rabbit with fork and garden trug, in a garden setting with flowers, showing a rabbit hutch(?) and a cold frame(?).
Inscribed (verso): Bedwell Lodge, 1891.
See also 'The Rabbits' Potting Shed' (*The Art*, p.190 and BP.431; cat.1001).
Pencil and grey wash, on card. 21.5 x 17
BP.1191   P.C.44   (*illustration p. 113*)

1007

PLATE XXXVI 'Golden corn' 1899 **(998)**

PLATE XXXVII Little pig in a tub 1899 (**1000**)

1011

1012

1012 A squirrel handing up nuts as a gift to another
squirrel, who is leaning out of a window in a
tree trunk.
Inscribed (verso): H.B. Potter. This is a very old
drawing. I think it may have been in the portfolio
before.
Pen-and-ink and grey wash, with chalky
highlights. 22 x 17.5
BP.429   S.14.F.B

1013 Tracing from a drawing showing cutlery, sugar
bowl, tongs, tea-pot, plates etc. dancing around
a Christmas cake with candles.
Pen-and-ink, on tracing paper. 31 x 16.5
BP.1267   Top Tray

1014 Study of a mouse with a ball of wool.
Pencil. W/m: Britannia. 16 x 10
BP.1015(iv)   P.C.12

1015 Three mice running away from a kitten.
These sketches are possibly an early version of the
mice running away from a kitten in *The Tale of
Johnny Town-Mouse*.
Pencil. W/m: Britannia. 16 x 16
BP.1015(v)   P.C.12

1016 Four studies of a mouse dancing.
Possibly illustrating the rhyme of *Three Blind Mice?*
Pencil. W/m: Britannia. 16.5 x 10
BP.1015(vi)   P.C.12

1017 Two sketches of a mouse in an egg-cup.
The first version of this illustration is in the *Ninny
Nanny Netticoat* manuscript (see BP.662;
cat.1156, 1157).
Pencil and pen-and-ink. W/m: /nson/60.
12.5 x 20
BP.1015(vii)   P.C.12

1018 A white mouse curled up asleep, dreaming about
Dutch cheese. Mice dance around the cheese
above his head.
Inscribed: The peculiar Dream of Mr Samuel
Whiskers upon the subject of Dutch Cheese.
Inscribed (verso): Studies of a tame white rat
'Sammy' from life. H.B. Potter.
W/c and pen-and-ink. 28 x 21.5
BP.262   S.4.F.C

1019 Sketches of mice dancing, including two mice
holding hands, and two dog studies.
The sketches are possibly early designs for the mice
dancing in *Ninny Nanny Netticoat* (see BP.662;
cat.1156, 1157).
Pencil and pen-and-ink. W/m: Britannia.
10 x 12.5
BP.387(a)   S.11.F.C
(Mounted with BP.387(b))

1020 Sketches of mice, including two mice dancing,
and studies of paws.
The sketches are possibly early designs for the mice
dancing in *Ninny Nanny Netticoat*.
Pencil and pen-and-ink. 13 x 12.5
BP.387(b)   S.11.F.C
(Mounted with BP.387(a))

1021 'The Mice in their Storeroom', with sacks of grain
and ears of wheat hanging up on the passage walls.
The setting of this picture is one of the back
passages at Bedwell Lodge, nr. Hatfield, and it was
drawn in the summer of 1891 (LL Cat.)
See also BP.286; cat.493.
Grey wash and pen-and-ink. 22 x 16
BP.430   S.14.F.B

1024

1022 Mother mouse with her three baby mice: one is
       on her knee; the other two are asleep in a cot
       (upper half).
       Inscribed: H.B.P.
       Mouse teaching its children to read: a big M is
       being drawn on a slate leaning against some books
       (lower half).
       Inscribed: H.B.P.
       Pen-and-ink. W/m: Britannia. 20.5 x 16.5
       BP.433(a,b)   S.14.F.B

1023 'The Mice in their Storeroom.'
       Study for BP.430; cat.1021.
       Verso: Three studies of a rabbit sitting; also rough
       sketch of three rabbits on seesaw.
       Pencil. 19.5 x 14.5
       BP.434   S.14.F.B

1024 A white mouse in a four-poster bed.
       Inscribed: Oct 26th 01.
       BP left this in the bedroom where she slept when
       she left Melford Hall after one of her visits – the
       mouse impersonates her. The bed had yellow
       hangings in that room. The drawing was given to
       Stephanie Hyde-Parker (LL Cat.)
       W/c and pen-and-ink. W/m: /6o/nson. 12 x 20
       BP.576   T.24.L

1025 Sketch of a mouse in a brass bedstead, with a table
       and medicine bottle beside it. Nearby is the doctor
       – a mole.
       Inscribed: Dr C. Aug '92.
       Caricature of Dr Culbard, the Potters' family
       doctor at Birnam, 1892. Described in the Journal as
       'kind and very fat and stuffy' (see also The Art).
       Pen-and-ink and pencil. W/m: Coat of arms [with
       monogram] S & H. 12.5 x 20
       BP.636(e)   T.29.R

1026 Studies of a mouse dancing.
       Inscribed (on folder): Sketches for rhymes (LL).
       The sketches are possibly early designs for the mice
       dancing in Ninny Nanny Netticoat (see BP.662;
       cat.1156, 1157).
       Pencil and pen-and-ink. W/m: Britannia.
       20.5 x 12
       BP.1015(iii)   P.C.12

1027 Sketch of a cat drinking from a cup and saucer on
       the floor.
       (Not sold.) Mentioned in a letter to Warne's
       (17 Jun 1926) when discussing copyrights of
       drawings sold to Nister (LL Cat.)
       W/c with pencil. 12 x 11
       BP.802   T.42.R

1027

1028 Sketch of a cat knitting and another sketch of the
head only.
Inscribed (verso): 100/62898 [or C2898].
A similar drawing was sold to Ernest Nister, and
used as part of one of the pictures in their children's
annuals (LL Cat.)
See BP.802; cat. 1027.
Pen-and-ink and pencil. 9.5 x 8.5
BP.511   S.19.F.C

A Frog he would a-fishing go (Nister)

The following drawings were done in 1894 and
offered to Ernest Nister in booklet form.
They were eventually used in one of Nister's
children's annuals to illustrate a set of verses by
someone else (see *Hist.*).

1029 The frog looking out of his house, standing on the
top of the steps watching the rain.
Inscribed (R): HBP; (L) in another hand(?): The
Tale of Jeremy Fisher.
Intended as the first page of the Nister booklet
done in 1894, but not bought by Nister and no
block made (LL Cat.)
Pen-and-ink. 14 x 20.5, mounted on brown
paper 20 x 27, inscribed (verso): A wet day.
H.B. Potter.
BP.507(a)   S.19.F.A

1030 The frog jumps into his boat.
(LL Cat.): Nister block no. 11283.
Rubbing of the block included with the drawing.
Pen-and-ink with pencil. 14 x 20
BP.507(b)   S.19.F.A
(Mounted with BP.507(c))

1031 The frog jumps into his boat: a study for BP.507(b).
Verso: Sketches of rabbits and a man walking.
Possibly studies for the Flopsy Bunnies?
Pencil. 14 x 20 (small segment cut out of the
paper)
BP.507(c)   S.19.F.A

1030

1042

1032 Sketch of the frog fishing in his boat (top) and (below) the frog going home empty-handed. Rubbing of Nister block no. 11284 (the frog fishing).
Pen-and-ink with pencil. 20.5 x 16
BP.507(d,e)   S.19.F.A

1033 The frog in his boat, fishing.
Pen-and-ink. 13.5 x 20
BP.507(f)   S.19.F.A

1034 The frog setting out on his way to fish.
Rubbing of Nister block no. 11282.
Pen-and-ink. 14.5 x 20.5
BP.507(g)   S.19.F.A

1035 The frog nearly catches a fish: a rough sketch.
Pencil. 10 x 15.5
Verso: The frog among leaves with a fishing net in his hands; also some other light pencil sketches. An unused drawing.
Pen-and-ink with pencil.
BP.507(h)   S.19.F.B

1036 The frog nearly catches a fish: a more finished version of BP.507(h).
Rubbing of Nister block no. 11285.
Pen-and-ink with pencil. 14.5 x 20.5
BP.507(i)   S.19.F.B

1037 The frog catches a fish which nips his fingers.
Pen-and-ink with pencil. 13.5 x 20
BP.507(j)   S.19.F.B

1038 The frog catches a fish which nips his fingers: similar to BP.507(j) but slightly more finished.
Rubbing of Nister block no. 11286.
Pen-and-ink with pencil. 13.5 x 20
BP.507(k)   S.19.F.B

1039 Study for the frog losing his fish.
Pen-and-ink with pencil. 10 x 16.5
BP.507(l)   S.19.F.B

1040 The frog losing his fish: a more finished work than BP.507(l).
Rubbing of Nister block no. 11287.
Pen-and-ink. 13.5 x 20
BP.507(m)   S.19.F.B

1041 The frog looking out of his house: similar to BP.507(a).
Not bought by Nister.
Pen-and-ink. 14 x 20.5
BP.507(n)   S.19.F.B

1042 The frog goes home empty-handed: a more finished version of BP.507(d).
Rubbing of Nister block no. 11288.
Pen-and-ink. 13.5 x 20
BP.507(o)   S.19.F.B

1043 The frog contents himself with a meal of grasshopper in his house: a sketch.
Pen-and-ink with pencil. 10.5 x 16.5
BP.507(p)   S.19.F.B

1044 The frog contents himself with a meal of
grasshopper: a more finished version of BP.507(p).
Rubbing of Nister block no. 11290.
Pen-and-ink. 14.5 x 20
BP.507(q)   S.19.F.B

1045 The fish are still laughing at him (all sitting in
his boat).
Rubbing of Nister block no. 11289.
Pen-and-ink with pencil. 14 x 18.5
BP.507(r)   S.19.F.B

1046 The fish are still laughing at him: another version
of BP.507(r).
Pen-and-ink. 14 x 19
BP.507(s)   S.19.F.B

1047 Series of sketches, most incomplete, of frogs'
heads, but including one of 'He succeeds, but the
fish nips his fingers'.
Inscribed (verso): Nister, 1894 (LL).
Original idea for *The Tale of Mr Jeremy Fisher*.
Pencil and pen-and-ink. W/m: St. Neot. 10 x 16.5
BP.1263(ii)   P.C.36

1048 'He tries again to catch a fish' (*Hist.* p. 180):
rough sketch of a frog in a boat, an umbrella
floating behind.
Inscribed (recto): Nister, 1894 (LL).
Verso: Sketches of frogs' heads, and a light sketch
of fish in a boat in top left-hand corner.
Original idea for *The Tale of Mr Jeremy Fisher*.
Pencil. 10.5 x 16.5
BP.1263(iii)   P.C.36

1049 'He succeeds, but the fish nips his fingers' (*Hist.*
p. 181): a sketch of a frog and a fish in a boat, with
an unfinished sketch of the frog at the side.
Inscribed (verso): Nister, 1894 (LL).
Original idea for *The Tale of Mr Jeremy Fisher*.
Pencil. 6.5 x 19
BP.1263(iv)   P.C.36

1050 'The fish are still laughing at him' (*Hist.* p. 182):
two light sketches at right angles to each other,
showing fish sitting in a boat.
Original idea for *The Tale of Mr Jeremy Fisher*.
Pencil. 10 x 16.5
BP.1263(viii)   P.C.36

1054(a)

1051 'The frog goes fishing' (*Hist.* p. 179), with a sketch
of a rabbit licking its paw, in the right-hand corner.
Inscribed (verso): Nister, 1894 (LL).
Original idea for *The Tale of Mr Jeremy Fisher*.
Pencil. 9 x 20.5
BP.1263(xiii)   P.C.36

1052 'The fish are still laughing at him' (*Hist.* p. 182).
Inscribed (verso): Nister, 1894 (LL).
Original idea for *The Tale of Mr Jeremy Fisher*.
Pencil. 10 x 16.5
BP.1263(ix)   P.C.36

1053 'He succeeds, but the fish nips his fingers' (*Hist.*
p. 181): sketch of a frog and a fish, at one end of
a lightly sketched boat.
Bottom of sheet, reversed: light pencil sketch for
'The fish are still laughing at him' (*Hist.* p. 182).
Original ideas for *The Tale of Mr Jeremy Fisher*.
Pencil and pen-and-ink. W/m: Britannia.
14 x 20.5
BP.1263(x)   P.C.36

Picture story about a guinea pig

1054 Five drawings inserted by their corners into a sheet
of lining paper. Against each picture is a line of
text in pencil, and each is inscribed: H.B.P.
(a) 'The perfidious friend assures the guinea pig it
won't hurt': dentist and friend examining the
guinea pig, who has a bandaged face.
(b) 'The guinea pig has doubts': the dentist and
friend confer.
(c) 'But they are overborne': a struggle between
dentist, friend and patient.
(d) 'The friend and the dentist take a professional
interest in the tooth but none whatever in the
victim': friend and dentist inspect the tooth.
(e) 'And go off discussing the successful operation':
back view of three departing guinea pigs.
The drawing (b) is reused in *The Fairy Caravan*, but
the text is different.
Pen-and-ink. 8 x 10
BP.554(a–e)   T.22

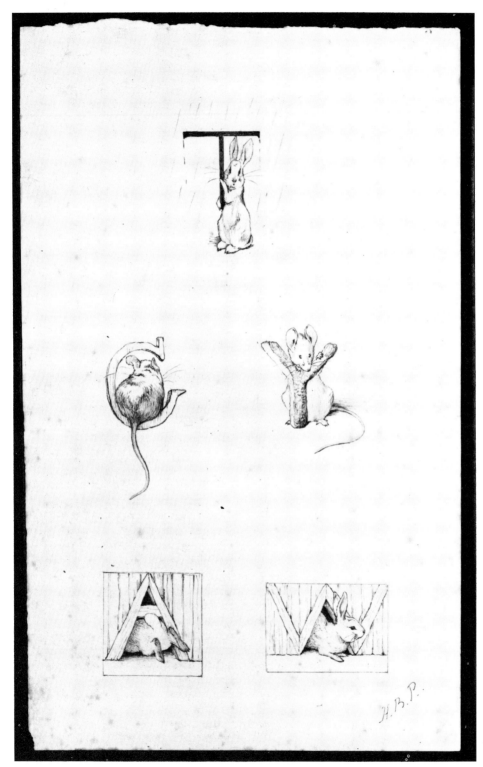

1061

PLATE XXXVIII *Rabbits' Christmas Party*: the rabbits arrive (**1003**)

PLATE XXXIX *Rabbits' Christmas Party*: around the hearth (**1005**)

PLATE XL From *Three Little Mice* (**1068**)

PLATE XLI (above) Page from the *Mrs Tittlemouse* manuscript (**1160**)

PLATE XLII (right) From the *Sly Old Cat* manuscript (**1275**)

1055 Six sheets of preliminary sketches for BP.554; cat.1054, some unused.
Pencil, but two sheets have some pen-and-ink work. 10 x 17; 10 x 14
BP.555(a–f) T.22

1056 Three sheets with rough preliminary sketches for BP.554(a); cat.1054.
Pen-and-ink and pencil. 8 x 10; 10 x 16; 16.5 x 10
BP.556(i) a–c T.22

1057 Five sheets with rough preliminary sketches for BP.554(b); cat.1054.
Pencil and pen-and-ink. 8 x 10 (each approx.)
BP.556(ii) a–e T.22

1058 Two sheets with rough preliminary sketches for BP.554(c); cat.1054.
Pencil and pen-and-ink. 8 x 10; 10 x 16
BP.556(iii) a,b T.22

1059 Two sheets with rough preliminary sketches for BP.554(d); cat.1054.
Pen-and-ink and pencil. 8.5 x 10; 8 x 10
BP.556(iv) a,b T.22

1060 Two sheets with rough preliminary sketches for BP.554(e); cat.1054.
Pen-and-ink and pencil. 8 x 10.5; 12.5 x 13
BP.556(v) a,b T.22

Alphabets

1061 Designs for a few letters of an alphabet: T,C,Y,A, and W. T is held up like an umbrella, by a rabbit in the rain. C has a mouse sitting on the letter, Y has a mouse peering through it. A is a gap in a fence with a rabbit disappearing through it, W is similarly a gap in a fence with a rabbit coming out.
Inscribed: H.B.P.
Pencil. 20 x 12.5
BP.440(b) S.14.F.C

1062 Designs for an alphabet: a rough sketch of C with a mouse sitting in it, and E with a mouse peering from behind the letter.
Below: a rough sketch of a cat carrying a shopping basket.
Possibly a study for Tabitha Twitchit in *The Pie and the Patty-Pan*?
Verso: Rough drawing of a cat, and a bent figure walking.
Pencil. W/m: St. Neot No. 16.5 x 10.5
BP.440(c) S.14.F.C

1063 Two drawings of cockatoos: one front view with an ornamental letter M and a spray of leaves above its head, the other back view, looking left, towards a lightly pencilled ornamental letter S.
Possibly copied from an illustration, by Beatrix or Rupert Potter.
Pen-and-ink. W/m: /od Paper/mond/are Road.
18 x 11
BP.1199 P.C.18

1064 Designs for an alphabet: two drawings of the letters C and Y, as in BP.440(b); cat.1061. C has a mouse sitting in it and Y a mouse peering over the top.
Inscribed: H.B.P.
Pencil. 10.5 x 20
BP.440(a) S.14.F.C *(illustration p. 120)*

Nursery Rhymes

I saw a ship

1065 Verses written out for Marjorie Moore(?) (LL).
2ff. Illustrations on a folded sheet.
1r. Inscribed: 'I saw a ship a-sailing . . .', showing a sailing ship.
1v. Inscribed: 'And 4 and 20 sailors . . .', showing sailors on a deck and up some rigging.
2r. Inscribed: 'The captain was a guinea-pig – The pilot was a rat', showing a guinea pig and rat pilot with a telescope.
2v. Inscribed: 'And the passengers were rabbits . . .', showing rabbits embarking on a ship.
Inscribed (on back): All of which will have to be carefully drawn, but I think the words are lovely. Just imagine the white mice letting down the bags of comfits into the hold!
May have originally been an idea for her 1905 *Appley Dapply* (LL Cat.)
Pen-and-ink. 18 x 11
BP.879 T.11

Three little mice sat down to spin

A booklet was planned which was to illustrate six of the eight lines of this rhyme, but nothing came of the project (LL Cat.)

1066 Three little Mice sat down to spin. Finished w/c showing three mice sitting in bent-wood chairs and working at their spinning wheels in a low panelled room with a loom and recessed window.
Inscribed: H.B.P.
W/c. 9.5 x 14, on card 14 x 21.5
BP.634(8) T.29.L

1067 Pussy passed by, and she peeped in. Finished w/c showing the mice turning in horror from their spinning wheels at the sight of a cat's face at the window.
Inscribed: H.B.P.
W/c. 9.5 x 14, on card 14 x 21.5
BP.634(9)   T.29.L

1068 'What are you at, my fine little Men?'
Finished w/c showing the mice in disarray, rushing from the window with their spinning wheels. The cat has pushed her face close to the window.
Inscribed: H.B.P.
W/c. 9.5 x 14, on card 14 x 21.5
BP.634(10)   T.29.L   (see PLATE XL)

1069 'Making coats for Gentlemen –.' Finished w/c showing the mice holding coats and a bale of cloth up to the window for the cat to see.
Inscribed: H.B.P.
W/c. 9.5 x 14, on card 14 x 21.5
BP.634(11)   T.29.L

1070 'Shall I come in, and cut off your threads?'
Finished w/c showing the mice closing the shutters and pushing at the cat's face with a broom.
Inscribed: H.B.P.
W/c. 9.5 x 14, on card 14 x 21.5
BP.634(12)   T.29.L

1071 'Oh no! Miss Pussy, you'd bite off our heads.'
Finished w/c showing the mice securing the shutters with iron bars.
Inscribed: H.B.P.
W/c. 9.5 x 14, on card 14 x 21.5
BP.634(13)   T.29.L

Cat. 1072–8: outlines, sewn together.

1072 Line sketch for title page showing three mice with distaffs.
Pen-and-ink. 12.5 x 20
BP.634(1)   T.29.L

1073 Line sketch showing the three mice spinning, with partly drawn spinning wheels and no background.
Pen-and-ink. 12.5 x 20
BP.634(2)   T.29.L

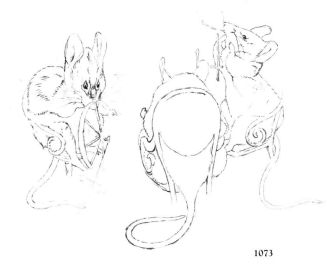

1073

1074 Line sketch showing the three mice turning to the window (the interior and spinning wheels have been left out).
Inscribed (by BP): Outlines; and (on one side): 7 coloured drawings/8 pen-and-ink (1 extra, coloured)/7 outlines.
This list refers to the number of sketches and finished paintings for this poem.
Pen-and-ink. 12.5 x 20
BP.634(3)   T.29.L

1075 Line sketch showing mice running from the cat at the window (no background).
Pen-and-ink. 12.5 x 20
BP.634(4)   T.29.L

1076 Line sketch showing mice with coats at the window.
Pen-and-ink. 12.5 x 20
BP.634(5)   T.29.L

1077 Line sketch showing mice closing the shutters against the cat (no background).
Pen-and-ink. 12.5 x 20
BP.634(6)   T.29.L

1078 Line sketch showing mice securing the window (no background).
Pen-and-ink. 12.5 x 20
BP.634(7)   T.29.L

1079 Title page: Three mice with distaffs.
Finished w/c, with title pencilled in.
Signed: H.B.P.
W/c. 9.5 x 14, on card 14 x 21.5
BP.634(14)   T.29.L

1080 Text page. With drawings of an oil-can,
screwdriver, bottle, spanner and thread with a
shuttle, under the text: Three little Mice sat down
to spin.
Pencil and sepia ink. 10 x 16.5
BP.634(15)   T.29.L

1081 Text page. With drawings of an ink pot and quill,
pencil, books and potted plants, under the text:
Pussy passed by, and she peeped in.
Pencil and sepia ink. 10 x 16.5
BP.634(16)   T.29.L

1082 Text page. With drawings of buttons, bobbins, a
pair of scissors and needle case, under the text:
'What are you at, my fine little Men?'
Pencil and sepia ink. 10 x 16.5
BP.634(17)   T.29.L

1083 Text page. With drawings of a tape measure and
pattern books, under the text: 'Making coats for
Gentlemen'.
Pencil and sepia ink. 10 x 16.5
BP.634(18)   T.29.L

1084 Text page. With drawings of a thimble, a pair of
scissors, pins and needles, pin-cushion and cotton
reels, under the text: 'Shall I come in, and cut off
your threads?'
Pencil and sepia ink. 10 x 16.5
BP.634(19)   T.29.L

1085 Text page. With drawings of a padlock, keys,
candle, match-box and snuffer, under the text:
'Oh no! Miss Pussy, you'd bite off our heads'.
Pencil and sepia ink. 10 x 16.5
BP.634(20)   T.29.L

1086 Drawing of a spinning wheel and distaff, intended
for the end of the booklet.
Sepia ink. 10 x 16.5
BP.634(21)   T.29.L

1086

1087 Finished w/c of the text page, BP.634(19);
cat.1084, showing the same arrangement of
thimble, scissors, pin-cushion and cotton reels.
W/c. 10 x 16
BP.634(22)   T.29.L

Tingle, Dingle, Dousy

1088 Set of three sheets pinned together. Sheets 1 and 2
show a mouse with its tail in the air; sheet 3 has
two sketches of a mouse (one in pencil, one in
pen-and-ink).
Verse inscribed on sheet 1: Tingle, dingle,
dousy [etc.].
Pencil and pen-and-ink. 13 x 8; 11 x 9; 20 x 10
BP.629(a–c)   T.28.R

1089 Three loose sheets with six illustrations of mice
on each sheet.
See also BP.629(a–c); cat.1088.
Pencil. W/m (d): Gurney. 20 x 10; 20.5 x 12.5;
20.5 x 10.5
BP.629(d–f)   T.28.R

SKETCH BOOKS

Beatrix Potter's sketch books are particularly interesting, dating as they do from childhood to maturity. But of course those in the Linder Bequest represent only a fraction of similar books which she must have used (and sometimes reused or destroyed) over her long artistic working life. The detailed entries are taken almost entirely from Leslie Linder's manuscript catalogue. In the later sketch books we have a chance to see not only the scenes and topics which immediately appealed to her, but also her search for the right background for some of her books. Likewise there are numerous sketches, many incomplete, of animals which subsequently appeared in her stories under now familiar names. The sketch books, few as they are here, nevertheless provide an invaluable insight into the influences upon the artist, and the way in which she went about her work.

1090 Drawing Book (age 8)

Sewn from sheets of thin paper (of the kind used for lining drawers). Edges cut roughly to size.

p.1 BP has written in copperplate pencil: Dalguise/Dunkeld, Perthshire.

p.2 Blank.

p.3 Inscribed: 1875 Dalguise. Painting of column [Mercat Cross of Dunkeld] standing on lawn in front of house – top part only. (Also, in pencil at top R.H., are two tiny outlines of a rabbit.)

p.4 Blank.

p.5 Inscribed: 1875 Dalguise. Rough painting of Dalguise garden at back of house with some trees, and distant fields.

pp.6–12 Blank.

Between pages 12 and 13 strips of folded paper are sewn in for mounting inserted pictures, which include one painting and two sheets of folded notepaper.

Drawing paper insert (14 x 15.5), inscribed: 1875 Dalguise. Two small watercolours of buildings, one inscribed: The duchess of Athole's model dairy. Pencil drawing of a building on verso.

Inserted sheet of '2 Bolton Gardens' folded notepaper, with a flower, leaf, bloom and what could be a 'root', in colour, in top left-hand corner, and inscribed: 1A, 1B, 1C [and] 1D.

On verso of front sheet are three butterflies in pencil.

Another [blank] sheet of notepaper.

p.13 Inscribed: Eggs. Four birds' eggs in colour.

p.14 Writing only: 1. Robin's egg. The egg is white with browney red spots. The Robin makes his nest in ivy or holes; it builds its nest in May. 2. Chaffinch's egg. The egg is light green with brown marks, it is found in May and built in low bushes.

p.15 Seven sketches of butterflies in pencil (on the first the pattern on the wings is shown).

pp.16–18 Blank.

p.19 Inscribed: Caterpillars. Twelve different ones are painted – seven of them crawling on leaves.

p.20 Contains writing about caterpillars. Text as follows: Tiger moth. 1. The caterpillar of the Tiger feeds on the nettle and hawthorn and is found in June, they are covered with black, white and red. They are found by road sides and lanes. Drinker. 2. The caterpillar is a dark brown with orange dots. I dont know what it eats, but I think it is the flowering nettle. It is found by hedges in May and June. Bombycidal. 3. The caterpillar eats sloe, it is a rare moth, the caterpillar is brown with yellow rings, it is hairy and found in June. Yellow tail. 4. The caterpillar feeds on hawthorn; it is yellow with a blue line along its sides and black dots. It is found on hedges in June.

[1–3 are written in ink, and 4–7 in pencil. 5–7 are further descriptions of caterpillars.]

p.21 Brown caterpillar on a stalk. Two other caterpillars in pencil. Many years later Beatrix Potter wrote against the brown caterpillar 'Bombycidae Trichiura Crataegi'.

pp.22–24 Blank.

Entry from LL Cat.

16.5 x 15

BP.740 T.40.L (*see* PLATE VI)

Tiger moth.

1. The caterpillar of the Tiger feeds on the nettle and both hawthorn and is found in June they are covered with black, white and red. They are found by road sides and lanes.

Drinker.

2. The cat.. is a dark brown with orange dots. I dont know what it eats, but I think it is the flower- -ing nettle. It is found by hedges in May and June

Bombycidal

3. The caterpillar eats sloe, it is a rare moth, the caterpillar is brown with yellow rings, it is has hairy and found in June.

Yellow tail

4. The cat.. feeds on haw- thorn; it is yellow with a blue line along its sides and black dots. It is found on hedges in June.

5 The cat.. is black with white spots its arch and feeds on the nee

6 The cat.. has red, black ochre streak along its sides and a white stre on its back, it has brown hairs it feeds on oar.

7 The caterpillar is gre with small

1091 Drawing Book (age 9)
Inscribed on cover: Helen Beatrix Potter, March
1876. Drawing of Potter crest. Pen-and-ink.

p. 1 Drawing in pencil of two rabbits skating.
Below: A house, hills behind. In the road in
front is a carriage with two rabbits in the back
and a rabbit coachman. Two other rabbits are on
horseback, and a third is walking – all rabbits are
clothed (also a boy's head). Inscribed: H.B.P.
1876. Pencil and pen-and-ink.

p. 2 Top: Aberfeldy bridge? Inscribed: H.B.P.
March 19 1876. W/c. Bottom: Drawing of
lighthouse, boats and coast. Inscribed: H.B.P.
1876. Pencil.

p. 3 Top: One rabbit skating, dressed in yellow.
Two rabbits walking in a high wind with a little
dog. One is holding his hat, the other holds an
umbrella which has blown inside-out. Inscribed:
March 21 1876. Bottom: Rabbits on ice – two
are dancing. One pushes an older rabbit who is
seated in a sledge-chair. Another pulls a sledge
in which there is a rabbit – a little dog runs in
front. Another rabbit looks on, his hands in his
pockets. Inscribed: March 21 1876. W/c and
pencil.

p. 4 Painting of four humming birds and a yellow
butterfly. One bird sits on a flower. Inscribed:
March 19 1876 H.B.P. W/c and pencil.

p. 5 Top: Painting of a girl driving two cows.
Inscribed: March 21 H.B.P. 1876. Bottom:
Painting of a rose and an iris. Inscribed:
March 21 H.B.P. 1876. W/c.

p. 6 Drawing of a church and chalet and drawing of
a shell. Pencil.

p. 7 Flowers. Inscribed: March 21 1876. W/c.

p. 8 Rough sketch of vase and flowers. Inscribed:
H.B.P. 1876 March 22. W/c.

p. 9 Rough sketch of flowers [bluebell, lily-of-the-
valley]. Inscribed: H.B.P. 1876 March 23. W/c.

p. 10 Rough drawing of leaves. Inscribed: H.B.P.
1876 March 23. Pencil.

p. 11 Drawings of humming birds and nest with
two eggs in it. Inscribed: H.B.P. 1876 April [2].
Pencil.

p. 12 Top: Drawing of three sheep. Bottom:
Drawing of horse and trough. Inscribed: H.B.P.
1876 April 3rd. Pencil.

p. 13 Drawing of birds (kingfishers and Chinese
jacanse [sic]). Inscribed: H.B.P. April [3rd].
Pencil.

p. 14 Wallflowers; also a Japanese lady. Inscribed:
1876 April 7. W/c and pencil.

1091 *(page)*

p. 15 Two rhinos [sic, i.e. hippopotamuses], two
roses and leaves. Pencil (hippopotamuses) and
w/c (roses).

pp. 16, 17 Unfinished flower drawings. W/c and
pencil.
Remaining sheets not used.
Entry from LL Cat.
14.5 X 11.5
BP.741   T.40.L

(LL Cat.): The preceding two drawing books were
given to Margaret Lane by Mr Heelis. Margaret
Lane was kind enough to give them to me together
with an odd sheet torn from a notebook
(see cat. 1092).

**1092 Sheet from notebook, written when BP was
seventy, concerning fungi, cancer research and
penicillin.**
BP recalls travelling back from Kew Gardens where
she was studying fungi, and overhearing a
conversation in the District Railway carriage about
Penicillium (LL). See *Journal* from p. 423 on.
The page was given by Mr Heelis to Margaret Lane;
later given to me with the Sketchbook (LL Cat.)
2ff; ink, on a sheet torn from a notebook.
17.5 X 11
BP.742   T.40.L

1094 (*page*)

1093 Drawing Book (age 10)
'Sketch Book' with limp green cloth cover.
The contents include:
Flower studies. Inscribed: May 1876. W/c and
  pencil.
Drawings of humming birds. Inscribed: May 2 '76
  (9 years 10 months). Pen-and-ink.
Drawing of clock and mice [copied from Mrs
  Blackburn's *The Pipits*]. Pen-and-ink.
Drawing of mouse carrying babies, and of a cat.
  Inscribed: Nos. 170, 144, 189.
Flower drawing: June 1876. W/c.
Drawing of an Australian scene with kangaroos and
  koala bears; also a sketch of a giraffe. Inscribed:
  H.B.P. November 22 1876. Pencil.
Milkmaid feeding ducks by a stream; copy after
  Walter Crane's 'Mrs Bond' in *The Baby's Opera*.
  W/c.
Drawing of eagles. Pencil.
Entry partly from LL Cat.
18 x 25.5
BP.743   T.40.R

1094 1902 Sketch Book
Sketch book, fawn canvas cover with elastic loop.
Including:
Painting of wallflowers. W/c.
Unfinished sketch of Mr Jeremy Fisher walking
  towards the rushes. Pencil and pen-and-ink.
Unfinished sketch of waterlilies. Pencil.
Painting of four-poster bed. W/c and pencil.
Painting of entrance gate in wall, background of
  fields and trees. Inscribed: Laund House Bolton
  Abbey July 2nd to July 8th '02. W/c and
  pen-and-ink.
Painting of cow sitting [sic] on the grass. W/c and
  pen-and-ink.
Landscapes. W/c.
Majority of pages are unused.
Entry from LL Cat.
14 x 23.5
BP.779   T.41.R

1095 1903 Sketch Book
Sketch book, fawn canvas cover with tapes.
First half mainly squirrel sketches and paintings for
The Tale of Squirrel Nutkin (1903).
Other end: cat sketches and paintings for *The Tale
of Benjamin Bunny* (1904).
9 pages: squirrels. W/c.
12 pages: squirrels. Pencil.
8 pages: cats. W/c.
7 pages: cats. Pencil.
Also two pages on which pencil sketches of mice
and rabbits appear.
Entry from LL Cat.
18 x 22.5
BP.775(a)   T.41.L

1096 BP removed three squirrel paintings from the 1903
Sketch Book (BP.775(a); cat. 1095) which she
sewed together at one corner, forming a 'set' –
all in brushwork.
1. Squirrel, front view.
2. Squirrel peeping out of his box.
3. Squirrel holding a nut in his paws.
17.5 x 22
Entry partly from LL Cat.
BP.775(b)   T.41.L

1099 (*page*)

1097 1904 Sketch Book (year approximate)
Sketch book, fawn canvas cover with elastic loop
and holder for pencil.
Including:
Painting of haycart in field surrounded by hills
(probably Cumberland).
Rough painting – believed to be hills at Newlands.
Painting of one of the small lakes, with hills in
background.
Pencil sketch of two cows, one being milked.
Painting of Esthwaite Water seen from the hillside.
Other rough w/c sketches believed to be around
Newlands.
Entry from LL Cat.
12.5 x 18.5
BP.780   T.41.R

1098 Solid Block Sketch Book
Fawn canvas cover with elastic loop.
Containing:
Landscape – probably Sidmouth.
Landscape – sloping hill [sic] and trees in
background.
Landscape – possibly Derwentwater; view across
with hills and mountains in background.
Part of a cottage – flowers growing up wall
(unfinished).
Brushwork – a forest of trees, in grey (probably
Cumberland?).
[Also pastel sketch of buildings, and an inserted
pencil sketch of the same.]
Entry from LL Cat.
18.5 x 26.5
BP.776   T.41.L

1099 1905 Sketch Book (year approximate)
Small sketch book, fawn canvas cover, elastic loop
and holder for pencil.
Including:
Sketches of magpies made at the Zoo, with pencil
notes about the bird.
Many sketches of birds.
Sketches of bears, cats and foxes.
Sketches of Rye?
Various landscapes.
Loose pencil sketch (12.5 x 10.5) of Ribby holding
a broom.
Entry from LL Cat.
13.5 x 9.5
BP.777   T.41.L

1100 1907 Sketch Book (year approximate)
Small sketch book, fawn canvas cover, elastic loop
and holder for pencil.
Including [starting from the back of the book]:
Painting believed to be Newlands – hills in the
    background, lake and trees in foreground.
Sketch of Keswick railway station platform. Pencil.
Sketch of Hill Top farmhouse. Pencil.
Painting of the entrance to Stoney Lane, three
    children and chickens in foreground.
Painting of Smithy Lane (as seen in *The Roly-Poly
    Pudding*).
Painting of Post Office, and Stoney Lane winding
    up the hillside.
Sketch of Hill Top, seen from farm. Pencil.
Painting of Buckle Yeat as seen from Tower
    Bank Arms.
Sketch: Rye, Feb 9th '07. Pencil.
Sketch of house: Croughton, Jan 7–10th '07.
    Pencil.
Entry from LL Cat.
9 x 13
BP.778   T.41.L

1101 Sketch Book
Stiff cloth cover. Filled with rough pencil sketches
believed to show the Sidmouth area.
Inscribed (on first page): Near Sidmouth Some of
these are backgrounds for Pig Robinson.
Entry from LL Cat.
13 x 18
BP.781   T.41.R

WORK BY MEMBERS OF THE POTTER FAMILY

In the past Beatrix Potter's work has been studied in isolation and her family's interest in the arts largely ignored. This section, though small and limited in scope, is a useful reminder of the artistic background to Beatrix Potter's early life. Her mother, Helen Leech, like most Victorian young ladies, had obviously been well taught in drawing and painting, and she continued to produce competent examples later in life, which suggests that she kept her interest in such activities. Rupert Potter retained throughout his life a genuine concern for art and artists, making regular visits to galleries and numbering painters such as Sir John Millais among his friends. That he was also a potentially good artist, at least in his younger days, can be seen from the sketch book which has survived, and from various attributable sketches in the collection (fine examples of his photographic work can be seen in a later section). But of all the family it was Beatrix's brother Bertram who showed the most complete dedication to art, leaving home and going off to live as a painter in Scotland, where he married and settled down. Although Beatrix Potter's art developed along completely different lines, and she was undoubtedly the most talented of her family, the atmosphere in which she grew up had certainly encouraged this talent to develop.

Helen Leech (Mrs Potter)

1102 View from a field of an inn and surrounding buildings.
Inscribed: Snake Inn Woodlands.
Inscribed (on folder): Not Beatrix Potter's – is it Helen Leech? (LL).
Brown wash and pencil. 20 x 29.5
BP.1223   P.C.30

1103 Landscape with trees and cliff.
Inscribed (verso): Helen Leech Burymelvich.
Pencil and w/c. 17 x 24.5
Verso: Caricatures of a man walking.
Pen-and-ink and w/c outline.
BP.752   T.40.R

Jane Ashton (Mrs Leech)

1104 Grandmother Leech's copybook for recording embroidery designs (sepia designs in back of notebook). Notebook half-bound in green morocco, with marbled boards.
Also other loose sheets relating to embroidery etc. contained within a pocket formed by two sheets sewn together.
Also in the notebook are stories by BP (*The Solitary Mouse, Wag by the Wa'*).
Two leaves of written text inscribed: Edging Small pattern [concerning instructions for embroidery patterns].
17ff. of designs. 2ff. of written text. W/m: 1831.
25 x 19
BP.667, 667(a–d)   T.32.L

Bertram Potter

1105 Unfinished study of BP by Bertram.
Inscribed: H.B.P. sketched by W.B.P.
Pencil. 33 x 23.5
BP.234   S.2.F.A

1106 Three studies of a hawk by Bertram, pasted on card; also studies of a cat and some fowls (by BP).
Inscribed: Studies of Birds. Hawks. W B Potter. Fowls etc. H.B. Potter.
Pen-and-ink and pencil. 17.5 x 25.5
Verso: Sketches of ducks and cats.
Pencil.
BP.645   T.29.R

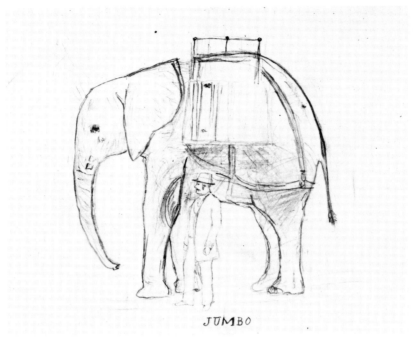

JUMBO

1110 (*page*)

1107 The stag and the dog or other tales (on cover).
Crudely sewn illustrated booklet.
Found with Beatrix Potter's papers: almost
certainly by Bertram when 8 or 9 years old
(LL Cat.)
10ff; pencil. 11 x 9
BP.785 T.42.L

1108 School exercise book (without cover).
Title: Dictation.
Specimens of ferns contained within the leaves.
16ff; pencil, on ruled paper. 20 x 15.5
BP.784 T.42.L

1109 Sketch book (without cover). Contains drawings
of animals with their names pencilled underneath.
Front page inscribed: Potter, Walter Bertram 1881
and 1882.
42ff. Pencil. 18 x 11.5
BP.786 T.42.L

1110 Sketch book (without cover). Contains
illustrations mainly of animals.
Aged 7 or 8? (LL Cat.)
21ff. Pencil and crayon. 17.5 x 11.5
BP.787 T.42.L

Cat.1111–1116, contained within an envelope
inscribed: Early drawings of W.B.P., and listed
below (except for BP.788(vii); cat.1313, which is a
postcard).

1111 Study of a grizzly bear.
Inscribed: 1882.
Black w/c and pencil on gummed paper. 12.5 x 15
BP.788(i) T.42.L

1112 Study of a grizzly bear.
Inscribed (verso): [Monogram] 1/2/83.
Pencil. 12 x 15.5
BP.788(ii) T.42.L

1113 Unfinished sketch of an alligator.
Pencil. 10 x 13
BP.788(iii) T.42.L

1114 Sketch of a lion.
Possibly BP's but contained within an envelope
of Bertram Potter's early work.
Pen-and-ink. 15.5 x 22
BP.788(iv) T.42.L

1115 Unfinished sketch of a lynx.
Pencil. 12 x 15
BP.788(v) T.42.L

1116 Study of ducks swimming near a river bank.
Pen-and-ink. W/m: Imperial Treasury de la Rue.
11.5 x 17.5
BP.788(vi)   T.42.L

1117 Sketch of a wren(?).
Inscribed (verso): [Monogram] Oct 1882.
Probably copy from a book on birds – Mrs
Blackburn? (LL Cat.)
Pencil, on card. 10.5 x 13.5
BP.789(b)   T.42.L

1118 Sketch of an unidentified bird.
Inscribed (verso): [Monogram] Oct 1882.
Probably copy from a book on birds – Mrs
Blackburn? (LL Cat.)
Pencil, on card. 9.5 x 11.5
BP.789(a)   T.42.L

1119 Shore of a lake with mountains (Esthwaite
Water?).
Inscribed: [Monogram] 1906.
W/c and pencil, framed by gold border. 37 x 27
BP.1247   P.C.31

1120 Sheep in a meadow in the snow.
Inscribed (verso): 'Winter' Copied from oil
painting by W.B. Potter. H.B. Potter.
W/c and pencil. 11 x 15, on card 15 x 20
BP.783   T.42.L

Rupert Potter

1121 Sketch Book. Plain paper boards.
Inscribed (inside cover): R. Potter Sept 1 1853.
Broughton in Furness. Dinting Lodge, Glossop.
Illustrations include bird studies, caricatures of
men and animals (bear playing flute, dog smoking a
pipe, and ducks flying, wearing hat and bonnet like
Jemima Puddle-Duck); also two students sitting in
arm-chairs reading newspapers with papers strewn
on the floor, inscribed: Temple life.
Pen-and-ink and w/c. 12.5 x 17
BP.782   T.42.L

1121 (*page*)

1123

1122 Church tower (incomplete). By Rupert Potter?
Pen-and-ink. 18.5 x 16.5
BP.1215   P.C.30

1123 A group of four dogs, two sitting and one lying
down.
Possibly copied from an engraving?
Pencil over a fawn wash, on card. 12 x 14
BP.1094   P.C.53

1124 Burrowing owl (*Speotyto cunicularia*).
Possibly copied from an engraving, *c.*1857?
Pencil, on card. 10.5 x 16
BP.1095(i)   P.C.53

1125 Two red-legged partridges (*Alectoris rufa*) in a
field setting.
Information from the Natural History Museum.
Possibly copied from an engraving, *c.*1857?
Pencil, on card. 19.5 x 20
BP.1095(ii)   P.C.53

1126 Kingfisher on a branch (*Alcedo atthis*).
Information from the Natural History Museum.
Possibly copied from an engraving, *c.*1857?
Verso: Faint sketch of cockatoo(?).
Inscribed: 6/6/57.
Pencil, on card. 18 x 17.5
BP.1095(iii)   P.C.53

1127 Hooded berry-eater (*Ampelion cuculatus*)(?), on a
branch.
Information from the Natural History Museum.
Possibly copied from an engraving, *c.*1857?
Pencil, on card. 19 x 16.5
BP.1095(iv)   P.C.53

COPIES OF WORK BY OTHER ARTISTS

This is a very slight section, but it is one that may well be added to, as more of the 'doubtful' items in this catalogue are recognised as copies rather than as original works. The Linder Bequest came to the V&A Library without any documentation. More has been acquired recently on the death of Miss Enid Linder. Undoubtedly Leslie Linder himself knew very well the sources from which he obtained much of his collection, but he did not record such facts in his own manuscript catalogue. As a result, doubt has sometimes arisen in the minds of all three cataloguers working on this volume as to whether all items were by the artist herself, partly by her, copied from her, or even copied by her from other works. The uneven nature of some of the sketches in this Collection may eventually lead to reattribution, when the provenance of the material is more fully studied.

1128 Study of a young gull.
Inscribed: Copied from Mrs Blackburn.
Inscribed (verso): Copy from Mrs Blackburn's bird.
(LL Cat.): Copy, in reverse, of Plate XXIV of the 1868 2nd edition of *Birds Drawn from Nature* by Mrs Hugh Blackburn (first picture in 'Part Second', on title page).
Pencil. 28 x 20
BP.420(b)   S.13.F.B

1129 Rough drawing of the same.
Inscribed: Copied from Mrs Blackburn.
Pencil. 27.5 x 20
BP.420(a)   S.13.F.B

1130 Robin perched on a sweet pea.
Inscribed: Copied from Mrs Blackburn.
(LL Cat.): Copy, in reverse, of Plate XLI of the 1868 2nd edition. BP's drawing is of the bottom figure in reverse, i.e. traced on paper, paper turned over and traced over on blank side so that the original pencil offset on to the drawing paper.
Pencil. 26.5 x 20
BP.419(a)   S.13.F.B

1131 Tracing of the same.
Inscribed (in ink) with monogram.
Pencil. 20.5 x 20
BP.419(b)   S.13.F.B

1132 Copy from a sketch by Constable: Sty Head Tarn, Borrowdale, Cumberland, dated Sunday 12th Oct 1806. Noon. (177–1888)
Inscribed: Copy from a sketch by Constable at S.K. Museum.
W/c. 11.5 x 25
BP.308   S.7.F.B

1133 Two copies from monochrome sketches by Constable: (i) Entrance to the Village of Edensor, dated 18 August 1801; (ii) View in Derbyshire, dated 1801. (247c-d–1888)
Inscribed: Copied S.K. Museum.
Grey wash with pencil. 35 x 25
BP.1020   P.C.23

1134 Study of a dead stag.
Inscribed (verso, in pencil): Copy from a lithograph after Sir E. Landseer drawn by Beatrix Potter.
Brown and black crayon, on grey paper. 33.5 x 44
BP.251   S.3.F.C

1134

WORK BY OTHER ARTISTS

This section is almost entirely concerned with *The Oakmen*. The original story-letter was written for one of her husband's nieces, but at a time when Beatrix Potter felt she was losing her skills (or perhaps her interest?) in such things. She therefore commissioned a well-known book illustrator to carry out her designs and purchased the illustrations from him. As a result we have the interesting experience of seeing Beatrix Potter's preliminary sketches and general ideas, together with their interpretation by E.A. Aris. The shock is considerable. The work was never published, mainly because of copyright difficulties, but one wonders if Beatrix Potter would ever have been satisfied with the very bright colours and very conventional style of Aris's work.

1136

The Oakmen, by E.A. Aris

Six watercolours by Aris for 'The Oakmen', ordered and paid for by BP.
(LL Cat.): They were not used because the story was never published owing to some doubts as to the plot being entirely original – with possible copyright risks.
All w/cs are signed: Ernest Aris 16 [i.e. 1916].
Each finished w/c is accompanied by BP's own suggestion of the illustration (in pencil), with pencil versions of the relevant part of the text and instructions as to colour etc. Material enclosed in folder inscribed: A toy town tale.
The letter 'a' distinguishes Aris's work, the letters 'b' and 'c' that of BP.

1135 Oakman sitting outside his house talking to two mice, by Aris.
W/c and pen-and-ink, on card. 19 x 14
BP.607(1a)   T.27.L

1136 Sketch by BP for BP.607(1a).
Inscribed: Gnome with red cap giving lump of sugar to mouse, plate on knee, bread & butter in hand. Doorway & steps leading up to tree-house behind.
Pencil. 20.5 x 16.5
BP.607(1b)   T.27.L

1137 Gnomes watching woodmen cutting down trees.
W/c and pen-and-ink, on card. 16.5 x 14
BP.607(2a)   T.27.L

1138 Two rough sketches by BP for BP.607(2a).
One is inscribed: Gnomes peeping round trees to watch woodcutters [etc.]; and: Light from this side. Pots & pans etc.
The other is partly in sepia ink.
Not sent to Aris.
Pencil and sepia ink. 20.5 x 16.5
BP.607(2b,2c)   T.27.L

1139 Gnomes talking to owl on wall.
W/c and pen-and-ink, on card. 19 x 14
BP.607(3a)   T.27.L

1140 Rough sketch by BP for BP.607(3a).
Pencil. 20.5 x 16.5
BP.607(3b)   T.27.L

1141 Sketch by BP for BP.607(3a).
Inscribed: Landscape rather blue. It seems to require a middle size figure somewhere in the middle distance. Gnomes talking to white owl on wall. I have a skin of a white barn owl [etc.].
Pencil. 20.5 x 16.5
BP.607(3c)   T.27.L

1142 Gnomes digging out door under tree stump.
W/c and pen-and-ink. 19 x 14
BP.607(4a)   T.27.L

1143 Sketch by BP for BP.607(4a).
Inscribed: Three gnomes digging out door under stump, which has been smothered with chips. White owl with lantern on fallen branch.
Pencil. 18 x 17
BP.607(4b)   T.27.L

1144 Gnomes leaving in their wagon.
W/c and pen-and-ink. 19 x 14
BP.607(5a)   T.27.L

1145 Sketch by BP for BP.607(5a).
Inscribed: Wagon loaded with boxes & furniture driven by gnomes, others following with bundles.
Pencil. 20.5 x 16
BP.607(5b)   T.27.L

1146 Gnomes unloading boxes and furniture.
W/c with pen-and-ink, on card. 19 x 14
BP.607(6a)   T.27.L

1147 Rough pencil sketches by BP for BP.607(6a).
Inscribed: Gnomes unloading boxes & furniture & carrying them into dugouts [etc.].
Pencil. 20.5 x 16.5
BP.607(6b)   T.27.L

Other items

1148 A country house surrounded by trees.
Inscribed (verso): Etched and printed by Beatrix Potter; also with initials etched on plate: BP.
Copy from a woodcut by Mr Alfred Parsons in Harpers Magazine.
1899? (LL Cat.)
14.5 x 20
BP.828   T.6

1149 Sketch of Camfield from the park. Artist unknown.
Inscribed: Camfield Place. Essendon Herts.
C. Dimsdale Esq.
Inscribed (on transparent cover): Mrs Edmund Potter's writing   Ex Mrs Gaddum (LL).
Pencil. 26 x 17.5
BP.1043   P.C.33

1150 Sketch of a boathouse by a lake.
Possibly by Bertram Potter?
Pencil, on unevenly cut sheet. 11 x 12.5
BP.1222   P.C.30

1151 Faint sketch of a harbour with buildings along a pier.
Verso: Sketches of pigs and cows feeding.
Pencil. 17.5 x 25.5
BP.750   T.40.R

PART II

Manuscripts, books, miscellaneous items and memorabilia

The remainder of this catalogue needs little comment, since the headings are self-explanatory. Among the most interesting items, because the least known, are the letters between Mr Thomas B. Potter and William Ewart Gladstone, but the whole sequence of family and business correspondence adds to the general appreciation of Beatrix Potter's background, life and work.

The entries for the books are taken entirely from Leslie Linder's own catalogue, since time did not permit a reappraisal of the various editions. Also in the final section are various miscellaneous groupings which indicate not only the great variety of Beatrix Potter's own interests, but also the wide area over which Mr Linder spread his net – no item was too small or too fragmentary for his collection, and some were very small indeed! Fortunately for posterity both Beatrix Potter and Leslie Linder were hoarders, and thus have provided in the V&A Library an unrivalled opportunity to study the art and writings of Beatrix Potter from every possible aspect.

MANUSCRIPTS: Literary

The Peter Rabbit books

Appley Dapply's Nursery Rhymes

1152 *1905 Book of Rhymes.* In a stiff red-covered exercise book; written out in ink or pencil, containing BP's own verses for her proposed 1905 *Appley Dapply.* Inscribed (inside cover): For N.D.W.; and: For Stephanie from Cousin B.
Sent to Norman Warne to look through. He initialled the rhymes he thought suitable: N.D.W. During the planning of the book he died and it was then put on one side. The MS was given to Stephanie Hyde-Parker. Two pages torn out were re-inserted in the book. These have been missing but were found again (LL Cat.)
Book picture of Mrs Tiggy-Winkle's head tipped in at the front, 2 w/cs of Lucie's (?) head tipped in at the back.
89ff. (57 blank); ink with pencil. 20 x 15.5
BP.618   T.28.L

1153 *1905 Book of Rhymes.* A four-page folded sheet of the rhymes intended for the early unpublished version of the book.
2ff; ink. 19.5 x 16
BP.626   T.28.R

1154 *1905 Book of Rhymes.* A single sheet of rhymes intended for the early unpublished version of the book: 'Appley Dapply, a little brown mouse', 'Knittery, knottery, 8, 9, 10', 'Peastraw and Parsnips', 'There once was an amiable guinea-pig'. Verso: 'Where are you going to, little dog Bell?'
1f; ink, on ruled foolscap paper. 33 x 20.5
BP.627   T.28.R

Cecily Parsley's Nursery Rhymes

1155 First MS of the 'Cecily Parsley' rhyme. Sewn into a booklet.
p.1 Two small pen-and-ink and w/c drawings – a barrel in a cellar and Cecily Parsley carrying a tray with three glasses of ale. In between, the verse: Cecily Parsley lived in a pen, And brewed good ale for Gentlemen.
p.3 Two small pen-and-ink and w/c drawings – green bottles and a cork-screw and two gentlemen rabbits smoking pipes and drinking ale by the kitchen fire. In between, the line: Gentlemen came every Day —.

p.5 Two small pen-and-ink and w/c drawings – a doorway in a wicker house with 'TO LET' on the door. A sign over the door – a quill pen on which hangs the notice 'The Pen Inn' – tells us it is Cecily Parsley's abode; below, three rats with writs and walking sticks look at the closed premises. BP has pencilled in: The bailiffs. In between, the line: Till Cecily Parsley ran AWAY.
p.7 Pen-and-ink and w/c drawing of Cecily Parsley running with a wheelbarrow into a burrow. Inscribed (on cover): Nursery Rhymes "Cecily Parsley" drawings original. Beatrix Potter. Jan '97.
4ff; pen-and-ink and w/c with pencil. 17.5 x 11
BP.661   T.30.R

Ninny Nanny Netticoat

1156 A folded sheet showing eleven mice dancing round a candlestick and hoisting a snuffer.
Inscribed: Ninny Nanny Netticoat/With a white petticoat/And a red Nose.
Second drawing (inside) shows four mice pushing a candle into a mousehole, and a solitary mouse looking puzzled.
Inscribed: The longer she stands/The shorter she grows. HBP. Aug 4th 97.
Inserted with BP.662(b) into another folded sheet, BP.662(c) (the cover), inscribed: Nursery Rhymes. 'Nanny Netticoat' Drawn by Beatrix Potter (sketch unfinished).
Pen-and-ink with pencil. 20 x 25.5
BP.662(a)   T.30.R

1156 *(detail)*

1158 *(page)*

1157 A folded sheet showing twelve mice dancing round a candlestick and hoisting a snuffer.
Inscribed: A Riddle. Ninny Nanny Netticoat/ With a white petticoat/And a red nose. . . /The longer she stands/The shorter she grows. Aug 97.
Second drawing (inside) shows four mice pushing a candle into a mousehole, and a solitary mouse looking puzzled.
Inscribed: Answer/A Candle.
Third drawing (on back) shows mouse in candlestick.
Inserted with BP.662(a) into another folded sheet, BP.662(c) (the cover).
Pen-and-ink with pencil. 20 x 25.5
BP.662(b)   T.30.R

Ginger and Pickles

1158 Seventeen drawings in sepia ink, and three in w/c, all mounted on blank pages of the MS. Written out (on one side of the page only) in a ruled exercise book, with the letters 'MSS' blind-stamped on cover. The illustration on f.3(v) has been removed (prior to entering LL's collection?) and 'we are producing from this' lightly pencilled on the page.
Inscribed (on title page): With love to Louie from Aunt Beatrix Christmas 1908.
48ff. (26 blank); pen-and-ink and w/c. 20 x 16
BP.603   T.26.R

1158 *(page)*

1160 (page)

1159 Second, enlarged version (text only). Written out in a ruled exercise book, with the letters 'MSS' blind-stamped on cover; 'N. Porter . . . 7 Sussex Place, South Kensington' trade card on inside front cover.

The back of the exercise book contains (upside down) a part of the draft text of *Idle Shepherd*; a small label with these words in pencil is stuck on the back cover.

24ff; ink. 20.5 x 16.5 (with separate inserted slip, 6 x 16)

BP.604 T.26.R

The Tale of Mrs Tittlemouse

1160 Eight watercolours, mounted on blank pages of the MS. Written out in a dark green leather-covered notebook with gold rules.

Fly-leaf inscribed: For Nellie, with love & best wishes for A Happy New Year Jan 1st 1910. The Tale of Mrs Tittlemouse.

30ff. (7 blank); pen-and-ink and w/c. 15 x 9

BP.598 T.26.L (see PLATE XLI)

The Tale of the Flopsy Bunnies

1161 Small fragment torn off a pencil draft of the opening page of *The Tale of the Flopsy Bunnies*, and including the word 'soporific'.

Verso: Rough sketch for Samuel Whiskers' coat of arms; also sketch of cottage.

1f; pencil. 5 x 16 (approx.)

BP.600 T.26.L

1162 (details)

The Roly-Poly Pudding

1162 Thirty-two drawings in sepia ink and two watercolours, mounted in the text. Written out (on one side of the page only) in a ruled exercise book with stiff black covers, blind-stamped 'Lamley & Co., publishers, South Kensington'. The title is written on the front endpaper and dated Christmas 1906.

The name and address of Winifred Warne appears at the top of the left front endpaper.

78ff. (44 blank); sepia ink and w/c. 23 x 17.5

BP.596 T.26.L

Peter Rabbit plays

1163 *The Tailor of Gloucester*: a play from the story by
BP, arranged by E. Harcourt Williams.
Title on first page.
Complete play written out by BP to show
E. Harcourt Williams exactly how she wanted it
presented, his first version being unsatisfactory and
his final version being based on hers (LL Cat.)
10ff; ink, on ruled exercise paper. 23 x 17.5
BP.689   T.36.L

1164 *Peter Rabbit* play (unfinished).
2ff; pencil, on poor quality paper. 26.5 x 19
BP.688   T.36.L

French translations of **Peter Rabbit books**

1165 *Peter Rabbit* translated by BP into French: *Le récit
de Pierre Lapereau*.
8ff; ink, on ruled exercise paper with comments by
Mlle Ballon (1912). 32.5 x 20.5
BP.699(1)   T.36.R

1166 *Peter Rabbit* translated by BP into French:
Pierre Lapin.
f.7: Criticism and comparison.
7ff; ink, on thin ruled exercise paper with
comments by Mlle Profichet(?) in red. The final
page consists of comparisons by BP between her
translation and that of Mlle Profichet. 24 x 20 etc.
BP.699(2)   T.36.R

1167 *Peter Rabbit* translated by BP into French: *Le récit de
Rémi Lapereau*.
Title on first page.
4ff; ink, with pencil corrections by BP on ruled
exercise paper. 32.5 x 20.5
BP.699(3)   T.36.R

1168 Unfinished French translation by BP: *L'histoire de
Pierre Lapereau*.
2ff; ink, on thin ruled exercise paper. 25 x 20
BP.699(4)   T.36.R

1169 *Benjamin Bunny* translated by BP into French:
Histoire de Jeannot Lapin.
Title on first page.
8ff; ink, on thin ruled exercise paper. 25 x 20
BP.703   T.36.R

1170 *Jemima Puddle-Duck* translated by BP into French:
Sophie Canétang.
Title on first page.
8ff; ink, on thin ruled exercise paper. 25 x 20
BP.702   T.36.R

1171 *The Flopsy Bunnies* translated by BP into French:
Histoire de la Famille Flopsaut.
Title on first page.
7ff; ink, on thin ruled exercise paper. 24.5 x 20
BP.700   T.36.R

1172 *Mrs Tiggy-Winkle* translated by BP into French:
Poupette à l'Épingle.
Title on first page.
8ff; ink, on thin ruled exercise paper. 25 x 20
BP.701   T.36.R

Books other than the Peter Rabbit books

Aesop's Fables

1173 *Grasshopper Belle and Susan Emmet*.
Title on first page.
About 1919 (LL Cat.)
2ff; ink, on ruled exercise paper. 25 x 20
BP.726   T.38.R

1174 *The fox and the stork*.
1f; draft, in ink, on a sheet from an exercise book.
20 x 15
BP.653   T.30.L

1175 Fables: *The folly of vanity* (three pages), *Sour grapes*
(three pages), *The frog's king* (four pages).
Later drafts, in ink, in an exercise book with a red
cover, labelled: Fables.
For earlier drafts, see BP.655; cat. 1176.
26ff. (21 blank); ink. 20 x 16
BP.654   T.30.L

1176 Dark green exercise book (earlier than BP.654;
cat. 1175) labelled: Fables; and (on back):
Demerara Sugar.
Early drafts occupy the first nine pages (*The folly of
vanity, Sour grapes* [*The frog's king*]); on pp. 17–22
are rough drafts for other fables: *The dog and his
bone, The hare and the tortoise*. The rest of the book
is filled with *The Fairy Caravan* material including
Demerara Sugar.
17ff. (3 blank); ink or pencil. 20 x 16
BP.655   T.30.L

1177 *Sour grapes, The folly of vanity,* end of *The frog's king,* opening paragraph of *The ant and the grasshopper.*
Last page inscribed (in pencil): Fables.
3ff; incomplete early drafts, in ink, on thick writing block paper. 25 x 20
BP.658(a–c)   T.30.L

1178 Concerning the Pisamours: material for *Grasshopper Belle and Susan Emmet.*
Material for a sequel to *The Fairy Caravan* (LL Cat.)
2ff; ink, on the back of torn *Sister Anne* proofs. 36 x 19; 25.5 x 19
BP.727(a)   T.38.R

1179 *Grasshopper Belle and Susan Emmet.*
Material for a sequel to *The Fairy Caravan* (LL).
2ff; ink, on *The Times* newspaper wrappers (torn).
Postmark: 1.iv.42. 20.5 x 15.5
BP.727(b)   T.38.R

1180 *The dog and his bone* (untitled): concerning Nettie the dog, and a bone.
2ff; ink, on ruled exercise paper. 20 x 16
BP.656(a,b)   T.30.L

1181 *The hare and the tortoise* (sheets untitled): concerning Ptolemy Tortoise and the Hare running in a race.
3ff; ink, on ruled exercise paper. 20 x 16
BP.657(a–c)   T.30.L

The Chinese Umbrella

1182 Typed copy of *The Chinese Umbrella.*
Warne's typed the copy of the story which was given by BP to Miss Chance; it concerned Tzuzee and Chuleh, her Pekinese dogs (LL Cat.)
6ff; on loose sheets, attached, and contained within red covers. 20.5 x 12.5
BP.601   T.26.L

Cinderella

1183 Chapter 1.
Title on first page.
The name of the town is left blank – but it was found on some of BP's rough drafts of *Cinderella* (LL Cat.)
2ff; final draft, in ink, on single sheets of ruled paper. 20 x 16.5
BP.704(i)   T.37.L

1184 Chapter 2.
5ff; final draft, in ink, on single sheets of ruled paper. 22.5 x 17.5
BP.704(ii)   T.37.L

1185 Chapter 3.
6ff; semi-final draft, in ink, on single sheets of ruled paper. 22.5 x 17.5
BP.704(iii)   T.37.L

1186 Chapter 4.
6ff; rough draft, in ink, on thin ruled exercise paper. 20 x 16.5
BP.704(iv)   T.37.L

1187 Chapter 5.
Inscribed on first page: Last chapter of Cinderella.
One line was added from an earlier draft.
5ff; final (unfinished) draft, in ink, on ruled exercise paper. 20 x 16.5
BP.704(v)   T.37.L

1188 Chapter 5.
4ff; early draft, in ink, on single sheets of ruled exercise paper. 22.5 x 17
BP.705(i)   T.37.L

1189 Chapters 1 and 2.
8ff; early draft, in ink, on single sheets of ruled exercise paper. 22 x 17
BP.705(ii)   T.37.L

1190 Chapters 1, 2 and 3.
8ff; early drafts, in ink, on thin ruled exercise paper. 25 x 20
BP.705(iii)   T.37.L

1191 Chapters 2 and 5.
5ff; very rough drafts, in ink, on galley proofs of *Sister Anne.* 30 x 19 etc.
BP.705(iv)   T.37.L

1192 Miscellaneous early drafts.
10ff; ink, in a red paper-covered exercise book with several loose sheets; also one sheet of notepaper. 20 x 16
BP.705(v)   T.37.L

1193 Preliminary notes: sheets numbered in pencil in the order in which they were found.
Verso: attached piece of blue paper with printed information on different type sizes.
These are preliminary notes giving the settings for the story and other details (LL Cat.)
18ff; preliminary notes in ink and pencil, on two sizes of notepaper and pages out of cash notebook; also one blank sheet inscribed (not in BP's hand): Cinderella? 16 x 10 etc.
BP.706   T.37.L

The Fairy Caravan

1194 The mouse and the wedding.
2ff; subject matter from p. 56 of 1929 edition of *The Fairy Caravan*; ink, on sheets of a small notebook with rounded corners. 13 x 8
BP.663(i)   T.31.L

1195 Matilda and Louisa Pussy-cat's shop.
Inscribed (in pencil): The Bandana Pocket-handkerchief. Describes how Sandy bought clothes for Tuppenny's part in the circus. Rather long, could be compressed.
3ff; subject matter from p. 56 (LL Cat.); early drafts, in ink, on ruled exercise paper. 20 x 16
BP.663(ii)   T.31.L

1196 Concerning Henny Penny.
3ff; relates to pp. 120–121 (LL Cat.); early draft, in ink (one side of page only), on ruled exercise paper. 20 x 16
BP.663(iii)   T.31.L

1197 Concerning Ribby, Tabitha and Mice.
3ff; relates to p. 180 (LL Cat.); early draft, in ink (one side of page only), on ruled exercise paper. 20 x 16
BP.663(iv)   T.31.L

1198 Concerning Cheese-box and the rats.
4ff; relates to p. 200 (LL Cat.); early draft, in ink (one side of page only), on ruled exercise paper. 20 x 16
BP.663(v)   T.31.L

1199 Concerning *The Fairy Caravan* characters travelling along by a brook.
5ff; relates to pp. 208–215 (LL Cat.); early draft of the end of Chapter XXII (one sheet missing), in ink (one side of page only), on ruled exercise paper. 20 x 16
BP.663(vi)   T.31.L

1200 Early draft concerning Fern Seed.
1f; ink, on poor quality paper. 21 x 14
BP.663(vii)   T.31.L

1201 Folded sheet with a feather attached, concerning the death of Charles (a cock) of *The Fairy Caravan*.
Inscribed: Beatrix Potter Nov 22. '29.
2ff; ink, on notepaper. W/m: Fairford. 15 x 10
BP.668   T.32.R

1202 Two other sheets concerning the death of Charles (also with a feather attached).
Each is inscribed as BP.668; cat.1201.
Charles of *The Fairy Caravan* died on Nov 17th 1929, less than three weeks of [sic] the publication of *The Fairy Caravan*. BP mounted the feathers in his memory (LL Cat.)
2ff; ink, on notepaper. W/m: Fairford. 15 x 10
BP.669, 670   T.32.R

1203 Two sketches of Charles of *The Fairy Caravan*.
Inscribed: Charles our cock. Silver Campine.
Verso: Rough sketch of horses by Hill Top.
Pencil. 17.5 x 10
BP.671   T.32.R

1204 Essay concerning Charles.
Inscribed: Beatrix Potter.
2ff; ink, on thin paper. 20 x 16.5
BP.673(a,b)   T.32.R

1205 Notes concerning Charles.
Rough drafts of final essay.
See also BP.673(a,b); cat.1204.
1f; ink, on thin paper. 20 x 16.5
BP.673(c)   T.32.R

1206 Notes concerning Charles.
Rough draft of an essay on Charles.
See also BP.673(a,b); cat.1204.
1f; ink, on ruled exercise paper. 20 x 16
BP.673(d)   T.32.R

1207 Folded sheet concerning Henny Penny, mother of Charles; also pen-and-ink illustration above the text.
Inscribed: Beatrix Potter Nov 21st '29.
2ff; ink, on notepaper. W/m: Fairford [C] ale/ JS & Co. No. 15 x 10
BP.672   T.32.R

1208 Notes concerning Henny Penny.
1f; ink, on thin ruled writing block paper. 15 x 20
BP.674   T.32.R

Sequel to The Fairy Caravan

1209 *Cherry Tree Camp* I.
Title on first page.
7ff; final draft, in ink (one side of page only),
on ruled writing block paper. 22 x 17
BP.664(i)   T.31.L

1210 *Xarifa and Tuppenny walk amongst the funguses.*
Inscribed: II.
3ff; final draft, in ink (one side of page only),
on ruled writing block paper. 22 x 17
BP.664(ii)   T.31.L

1211 Leading up to *The Tale of the Idle Shepherd Boy.*
Inscribed in pencil (at top of sheet): III. I have just
put these numbers for order, of course it might
require splitting up.
Inscribed (on final sheet): This is about a quarter
of the whole tale of the Shepherd. It ends alright.
It is the story of the calling 'Wolf! Wolf!'.
The pencil remarks were intended for Bertha
Mahony Miller, as there was some possibility of
the text being used for the *Horn Book Magazine*
(LL Cat.)
See also BP.604; cat.1159.
10ff; final draft, in ink (one side of page only),
on ruled writing block paper. 22 x 17
BP.664(iii)   T.31.L

1212 Tea-party of mice and birds.
Inscribed: IV.
8ff; final draft, in ink (one side of page only),
on ruled writing block paper. 22.5 x 17.5
BP.664(iv)   T.31.L

1213 Leading up to and including *The Tale of Little Red
Riding Hood.*
Inscribed: V.
11ff; final draft, in ink (one side of page only),
on ruled writing block paper. 22.5 x 17.5
BP.664(v)   T.31.L

1214 Xarifa stays in the Hollow Ash.
5ff; ink (one side of page only), on thin ruled
exercise paper. 20 x 16
BP.664(vi)   T.31.L

1215 Concerning Billy Brown Shrew.
Reference to a story about Smeralda Bangs and the
Moppets.
The story exists only unfinished, in code (LL Cat.)
6ff; draft, in ink (one side of page only), on ruled
exercise paper. 20 x 16.5
BP.664(vii)   T.31.L

1216 Concerning Bird's Place, a garden in Wales.
2ff; ink, on ruled exercise paper. 20 x 16
BP.664(viii)   T.31.L

1217 Joseph Mouse.
Title on first page (in pencil).
6ff; draft based on *The Solitary Mouse*, in ink,
on ruled exercise paper. 20 x 16
BP.664(ix)   T.31.L

1218 Inscribed (in pencil): (Discussion about engaging a
fresh performer).
Duplicate inscribed (at top of first sheet):
Concerning the Tail-less Fox, leading up to *The
Fox and the Crow.*
13ff; early draft with many corrections, in ink, on
thin writing block paper. 25 x 20
BP.664(xi)   T.31.L

1219 Inscribed: This follows Joseph Mouse.
Inscribed (on final sheet) with reference to Goody
Simpson and a list (in pencil): follows – the story of
Kirsteen Kettle, follows – the incident of Sophy &
Price the hares, follows – the flowers that sing in
the Bog, follows – Pony William's adventure (fell
through barn floor & stuck) [etc.].
Goody Simpson later became Sally Benson in the
story of *Wag-by-Wall* (LL Cat.)
2ff; draft, in ink, on ruled exercise paper. 20 x 16
BP.664(x)   T.31.L

1220 Concerning *The Oakmen.*
Draft with many corrections (two pages cancelled).
13ff; ink, on ruled writing paper.
25 x 20; 22.5 x 17.5
BP.664(xii)   T.31.L

1221 Two drafts, numbered 13 and 14, of Chapter I.
13: 6ff; ink, on thin writing block paper, with 3ff.
on thicker writing block paper. 25.5 x 20 etc.
14: 8ff. 22.5 x 17.5 etc.
BP.664(xiii, xiv)   T.31.R

1222 Two drafts of Chapter II, also one sheet numbered
15, listing Latin names of fungi.
15: 5ff; ink (one side of page only), on ruled
exercise paper. 20 x 16; 11 x 16
16: 3ff. 25 x 20
BP.664(xv,xvi)   T.31.R

1223 Two drafts of Chapter IV, numbered 17 and 18.
17 inscribed (on first page): Not very suitable
depends too much on flowers and birds.
17: 5ff. 18: 5ff. Early drafts, in ink, with pencil
corrections, on ruled exercise paper. 20 x 16
BP.664(xvii, xviii)   T.31.R

1224 Draft of Chapter V, numbered 19.
Inscribed (on first page): Follows the teaparty &
Elly Campane.
Inscribed (on final page, in pencil): Follows the
Tale of Second Cousin Mouse (Bluebeard) [etc.].
5ff; ink, on ruled exercise paper. 20 x 16
BP.664(xix)   T.31.R

1225 Early draft of Chapter V, numbered 20.
5ff; ink, on ruled exercise paper. 20 x 16
BP.664(xx)   T.31.R

1226 *The Solitary Mouse*, by Beatrix Potter (copyright
reserved).
Title on first page.
Rough sheets from drafts sent to Bertha Mahony
Miller for use in the *Horn Book Magazine*. It was,
however, never published (LL Cat.)
9ff; ink on ruled exercise paper. 1f. missing.
23.5 x 16
BP.664(xxi)   T.31.R

1227 Concerning Joseph Mouse.
6ff; earlier draft, in ink (one side of page only),
on thin writing block paper. 25 x 20
BP.664(xxii)   T.31.R

1228 Two drafts, numbered 23 and 24, following *Joseph
Mouse*, leading to *Goody Simpson*.
23: 3ff. 24: 6ff. Rough drafts (23 an earlier draft
than 24), in ink, on ruled writing block paper.
25 x 20
BP.664(xxiii,xxiv)   T.31.R

1229 End of Chapter V, about Belinda Woodmouse,
leading to *Bluebeard*.
3ff; draft, in ink, on thin ruled exercise paper.
20 x 16.5
BP.664(xxv)   T.31.R

1230 Two drafts of *The Tail-less Fox*, leading to *The Fox
and the Crow*, numbered 26 and 27.
26: 9ff. 27: 7ff. Drafts, in ink, on ruled exercise
paper. 20 x 16
BP.664(xxvi,xxvii)   T.31.R

The Fairy Clogs

1231 Title on first page.
Inscribed (in pencil): Written at Hill Top [on]
Sunday Nov. 5. '11.
5ff; early draft of *The Fairy Clogs*, in ink, on ruled
exercise paper. 20 x 16
BP.715   T.38.L

1232 Title on first page.
Inscribed (in pencil): Hill Top Farm Nov 5.11
Sunday [eve].
Labelled (on cover): Carrier's Bob. A northern
garland [incorrect title].
One of four stories accepted by and printed in
Country Life in 1913 (LL Cat.)
22ff. (14 blank); ink, in a green-covered exercise
book. 20 x 16
BP.709   T.38.L

1233 MS containing three stories: *The Fairy Clogs*,
inscribed (on first page): Sunday Nov 5 11; also
Carrier's Bob, inscribed (in pencil): Aug 1911;
and *The Mole-catcher*, inscribed (in pencil):
29th Oct '11.
These three stories, together with *The Pace-eggers*,
were printed in *Country Life* in 1913.
See also BP.711, 714, 712, 713; cat. 1277–1278,
1284–1285.
23ff. (5 blank); ink, with pencil corrections, in a
black-covered exercise book. 20 x 16
BP.710   T.38.L

Fairy Tales

1234 *Red Riding Hood*.
Title on cover and title page; the latter inscribed:
adapted from the French of M. Perrault.
51ff. (34 blank); ink, with notes in faint pencil:
Revised copy elsewhere; in a black-covered semi-
stiff exercise book. 16.5 x 10
BP.616   T.27.R

The Tale of the Faithful Dove.

There is a town — a little old red-roofed town that I know — a city of gates and walls. It has steep cobled streets that mount — like the ribs of a crown; to the grey flint church on the summit.

The gold weather-cock glitters in the sunshine; and the pigeons wheel round in short sharp flights. As they turn and tumble their wings show white against the dark clouds over the sea.

Sometimes on hot harvest days they fly out to the cornfields; but always with an eye on safety and their nests in the Ypres Tower, high up on the walls of the town. And the other eye for the falcons across the marsh at Camber.

But more often they peck about in the grass-grown streets, amongst the cobble-stones of the market-place, or in a dusty yard of the flour-mill down by the river.

"Why should a pigeon risk his tail in Winchelsea Marsh while there is corn in Rye?" said Mr Vidler, bobbing and bowing and strutting around.

1236 (page)

1235 *Fairy Tales.*
Title inscribed on cover. On title page: Red Riding Hood (revised text), adapted from the French of M Perrault. On f. 15r: The Molecatcher's Burying; on f. 22r: The Fairy in the Oak. Written for two little New Zealand Fairies, by promise.
Faint pencil note relating to *The Mole-catcher's Burying*: Written at Sawrey Oct 29 '11.
Faint pencil note facing opening of *The Fairy in the Oak*: 'Dryadasque puellis/For tis my faith that every flower enjoys the air it breathes'.
'The Fairy in the Oak' was rewritten in 1929 as the last chapter in *The Fairy Caravan* (LL Cat.)
64ff. (21 blank); ink, in a black-covered semi-stiff exercise book. 16.5 x 10
BP.617   T.27.R

The Tale of the Faithful Dove

1236 Title on first page.
Inscribed (opposite title, in pencil): Founded upon fact, but the incident occurred at another seaside town, I think Folkestone or Dover; and (in ink): 'Da schliefen auch die Tauben auf dem Dache'. Dornröschen [There slept also the doves on the roof. Briar Rose].
Inscribed (below): Hastings Feb. 4th–14th, '07.
76ff. (55 blank); ink, in a hard-backed exercise book with a marbled cover. 22.5 x 17.5
BP.685   T.35.R

147

1237 Carbon copy of typescript of *The Faithful Dove*.
In 1955 Warne's published *The Tale of the Faithful Dove* in a New York trade edition, and in a limited numbered edition of 100 copies in London (LL Cat.)
3off. 24 x 18
BP.686   T.35.R

1238 Receipt for copy no. 1 of limited edition: Bought of Frederick Warne & Co. by L. Linder. B. Potter. Faithful Dove No. 1 3/6.
To obtain copyright, a copy has to be actually sold (LL Cat.)
BP.687   T.35.R

The Idle Shepherd Boy

1239 Title on cover and first page.
The story was later incorporated into the sequel to *The Fairy Caravan* (LL).
See also BP.604; cat.1159 and BP.664 (iii); cat.1211.
16ff. (10 blank); final draft, in ink, in a blue paper-covered exercise book. 20 x 16.5
BP.605(a)   T.26.R

1240 Loose sheet of an early draft (partly in code) inserted in the end of the exercise book. Dated Oct. 1911.
1f; ink, on a ruled sheet from an exercise book (BP.605(a); cat.1239). 20 x 16
BP.605(b)   T.26.R

1241 Rough drafts.
6ff; ink, with pencil corrections, on ruled exercise paper. 20 x 16.5
BP.605(c)   T.26.R

1242 Rough draft.
Inscribed (verso): And next season Timmy and Goody Tiptoes (line from MS of *The Tale of Timmy Tiptoes*).
See also BP.605(a); cat.1239.
1f; ink, on ruled exercise paper. 20 x 16
BP.605(d)   T.26.R

Kitty-in-Boots

1243 MS version of what was intended to be the 1914 book in the Peter Rabbit series (believed to be 2nd draft).
Inscribed (on cover): Four proofs in slip.
Assumed to be the MS from which the type was set (LL Cat.)
14ff. (2 blank); ink (one side of page only), in an exercise book with orange paper cover entitled: The St. Paul's Exercise Book. 20.5 x 16.5
BP.612   T.27.R

1244 Another draft (believed to be the first: LL Cat.).
Most of the pages are loose.
28ff. (14 blank); ink (one side of page only), with pencil corrections, in an exercise book with green paper cover entitled: The Monster Exercise Book.
20.5 x 16.5
BP.613   T.27.R

1245 Beginning of *Kitty-in-Boots* (untitled).
2ff. (1 blank); ink, on thin ruled paper. 25 x 19.5
BP.614   T.27.R

The Oakmen

1246 First page inscribed above text (in pencil): I have given P.p. [i.e. Prickle-pin] to the Oakmen, to have for a little dog. I hope they will be very kind to him, he was *such* a nice little animile – such a soft [waistcoat] under his prickles.
Text of *The Oakmen* copied by BP from Nancy [Hudson]'s copy (LL Cat.)
19ff; ink, in a green paper-covered sketch book with blank spaces to indicate the position of the illustrations; one pencil sketch. Loose insertions at back of book: 2ff. with very rough sketches of a man digging. 13 x 18
BP.606   T.27.L

Rhymes

1247 'I will go back to the hills again' (first line).
Written shortly before BP's death (LL Cat.)
1f; ink, on plain paper. 13 x 11.5
BP.623   T.28.R

1248 *The Tom-tit's Song*: eleven two-line verses.
Title on first page.
Verso inscribed with detailed comments by BP.
1f; ink. 20 x 16
BP.631(a)   T.28.R

1249 Early draft of *The Tom-tit's song* [sic].
Title on first page.
1f; draft, in ink, on ruled exercise paper. 13 x 16
BP.631(b)   T.28.R

1250 'The wanderings of a small black cat' (first line).
Inscribed: For Betty Harris in remembrance of a
perfect day. August 5th 1930.
1f; ink, on plain paper. W/m: Savernake
Superfine. 32 x 20.5
BP.728   T.39.L

1251 Verses headed by BP: either Over the Hills & Far
Away or "Butter-cup Land".
2ff; ink and pencil, on ruled exercise paper.
21 x 16.5
BP.630(a,b)   T.28.R

1252 Three verses beginning: 'Now happy be the
bridegroom'.
1f; pencil, on a ruled sheet of notepaper. 17.5 x 11
BP.632   T.28.R

Sister Anne

1253 75ff; printer's manuscript, in ink, on ruled block
paper; with corrections in pencil by the publisher.
22.5 x 17.5
BP.678   T.33.R

Cat.1254–1261: BP arranged the drafts into sets
secured by a paper clip. They are in the order in
which she left them (LL Cat.); several have pencil
corrections. No sheets for Chapter 7.

1254 Chapter 1: The Tale of the Second Cousin Mouse.
8ff; draft for Chapter 1 with a duplicate of p.3, in
ink, on ruled block paper. 22.5 x 17.5
BP.680(i)   T.34.L

1255 Chapter 2.
10ff; early draft, in ink, on ruled block paper.
22.5 x 17.5
BP.680(ii)   T.34.L

1256 Chapter 3.
13ff; early draft, in ink, on ruled block paper.
22.5 x 17.5
BP.680(iii)   T.34.L

1257 Chapter 4.
9ff; early draft, in ink, on ruled block paper.
22.5 x 17.5
BP.680(iv)   T.34.L

1258 Chapter 5.
12ff; early draft, in ink, on ruled block paper.
22.5 x 17.5
BP.680(v)   T.34.L

1259 Chapter 6.
3ff; ink, on ruled block paper. 22.5 x 17.5
BP.680(vi)   T.34.L

1260 Chapter 8.
6ff; early draft, in ink, on ruled block paper.
22.5 x 17.5
BP.680(vii)   T.34.L

1261 Chapter 9.
10ff; ink, on ruled block paper. 22.5 x 17.5
BP.680(viii)   T.34.L

Cat.1262–1274: BP assembled these drafts in sets.
They are not necessarily in page order (LL Cat.)

1262 Chapter 1, numbered 1 and 2.
7ff. and 2ff; two early drafts, in ink with pencil
corrections, on exercise paper. 20 x 16.5
BP.681(i,ii)   T.34.R

1263 Chapter 3, numbered 3.
13ff; early draft, in ink, on plain and ruled exercise
paper. 20 x 16.5
BP.681(iii)   T.34.R

1264 Chapter 4, numbered 4.
8ff; early draft, in ink, on ruled exercise paper.
22.5 x 17.5
BP.681(iv)   T.34.R

1265 Chapter 4, numbered 5.
5ff; early draft, in ink, on ruled exercise paper.
22.5 x 17.5
BP.681(v)   T.34.R

1266 Chapter 4, numbered 6.
4ff; early draft, in ink, on ruled exercise paper.
22.5 x 17.5
BP.681(vi)   T.34.R

1267 Chapter 5, numbered 7.
8ff; early draft, in ink, on ruled exercise paper.
22.5 x 17.5
BP.681(vii)   T.34.R

1268 Chapter 5, numbered 8.
2ff; early draft, in ink, with pencil corrections, on ruled exercise paper. 22.5 x 17.5
BP.681(viii)   T.34.R

1269 Chapter 9, numbered 9.
8ff; ink, with pencil corrections, on ruled exercise paper; also one thin sheet. 22.5 x 17.5
BP.681(ix)   T.34.R

1270 Early sheets, numbered 10–13.
12ff; early drafts, in ink, on ruled exercise paper. 22.5 x 17.5
BP.681(x–xiii)   T.34.R

1271 Early sheets, also notes on *The Fairy Caravan* characters, numbered 14.
13ff; early drafts, in ink, on ruled exercise paper. 22.5 x 17.5
BP.681(xiv)   T.34.R

1272 Early unsorted sheets, numbered 15.
10ff; early drafts, in ink. 20 x 14 etc.
BP.681(xv)   T.34.R

1273 Early sheets, numbered 16.
8ff; ink, on thin ruled exercise paper; also one plain sheet. 20 x 16.5
BP.681(xvi)   T.34.R

1274 Early sheets of Chapter 1, numbered 17 and 18.
12ff; one very rough early draft; also a more finished draft, in ink, fastened by paper clips. 25.5 x 20
BP.681(xvii,xviii)   T.34.R

The Sly Old Cat

1275 Folding panorama in wallet form with text (14ff.) and w/cs (14) mounted on alternate pages.
Title on inside front cover; blue cloth boards with silver clasp.
Dated (on last w/c): March 20th '06.
Presented to Nellie Warne and bound for her by Warne's (LL Cat.)
11.5 x 9.5 (folded)
BP.597   T.26.L   (*see* PLATE XLII)

1276 Rough sketch for the panorama, showing the cat pouring out tea for the rat, who is seated at the table.
Inscribed (verso): Sly Old Cat (LL).
Pencil, with some pen-and-ink. 15 x 12.5
BP.1092   P.C.50

Stories (short & fragmentary)

Carrier's Bob
1277 Title on first page.
See BP.714; cat.1278 for a later draft, and see also BP.710; cat.1233.
3ff; early draft, in ink, on foolscap paper. 32.5 x 20
BP.711   T.38.L

1278 Title on first page.
See BP.711; cat.1277 for earlier draft.
3ff; latest draft, in ink, on ruled foolscap paper. 32.5 x 20
BP.714   T.38.L

Elinor's Awmry
1279 Title on first page.
1909? (LL Cat.)
2ff; ink, on ruled exercise paper. 20 x 16
BP.719(c)   T.38.R

Flittermouse and Fluttermouse
1280 Title on first page.
2ff; ink and pencil, on ruled exercise paper. 20 x 16.5
BP.708   T.37.R

Llewellyn's Well
1281 Title on cover.
Inscribed (on cover): Llewellyn's Well. Made & part written at Gwaynynog, Denbigh.
In a brownish paper-covered exercise book.
Loosely inserted in the back are sheets of MS for another story about a 'wickid [sic] Princess' and a necklace.
16ff. (12 blank); ink. 20.5 x 16.5
BP.707(a)   T.37.R

1282 Title on first page.
6ff. (3 blank); earlier draft, in ink, with corrections (unfinished), in a mottled stiff-covered exercise book. 23 x 18
BP.707(b)   T.37.R

1283 Early drafts relating to *Llewellyn's Well*.
10ff; ink, on various types of ruled exercise or letter paper. 20 x 16 etc.
BP.707(c)   T.37.R

The Mole-catcher's Burying

1284 Early draft (untitled).
Inscribed (in pencil): Sunday 29 Oct. 11. Hill Top.
Later draft in *Red Riding Hood* Notebook (see
BP.617; cat.1235, and see also BP.710; cat.1233).
1f; ink, on ruled foolscap paper. 32.5 x 20
BP.712   T.38.L

Pace-eggers

1285 Title on first page.
5ff; final draft, in ink, on thin ruled exercise paper.
25 x 19.5
BP.713   T.38.L

The Solitary Mouse

1286 Contained within Grandmother Leech's copybook
of embroidery designs (see BP.667 etc.; cat.1104).
Title on first page.
Four and a half pages of introductory material
telling of country dancing and of the wild ponies
on Troutbeck Tongue, which gave her the first idea
of a Fairy Caravan (LL Cat.)
The story was sent to Mrs Bertha Mahony Miller
for possible use in the *Horn Book Magazine*.
15ff; introduction and story, in ink, on pages of the
copybook. 25 x 20
BP.667   T.32.L

Tale of Little Snow Drop

1287 Title on first page. Unfinished.
1f; pencil, on ruled exercise paper. 20 x 16
BP.716   T.38.R

Wag-by-Wa'

1288 *The Little Black Kettle.*
Inscribed: Wag by Wa' Nov 25 '09.
2ff; first draft of the story, in ink, on plain paper.
20.5 x 16.5
BP.684(a)   T.35.L

1289 *The Little Black Kettle.*
Title on first page.
2ff; an early draft, in ink, on plain paper.
20.5 x 16.5
BP.684(b)   T.35.L

1290 *Wag by the Wa'.*
Contained within Grandmother Leech's copybook
of embroidery designs (see BP.667 etc.; cat.1104).
8ff; *The Fairy Caravan* version of the story, in ink,
on pages of the copybook. 25 x 20
BP.667   T.32.L

1291 *Wag-by-Wa'.*
Title on first page.
Copy of MS, sent to Mrs Bertha Mahony Miller for
publication in the *Horn Book Magazine* (LL Cat.)
2ff; ink on folded ruled foolscap paper. 33 x 20
BP.682   T.35.L

1292 *Wag-by-the-Wall.*
Title on first page.
2ff; early draft with corrections, in ink, on plain
paper. 19 x 15.5
BP.683(a)   T.35.L

1293 *Wag-by-the-Wall.*
2ff; odd sheets of an early draft, in ink, on ruled
exercise paper. 20 x 16
BP.683(b)   T.35.L

1294 *Wag-by-the-Wall.*
1f; odd sheet of an early draft, in ink, in ruled
exercise book. 23 x 18
BP.683(c)   T.35.L

1295 *Wag-by-the-Wall.*
1f; odd sheet of an early draft, in ink, on a sheet
torn from a cash book with red margins. 22.5 x 18
BP.683(d)   T.35.L

Miscellaneous writings

1296 Essay concerning elderflowers.
Inscribed: Aug 28.
1f; ink, on ruled exercise paper. 20 x 16
BP.718   T.38.R

1297 When is a house unoccupied, & non rateable?
Possibly extract from *Irish Guardian* (LL Cat.)
1f; ink, on ruled exercise paper. 11.5 x 20.5
BP.719(b)   T.38.R

1298 Memories of Old Katie Macdonald (the first Mrs
Tiggy-Winkle).
1f; ink, on a fragment of *Yorkshire Post* newspaper
wrapper. 28.5 x 10
BP.720(a)   T.38.R

1299 Another memorandum on fragment of *Yorkshire
Post* wrapper, possibly concerning farming matters.
1f; ink. 17 x 13.5
BP.720(b)   T.38.R

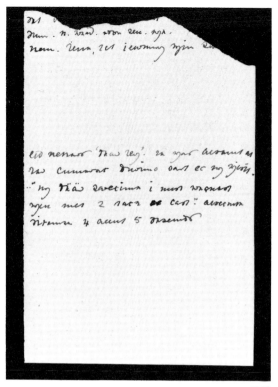

1300

1300 Notes including the verse: 'Cecily Parsley lived in a pen' etc. and 'My dear Caroline I must request you not to talk so fast'.
Code writing of the period 1884–1886 (LL Cat.)
See p.315 of *Journal*.
1f; closely written in ink, on plain paper.
16.5 x 5.5
BP.721   T.38.R

1301 Peermingle. The beginning of a story of a cockleshell fairy.
See *Red Riding Hood* Notebook for the final version (BP.617; cat.1235).
Code writing.
1f; ink, on ruled exercise paper. 20 x 16.5
BP.722   T.38.R

1302 Notes about local people, and concerning Jonathon.
Inscribed: Oct 9. 24.
3ff; ink, on various kinds of ruled paper.
19.5 x 18 etc.
BP.723(a,b)   T.38.R

1303 Miscellaneous information concerning ants (the Pisamours): material for *Grasshopper Belle and Susan Emmet*.
1f; ink, on ruled exercise paper. 20.5 x 16
BP.725   T.38.R

1304 Of timber (newspaper article: LL Cat.).
Title on first page.
Inscribed: Copy.
2ff; later draft, in ink, on ruled exercise paper.
22.5 x 17.5
BP.729(a)   T.39.L

1305 Of timber.
1f; early incomplete draft, in ink, on ruled exercise paper. 22.5 x 17.5
BP.729(b)   T.39.L

1306 Hedgehogs (letter sent to *The Field*: see *Hist.*).
Title on first page.
2ff; later draft, in ink, on ruled exercise paper.
20.5 x 16.5
BP.730(a)   T.39.L

1307 Hedgehogs (letter sent to *The Field*: see *Hist.*).
2ff; early draft, in ink and pencil, on ruled exercise paper. 20.5 x 16.5
BP.730(b)   T.39.L

1308 Wasted land.
Title on first page.
2ff; ink, on ruled exercise paper. 22.5 x 17.5
BP.731   T.39.L

1309 Notes on Crompton family history, copied from Baines' *History of Lancashire*. Concerning the history of Abraham Crompton and Chorley Hall; also notes concerning the Hayhursts: information supplied by Edith Gaddum, Feb 18th '22.
2ff; ink, on ruled foolscap paper. 32.5 x 20.5
BP.732   T.39.L

1310 Copy by BP of J[ohn] Crompton's account of an execution on Tower Hill, 1715.
Inscribed (on first page): London Feb 25.1715; and (on f.3, in pencil): on two pages, mended, carefully. [Very] good clear round hand.
3ff; ink, on ruled exercise paper. 25 x 20
BP.733   T.39.L

1311 Sheet of proposed amendments for the *Sequel to The Fairy Caravan*, sent to Bertha Mahony Miller (BP's copy), together with sheet of amendments to introduction of BP's article.
2ff; ink. 26.5 x 21; 25.5 x 20
BP.723(c)   T.38.R

MANUSCRIPTS:
Correspondence

Personal correspondence

Family

1312 Two unused sheets. Headed: 2, Bolton Gardens, South Kensington. S.W.
Envelope with Potter crest.
15 x 10; 8 x 11
BP.800   T.42.R

1313 Postcard to [unknown] from Bertram Potter. Headed: Eiffel Tower. 6 Sep 1889. Concerning the Eiffel Tower.
The postcard is in an envelope of Bertram Potter's early drawings.
9 x 14
BP.788(vii)   T.42.L

1314 Ashton, T. to Rupert Potter. Concerning his mother's death. 12 Sep 1891. Prestbury Hall. Inscribed (verso) by BP: Condolences on my grandmother's death [Grandmother Potter].
2ff. 17.5 x 11
BP.796   T.42.R

1315 Gaskell, W. to BP. 19 Dec 1874. Plymouth Grove. Thanking BP for a comforter.
2ff; with envelope. 18 x 11.5
BP.798(i)   T.42.R

1316 Gaskell, W. to BP. No date. Inscribed (on separate sheet): Honey-bee to Honey-bee.
2ff; greetings card with coloured illustration.
17.5 x 11
BP.798(ii)   T.42.R

1317 Gaskell, W. to BP. 23 Aug 1877. Talladh-a-Cheithe. Concerning a holiday in Scotland.
2ff. 17.5 x 11
BP.798(iii)   T.42.R

1318 Gladstone, W.E. to Thomas B. Potter. 24 Jul 1865. Hawarden. Thanking TP for his congratulations. In connection with an election?
1f. 18 x 11
BP.739(i)   T.39.R

1315

1319 Gladstone, W.E. to Thomas B. Potter. 27 Mar 1866. 11 Carlton House Terrace. Thanking him for a letter and regretting that he cannot go to Liverpool.
2ff. (1 blank) 18 x 12
BP.739(ii)   T.39.R

1320 Gladstone, W.E. to Thomas B. Potter. 21 Jun 1866. 11 Carlton House Terrace. Concerning political matters.
1f. 19 x 12
BP.739(iii)   T.39.R

1321 Gladstone, W.E. to Thomas B. Potter. 22 Feb 1867. 11 Carlton House Terrace. Declining an invitation to join the Cobden Club.
1f. 18 x 11
BP.739(iv)   T.39.R

1322 Gladstone, W.E. to Thomas B. Potter. 26 Sep 1867. Hawarden. Declining hospitality, also an apology for being unable to help Lancaster institutions.
2ff. 17.5 x 11
BP.739(v)   T.39.R

1323 Gladstone, W.E. to Thomas B. Potter. 27 Oct 1867. Hawarden. Concerning Parliamentary matters.
2ff. 17.5 x 11
BP.739(vi)   T.39.R

1324 Gladstone, W.E. to Thomas B. Potter. 1 Apr 1868. 11 Carlton House Terrace. Concerning a motto for the Cobden Club.
2ff. 13 x 8.5
BP.739(vii)   T.39.R

1325 Gladstone, W.E. to Thomas B. Potter. 28 Dec 1868. 10 Downing Street. Concerning election matters and the vote.
2ff. 9 x 11.5
BP.739(viii)   T.39.R

1326 Gladstone, W.E. to Thomas B. Potter. 22 Jan 1869. Hawarden. Concerning voting by ballot at Manchester.
1f. 18.5 x 12
BP.739(ix)   T.39.R

1327 Gladstone, W.E. to Thomas B. Potter. 27 Jan 1869. 10 Downing Street. Concerning 'freedom of the vote'.
2ff. 18.5 x 12
BP.739(x)   T.39.R

1328 Gladstone, W.E. to Thomas B. Potter. 25 Mar 1869. 11 Carlton House Terrace. Thanking TP for his congratulations.
2ff. (1 blank); with envelope. 19 x 12
BP.739(xii)   T.39.R

1329 Gladstone, W.E. to Thomas B. Potter. 28 Apr 1869. 11 Carlton House Terrace. Concerning Club matters in relation to the French Government.
2ff. 18 x 12
BP.739(xiii)   T.39.R

1330 Gladstone, W.E. to Thomas B. Potter. 10 Jun 1869. 11 Carlton House Terrace. Declining an invitation to the Club.
2ff. 18.5 x 12
BP.739(xiv)   T.39.R

1331 Gladstone, W.E. to Thomas B. Potter. 21 Jan 1870. 10 Downing Street. Concerning a meeting of Parliament.
1f; with envelope. 23 x 18
BP.739(xvi)   T.39.R

1332 Gladstone, W.E. to Thomas B. Potter. 20 Apr 1871. 11 Carlton House Terrace. Declining Mr Potter's request as he is on vacation.
2ff. 18 x 11.5
BP.739(xvii)   T.39.R

1333 Gladstone, W.E. to Thomas B. Potter. 3 Nov 1872. Hawarden. Concerning the 'Italian cause' and other political matters.
2ff. 18 x 11
BP.739(xviii)   T.39.R

1334 Gladstone, W.E to Thomas B. Potter. 2 Dec 1872. 10 Downing Street. Thanking him for a letter.
2ff; with black border. 18.5 x 12
BP.739(xix)   T.39.R

1335 Gladstone, W.E. to Thomas B. Potter. 6 Aug 1874. 21 Carlton House Terrace. Concerning a possible meeting of radicals.
2ff; with envelope, all with black border.
11.5 x 17.5
BP.739(xx)   T.39.R

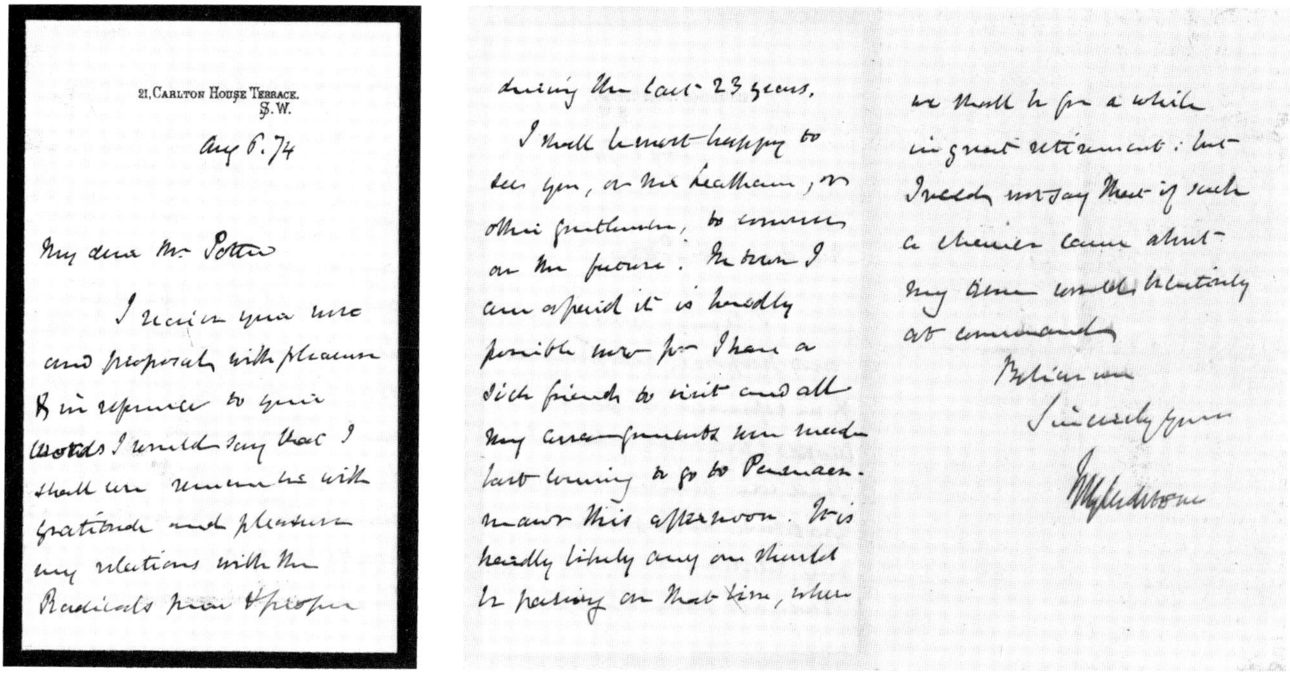
21, Carlton House Terrace.
S.W.
Aug 6. 74

My dear Mr Potter

I receive your kind proposal with pleasure & in response to your words I would say that I shall ever remember with gratitude and pleasure my relations with the Radicals [illegible] during the last 23 years.

I shall be most happy to see you, or Mr Leatham, or other gentlemen, to converse on the future. But I am afraid it is hardly possible now for I have a sick friend to visit and all my arrangements were made last evening to go to Penmaenmawr this afternoon. It is hardly likely any one should be passing on that line, where we shall be for a while in great retirement: but I need not say that if such a chance came about my time would be entirely at command.

Believe me
Sincerely yours
W E Gladstone

1335

1336 Gladstone, W.E. to Thomas B. Potter. 28 Aug 1874. Hawarden. Thanking him for a letter.
2ff. (1 blank); with black border. 18 x 11.5
BP. 739(xxi) T. 39. R

1337 Gladstone, W.E. to Thomas B. Potter. 15 Oct 1874. Hawarden. Concerning political matters including the Suez Canal.
2ff; with black border. 18.5 x 12
BP. 739(xxii) T. 39. R

1338 Gladstone, W.E. to Thomas B. Potter. 2 Dec 1874. Hawarden. Concerning the Catholic questions.
2ff; with black border. 18.5 x 12
BP. 739(xxiii) T. 39. R

1339 Gladstone, W.E. to Thomas B. Potter. 18 Oct 1875. Hawarden. Concerning religious matters.
2ff; with black border. 10.5 x 15
BP. 739(xxiv) T. 39. R

1340 Gladstone, W.E. to Thomas B. Potter. 28 Dec 1875. Hawarden. Concerning the Liberal Party.
2ff; with black border. 18.5 x 12
BP. 739(xxv) T. 39. R

1341 Gladstone, W.E. to Thomas B. Potter. 3 Jan 1876. Hawarden. Concerning Parliamentary matters.
2ff; with black border. 18.5 x 12
BP. 739(xxvi) T. 39. R

1342 Gladstone, W.E. to Thomas B. Potter. 4 Feb 1876. 4 Carlton Gardens. Concerning political matters, including a mention of the Suez Canal.
2ff; with black border. 11.5 x 18.5
BP. 739(xxvii) T. 39. R

1343 Gladstone, W.E. to Thomas B. Potter. 25 Aug 1876. Hawarden. Concerning political matters, including the Eastern Question.
2ff. 18 x 11
BP. 739(xxviii) T. 39. R

1344 Gladstone, W.E. to Thomas B. Potter. 11 Nov 1876. Concerning Egypt and other political matters.
2ff. 17.5 x 11
BP. 739(xxix) T. 39. R

1345 Gladstone, W.E. to Thomas B. Potter. 16 Jan 1877. Concerning the Cobden dinner.
2ff. 17.5 x 11
BP. 739(xxx) T. 39. R

1346 Gladstone, W.E. to Thomas B. Potter. 16 Nov 1877. Hawarden. Concerning political matters.
2ff. 18.5 x 11.5
BP. 739(xxxi) T. 39. R

1347 Gladstone, W.E. to Thomas B. Potter. 21 Nov 1877. Killruddery, Bray. Comments on Disraeli.
2ff. 17.5 x 11
BP. 739(xxxii) T. 39. R

1348 Gladstone, W.E. to Thomas B. Potter. 3 Dec
1877. Hawarden. A denial of rumours.
2ff. 11.5 x 9
BP.739(xxxiii)   T.39.R

1349 Gladstone, W.E. to Thomas B. Potter. 1 Aug
1886. 21 Carlton House Terrace. Concerning
political matters.
2ff. 17.5 x 11
BP.739(xxxiv)   T.39.R

1350 Gladstone, W.E. to Thomas B. Potter. 24 Apr
1888. House of Commons. Concerning a possible
attack on Mr Potter.
2ff; with envelope. 12 x 18.5
BP.739(xxxv)   T.39.R

1351 Gladstone, W.H. to Thomas B. Potter. 19 Mar
1869. 10 Downing Street. Thanking TP on his
father's behalf for a volume of Cobden's works.
1f. 18 x 11.5
BP.739(xi)   T.39.R

1352 Gladstone, W.H. to Thomas B. Potter. 23 Nov
1869. Hawarden. Thanking TP on his father's
behalf.
2ff. 18 x 12
BP.739(xv)   T.39.R

1353 Potter, J. to Rupert Potter. 10 Oct 1874. Camfield.
Concerning a visit from Mr Bright, and other
family matters.
2ff; with envelope. 17 x 11
BP.797   T.42.R

1354 Potter, H.B. to Rupert Potter. Also on same sheet,
Rupert Potter to HBP. No year given, but probably
before 1875. Concerning her cold.
1f. 17.5 x 11.5
BP.794(i)   T.42.R

1355 Potter, H.B. to Rupert Potter. 3 Apr 1883.
10 Larkstone Road, Ilfracombe. Mainly concerning
scenes at Watermouth Harbour.
Inscribed (on envelope): Worth keeping.
An early impression leading to Pig Robinson.
1f. 18 x 11
BP.794(ii)   T.42.R

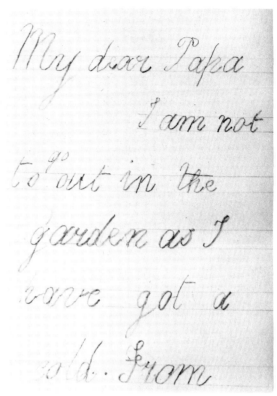

1354 (*page*)

1356 Potter, R. to HBP. 2 Mar 1874. Dalguise.
Concerning his stay at Dalguise.
1f. 18 x 11.5
BP.793(i)   T.42.R

1357 Potter, R. to HBP. 1874. Dalguise.
With illustrations of a dog ('Sandy').
2ff. 18 x 11.5
BP.793(ii)   T.42.R

1358 Potter, R. to Edmund Potter. 22 Sep 1846.
Concerning a holiday in Cumberland.
Includes a postmark, stamps and two wax seals.
2ff. 22.5 x 18.5
BP.793(iii)   T.42.R

1359 Potter, W.B. to HBP. 12 Oct. No year given.
Concerning animals, including the stuffing of one
of their bats.
2ff. 16 x 19.5
BP.795   T.42.R

far along the ground as possible, in a given number of strokes. Mr Hollins has joined. I should advise you to boil that dog's skull in soda if you can get a pan. Mrs Hollins gave me a very fine crysalis which one of the servants had found, on the Downs. I think it is a Privet Hawk from the curious nose it has. I don't think it is quite so big as the one we had last year. I will send it by post if you think it would be safer at home. I have no more time to write now, & nothing more I think to say.

I remain your affectionate brother
WB Potter

The Grange
Oct 12th

Dear B.

I have just received your letter. I suppose from what you say you will have to let lose the long-eared bats, as they will not eat meat. It is a great pity they are not easier to feed. As for the other, I think it would be almost wrong to let it go, as we might never catch another of that kind again. If he cannot be kept alive as I suppose he can't, you had better kill him, & stuff him as well as you can. Be also sure to take his measurements most carefully

before you stuff him. That is, the length of head, body, tail, Humerus, Radius Femoris, Tibia, pollex & claw, & also the fingers; & in other words all the bones of its wings & legs. I do not know what you had better do to keep the wings stretched out, perhaps if you pinned them out like the bat you got at Edinburgh, but take care if you do so to put some cotton wool behind its back so that it will not be flat. I should not do so much at its head, as it can't smell much. I am glad to hear that the heron is no worse than it was, perhaps it can be improved. Is it not very late for swallows? I saw some on Sunday. I am sorry to hear of Adolphus' illness. It has gone very

cold here, but today it is very bright & fine. There was a little snow this morning about half past six. I am afraid nearly all the chance of my procuring a snake is gone, it is too cold for them. It gets dark so soon now, that it is not worth my while to go out walking on a half holiday. as unless you go a long way the country about here is rather dull, now that the summer is over. They have got up a Golf Club here, & play on the links, near Compton Place. It is seems a rather slow game, & is played with a wooden stick, & an india rubber ball. Each player has a ball & about half a dozen sticks, & the object of the game seems to be to hit the ball as

1359

157

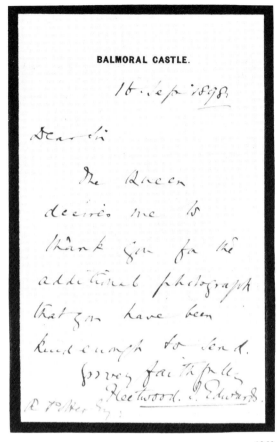

BALMORAL CASTLE.

16 Sep 1898

Dear Sir

The Queen desires me to thank you for the additional photograph that you have been kind enough to send.

Yours faithfully,
Fleetwood. J. Edwards.

R. Potter Esq.

1360

1360 Victoria, Queen of Great Britain and Ireland, to Rupert Potter. 16 Sep 1898. Balmoral Castle. Acknowledgement by the Queen's secretary of an additional photograph sent by RP to the Queen. (LL Cat.): Photograph of one of the Queen's grandchildren taken in Millais' studio – believed to be the 1882 portrait of Princess Marie of Edinburgh which Millais painted for the Queen.
2ff. (1 blank); with black border, and envelope.
18 x 12
BP.799   T.42.R

Friends

1361 Potter, H.B. to Delmar Banner. 8 Sep 1936. Castle Cottage. Concerning the settlement of Esthwaite Hall Estate.
1f. 23 x 17.5
BP.805(i)   T.3

1362 Potter, H.B. to Delmar Banner. 14 Sep 1936. Castle Cottage. Concerning the purchase of property.
3ff. 22.5 x 17.5
BP.805(ii)   T.3

1363 Potter, H.B. to Delmar Banner. 23 Sep 1936. Castle Cottage. Suggesting that the Banners buy a cottage called 'The Brow'.
1f. 22.5 x 17.5
BP.805(iii)   T.3

1364 Potter, H.B. to Delmar Banner. 28 Sep 1936. Castle Cottage. Further concerning the purchase of the cottage.
1f. 22.5 x 17.5
BP.805(iv)   T.3

1365 Potter, H.B. to [Delmar] Banner. 4 Oct 1936. Castle Cottage. Further concerning available property for purchase.
1f. 17.5 x 11
BP.805(v)   T.3

1366 Potter, H.B. to Delmar Banner. 11 Oct 1936. Castle Cottage. Asking Mr Banner to lunch.
1f. 17.5 x 11
BP.805(vi)   T.3

1367 Potter, H.B. to Delmar Banner. 13 Oct 1936. Castle Cottage. Informing Mr Banner that 'The Brow' is no longer available.
1f. 17.5 x 11
BP.805(vii)   T.3

1368 Potter, H.B. to Delmar Banner. 18 Oct 1936. Castle Cottage. Further concerning the selling of 'The Brow'.
1f. 17.5 x 11
BP.805(viii)   T.3

1369 Potter, H.B. to Delmar Banner. 23 Oct 1936. Castle Cottage. Concerning the selling of Mr Banner's house, with a request to return a BP sketch.
1f. 17.5 x 11
BP.805(ix)   T.3

1370 Potter, H.B. to Delmar and Josephine Banner. 1 Dec 1936. Castle Cottage. Concerning the woodcuts of Josephine 'Pigwig' Banner and the sale of Esthwaite Hall.
2ff. 17.5 x 11
BP.805(x)   T.3

1371 Potter, H.B. to Delmar and Josephine Banner. 2 Sep 1937. Castle Cottage. Concerning village matters.
2ff. 17.5 x 11
BP.805(xi)   T.3

1372 Potter, H.B. to Delmar Banner. 7 Oct 1937. Castle Cottage. Concerning the purchase of a painting, with notes on trees.
2ff. 17.5 x 11
BP.805(xii)   T.3

1373 Potter, H.B. to Delmar and Josephine Banner. 17 Dec 1937. Castle Cottage. Concerning the snow.
2ff. 17.5 x 11
BP.805(xiii)   T.3

1374 Potter, H.B. to Elizabeth Booth. 12 Jun 1943. Castle Cottage. Concerning her Peter Rabbit Books, particularly *The Tailor of Gloucester*.
2ff; Xerox copy with envelope. 27.5 x 21.5; 21 x 16 (size of letter)
BP.820   T.4

1375 Potter, H.B. to Benita Gaddum. 22 Oct 1930. Sawrey. Concerning a Nursing Trust.
2ff. 22.5 x 17
BP.807(i)   T.3

1376 Potter, H.B. to Benita Gaddum. 7 Nov 1930. Sawrey. Further concerning a Nursing Trust.
1f. 22.5 x 17
BP.807(ii)   T.3

1377 Potter, H.B. to Benita Gaddum. 29 Nov 1930. Sawrey. Further concerning a Nursing Trust.
1f. 22.5 x 17
BP.807(iii)   T.3

1378 Potter, H.B. to Josephine Banner. 28 Jan 1938. Castle Cottage. Concerning the *Music Book*, and an explanation of the method of reproduction used for her drawings.
1f. 25 x 20
BP.805(xv)   T.3

1379 Potter, H.B. to Josephine Banner. 28 Feb 1938. Castle Cottage. Further concerning the *Music Book*.
1f. 25 x 20
BP.805(xiv)   T.3

1380 Potter, H.B. to Josephine Banner. 26 Jun 1939. Castle Cottage. Concerning her own and Mrs Banner's illnesses.
1f. 17.5 x 11.5
BP.805(xvi)   T.3

1381 Potter, H.B. to Josephine Banner. 7 Mar 1943. Castle Cottage. Concerning country matters: plants and animals around Sawrey.
2ff. 17 x 24.5 (folded)
BP.805(xvii)   T.3

1382 Potter, H.B. to [Josephine Banner]. No date. Note and newscutting (1938?) with separate rough sketch: caricatured self-portrait.
Inscribed: HBH a portrait hows that??! Motto 'Keep smiling'.
Note is written on back of ICAA Christmas card insert.
2ff. (and newscutting) 12.5 x 10; 7 x 11
BP.806   T.3

1383 Potter, H.B. to [Josephine Banner] (fragment). No date. Concerning the spoiling of Coniston Valley. Attributed by LL.
2ff. 17.5 x 11
BP.805(xviii)   T.3

1384 Potter, H.B. to Mrs Hall. 11 Aug 1942. Castle Cottage. Expressing disapproval of goat keeping.
2ff. 17 x 22
BP.807(iv)   T.3

1385 Potter, H.B. to Margaret Hammond. 1 Apr 1922. Sawrey. Concerning the renting of Castle Cottage to Miss Hammond and Miss Mills.
1f. 25 x 20
BP.803(ii)   T.3

1386 Potter, H.B. to Margaret Hammond. 19 Apr 1922. Sawrey. Further details concerning the renting of Castle Cottage.
1f. 17.5 x 22
BP.803(i)   T.3

1387 Potter, H.B. to Margaret Hammond. 18 Jul 1924. Sawrey. Mainly concerning the garden at Sawrey.
1f. 23.5 x 18
BP.803(iii)   T.3

1388 Potter, H.B. to Margaret Hammond. 22 Jun 1929. Castle Cottage. Concerning Castle Cottage, Sawrey.
2ff. 17.5 x 11.5
BP.803(iv)   T.3

1389 Potter, H.B. to Cecily Mills. 8 Jul 1933. Instructions as to the keeping of a turkey.
2ff; with black border. 15 x 10
BP.803(v)   T.3

1390 Potter, H.B. to Margaret Hammond. 15 Oct 1936. Castle Cottage. Concerning the weather and farming matters.
1f. 17.5 x 11
BP.803(vi)   T.3

1391 Potter, H.B. to Margaret Hammond and Cecily Mills. 30 Sep 1936. Sawrey. Concerning village matters; also rough sketches of dog and hen.
2ff. 11 x 5
BP.803(vii)   T.3

1392 Potter, H.B. to Margaret Hammond. 7 Nov 1938. Higher Babington, Wirral. Mainly concerning a stay in hospital.
1f. 17.5 x 11
BP.803(viii)   T.3

1393 Potter, H.B. to Margaret Hammond. No date. Concerning the elderflower's medicinal properties.
1f. 22.5 x 17.5
BP.803(ix)   T.3

1394 Potter, H.B. to Margaret Hammond. No date. Tower Hotel, Hawick. Concerning a holiday in the Cheviots.
1f. 13 x 20.5
BP.803(x)   T.3

1395 Potter, H.B. to Cecily Mills. No date. Informing Miss Mills that letters will be left with her while BP is on holiday.
1f. 17.5 x 11
BP.803(xi)   T.3

1396 Potter, H.B. to Cecily Mills. No date. Concerning BP's illness.
1f; torn from exercise book. 8 x 17
BP.803(xii)   T.3

1397 Potter, H.B. to Cecily Mills. No date. Castle Cottage. Mainly concerning a Post Office sale.
1f. 25 x 20
BP.803(xiii)   T.3

1398 Potter, H.B. to [Margaret Hammond and Cecily Mills]. 22 Nov 1929. Sketch of 'Kiltie' (MH and CM's dog), with a note about his identity. Believed to have been inserted in Miss Hammond's copy of the privately printed version of *The Fairy Caravan*, 1929. Kiltie was called 'Sandy' in *The Fairy Caravan* (LL Cat.)
2ff; headed with pen-and-ink sketch. 15 x 10
BP.804   T.3

1399 Potter, H.B. to Margaret Hammond and Cecily Mills. 30 Mar 1939. Liverpool Hospital. Concerning BP's failing health and instructions as to the placing of her belongings should she not recover.
1f; pencil. 22.5 x 17
BP.803(xv)   T.3

1400 Potter, H.B. to Margaret Hammond. 12 Jul 1939. Liverpool Hospital. Concerning her stay in hospital.
1f. 17.5 x 11
BP.803(xiv)   T.3

1401 Potter, H.B. to Margaret Hammond. No date. Liverpool Hospital. Concerning BP's illness.
1f; pencil. 17.5 x 11
BP.803(xvi)   T.3

1402 Potter, H.B. to Margaret Hammond. No date. Liverpool Hospital. Concerning her stay in hospital.
1f; pencil. 17.5 x 11
BP.803(xvii)   T.3

1403 Potter, H.B. to Margaret Hammond. No date. Liverpool Hospital. Concerning BP's stay in hospital.
Verso: Note written by Nurse Edwards.
2ff; pencil. 25 x 20
BP.803(xviii)   T.3

1404 Potter, H.B. to Dr Henderson. 10 Feb 1931. Sawrey. Concerning the Nursing Association.
1f; typed copy. 26 x 21
BP.810(i)   T.3

1405 Henderson, Dr to Benita Gaddum. 11 Feb 1931. Kendal. Further concerning the Nursing Association.
With Dr Henderson's letter is enclosed the typed copy of BP's letter (BP.810(i); cat.1404).
1f. 26 x 20.5
BP.810(ii)   T.3

1406 Potter, H.B. to Margaret Hough. 4 Nov 1913. Sawrey. Concerning *The Tale of Pigling Bland* (which BP sent to Margaret Hough with the letter).
2ff. 17.5 x 11
BP.818(i)   T.4

1407 Potter, H.B. to Margaret Hough. 30 Dec 1924. Sawrey. Concerning the wet summer etc.; also a mention of the forthcoming *Jemima Puddle-Duck* painting book.
2ff. 16.5 x 12.5
BP.818(ii)   T.4

1408 Potter, H.B. to Miss Jump. 24 Feb 1920. Sawrey. BP's reasons for giving up illustrating (Miss Jump had sent her verses to illustrate).
2ff. 17.5 x 11
BP.814   T.4

1408a Potter, H.B. to Mr Macdonald. 2 Oct 1940. Sawrey. Concerning rent and Bridge End.
1f; Xerox copy. 19 x 14.5
BP.1572   T.3

1408b Potter, H.B. to Mrs Macdonald. 26 Jun 1942. Castle Cottage. Concerning a leaking roof etc.
1f; Xerox copy. 19.5 x 12; 17.5 x 11 (size of letter)
BP.1573   T.3

1409 Potter, H.B. to Bertha Maloney [i.e. Mahony]. 20 May 1927. Sawrey. Rough draft of a letter concerning BP's intention to sell drawings in order to help the National Trust to buy land.
1f; with pen-and-ink sketch of Peter Rabbit.
20 x 16
BP.815   T.4

1410 Potter, H.B. to Annie Moore. 26 Nov 191[8]. Sawrey. Concerning BP's state of health and social matters.
2ff; Xerox copy. 21 x 16.5; 17.5 x 11.5 (size of letter)
BP.1491   T.8

1411 Potter, H.B. to Mrs Louise Warne. 26 Sep 1905. 8 Bedford Square. Concerning Norman Warne's tombstone, the Warne family's generosity to her, and her intention to write to Winifred: 'It is so much more satisfactory to address a real live child – secret of the success of Peter Rabbit'.
2ff; with black border. 15 x 10
BP.811   T.4   (*illustration overleaf*)

1412 Potter, H.B. to Miss West. 24 May 1943. Castle Cottage. Thanking her for the posy.
1f. 17.5 x 11
BP.816   T.4

1413 Potter, H.B. to Mrs Wicksteed. 17 Jan 1902. Bolton Gardens. Concerning *The Tailor of Gloucester* and details of BP's progress with *The Tale of Squirrel Nutkin*.
(LL Cat.): Letter sent with a copy of the privately printed *Tailor of Gloucester*.
2ff. 15 x 9.5
BP.812   T.4

1414 Potter, H.B. to George Wilson. 12 Sep 1935. Postcard concerning trees and farm repair work.
9 x 14
BP.808(iv)   T.3

1415 Potter, H.B. to George Wilson. 10 Feb 1941. Sawrey. Postcard concerning the felling of trees.
9 x 14
BP.808(i)   T.3

1416 Potter, H.B. to George Wilson. 13 Jul 1941. Sawrey. Concerning farm matters.
1f. 22.5 x 14
BP.808(v)   T.3

1417 Potter, H.B. to George Wilson. 3 Oct 1941. Sawrey. Further concerning farming matters.
1f. 20 x 16
BP.808(vi)   T.3

1418 Potter, H.B. to George Wilson. 16 Oct 1941. Sawrey. Further concerning farming matters.
1f. 20 x 16
BP.808(vii)   T.3

1419 Potter, H.B. to George Wilson. 28 Oct 1942. Sawrey. Postcard concerning the dangerous state of the cottage porch.
9 x 14
BP.808(ii)   T.3

8 Bedford Square
Sept 26ᵗʰ 05.

Dear Mrs Warne,

Thank you so much for the sweet photograph of Winifred and her little sister. I should have liked it and admired it even if they had been strangers, but I have heard Norman talk so often about the children that they seem like little friends.

I am going back to north Wales tomorrow, and afterwards to the Lakes for sketching, which has got sadly neglected this summer — I hope there is a chance of a fine October after so much damp weather.

I expect I shall get back to London about the end of October, I will write to you as soon as I get back and ask when I may come over to lunch. I cannot tell you how grateful I have felt for the kindness of all of you; it has been a real comfort & pleasure to stay in this house —

I shall be amused to introduce "Mrs Tiggy" to Winifred; Louie has seen her here, she didn't make much remark at the time, but seems to have had plenty to say about it when she got home.

I hope I shall write Winifred lots of letters, it is much more satisfactory to address a real live child; I often think that that was the secret of the success of Peter Rabbit, it was written to a child — not made to order —

Millie & I went up to Highgate yesterday, the stone is put back quite neatly again; it seems to want something planting at the back, there is much untidy trampled earth where the hawthorn was cut down. I don't believe grass will ever grow well under the fir tree, I was wondering whether white Japanese anemonies would grow there it is rather shaded, Millie says you have them in your garden & know their habits.

I think I never saw a better photograph of a baby, it is a delightfully pretty group. I remain yrs sincerely

Beatrix Potter.

1411 (to Mrs Warne)

1420 Potter, H.B. to George Wilson. 15 Dec 1942. [Sawrey.] Postcard concerning farming matters and trees.
9 x 14
BP.808(iii)   T.3

1421 Potter, H.B. to George Wilson. 12 Oct 1943. Sawrey. Further concerning farming matters.
1f. 18.5 x 16
BP.808(viii)   T.3

1422 Potter, H.B. to George Wilson. 13 Oct 1943. Sawrey. Concerning farming matters.
1f. 18 x 11
BP.808(ix)   T.3

1423 Potter, H.B. to George Wilson. 24 Jan. No year given. Sawrey. Further concerning farming matters.
1f. 19 x 15.5
BP.808(x)   T.3

1424 Potter, H.B. from William Wood. 31 Oct 1930. Hawick. Application for a 'double-shepherd's place' on one of BP's farms.
1f. 22.5 x 17.5
BP.819   T.4

1425 Potter, H.B. to Miss Gertrude Woodward. 24 Sep 1913. Bolton Gardens ('in train'). Concerning servants and other family matters.
1f; file copy; pencil. 21 x 14
BP.813   T.4

1426 Potter, H.B. to Barbara [no surname given]. 13 Dec 1911. Hill Top Farm. Sending her a copy of *The Tale of Timmy Tiptoes*; also concerning an early flying machine trial on Windermere.
2ff. 15 x 10
BP.817   T.4

1427 Potter, H.B. to an unknown correspondent. 27 Dec 1939. Castle Cottage. Information concerning her books.
Letter mounted with typed copy in red booklet containing answers to a questionnaire (see BP.834(a); cat.1925).
3ff. 17.5 x 11.5
BP.834(b)   T.7

1428 Potter, H.B. to an unknown correspondent. 3 Dec 1896. 2 Bolton Gardens. Concerning Sir H. Roscoe's request for the correspondent to examine BP's fungus drawings.
2ff; Xerox copy. 32.5 x 21.5; 15 x 19.5 (size of letter)
BP.821(xiii)   T.5

Miniature letters

For transcripts, see *Hist.*

1429 Original text written out by BP, 1907–12(?). BP made drafts of her miniature letters so that she might refer to them when sending fresh letters to the children. The wording is sometimes slightly different in the letters (LL Cat.)

Page 1
1 Text of letter from Ribby to Tabitha Twitchit.
2 Text of letter from Tabitha Twitchit to Cousin Ribby.
See letter BP.578(12); cat.1448.
3 Text of letter from Ribby to Duchess.
See letter BP.578(13); cat.1449.
4 Text of letter from Duchess to Ribby.
5 Text of letter from Squirrel Nutkin to Mr Old Brown, Owl Island.
See letter BP.578(3); cat.1439.
6 Text of letter from Squirrel Nutkin to Mr Brown Esq, Owl Island.
See letter BP.578(4); cat.1440.
7 Text of letter from Squirrel Nutkin to Mr O. Brown Esq, Owl Island.
See letter BP.578(2); cat.1438.

Page 2
8 Text of letter from Squirrel Nutkin to The Right Honourable Old Brown Esq, Owl Island.
9 Text of letter from Twinkleberry Squirrel to O. Brown Esq, M.P., Owl Island.
See letter BP.578(1); cat.1437.
10 Text of letter from Squirrel Nutkin to Dr Maggotty, The Dispensary.
11 Text of letter from Matthew Maggotty, M.D. to Squirrel Nutkin Esq, Derwent Bay Wood.
12 Text of letter from Squirrel Nutkin to Dr Maggotty Esq, M.D., The Dispensary.
13 Text of letter from M. Maggotty, M.D. to Squirrel Nutkin Esq, Derwent Bay Wood.
14 Text of letter from Squirrel Nutkin to Dr Maggotty.

Page 3

15 Text of letter from Miss Lucinda Doll to Mrs Tom Thumb, Mouse Hole.

16 Text of letter from Hunca Munca to Miss Lucinda Doll, Doll's House.
See letter BP.578(7); cat.1443.

17 Text of letter from Peter Rabbit to Mr McGregor, Gardener's Cottage.

18 Text of letter from [Mrs] Jane McGregor to Master Peter Rabbit, Under Fir tree.

19 Text of invitation from Mr Alderman Ptolemy Tortoise to Mr Jeremy Fisher.

20 Text of invitation from Mr Alderman Ptolemy Tortoise to Sir Isaac Newton, The Well House.
See letter BP.578(10); cat.1446.

21 Text of letter from Mr Jeremy Fisher to Mr Alderman Ptolemy Tortoise, Melon Pit.

22 Text of acceptance from I. Newton to Alderman P. Tortoise, Melon Pit, South Border.
See letter BP.578(11); cat.1447.

Page 4

23 Text of letter from Peter Rabbit to Master Benjamin Bunny, The Warren.

24 Text of letter from [Mrs] Josephine Rabbit to Mrs Tiggy-Winkle, Cat Bells.

25 Text of letter from Mrs Tiggy-Winkle to Mrs Rabbit, Under Fir tree.
See letter BP.578(14); cat.1450.

26 Text of letter from [Mrs] Josephine Rabbit to Mrs Tiggy-Winkle.

Page 5

27 Text of letter from Tom Thumb to Miss Lucinda Doll, Doll's House.
See letter BP.578(6); cat.1443.

28 Text of letter from Miss Lucinda Doll to Mr T. Thumb, The Mouse Hole.
See letter BP.578(9); cat.1445.

29 Text of letter from Thomas Thumb to Miss Lucinda Doll, Doll's House.
See letter BP.578(5); cat.1441.

Page 6

30 Account: From Messrs Ginger & Pickles, for groceries to Miss Lucinda Doll.

31 Text of letter from Miss Lucinda Doll to Messrs Pickles & Ginger [sic].

32 Text of letter from Messrs Ginger & Pickles to Miss Lucinda Doll.

33 Text of letter from William Potatoes (witnesses Gilbert Cat and John Stoat Ferret) to Samuel Rat, High Barn.

34 Text of letter from Cock Robin to Miss Jenny Wren, The Nest, Beech Hedge.

35 Text of letter from Jenny Wren to Cock Robin Esq, The Holly Bush.

36 Text of invitation from Sally Henny Penny to . . . the Puddle Duck Family, Farm yard.

Page 7

37 Text of letter from Samuel Whiskers to Farmer Potatoes, The Riddings.

38 Text of letter from Ribby to Mrs Rebeccah Puddle Duck, Farm Yard.

39 Text of letter from Tom Titmouse to Jack Sparrow, The Eaves.

40 Text of letter from the little Red Ants to the Cricket, Buckle Yeat.

41 Text of letter from the Cricket to the little Red Ants, Hill Top Farm.

42 Text of letter from Miss Lucinda Doll to Mrs T. Thumb [Hunca Munca], The Mouse Hole.
See letter BP.578(8); cat.1444.

Page 8

43 Text of letter from Samuel Whiskers to Mr Obadiah Rat, Barley Mill.

44 Text of invitation from Sally Henny Penny to Master Tom Kitten, Hill Top Farm.

45 Text of letter from T. Kitten to Miss Sally Henny Penny, Barn Door.

46 Text of letter from the Puddle Ducks to Miss Sally Henny Penny, Barn Door.

47 Text of letter from Rebeccah Puddleduck [sic] to Mrs Ribston Pippin, Lakefield Cottage.

4ff. 20 x 16
BP.581   T.24.L

Letters from Mrs Flopsy Bunny and each of her six children to Master John Hough

1430 Letter from First Flopsy Bunny.
1f. 70 x 40mm
BP.579(1)

1431 Letter from 2nd Flopsy Bunny.
1f. 67 x 40mm
BP.579(2)

1432 Letter from 3rd (Miss) F. Bunny.
1f. 56 x 32mm
BP.579(3)

1433 Letter from 4th (Miss) F. Bunny.
1f. 40 x 32mm
BP.579(4)

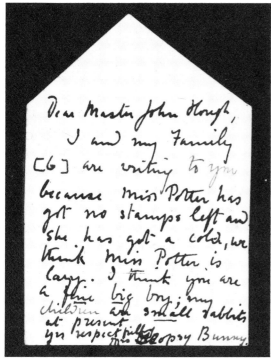

1436

1434 Letter from 5th Miss F. Bunny.
1f. 49 x 29mm
BP.579(5)

1435 Letter from 6th Master F. B.
1f. 38 x 25mm
BP.579(6)

1436 Letter from Mrs Flopsy Bunny.
1f. 68 x 48mm
BP.579(7)

Cat. 1430–1436 written by BP in brown ink.
BP.579(1–7)   T.24.L

Letters to Hilda Moore

1437 Letter from Twinkleberry Squirrel to O. Brown
Esq, M.P., Owl Island.
1f. 90 x 44mm
BP.578(1)

1438 Letter from Squirrel Nutkin to Old Mr Brown Esq,
Owl Island.
1f. 53 x 45mm
BP.578(2)

1439 Letter from Squirrel Nutkin to Mr Brown, Owl
Island.
1f. 69 x 34mm
BP.578(3)

1440 Letter from Squirrel Nutkin to Mr Old Brown Esq,
Owl Island.
1f. 78 x 34mm
BP.578(4)

1441 Letter from Thomas Thumb to Miss Lucinda Doll,
Doll's House.
1f. 93 x 53mm
BP.578(5)

1442 Letter from Thomas Thumb to Miss Lucinda Doll,
Doll's House.
1f. 90 x 45mm
BP.578(6)

1443 Letter from Hunca Munca to Miss Lucinda Doll,
Doll's House.
1f. 92 x 36mm
BP.578(7)

1444 Letter from Miss Lucinda Doll to Mrs Thomas
Thumb [Hunca Munca], Mouse Hole.
1f. 78 x 73mm
BP.578(8)

1445 Letter from Miss Lucinda Doll to Mr T. Thumb,
Mouse Hole.
1f. 90 x 32mm
BP.578(9)

1446 Invitation from Mr Alderman Ptolemy Tortoise to
Sir Isaac Newton, The Well.
1f; on a Potter invitation card. 42 x 90mm
BP.578(10)

1447 Letter from I. Newton to Mr Alderman Ptolemy
Tortoise, The Melon Pit.
1f. 38 x 124mm
BP.578(11)

1448 Letter from Tabitha Twitchit to Mrs Ribston
Pippin, Lakefield Cottage.
1f. 44 x 91mm
BP.578(12)

1449 Letter from Ribby to Mrs Duchess, Belle Green.
1f. 53 x 92mm
BP.578(13)

1450 Letter from Mrs Tiggy-Winkle to Mrs Rabbit, Sand
Bank, Under Fir-tree.
1f. 44 x 99mm
BP.578(14)

BP.578(1–14)   T.24.L

Letters to Miss Margaret Hough

1451 Letter from Peter Rabbit. With two little drawings
of pigs.
1f. 75 x 41mm
BP.580(1)

1452 Letter from Benjamin Bunny.
1f. 78 x 40mm
BP.580(2)

1453 Letter from Mrs Tabitha Twitchit. With a drawing
of a cat.
1f. 68 x 40mm
BP.580(3)

1454 Letter from Mrs Tiggy-Winkle. With drawings of
three Christmas crackers.
1f. 75 x 36mm
BP.580(4)

1455 Letter from 'All the little animals and birds'.
1f. 80 x 35mm
BP.580(5)

1456 A greeting: 'Happy New Year'. With drawings of
three ducks.
1f. 69 x 41mm
BP.580(6)

1457 A greeting: 'A Merry Christmas – from Tom
Thumb and Hunca Munca'. With drawings of two
little mice.
1f. 32 x 16mm
BP.580(7)

1458 A greeting: 'Merry Xmas'. With drawings of four
little rabbits.
1f. 42 x 29mm
BP.580(8)

BP.580(1–8)   T.24.L

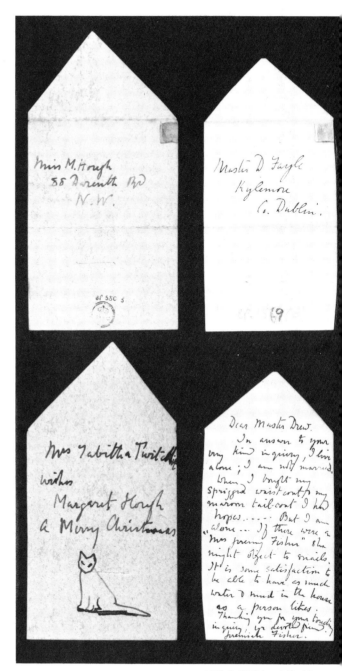

1453 & 2123 (see Addenda)

1459 Xerox copies of four miniature letters to Miss
Marjorie Moller.
Sent by the Free Library of Philadelphia, USA
(to which they belong).
2ff. 24 x 20
BP.580(a)   T.24.L

1460

1460 Mail-bag. A small cotton-twill bag marked 'G.P.O.' in thick letters, with a red string draw-thread at the neck.
Made by BP and delivered, with letters, to the Moore children.
10 x 10
BP.577   T.24.L

Picture letters

1461 Potter, H.B. to Walter Gaddum. 6 Mar 1897. Concerning a squirrel, Peter Rabbit (her pet rabbit), an owl and other animals.
2ff; 10 pen-and-ink sketches.   17 x 11
BP.876(i)   T.11

1462 Potter, H.B. to Walter Gaddum. 14 Jan 1899. Robertson Terrace, Hastings. Concerning a sparrowhawk and Barbary falcon.
2ff; on grey paper; 2 pen-and-ink sketches.
17.5 x 11
BP.876(ii)   T.11

1463 Potter, H.B. to Eric Moore. 28 Mar 1894. Pendennis Hotel, Falmouth. Concerning a pig on board ship and its escape on to a desert island. Probably the preliminary idea for *The Tale of Little Pig Robinson*.
4ff; file copy; 8 pen-and-ink sketches.   11 x 8
BP.877   T.11

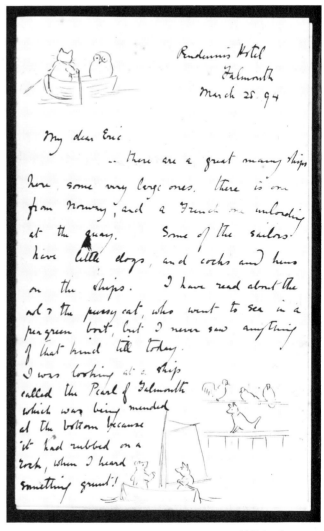

1463 *(page)*

1464 Potter, H.B. to Marjorie Moore. 23 Aug 1898. Waverley, Dumfries. Concerning her Scottish journey.
2ff. 17.5 x 11
BP.878(i)   T.11

1465 Potter, H.B. to Marjorie Moore. 13 Jan 1899. Hastings. Concerning a Manx cat and various kinds of carriage.
2ff; on grey paper; 3 pen-and-ink sketches.
18.5 x 10.5
BP.878(ii)   T.11   *(illustration overleaf)*

a great many carriages, one fat
old gentleman always amuses
me, he has the very smallest
grey ponies in little blue & red
coats.

My pony must be having a lazy
time, I shall come and see you
some day when it is fine.
yrs. aff. Beatrix Potter.

1465 (page)

1466 Potter, H.B. to Marjorie Moore. 26 Jan 1900.
Winchelsea. Concerning school, attacks
of 'flu' etc.
2ff; 4 pen-and-ink sketches. 15.5 x 10
BP.878(iii) T.11

1467 Potter, H.B. to Marjorie Moore. 24 Apr 1900.
2 Croft Terrace, Tenby. Concerning the seaside.
2ff; 3 pen-and-ink sketches. 18 x 11
BP.878(iv) T.11

1468 Potter, H.B. to Norah Moore. 25 Sep 1901.
Lingholme [sic], Keswick. Concerning *The Tale of
Squirrel Nutkin* and Old Brown.
Letter stitched with cotton, inserted into
cardboard folder with blue cord ties.
Inscribed (on cover): The original illustrated MS
[in letter form] of "The Tale of Squirrel Nutkin" by
Beatrix Potter.
Inscribed (on back of cover, in pencil): 1135 words
12 drawings (Book contains 1210 words) Peter R.
377 words.
8ff; pen-and-ink sketches. 18 x 11
BP.880 T.11

If I have not, you will
say I ought to go to school
too, and learn
out of a big
spelling book.
I expect when I see you again,
you and Frida will have grown
so big I shall
not know you!
I believe I
haven't seen you since last
July, it is quite shocking.
It is all because of my poor old
pony being dead; when I went

to drive to Wandsworth in the
big carriage, my Mamma
wants to drive
the other
way;
and when your Mamma
wanted to call at Bolton
Gardens at Christmas, I
could not ask her to come,
because we had influenza in
the house. I hope you
did not have

1466 (page)

Business correspondence

Artists

1469 Aris, E.A. to BP. 18 Sep 1916. Hornsey. Sending drawings for *The Oakmen*.
2ff. 25 x 19.5
BP.608   T.27.L

1470 Aris, E.A. to BP. 21 Nov 1917. Colchester Mil. Hospital. EA claims his use of the name 'Peter Rabbit' for a character in his story is coincidental and not borrowed from BP.
2ff. 20.5 x 16.5
BP.609   T.27.L

1471 Potter, H.B. to Ernest Aris. 23 Nov [1917]. Draft of a letter disallowing claim that EA has not heard of Peter Rabbit.
1f. 24.5 x 19.5
BP.610   T.27.L

1472 Potter, H.B. to Nancy Hudson. No date. Concerning the felling of an oak tree and a robin who lives with the Oakmen. With a rough drawing of a robin, and also of BP and Ethel Green cutting firewood.
1f; file copy. 21 x 17.5 (torn)
BP.611   T.27.L

Publishers

1473 Nister E. to BP. 25 May 1894. Concerning payment for the frog drawings submitted for publication.
Inscribed on three separate occasions by BP (on sheet 2, verso): May 29th accepted 7/6 each for three. 25/- for frogs. Some years later bought back frogs for £3 (3) and made it into Mr Jeremy Fisher. 'Nister's' was an unattractive German(?) firm, but it was my first start at having anything published. H.B.H.
2ff. 25 x 19.5
BP.790(i)   T.42.R

1474 Nister, E. to BP. 30 May 1894. London. Further concerning payments for the frog drawings.
Verso: Copy of BP's reply to Nister.
1f; headed. 25.5 x 19.5
BP.790(ii)   T.42.R

1475 Nister, E. to BP. 2 Jun 1894. London. Further concerning the frog drawings.
1f; headed. 25 x 19.5
BP.790(iii)   T.42.R

1476 Nister, E. to BP. 4 Jun 1894. London. Further concerning the frog drawings.
1f; headed. 25 x 19.5
BP.790(iv)   T.42.R

1477 Nister, E. to BP. 5 Jun 1894. Payment form stating sum owed to BP.
2ff. (1 blank); headed. 20 x 13
BP.790(v)   T.42.R

1478 Potter, H.B. to Ernest Nister. 2 Jun 1894. 2 Bolton Gardens. Asking for return of frog drawings.
2ff; file copy with corrections. 15 x 9.5
BP.791   T.42.R

1479 Potter, H.B. to Mr Wilfred Evans. 9 Jan 1910. 2 Bolton Gardens. Concerning printing of tariff reform leaflet.
2ff. 15 x 10
BP.738(i)   T.39.R

1480 Potter, H.B. to W. Evans. 11 Jan 1910. Hill Top, Sawrey. Further concerning the tariff reform leaflet.
2ff. 15 x 10
BP.738(ii)   T.39.R

1481 Potter, H.B. to W. Evans. 28 Feb 1910. 2 Bolton Gardens. Concerning ideas for a leaflet on the shortage of horses; also further concerning the tariff reform leaflet.
2ff. 15 x 10
BP.738(iii)   T.39.R

1482 Potter, H.B. to W. Evans. 4 Mar 1910. 2 Bolton Gardens. Further concerning leaflets.
2ff. 15 x 10
BP.738(iv)   T.39.R

1483 Potter, H.B. to W. Evans. 8 Mar 1910. 2 Bolton Gardens. Further concerning leaflets.
2ff. 18 x 11
BP.738(v)   T.39.R

1484 Potter, H.B. to W. Evans. 15 Mar 1910. 2 Bolton Gardens. Further concerning leaflets.
1f. 15 x 10
BP.738(vi)   T.39.R

1485 Potter, H.B. to W. Evans. 18 Mar 1910. Hill Top, Sawrey. Further concerning leaflets.
2ff. 15 x 10
BP.738(vii)   T.39.R

1486 Potter, H.B. to W. Evans. 22 Mar 1910. 2 Bolton Gardens. Concerning distribution of leaflets.
2ff. 17.5 x 11
BP.738(viii)   T.39.R

1487 Potter, H.B. to W. Evans. 28 Mar 1910. Teignmouth. Concerning leaflets, including the Horse leaflet.
2ff. 16 x 10
BP.738(ix)   T.39.R

1488 Potter, H.B. to W. Evans. 4 Apr 1910. Teignmouth. Further concerning distribution of leaflets.
2ff. 16 x 10
BP.738(x)   T.39.R

1489 Potter, H.B. to W. Evans. 6 Apr 1910. 2 Bolton Gardens. Thanks for letters sent to BP concerning the leaflets.
2ff. 16 x 10
BP.738(xi)   T.39.R

1490 Potter, H.B. to W. Evans. 13 Apr 1910. 2 Bolton Gardens. Further concerning replies to the tariff reform leaflets and the posting of the Horse leaflets.
2ff. 18 x 11
BP.738(xii)   T.39.R

1491 Potter, H.B. to W. Evans. 17 Apr 1910. 2 Bolton Gardens. Further concerning the posting of the Horse leaflets and royalties in connection with foreign translations.
2ff. 18 x 11
BP.738(xiii)   T.39.R

1492 Potter, H.B. to W. Evans. 22 Apr 1910. 2 Bolton Gardens. Concerning the receipt of letters in connection with the leaflets.
2ff. 18 x 11
BP.738(xiv)   T.39.R

1493 Potter, H.B. to W. Evans. 16 May 1910. 2 Bolton Gardens. Concerning the reprint of the tariff reform leaflet.
2ff. 18 x 11
BP.738(xv)   T.39.R

1494 Potter, H.B. to W. Evans. 10 Jul 1913. Lindeth Howe, Windermere. Concerning an interest in his firm and an illness (slowing up her progress with a book – *The Tale of Pigling Bland* ?).
2ff. 18 x 11
BP.738(xvi)   T.39.R

1495 Potter, H.B. to Alexander McKay. 13 [or 14] Jul [1932?] File copy of a letter returning printer's proofs of *Sister Anne*, remarking on the absence of errors and asking for an agreement.
1f. 22 x 17
BP.679   T.33.R

1496 Warne, F., & Co. to BP. 16 Dec 1901. Chandos House, Bedford Street, London. Concerning the printing of Warne's edition of *The Tale of Peter Rabbit*.
1f; headed and typed. 25.5 x 20
BP.821(ii)   T.5

1497 Warne, F., & Co. to BP. 21 Dec 1901. London. Acknowledging receipt of the privately printed edition of *The Tale of Peter Rabbit*; also particulars concerning copyright.
2ff; headed. 20 x 12.5
BP.821(iii)   T.5

1498 Warne, F., & Co. to BP. 13 Jan 1902. London. Concerning preparations for reproduction of illustrations with Hentschel's blocks.
2ff; headed, with envelope. 20 x 12.5
BP.821(iv)   T.5

1499 Warne, F., & Co. to BP. 17 Jan 1902. London. Further concerning Hentschel's blocks.
2ff; headed. 20 x 12.5
BP.821(v)   T.5

1500 Warne, F., & Co. to BP. 7 May 1902. London. Concerning a revised offer of royalties.
1f; headed and typed. 25 x 20
BP.821(vi)   T.5

1501 Warne, N. to BP. 26 May 1902. London. Letter accompanying a draft of the agreement.
1f; headed and typed. 25.5 x 20
BP.821(vii)   T.5

1502 Warne, N. to BP. 29 May 1902. London. Further concerning royalties.
1f; headed and typed. 25.5 x 20
BP.821(viii)   T.5

1503 Warne, N. to BP. 2 Jun 1902. London. Letter accompanying proofs of first four blocks received for *The Tale of Peter Rabbit*.
1f; headed and typed. 20 x 12.5
BP.821(ix) T.5

1504 Warne, F., & Co. to BP. 24 Jun 1902. London. Concerning remaining eight block proofs of *The Tale of Peter Rabbit*, and cover design.
2ff; headed and typed. 25.5 x 20
BP.821(x) T.5

1505 Warne, F., & Co. to BP. 16 Aug 1902. London. Concerning first proof of the colour plates for *The Tale of Peter Rabbit*.
1f; headed and typed. 25.5 x 20
BP.821(xi) T.5

1506 Potter, H.B. to Fruing (?) Warne. 12 Aug 1916. Sawrey. Concerning E. Aris as possible illustrator for *The Sly Old Cat*.
4ff; Xerox copy. 20 x 25; 17.5 x 11.5 (size of letter)
BP.1485 T.5

1507 Potter, H.B. to Fruing Warne. 13 Jan 1927. Sawrey. Concerning the Harrap correspondence and proposed plan for an almanac.
1f. 17.5 x 11
BP.823 T.5

1508 Harrap, G. to Fruing Warne. 10 Jan 1927. Concerning the inclusion of Peter Rabbit in one of their stories, with proof of final paragraph of story and an acknowledgement note.
1f; typed copy of letter. 26 x 20
BP.824 T.5

1509 Warne, N. to BP. 25 May 1905. London. Mainly concerning *The Pie and the Patty-Pan*.
2ff. 20 x 12.5
BP.822(i) T.5

1510 Warne, N. to BP. 26 May 1905. London. Further concerning *The Pie and the Patty-Pan*.
2ff; headed, with envelope. 20 x 12.5
BP.822(ii) T.5

1511 Warne, F., & Co. to Canon H.D. Rawnsley. 18 Sep 1901. Concerning Warne's edition of *The Tale of Peter Rabbit*. They prefer BP's text to Rawnsley's.
1f. 22.5 x 17.5
BP.821(i) T.5

Translators

1512 Ballon, Mlle Victorine to BP. 30 Aug 1912. Honfleur. Concerning BP's approval of her translation.
2ff. 17.5 x 27 (folded)
BP.694 T.36.R

1513 Hertz, Miss A.R. to BP. 16 Oct 1918. Paris. Postcard requesting a French edition of *The Tale of Peter Rabbit*.
14 x 9
BP.696 T.36.R

1514 Potter, H.B. to Frederick Warne & Co. 15 May 1912. 2 Bolton Gardens. Concerning Mlle Ballon's French translation.
2ff. 17 x 11.5
BP.693 T.36.R

1515 Potter, H.B. from Frederick Warne & Co. 15 Feb 1913. Chandos House. Sending two sets of proofs of *The Tale of Benjamin Bunny*.
1f. 20.5 x 15.5 (torn edge)
BP.695 T.36.R

1516 Potter, H.B. from Frederick Warne & Co. 8 Nov 1918. Chandos House. Concerning the possibility of publishing French translations in GB, *The Tale of Johnny Town-Mouse*, and Grimwades china.
3ff. 26 x 20.5
BP.697 T.36.R

1517 Brown envelope addressed to Mlle Victorine Ballon.
It contained proofs of the French translation (LL Cat.)
26 x 21.5
BP.698 T.36.R

Linder correspondence

1518 Ludbrook, S. to Leslie Linder. 3 Feb 1968. Greenhowe, Hawkshead. Concerning the Nursing Association, in reply to a query from LL.
2ff; typed. 22 x 20
BP.810(iii) T.3

1519 Warne, F., & Co. to Leslie Linder. 18 Mar 1968. Chandos House. Concerning a list of BP's books. Enclosed is a typed copy giving the publication date announcements of BP titles (see BP.1483(b); cat.1915).
1f; typed. 26 x 20.5
BP.1483(a)   T.5

1520 Warne, F., & Co. to Leslie Linder. 15 Jan 1970. Chandos House. Information concerning *Timmy Tiptoes*.
1f. 26 x 20.5
BP.1484   T.5

1521 Hough, M. to Miss Pye. No date. Hollyhocks, Langton Maltravers, Swanage. Concerning M. Hough's decision to sell to Leslie Linder the miniature letters sent to her by BP.
1f. 17.5 x 13.5
BP.1494   T.24.L

1522 Evans, R. to Charles Rare Books. 26 Oct 1955. 154 Clerkenwell Road. Concerning BP's election poster.
1f. 25.5 x 20
BP.1497   T.39.R

1523 Gatey, Heelis & Co. to Leslie Linder. 14 Feb 1968. Ambleside. Concerning the Nursing Association.
1f. 25 x 20
BP.1482   T.4

1524 Boultbee, Mrs W. to Leslie Linder. 9 Oct. No year given. The Vicarage, Maldon. Concerning the *Journal*.
See the Warne Family Tree sent with the letter (BP.1481(b); cat.1918).
1f. 17.5 x 13.5
BP.1481(a)   T.4

1525 Warne, F., & Co. to BP. 9 Jul 1940. Concerning the original illustrations for the Peter Rabbit Books etc.
1f; typed copy. 26 x 20.5
BP.821(xii)   T.5

1526 Lane, M. (Countess of Huntingdon) to Leslie Linder. 16 Mar 1966. Blackbridge House, Beaulieu. Concerning a sketch book and other drawings.
1f. 25 x 20
BP.1500   T.40.R

1527 Lane, M. (Countess of Huntingdon) to Leslie Linder. 4 Dec 1963. Westmead House, Roehampton. Concerning BP's 1876 sketch book and her code writing.
2ff. 17.5 x 13.5
BP.1499   T.40.R

1528 Opie, I. and P. to Leslie Linder. 19 Oct 1971. Westerfield House, West Liss, Hampshire. Concerning a version of *The Two Sisters* which BP adapted for *Sister Anne*.
1f. 25.5 x 20.5
BP.1496   T.33.L

1529 Voyce, J. to Leslie Linder. 7 Oct 1969. City Library, Gloucester. Concerning a *Cecily Parsley* w/c which came to light as a result of the *Tailor of Gloucester* exhibition held in the City Library.
1f. 20 x 15.5
BP.1495   T.30.R

1530 Kensington and Chelsea Public Libraries to Leslie Linder. 24 Aug 1967. Central Library, Phillimore Walk. Concerning 2 Bolton Gardens.
Enclosed with it is a Xerox of 1895 map showing Bolton Gardens (see BP.1487(b); cat.1917).
1f; typed. 25.5 x 20
BP.1487(a)   T.7

1531 Kensington and Chelsea Public Libraries to Leslie Linder. 7 Dec 1967. Central Library, Phillimore Walk. Concerning the demolition of 2 Bolton Gardens.
1f; typed. 25.5 x 20
BP.1488   T.7

BOOKS

It was originally intended to catalogue the books in detail, but unfortunately time and staff did not permit an accurate bibliographic study of the works. Most of the entries printed here are taken almost directly from Leslie Linder's manuscript catalogue, which did not contain the 'BP' numbers to be found on other material in the collection. This catalogue lists most of the items in alphabetical order and has added the 'BP' numbers, which should simplify identification. All books are in paper-covered boards unless otherwise stated.

The order of the books under each title is according to Mr Linder's own placing.

The Peter Rabbit books

Appley Dapply's Nursery Rhymes

1532 Green with dust jacket; first edition; mint copy.
Inscribed: Published Oct. 30. 17. 1st edition.
(BP's copy)
BP. 147

1533 Green; first edition.
Inscribed: For Annie B. Moore with love from 'Beatrix Potter' Dec. 8. 17.
BP. 146

Cecily Parsley's Nursery Rhymes

1534 Red; first edition; also dust jacket from another first edition.
Inscribed: For Miss Owen With all good wishes for Christmas & New Year Dec 22. 22. from 'Beatrix Potter'.
(BP's copy)
BP. 153

1535 Red; first edition.
Inscribed: For Isabel Wishing her a Merry Christmas from Mrs Heelis Dec 22. 22.
BP. 152

Ginger and Pickles

1536 Olive-green with dust jacket; first edition, 1909 on title page; mint copy.
(BP's copy)
BP. 121

1537 Pale green; first edition, 1909.
Inscribed: For Mrs Moore With love and best wishes from Beatrix Potter Christmas 1909.
BP. 122

1538 Grey; later large format; shaped back but flat. Different pictures of biscuit tin and case of soap from those in the English small format edition (LL Cat.)
(BP's copy)
BP. 125

1539 Dark buff; large format.
Inscribed: To Isabel from 'Beatrix Potter'; also inscribed: To Isabel From Mother Easter 1924.
BP. 124

1540 Cream; small format.
Inscribed: 'Beatrix Potter'.
Pictures of biscuit tin and case of soap as those in the American edition.
BP. 127

1541 Buff; late large format edition; nearly mint.
BP. 123

The Pie and the Patty-Pan

1542 Maroon with dust jacket; first edition, 1905 on title page; mint copy.
(BP's copy)
BP. 154

1543 Brown; dedication copy.
Inscribed: For Joan Moore with love from Beatrix Potter. Nov 16th 05.
BP.155

1544 Brown with dust jacket; second printing; plain mottled lavender endpapers; mint copy.
(BP's copy)
BP.157

1544a Blue with dust jacket; as cat. 1544.
(BP's copy)
BP.158

1545 Later edition with dust jacket; large format (with 85mm diameter picture on cover); *The Pie and the Patty-Pan* design on endpapers; mint copy.
(BP's copy)
BP.156

1546 Red; large format; *The Pie and the Patty-Pan* endpapers.
Inscribed: To Isabel from 'Beatrix Potter'; also inscribed by Mrs Mackereth: To Isabel. From Mother. May 11th 1924.
BP.159

1547 Modern copy with notes about the pictures etc., written by Mrs Brockbank (daughter of Mrs Rogerson, who owned 'Duchess').
Mrs Brockbank lived at Lakefield Cottage
(LL Cat.)
BP.161

1548 Maroon; second printing; plain mottled lavender endpapers.
BP.160

The Roly-Poly Pudding
(later *The Tale of Samuel Whiskers*)

1549 Red; first small format edition; shabby; front corners eaten off by dog?
Inscribed: Olive from Yvonne Xmas 1930, to remind her of all the nice places in Sawrey, where she saw Peter Rabbit and Beatrix Potter.
BP.107

1550 Maroon cloth; first edition, 1908 with [All rights reserved] on title page; cover picture and back endpaper missing.
Inscribed: For Mrs Moore with love from Beatrix Potter Christmas 1908.
BP.100

1551 Cream boards, cloth spine; cheaper large format edition; some text on coated paper with picture on other side.
BP.103

1551a As cat. 1551, but mint copy.
(BP's copy)
BP.104

1552 Maroon cloth; large format edition with bevelled edges.
Inscribed: To Isabel from Mrs Heelis in remembrance of the Old Farm House, May 1927; also inscribed by Mrs Mackereth: To Dear Isabel from mother Xmas 1920.
BP.101

1553 Red; first small format edition.
Inscribed: To Isabel with love from Mrs Heelis 'Beatrix Potter' Christmas, 1926.
BP.105

1554 Maroon cloth; first edition, second printing, without [All rights reserved].
Inscribed: With love from Mary.
BP.99

1554a As cat. 1554, but one front endpaper leaf missing.
BP.148

1555 Red; first small format edition.
Inscribed: 'Beatrix Potter'.
Some pictures chalked by a child.
Ex Mrs Whittaker.
BP.106

The Story of a Fierce Bad Rabbit

1556 Panoramic; green; first edition, London & New York; mint copy.
(BP's copy)
BP.162

1557 Panoramic; first edition, London & New York.
Inscribed: For Joan from Miss Potter with love & wishing her a Merry Christmas 1906.
Joan Moore was then 10 years old (LL Cat.)
BP.163

1558 Panoramic; olive-green; second printing(?), New York & London; shabby.
BP.164

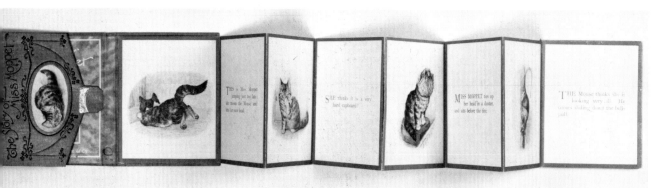

The Story of Miss Moppet

1559 Panoramic copy; first edition, London & New York; mint copy.
(BP's copy)
BP.165

1560 Small book format; grey.
Inscribed: For Isabel from 'Beatrix Potter'.
BP.167

1561 Panoramic; grey; first printing, London & New York; shabby; front cover picture missing.
BP.166

The Tailor of Gloucester

1562 Privately printed; pink; Rupert Potter's bookplate, printed in Gothic lettering: Rupert Potter.
Inscribed: Dec 18. 1902.
(BP's copy)
BP.39

1563 Privately printed; Rupert Potter's Lincoln's Inn bookplate, printed in Gothic lettering: Rupert Potter/Lincoln's Inn.
Two pencil sketches (both 3.5 x 4) have been tipped in above and below the bookplate:
(i) Cecily Parsley and wheelbarrow; (ii) Cecily Parsley making cider.
(BP's copy)
BP.40

1564 Privately printed.
Inscribed: To Mrs Wicksteed from Beatrix Potter Jan 17th '03.
Picture of Tailor lifting cups off dresser is missing.
BP.42

1565 Privately printed.
Inscribed: For Mrs Banner, with kind regards from Beatrix Potter, Oct 7.35.
BP.41

1566 Privately printed.
Inscribed (on cover): Imperfect.
BP has cut out parts of the text and removed some of the pictures for pasting in her two *The Tailor of Gloucester* MSS.
Also some rewriting of the text for Warne's edition, and lines counted in some of the paragraphs.
Front endpaper: pencil designs for endpapers.
Back endpaper: coloured designs for endpapers.
Cutting from a 1931 book sale catalogue re a book by Ralph Wallis, printed for the author in 1668: 'Room for the Cobbler of Gloucester and his Wife'.
He was known as the 'Cobbler of Gloucester'
(LL Cat.)
(BP's copy)
BP.44

1567 Privately printed.
Inscribed (on cover): Imperfect.
Some of the text has been cut out and some pictures removed, as for previous copy.
Back endpaper: pencil sketches of the Mayor.
BP has experimented with scroll designs above and below some of the pictures.
(LL Cat.) (These designs were never used) i.e. see 'Rats dancing' [BP.471; cat.790], 'Mice and teacups' [BP.472–473; cat.791–794], 'Three little mice sat down to spin' [BP.634; cat.1066ff].
(BP's copy)
BP.43

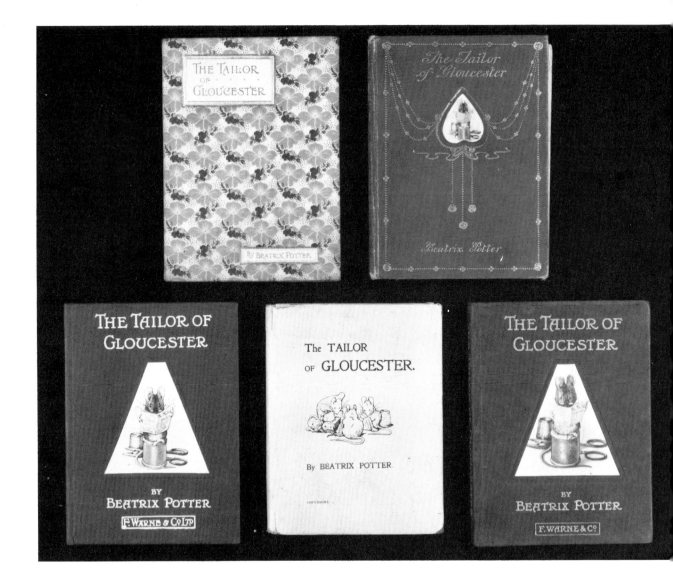

1568 Privately printed.
Inscribed: 500 copies, printed Dec. 1902.
(BP's copy)
BP.45

1569 Maroon with dust jacket; first Warne's edition.
Inscribed: Oct 16th '03 from Mr Warne.
(BP's copy)
BP.50

1570 De-luxe flowered art fabric; first edition.
Inscribed: To Ethel with love from B. Nov 10th '03.
Ethel Hyde-Parker was the mother of Stephanie
Duke.
Frontispiece: Mouse on cotton reel; other copies
had the usual frontispiece (LL Cat.)
(BP's copy)
BP.55

1571 Maroon leather; first edition.
Origin of this copy unknown, may have been a
special one-off binding? The mouse on cotton reel,
and the usual frontispiece picture were both
printed on one sheet. They were then separated
and used individually for the fabric-bound copies.
In this particular copy, they were not separated,
but both pictures were *sewn* into the book, the
usual frontispiece facing the title page (LL Cat.)
BP.51

1572 Maroon; first edition.
Inscribed: To Mrs Dixon with love from Beatrix
Heelis Dec. 23rd 1916. This is my own favourite
amongst my little books.
BP.49

1573 Maroon; first edition; endpapers: design 1 occurring four times.
Inscribed: For Mrs Moore with love from Beatrix Potter. Nov 19th '03.
BP.52

1574 Maroon; second printing, 1903 on title page; endpapers: designs 1 and 2 occurring twice.
Inscribed: J. E. Moore.
BP.53

1575 Privately printed; pink; back strip partly missing, cover shabby; copy belonging to the Moore family; not inscribed.
BP.48

1576 Blue-grey.
Inscribed: To Isabel from 'Beatrix Potter' May 1927.
BP.57

1577 Yellow; late edition, *c.*1930–35.
Inscribed: For Celia Norah Edwards with love from Beatrix Potter Ap. 1939.
Given to Nurse Edwards on returning from Liverpool Hospital after a serious operation; period believed to be last week in March to early April. Not given at the same time as the 'Lady Mouse' and 'Gentleman Mouse' paintings (BP.473(a,b); cat.793–794). All were given to Dr Renshaw in exchange for one of his oil paintings (LL Cat.)
BP.58

1578 Privately printed edition; pink; mint copy.
BP.47

1578a As cat.1578, but worn, with frayed spine.
BP.46

1579 Blue-grey decorated cloth; 1903 on title page but bound 1904; endpapers: designs 2 and 3; poor condition.
BP.56

1580 De-luxe flowered art fabric; first edition; standard frontispiece; endpapers: design 1 occurring four times.
BP.54

The Tale of Benjamin Bunny

1581 Grey; first edition; mint copy.
Inscribed: Aug. 25 1904 published Sept 29th.
(BP's copy)
BP.59

1582 Tan with dust jacket; 1905 printing; mint copy.
Inserted slip of paper inscribed: 1st and early editions to be kept.
(BP's copy)
BP.60

1583 Grey.
Inscribed: To Isabel from Beatrix Potter.
BP.62

1584 Cream; endpapers: designs 8 and 9.
Inscribed: Beatrix Potter Nov. 6th 40 That's the lot Without a Blot!
The last book to be signed in a set of post-war editions. (A request from a friend – for a friend.)
(LL Cat.)
BP.63

1585 Cream; endpapers: designs 8 and 9.
Inscribed: Beatrix Potter June 11 42.
BP.64

1586 Grey; with the first edition pictures; endpapers: designs 6 and 7; mint copy.
BP.61

The Tale of Jemima Puddle-Duck

1587 Grey; first edition.
Inscribed: Betsy Cannon from Miss Potter.
Aug 22nd 1908.
Ex Sotheby.
BP.111

1588 Green decorated cloth; first edition.
Inscribed: For Mrs Edmondson with kind regards from Beatrix Potter Oct 16. 08.
BP.110

1589 Green; first edition.
Half-title inscribed: 'For Jemima', at Sawrey camp from Beatrix Potter July 28 43.
The child's name 'Florence Dawson' is also on this page. Given on the *last* birthday of Beatrix Potter (LL Cat.)
BP.108

1590 Green; first edition.
Inscribed: For Marjorie Moore with love and best
wishes from Beatrix Potter Oct 3rd 08.
BP.109

1591 Grey.
Inscribed: Love to Isabel [Mackereth] from Mrs
Heelis in remembrance of Hill Top Farm, Sawrey.
May. 1927.
John and Mrs Mackereth at one time ran Hill Top
Farm for Mrs Heelis.
BP.112

1592 Grey; first edition.
Believed to have been used for Braille; has been
repaired. For reference purposes only (LL Cat.)
BP.113

The Tale of Johnny Town-Mouse

1593 Brown; first edition.
Inscribed: For Mrs Moore with love from Beatrix
Heelis. Nov. 26. 18.
Including two-page letter sending the book to Mrs
Moore. 26 Nov 1918. Sawrey.
BP.149

1594 Brown; first edition; shabby; Stephen Leech's
bookplate.
Inscribed: For Stephen Leech from 'Beatrix Potter'
Sept 4th. 20.
BP.150

1595 Brown; first edition (no 'n' in London).
Inscribed: For Isabel with love from Mrs Heelis
Dec. 7. 18.
BP.151

The Tale of Little Pig Robinson

1596 Warne's first edition with dust jacket.
Inscribed: For Annie B. Moore with love from
'Beatrix Potter', Nov 8th 1930.
BP.168

1597 Second printing of 1930 with dust jacket; large
format edition; mint copy.
Inscribed: Beatrix Potter.
(BP's copy)
BP.170

1598 Warne's edition, 1930 reprint; mint copy.
(BP's copy)
BP.169

1599 First edition with dust jacket.
Inscribed: For Isabel Mackereth with love from
Mrs Heelis, Beatrix Potter Nov. 4 1930.
With original brown paper addressed by Beatrix
Potter: Mrs W. Mackereth, Sawrey Ground,
Crosby, Nr. Maryport. Postmark Nov. 4. 30.
Stamp 6d. Sawrey Parcel Post 5 pm 4 No/.
BP.171

1600 1930 reprint.
BP.172

The Tale of Mr Jeremy Fisher

1601 Blue decorated cloth with dust jacket; first edition;
mint copy.
(BP's copy)
BP.91

1602 Red.
Inscribed: To Isabel from Beatrix Potter.
BP.93

1603 Modern copy.
Written in by Stephanie Hyde-Parker (Mrs Mary
Stephanie Duke), to whom the book was dedicated
(LL Cat.)
BP.94

1604 Red; first edition.
BP.92

The Tale of Mr Tod

1605 Fawn; first edition; mint copy.
(BP's copy)
BP.137

1606 Grey with dust jacket; first edition; mint copy.
(BP's copy)
BP.135

1607 Grey; first edition; mint copy.
(BP's copy)
BP.136

1608 Grey; first edition; copy belonging to the Moore
family; not inscribed.
BP.140

1609 Fawn; first edition.
Inscribed (by Marjorie Moore): Marjorie.
BP.139

1610 Buff.
Inscribed: Love to Isabel from 'Beatrix Potter'.
BP.141

1611 Grey; first edition.
Marked up for Braille in pencil.
BP.138

The Tale of Mrs Tiggy-Winkle

1612 Brown with dust jacket; first edition; mint copy.
(BP's copy)
BP.81

1613 Green; first edition; faded spine, otherwise
mint copy.
(BP's copy)
BP.82

1614 Blue decorated cloth with dust jacket; first edition;
mint copy.
(BP's copy)
BP.83

1615 Green; first edition; shabby; copy belonging to the
Moore family; not inscribed.
BP.84

1616 Buff.
Inscribed: For Isabel with love from 'Beatrix
Potter'.
BP.86

1617 Modern copy, with notes about the pictures etc.,
written by Lucie Carr (the Lucie of Mrs Tiggy-
Winkle: LL Cat.).
BP.87

1618 Brown; endpapers: designs 6 and 7.
How Keld picture, p.20 still has wording.
BP.85

The Tale of Mrs Tittlemouse

1619 Cream; first edition; frontispiece missing.
Inscribed: For Hilda with love from Beatrix Potter
Sept 21st 10.
Hilda Moore was then 8 years old (LL Cat.)
BP.128

1620 Buff.
Inscribed: To Isabel from 'Beatrix Potter'; also
inscribed: To Isabel From Mother, May 11th 1926,
Sawrey.
BP.130

1621 Blue-grey; first edition.
BP.129

The Tale of Peter Rabbit

1622 Privately printed; pale olive-green; flat back;
Rupert Potter's bookplate.
Inscribed: Dec. 16. 1901; and (in pencil) by BP:
1st printing 250 copies.
(BP's copy)
BP.6

1622

1623 Privately printed; pale olive-green; flat back.
Inscribed: For Miss Owen from 'Beatrix Potter'
(Beatrix Heelis) Jun [1]5. 17. With kind regards.
The 1st edition, 250 copies. Christmas 1900
(a mistake for 1901: LL Cat.).
(BP's copy)
BP.5

1624 Privately printed; olive-green; round back; Rupert
Potter's bookplate.
Inscribed (in pencil) by BP: 2nd printing 200.
(BP's copy)
BP.7

1625 Privately printed; olive-green; round back; Rupert
Potter's bookplate.
Inscribed (in ink) by BP: 200 copies printed
Feb. 1902.
(BP's copy)
BP.4

1626 Privately printed; olive-green; round back;
mint copy.
(BP's copy)
BP.2

1627 Privately printed; olive-green; round back; mint
copy, backstrip faded.
(BP's copy)
BP.1

1628 Grey; first Warne's edition; plain endpapers.
Inscribed: 1st edition.
(BP's copy)
BP.9

1629 Emerald-green cloth with dust jacket; first Warne's
edition; plain endpapers; Rupert Potter's
bookplate.
Inscribed: Oct. 1902.
(BP's copy)
BP.10

1630 Olive-green cloth with dust jacket; first Warne's
edition; plain endpapers; Rupert Potter's
bookplate.
Inscribed: Oct. 1902.
(BP's copy)
BP.11

1631 Dark green; fourth printing (with 'shed' in place of
'wept'); plain endpapers.
Slip of paper inserted, inscribed: 4th edition, shed
instead of wept, see p.51.
(BP's copy)
BP.14

1632 Dark brown; first edition, fifth printing; coloured
pictorial endpapers: design 1 occurring four times.
(BP's copy)
BP.15

1633 Dark brown; sixth printing; endpapers: designs
1 and 2.
BP.16

1634 Dark brown with dust jacket; seventh printing;
endpapers: designs 2 and 3.
Inscribed: Early edition.
(BP's copy)
BP.17

1635 Dark brown; eighth printing; endpapers: designs
2 and 4.
(BP's copy)
BP.18

1636 Dark brown with dust jacket; first printing with
blocks re-engraved, Sept. 1907, ninth printing?
Inscribed: New plates Autumn 1907. Early copy to
be kept H.B.P.; also inserted slip of paper inscribed
(in ink): New blocks, first time of re-engraving first
printing – see p.68.
(LL Cat.): A slightly different picture occurs on
p.81, and a quite different picture of Peter in
wheelbarrow occurs on p.68. (These two new
blocks appear to have been used between 1907
and 1911.)
(BP's copy)
BP.20

1637 Dark green; later printing using the new pictures
on pp.68 and 81; endpapers: designs 5 and 6.
(BP's copy)
BP.21

1638 Dark green; faulty copy of seventh printing; sheets
out of order.
(BP's copy)
BP.19

1639 Privately printed; pale olive-green; flat back; worn
to state of loose sections only; copy belonging to
the Moore family; not inscribed.
BP.8

1640 Pirated edition by Henry Altemus Co.: first
edition, 1904 (from Warne's fourth printing),
with dust jacket.
Against the picture of Mrs McGregor and the pie,
Warne's have written (in pencil): New. BP added
(in pencil): No it is not new, we left it out of our
last edition. B.P.
(BP's copy)
BP.26

1641 Pirated edition, as cat. 1640; mint copy.
(BP's copy)
BP.27

1642 Grey with dust jacket.
Inscribed: To Isabel from Beatrix Potter.
BP.12

1643 Buff; endpapers: designs 8 and 9.
Inscribed: Beatrix Potter Nov 6th 1940.
BP.22

1644 Privately printed; olive-green; second printing;
round back.
BP.3

1645 Dark green; fourth printing; plain leaf-pattern
endpapers.
BP.13

1646 Red cloth library binding; endpapers: designs
4 and 5; mint copy.
Experimental copy using 1907 sheets with the
different pictures on pp.68 and 81. Believed to
be one of two copies (LL Cat.)
Ex Warne.
BP.24

1647 Cream; recent edition from new blocks, 1958.
Inscribed (by Mr Priddle): With kind regards from
R.A.V. Priddle, 1st edition from new original
blocks 20th February 1958.
BP.23

1648 Specially bound copy from an ordinary *Peter Rabbit*,
adding new material, and submitted to Warne's in
1952 to arouse their interest in producing some
form of book which included new Beatrix Potter
material (LL Cat.)
Inscribed: Special edition limited to 2 copies.
No.2.
(LL Cat.): Warne's were given 'No. 1', which
eventually led to the planning of *The Art*. (See
article in *The Horn Book Magazine* when *The Art*
was first published.)
BP.25

The Tale of Pigling Bland

1649 1916 printing; *Sly Old Cat* mentioned on
endpapers.
BP.145

1650 Green with dust jacket.
Inscribed: Love to Isabel from 'Beatrix Potter'; also
inscribed: To Isabel from Mother, May 11th 1925.
BP.144

1651 Green-grey; first edition.
BP.143

The Tale of Squirrel Nutkin

1652 Grey with dust jacket.
Inscribed: 1st edition.
(BP's copy)
BP.67

1653 De-luxe flowered art fabric with dust jacket; second
or third printing, 1903 on title page; mint copy.
Apparently there were no first printing sheets
bound in fabric (LL Cat.)
(BP's copy)
BP.70

1654 Dark blue with dust jacket; first edition; mint copy.
(BP's copy)
BP.69

1655 Brown with dust jacket; first edition; mint copy.
Inscribed: One of [some] copies. Copy bound for
Liberty Oct 1903.
Title page embossed at bottom left: L. Bates/
Booksellers Stationers/Buxton.
Liberty's have no record of these specially bound
copies (LL Cat.)
(BP's copy)
BP.68

1656 Grey; second or third printing, 1903 on title page;
copy belonging to the Moore family; not inscribed.
BP.72

1657 Grey.
Inscribed: For Isabel from Mrs Heelis 'Beatrix
Potter'.
BP.73

1658 Grey; second or third printing, 1903 on title page.
BP.71

The Tale of the Flopsy Bunnies

1659 Dark green; first edition.
Inscribed: For Betsy Cannon from Miss Potter
Aug. 31st 09.
Ex Sotheby.
BP.118

1660 Brown with dust jacket.
Inscribed: To Isabel from 'Beatrix Potter'.
BP.119

The Tale of Timmy Tiptoes

1661 Decorated red cloth; first edition; mint copy.
BP.133

1662 Dark olive-green.
Inscribed: For Isabel from Beatrix Potter.
BP.132

1663 Dark olive-green; endpapers: designs 8 and 9;
unsigned copy, but belonged to BP (copy later
presented to the Moore family?).
BP.134

1664 Brown; first edition.
BP.131

The Tale of Tom Kitten

1665 Greenish-brown with dust jacket; first edition;
mint copy.
(BP's copy)
BP.96

1666 Green; first edition.
Inscribed: For Betsy Cannon from Miss Potter.
Sept 10th 1907.
Ex Sotheby.
BP.97

1667 Brown.
Inscribed: Love to Isabel from 'Beatrix Potter'; also
inscribed: To Isabel From Mother Xmas 1925.
BP.98

The Tale of Two Bad Mice

1668 Light grey with dust jacket; first edition; mint copy.
Recently inscribed: Winifred M.L. Warne.
(BP's copy)
BP.76

1669 De-luxe red decorated cloth; first edition;
mint copy.
Inscribed (by BP): Sept 21st 04; also inscribed:
Winifred M. L. Warne.
Cover design believed to be by BP.
BP.77

1670 Red; first edition; shabby.
Inscribed (by Marjorie Moore): Marjorie.
BP.78

1671 Brown; *c.* 1930 edition; shabby.
Inscribed: Olive Parkinson from her Grandma,
on her 7th birthday, Aug 17. 1930. Beatrix Potter
hopes Olive will meet Peter Rabbit and the Two
bad Mice in Sawrey. There are some *very* bad mice
at Castle Cottage, they have eaten 4 lbs of
marmalade! (all in BP's writing: LL Cat.)
BP.80

1672 Red.
Inscribed: To Isabel from Beatrix Potter; also
inscribed: Winifred M. L. Warne.
BP.79

Foreign-language editions of the Peter Rabbit books

Afrikaans

The Tale of Peter Rabbit

1673 Dark brown; mint copy.
(BP's copy)
BP.38

American

Ginger and Pickles

1674 Buff; early large format American edition.
Warne's have written 'American Edition' on dust
jacket. Money values have been converted to
dollars.
Same pictures of biscuit tin and case of soap as in
the English small format edition (LL Cat.)
(BP's copy)
BP.126

The Roly-Poly Pudding

1675 As English large format edition; worn, wanting
front endpaper.
BP.102

The Tale of Little Pig Robinson

1676 First edition with dust jacket; mint copy.
(BP's copy)
BP.173

1677 Copy with inscription by Margery McKay
Cridland, dated 7 Oct 1962.
BP.174

1678– Two copies of American edition.
1679 (BP's copies: see LL Cat.)

The Tale of Benjamin Bunny

1680 Recent, *c.*1952; spelling 'muffatees' on p.15 not yet
corrected.
BP.65

The Tale of Squirrel Nutkin

1681 New York edition, *c.*1952.
BP.75

The Tale of Peter Rabbit

1682 Yellow; cheap American edition, 30,000 copies,
1951.
22.5 x 15
BP.30

1683 *Unused.*

Dutch

The Tale of Peter Rabbit

1684 Dark green with plain transparent dust jacket;
published under licence by Nijgh & van Ditmar's,
Rotterdam; plain mottled-green endpapers;
mint copy.
Inscribed: H.B. Potter, Nov 8th 1912.
(BP's copy)
BP.117

The Tale of Jemima Puddle-Duck

1685 Dark grey; published under licence by Nijgh &
van Ditmar's, Rotterdam; plain mottled-green
endpapers; mint copy.
Inscribed: H.B. Potter, Nov 8th 1912.
(BP's copy)
BP.36

French

The Tale of Peter Rabbit

1686 Dark brown; pre-war copy, 1907–1911 sheets with
the different pictures on pp.68 and 81, and an all-
French title page: Londres et New York, Frederick
Warne & Cie; translators: V. Ballon et J. Profichet;
endpapers: designs 6 and 7.
Although inscribed: For Janie Watt Brown from
Beatrix Potter Oct 22nd 20. Sawrey, the copy was
in BP's possession at her death, so cannot have
been given? (LL Cat.)
(BP's copy)
BP.31

1687 Brown; post-war copy, 'Ltd.' now added; only
V. Ballon given as translator (current editions
acknowledge *both* translators as in BP.31; cat.1686);
usual pictures; plain mottled-grey endpapers.
Warne's were 'Limited' in 1918. Assumed first
edition in French, 1921 (LL Cat.)
(BP's copy)
BP.32

1688 Brown; assumed first French (trade) edition;
translator: V. Ballon; endpapers: designs 8 and 9.
Inscribed: A story for the little Storeys and a merry
Christmas from Mrs Heelis Dec 24.26.
Although inscribed to Tom Storey's children, this
copy cannot have been given because it was
amongst BP's possessions when she died (LL Cat.)
BP.33

The Tale of Squirrel Nutkin

1689 Blue-grey; assumed first edition, 1931; translator:
Jeanne Fish; endpapers: designs 8 and 9; mint copy.
(BP's copy)
BP.74

The Tale of Benjamin Bunny

1690 Grey; assumed pre-first [sic] edition, 1921;
translator: V. Ballon [sic]; plain mottled-grey
endpapers; mint copy.
(BP's copy)
BP.66

1694

The Tale of Mrs Tiggy-Winkle

1691 Blue-green; first edition; translators: Victorine
Ballon and Julienne Profichet; endpapers: designs
8 and 9; mint copy.
Inscribed: May 1922 published.
(BP's copy)
BP.88

1692 Blue-green; assumed first edition, 1922;
endpapers: designs 8 and 9; mint copy
(same as BP.88; cat.1691).
(BP's copy)
BP.89

The Tale of Jemima Puddle-Duck

1693 Blue-green; assumed first edition, 1922; translators:
Victorine Ballon and Julienne Profichet; endpapers:
designs 8 and 9; mint copy.
(BP's copy)
BP.114

1694 Blue-green; first edition, 1922; translators:
Victorine Ballon and Julienne Profichet;
endpapers: designs 8 and 9; mint copy.
Inscribed: Published May 1922.
(BP's copy)
BP.115

The Tale of Mr Jeremy Fisher

1695 Orange-brown; first edition, 1940; translator:
M.A. James; mint copy.
Inscribed on half-title: French translation
Feb. 1940.
(BP's copy)
BP.95

The Tale of the Flopsy Bunnies

1696 Pale olive-green; assumed first edition, 1931;
mint copy.
(BP's copy)
BP.120

German

The Tale of Mrs Tiggy-Winkle

1696a Paper; printed in Essen, 1947?; translated by
Capt. L.E. Jellinek; English title and coloured
illustration (not by BP) on front; 12pp; cover
missing.
BP.1433

The Tale of Peter Rabbit

1697 Pale olive-green; endpapers: designs 8 and 9;
mint copy.
In Gothic type throughout and on cover.
Including Warne's printed sheet addressed:
Mrs Heelis, Castle Cottage, Sawrey nr Ambleside.
(BP's copy)
BP.34

1698 Pale olive-green; endpapers: designs 8 and 9;
mint copy.
In roman type throughout.
(BP's copy)
BP.35

Welsh

The Tale of Jemima Puddle-Duck

1699 Green; assumed first edition, 1924; mint copy.
(BP's copy)
BP.116

The Tale of Mrs Tiggy-Winkle

1700 Pale grey; assumed first edition, 1932; mint copy.
(BP's copy)
BP.90

The Tale of Peter Rabbit

1701 Pale olive-green; assumed first edition, 1932;
mint copy.
(BP's copy)
BP.37

The Tale of Mr Tod

1702 Light grey-blue; first edition, 1963. Translated by
Miss Mari D. Evans, prizewinner of the
Pembrokeshire Welsh Book Society, for the
translation into Welsh of an English children's
book. First published March 9th 1963.
BP.142

Books other than the Peter Rabbit books

The Fairy Caravan

1703 Privately printed edition; grey cover with dark grey
spine and black lettering. Title page: The Fairy
Caravan, by Beatrix Heelis ('Beatrix Potter').
Copyright of the Author 1929. Opposite title page:
Copyrighted in the United States by the David
Mc.Kay Company, Philadelphia. Registered at
Stationers' Hall, London, by the Author. Some
pages uncut. Plain endpapers.
Sixteen first sections printed at Ambleside and ten
half-titles (LL Cat.)
228pp; 6 colour illustrations including frontispiece,
62 black-and-white illustrations. 22.5 x 17
BP.177

1704 Unbound copy. Title page as BP.177; cat.1703.
Worn condition.
BP.882(a)   Photographs Safe

1705 Unbound copy. Title page as BP.177; cat.1703.
Worn condition.
BP.882(b)   Photographs Safe

1706 Title page as BP.177; cat.1703. In fairly good
condition.
Inscribed (inside front board, in pencil): This copy
of the book is No. 4.
Inscribed (on next sheet): To John Mackereth in
remembrance of Hill Top and the Sheep. With
kind regards to all at Sawrey ground from Beatrix
Heelis. Oct 26th 1929.
BP.183

1707 Title page as BP.177; cat.1703. In fairly good
condition.
Inscribed (on endpaper, in pencil): This copy
is no. 5.
Inscribed (on next sheet): To Mary Hutton from
Beatrix Heelis Oct. 26th '29.
BP.182

1708 Title page as BP.177; cat.1703. In slightly worn
condition.
Copy given to Mrs Susan Ludbrook by Capt Duke.
Inscribed (by Mrs Ludbrook): Susan Ludbrook,
At Hilltop, Near Sawrey, A gift from Captain
Duke 1940.
Inscribed (on piece of paper tipped on to
endpaper): Passed on to Mr L. Linder, November
'59 for his collection, in memory of the years of
happy service I spent, in Hilltop, Near Sawrey, as
Curator of The Beatrix Potter Memorial House
1946 to 1958. Susan Ludbrook.
BP.184

1709 Title page as BP.177; cat.1703. Mint copy.
BP.180

1710 Title page as BP.177; cat.1703. Mint copy.
BP.178

1711 Title page as BP.177; cat.1703. Mint copy.
BP.179

1712 First English edition, 1952. Green cover with dark
blue lettering and yellow dust jacket. Title page:
The Fairy Caravan, by Beatrix Potter, Author of
'The Tale of Peter Rabbit', etc. Frederick Warne &
Co. Ltd., London and New York. In good
condition.
Inscribed (by Mr Herring): To Mr Leslie Linder
from W.A. Herring. A memento of our visit to
Sawrey, May 17th to 28th 1952. 24.7.52.
224pp; 6 colour illustrations and 2 monochrome
(green) illustrations. 20 x 14.5
BP.185

1713 Another (American) edition. Dark green cover with colour illustrations pasted on, black lettering and cream dust jacket. Title page: The Fairy Caravan by Beatrix Potter, Author of the famous 'Peter Rabbit' books. Philadelphia, David McKay Company. Washington Square. Title page verso: Copyright, 1929, by David McKay Company. Mint copy.
228pp. 21 x 16
(BP's copy)
BP.181

Sister Anne

1714 Blue cover with gold lettering and pink dust jacket. Title page: Sister Anne, by Beatrix Potter, Author of the Fairy Caravan, Little Pig Robinson, etc. Illustrated by Katharine Sturges, Philadelphia. David McKay Company, Washington Square. First edition, 1932. Plain endpapers. In good condition. 158pp; 13 black-and-white illustrations including frontispiece. 19.5 x 13
BP.186

The Tale of the Faithful Dove

1715 Yellow dust jacket with green lettering. Title page: The Tale of the Faithful Dove, by Beatrix Potter, Author of 'The Tale of Peter Rabbit,' etc. Frederick Warne & Co. Ltd., London and New York. Title page verso: Copyright, 1955 by Frederick Warne & Co., Ltd. First edition limited to 100 copies. Mint copy.
Inscribed: No. 1.
32pp. 14 x 11
BP.193

1716 Fawn cover with blue lettering; blue paper dust jacket with white lettering and illustrated. Title page: The Tale of the Faithful Dove, by Beatrix Potter, Author of 'The Tale of Peter Rabbit,' etc. Frederick Warne & Co. Inc., New York. Title page verso: Copyright, 1956 by Frederick Warne & Co., Inc. First edition. Plain endpapers. In good condition.
Inscribed: Corrected copy [ref: Hill Top M.S]. It contains a sheet with proposed corrections by LL.
28pp; 7 black-and-white illustrations (not by BP). 18.5 x 11.5
BP.195

1717 As BP.195; cat.1716. In good condition.
18.5 x 11.5
BP.194

Wag-by-Wall

1718 Green cover with gilt lettering and yellow dust jacket (hand-made). Title page: Wag-By-Wall, by Beatrix Potter, Author of 'The Tale of Peter Rabbit,' etc. Frederick Warne & Co., Ltd., London and New York. Title page verso: Copyright, London 1944. First edition limited to 100 copies. Plain endpapers. Mint copy.
Inscribed (by BP): No. 1.
This little story was written by Beatrix Potter late in the autumn of 1943 for publication in the Anniversary Number of The Horn Book Magazine (USA), May 1944.
24pp. 13.5 x 10.5
(BP's copy)
BP.187

1719 As BP.187; cat.1718.
Inscribed: No. 10; also inscribed: To Miss Hammond and Miss Mills 'In memory' Xmas 1944. W. Heelis.
14 x 10.5
BP.188

1720 As BP.187; cat.1718.
Inscribed: To Miss Hammond. 'In memory' W. Heelis. Xmas 1944.
15.5 x 11
BP.189

1721 As BP.187; cat.1718, without dust jacket.
(BP's copy)
15.5 x 11
BP.192

1722– American edition. Grey cover with engraved
1722a illustrations and red lettering. Title page: Wag-by-Wall, by Beatrix Potter, with decorations by J.J. Lankes, Boston. Title page verso: Copyright 1944 by The Horn Book Inc. Colophon: This first edition of Wag-by-Wall set in Scotch Roman and printed on Flemish Book laid paper at the printing press of Thomas Todd on Beacon Hill, Boston. Patterned orange endpapers. In good condition. 30pp; 5 black-and-white illustrations, including title page; also 1 photograph on front. 15.5 x 11
(2 copies including BP's copy)
BP.190, 191

Miscellaneous editions

Peter Rabbit Fold-A-Way Edition

1723 Pirated edition by Reilly & Lee Co., Chicago, April 1920. Paper cover, containing cut-outs. Inscribed (by Mr Warne): This may interest you. It is a piracy from U.S.A. – some copies of which were offered for sale here – but we have stopped the importation and made them return the stock. 16ff; coloured pictures on one side only.
19.5 x 14.5
(BP's copy)
BP.28

The Tale of Peter Rabbit with Puzzle Pictures

1724 Green cloth with dust jacket. Henry Altemus Company, 1907. Coloured frontispiece: Mrs Rabbit with basket.
72pp; 30 line drawings crudely based on original pictures. 21 x 16
(BP's copy)
BP.29

Peter Rabbit's Almanac for 1929

1725 Fawn with dust jacket.
Inscribed (on half-title): Beatrix Potter.
Ex Mrs Whittaker (LL Cat.)
BP.197

1726 Fawn; mint copy.
(BP's copy)
BP.196

1727 Fawn; spine slightly damaged.
BP.200

1728 Buff.
Inscribed: For Mrs Mackereth and John Mackereth with kindest remembrance from 'Beatrix Potter'.
BP.199

1729 Inscribed: For Annie B. Moore with love from Beatrix Heelis 'Beatrix Potter' Dec 17th 28.
BP.198

Toy pictures

Three toy pictures with movable flaps, made for Walter Gaddum.

1730 Rabbit hutch: door on right opens to reveal rabbit. Probably 1889 (LL Cat.)
W/c, wash and pencil, mounted on linen. 24 x 28
BP.551   T.22

1731 Mousehole in wainscot: a panel opens to reveal mice climbing down ladder while another mouse waits outside; flap below opens to reveal three mice at table and three empty chairs.
Inscribed: H.B.P. 1890.
W/c and pen-and-ink, mounted on card. 21.5 x 17
BP.552   T.22   (see PLATE XLIII)

1732 'Benjamin Bunny & Son Greengrocers': shop with fruit and vegetables in barrels and baskets (two lids open to reveal the contents); Benjamin Bunny wears a blue apron.
Inscribed: H.B.P. 1891.
W/c and pen-and-ink, mounted on linen, with silk tasselled loop. 18 x 25.5
BP.553   T.22

Working and special copies

1733 The Tailor of Gloucester; privately printed; pink boards.
Used by BP when planning Warne's first edition, 1903. Includes various designs for endpapers (some coloured). Loose pencil sketches for colour illustrations inserted (a few are additions). Text throughout altered. Quotation from Richard III on title page.
BP.593

1734 The Tale of Peter Rabbit; privately printed; light olive-green boards; first edition, Oct 1902; flat back.
Used by BP when planning Warne's edition. Cover inscribed: Working Copy 2 Bolton Gdns SW. Proof of frontispiece inserted; text altered in parts; 3 pictures hand-coloured.
BP.585

Cat. 1735–1736 are specially bound volumes, formerly belonging to Rupert Potter.

1735   Half-bound in blue calf with blue marbled boards. Rupert Potter's bookplate. Headband; edges not gilt; decorated ribbed spine.
Titles: Squirrel Nutkin (first edition); Tailor of Gloucester (first edition); Two Bad Mice (first edition).
(BP's copy: LL Cat.)
BP.176

1736   Half-bound in dark green calf with green marbled boards. No bookplate. Headband; edges not gilt; decorated ribbed spine.
Titles: Benjamin Bunny (first edition); Two Bad Mice (first edition); Peter Rabbit (seventh [or sixth] printing).
(BP's copy: LL Cat.)
BP.175

Dummies and printer's proofs

1737   *The Tale of Johnny Town-Mouse*; dummy. Blue with flat back.
Carbon copy of Warne's typescript of BP's written MS has been cut up and pasted in a copy of *Mrs Tittlemouse*. Under each of the *Mrs Tittlemouse* pictures Warne's have pencilled the new title indicating where the *Johnny Town-Mouse* pictures are to be placed and have written on title page: The Tale of Timmy Willie. BP has amended it (in pencil) to: The Tale of a Country Mouse.
An inserted piece of paper is inscribed: The Tale of Johnny Town-Mouse.
Amendments by BP, and inserted pencil sketches.
14 X 10.5
BP.207

1738   *Kitty-in-Boots*; dummy. Fawn with round back.
Cuts from one of four sets of galley proofs of *Kitty-in-Boots* pasted in the pages of the dummy by BP. Some of the proofs are edited in pencil by BP. Also indicated (in pencil): endpapers, title, half-title etc. The strips of the galley proofs occupy twenty-one pages. Three sets are missing and galley proofs of the last 1500 words (approximately) are missing. Good condition.
Cuts for four pages are missing (LL Cat.)
The text of the missing items has been taken from the MS by LL.
13.5 X 10
BP.211

1739   *Kitty-in-Boots*; dummy (not used). Some coated pages. Fawn cover with round back.
Inscribed (in pencil): 1–8 [to indicate sections of the book. Endpapers indicated in pencil].
13.5 X 10
BP.210

1740   *Peter Rabbit's Almanac for 1929*; dummy. White cloth.
BP has pencilled the order of contents and given the subject matter for some of the pictures.
Loose pencil drawing (8.5 x 7) of robin and rabbit's head.
Squirrel border design formerly inserted (see BP.478; cat.950).
12 X 9
BP.213

1741   *The Tale of Pigling Bland*; dummy. Grey with round back. Some coated pages to indicate position of illustrations. Mint copy.
One pencil sketch inserted between the leaves: Pigwig sitting on a chair in front of a bowl.
14 X 10
BP.208

1741a   As BP.208; cat.1741. Blue.
14.5 X 11
BP.209

1742   *The Tale of Two Bad Mice*; experimental dummy.
Inscribed (on half-title, in pencil): The Tale of the Doll's House; frontispiece: colour illustration (taken from *Tailor of Gloucester* to indicate position of colour illustration); inscribed (on title page): The Tale of Two Mice ('Doll's House' [erased]) & Hunca Munca. By Beatrix Potter. Black-and-white [within pencil oval]. London & New York. Frederick Warne & Co; inscribed (on title page verso): black and white print [within pencil oval]; cut-outs from *Tailor of Gloucester* tipped in to indicate position of text and illustrations.
17 X 12
BP.212

1743   *Sister Anne*; galley proofs. Containing a few printer's errors only.
33ff. 60 X 19
BP.677   T.33.R

1744 *The Fairy Caravan*; galley proofs of the new first section, printed at Ambleside.
Inscribed (not in BP's writing): Rough proof; and (by BP): Registered at Stationers Hall London, by the Author.
One of the proofs has seven sketches of dogs, including 'Nip'.
4ff; page proofs of this section: 20pp. 72 x 17 etc.
BP.676(a,b)   T.33.L

1745 *The Tale of Pigling Bland*; galley proofs.
Inscribed: Corrected for Bedford St. Stamped: Proof F. Warne & Co. 26 Apr 1913.
Corrections by Warne's in ink, and by BP in pencil, to improve text and add extra material.
7ff. 75 x 21 etc.
BP.675   T.33.L

Music books

1746 *The Peter Rabbit Music Books*. Paper cover with colour illustrations. Title page: The Peter Rabbit Music Books for Pianoforte. Music by Christopher Le Fleming, with illustrations by Beatrix Potter. Book I. Six Easy Pieces [with titles]. Book II. Six Easy Duets [with titles]. J. & W. Chester, Ltd., 11, Great Marlborough Street, London W1. Frederick Warne & Co., Ltd., London and New York.
First edition, 1935. Near mint condition.
20pp; 6 black-and-white illustrations. 30.5 x 24
BP.1119

1746a Xerox of letter. Potter, H.B. to Mr Le Fleming. 13 Sep 1935. Castle Cottage, Sawrey. Concerning the Music Books. 2ff. 20.5 x 11.5
Xeroxes of 18 sketches for illustrations. 20 x 12 etc.
Pencil designs for two pages of Music Book.
p.7: squirrels, owl's back (R) and owl's eyes (L).
16.5 x 24
p. 8: Old Brown, Squirrel Nutkin and other squirrels. 17 x 24.5
BP.1119(a)

1747 *The Peter Rabbit Music Books*. Title page as BP.1119; cat.1746. Copy faulty: has interior of Book 1 (with six black-and-white illustrations), and hard-backed cover (with transparent jacket) of Book 2 [sic]. Mint copy.
31 x 24.5
BP.1121

1748 *The Peter Rabbit Music Books*. Book 2. Paper cover. Title page as BP.1119; cat.1746. Colour illustrations. Near mint condition.
32pp; 12 black-and-white illustrations. 30.5 x 24
BP.1120

1749 Drawing for Book 2, Duet no. 3 of *The Peter Rabbit Music Books*, published by J. & W. Chester and Frederick Warne.
Shows Two Bad Mice running away from the Doll's House carrying a chair and a ham.
Drawn in 1935.
BP's original drawings inked over for the publishers (LL Cat.)
Pencil. W/m: I & JS/1861. 11.5 x 18
BP.692   T.36.L

Plays

1750 *Squirrel Nutkin*. Title page: Squirrel Nutkin. A children's play. Adapted by Beatrix Potter from her original story. Music adapted and arranged from traditional tunes by Christopher Le Fleming. Frederick Warne & Co. Ltd., London, New York.
First edition, 1967.
24pp. 28.5 x 22.5
BP.1122

1751 *Ginger and Pickles*. Yellow cover with one illustration (adapted from the book) and blue lettering. Title page: Ginger and Pickles. A play in one act, from the Story by Beatrix Potter. Adapted by E. Harcourt Williams. Opposite title page: Frederick Warne & Co., Ltd., Chandos House, Bedford Court, London WC2. Colophon: Frederick Warne & Co., London and New York.
First edition, 1931. Near mint condition.
20pp. 18 x 11
(BP's copy: LL Cat.)
BP.218

1752 *Ginger and Pickles*. Title page as BP.218; cat.1751.
In fairly good condition.
18 x 11
(BP's copy: LL Cat.)
BP.217

1753 *The Tailor of Gloucester.* Yellow paper cover with green lettering. Title page: The Tailor of Gloucester. A play from the story by Beatrix Potter. Adapted by E. Harcourt Williams. Opposite title page: Frederick Warne & Co., Ltd., Chandos House, Bedford Court, London, WC2. Colophon: Published by Frederick Warne & Co. Ltd., London and New York. First edition, 1930. In fairly good condition.
16pp. 18 x 11
(BP's copy: LL Cat.)
BP.215

1754 *The Tailor of Gloucester.* Title page as BP.215; cat.1753. In good condition.
18 x 11
(BP's copy: LL Cat.)
BP.214

1755 *Mr Samuel Whiskers.* Yellow cover with illustration (adapted from the original story) and red lettering. Title page: Mr Samuel Whiskers. A play in three scenes and an epilogue, from the story of 'The Roly-Poly Pudding' by Beatrix Potter. Adapted by Theron H. Butterworth. Opposite title page: Frederick Warne & Co., Ltd., Chandos House, Bedford Court, London WC2. Colophon: Frederick Warne & Co., Ltd., London and New York. First edition, 1933. Near mint condition. No illustrations.
20pp. 17.5 x 11
(Not BP's copy?)
BP.216

1756 *The Tailor of Gloucester.* Drawing for the cover picture of the play: a gentleman mouse bowing to a lady mouse.
See also BP.690(b); cat.1757.
Pen-and-ink and pencil. 17 x 16.5
BP.690(a)　T.36.L

1757 *The Tailor of Gloucester.* Drawing for the cover picture of the play.
The final version of BP.690(a); cat.1756, squared up for the printer.
Inscribed (by Warne's: LL Cat.): The Tailor of Gloucester play; and: 2¾ ins. wide.
Inscribed (verso): Warne no. 11.
Pen-and-ink with pencil. W/m: Bath/Post/ Newton/Mill. 22.5 x 17.5
BP.690(b)　T.36.L

1758 *The Tailor of Gloucester.* Printer's proofs of the cover picture for the play.
For preliminary drawings, see BP.690(a,b); cat.1756–1757.
12.5 x 19
BP.690(c)　T.36.L

Miscellaneous books

1759 Jenkins, J. *Jenkins' vest-pocket lexicon: an English dictionary of all except familiar words* [etc.]. London: Kegan Paul, Trench, Trubner & Co., 1890.
Red cover. 8 x 5.5
BP.1272　T.10

1760 National Book League: *Beatrix Potter Centenary Catalogue 1966.* Green cover with black and white lettering. Title page: Beatrix Potter, 1866–1943. Centenary Catalogue 1966. National Book League, 7 Albemarle St, London W1. Title page verso: This catalogue has been prepared for the National Book League by Mr Leslie Linder. Frederick Warne & Co. Ltd. Made and printed in Great Britain by W. & J. Mackay & Co. Ltd. Near mint condition.
Inscribed (inside cover): Noël Moore.
110pp; 12 black-and-white photographs of various items listed in catalogue, and 1 colour photograph.
21.5 x 14
BP.883(a)　Photographs Safe

1761 As cat.1760. Mint condition.
BP.883(b)　Photographs Safe

1762 As cat.1760. Unbound, with loose pages and board covers separate.
BP.883(c)i　Photographs Safe

1763 As cat.1760. Mint condition.
BP.883(c)ii　Photographs Safe

1764 National Book League: *Beatrix Potter Centenary Catalogue.* Unbound proof with corrections in red by Leslie Linder.
BP.883(d)　Photographs Safe

1765 Weatherly, Frederic E. *A Happy Pair.* Illustrated by BP. London: Hildesheimer & Faulkner (Germany printed, 1890).
14pp; 7 colour illustrations (1 on back cover).
12 x 10
BP.564　T.23.R

MISCELLANEOUS OBJECTS

Christmas cards etc

1766 Designs for ICAA Christmas cards, showing two drawings: a rabbit smoking a pipe and a rabbit as a postman.
Early versions of two illustrations in *A Happy Pair* by F. Weatherly (see BP.564; cat.1765).
Pen-and-ink. 12.5 x 20
BP.1147   P.C.16

1767 Design for Hildesheimer and Faulkner.
A gentleman and a lady rabbit walking through the snow under an umbrella.
Inscribed: H.B.P.
Study for an illustration in *A Happy Pair* by F. Weatherly (see BP.564; cat.1765).
W/c. 18 x 13.5
BP.1474   S.14.F.B   (*see* PLATE XLIV)
(Re-mounted with BP.1475)

1768 Design for Hildesheimer and Faulkner. Two rabbits in hats and top coats, with walking sticks, walking through the snow.
Inscribed: H.B.P.
Inscribed (verso): From Beatrix Potter.
Christmas 1894.
The design was reused for the *Appley Dapply* frontispiece.
Both BP.1475 and 1474 were originally mounted on brown paper inscribed (in pencil): 2 pictures given to Moore children (Marjorie & Joan).
W/c. 18.5 x 13.5
BP.1475   S.14.F.B
(Re-mounted with BP.1474)

1769 Design for Hildesheimer and Faulkner. Lady rabbit and gentleman rabbit passing in the street.
Inscribed: H.B.P.
Inscribed (verso): Beatrix Potter. 2 Bolton Gardens. June '90.
One of the designs submitted to Hildesheimer and Faulkner in 1890.
See BP.443(b); cat.1770 for the unfinished version.
W/c with pen-and-ink. W/m: Regina Note.
17.5 x 11.5
BP.443(a)   S.15.F.A

1770 Design for Hildesheimer and Faulkner. Study for BP.443(a); cat.1769. Lady rabbit and gentleman rabbit passing in the street.
Pen-and-ink and pencil. W/m: Victoria [and Queen's head]. 14 x 11.5
BP.443(b)   S.15.F.A

1771 Design for Hildesheimer and Faulkner. Mice on a bench playing musical instruments.
Inscribed: H If you choose either of the mice I would draw the heads more carefully.
Inscribed (verso): Beatrix Potter 2 Bolton Gardens SW.
Sketches submitted to Hildesheimer and Faulkner in 1890. Later published as Christmas and New Year cards. See *Journal*, p.201.
Pencil and pen-and-ink. W/m: Victoria Regina [and Queen's head]. 17.5 x 11.5
BP.444   S.15.F.A

1772 Design for Hildesheimer and Faulkner. Sketch of mice dancing.
Inscribed (below): 1.
See *Journal*, p.201.
Pencil and pen-and-ink. W/m: Regina Note.
17.5 x 11.5
BP.445   S.15.F.A

1773 Design for Hildesheimer and Faulkner. Sketches of mice dancing.
The sketches are studies for BP.445; cat.1772.
See *Journal*, p.201.
Pencil. 17.5 x 11.5
BP.446   S.15.F.A

1774 Design for Hildesheimer and Faulkner. Sketch of two rabbits, one of whom is carrying a plum pudding.
Marked 'E' in corner and inscribed (in pencil): Plum pudding – holly on the wall – brown rabbit – white rabbit – red tiles.
Used as a Christmas and New Year card (LL Cat.)
Pencil. W/m: Victoria Regina [and Queen's head].
17.5 x 11.5
BP.1472   S.15.F.A

1775 Design for Hildesheimer and Faulkner. Tarts on a dish with a partly cut cake, a silver jug, two wineglasses and a bottle beside it.
Inscribed (above): Who Stole the Tarts? also: H.B.P.
Inscribed (verso): Suggestion for making up mice, or as separate cards with motto printed on the floor.
Above this inscription is an indication as to spacing, above which is inscribed: Verse [in square brackets].
W/c and pencil. W/m: Regina Note.   10 x 12.5
BP.447   S.15.F.A

1776 Design for Hildesheimer and Faulkner. Two faint sketches: one of the lady rabbit and gentleman rabbit passing in the street, the other of two rabbits under an umbrella (the Happy Pair).
W/c and pencil. W/m: Regina Note. 18 x 12
Verso: Two sketches of mice playing musical instruments and mice dancing.
Pencil.
BP.448 S.15.F.A

1777 Design for Hildesheimer and Faulkner. A fox carrying a goose arrives at the door of a house where three fox faces look out of a window (R).
Marked 'F' and inscribed: Window to open, or if preferred, I would draw it open; also inscribed (by tree): Tree to be moved further in.
Inscribed (verso): Beatrix Potter, 2 Bolton Gardens, S.W.
Pencil and pen-and-ink. W/m: E Towgood. 17 x 18
BP.449 S.15.F.A

1778 Design for Hildesheimer and Faulkner. A fox with a snowball in one hand, at the door of a house. Another fox looks out. Two foxes are at an upper window, one with a snowball.
Marked 'G' and inscribed: Throwing snow off the window sill.
Inscribed (verso): Beatrix Potter, 2 Bolton Gardens, S.W.
Pencil. W/m: Fine. 17 x 21
BP.450 S.15.F.A

1779 Design for Hildesheimer and Faulkner. A fox with a goose over its shoulder at the door of a house. The fox is coloured in, but the background is unfinished.
W/c, pen-and-ink and pencil. W/m: Regina Note. 17.5 x 11.5
BP.451(a) S.15.F.A

1780 Design for Hildesheimer and Faulkner. Two rough sketches, one of a fox with a goose over its shoulder looking up at a window, the other of a fox sweeping below the window; also two small sketches of heads at a window.
Verso: Three rough sketches of mice on a wall, playing musical instruments.
Pencil. 11 x 11
BP.451(b) S.15.F.A

1781 Design for Hildesheimer and Faulkner. Sketches of a fox with a goose over its shoulder; also of a fox looking out of a window and holding a snowball (studies for BP.449–450; cat.1777–1778).
Verso: Faint sketch of a fox throwing a snowball.
Pencil, on torn sheet. W/m: Fine. 17 x 21.5
BP.451(c) S.15.F.A

1782 Design for a Christmas card, in the form of a nest with a mouse inside.
Inscribed: H.B.P.
See BP.442(a); cat.1787 for the outside of the nest.
Early design for a Hildesheimer and Faulkner Christmas card. The final design shows mice in a coconut (see BP.565; cat.1788).
W/c with pen-and-ink. 7 x 7
BP.442(b) S.15.F.A (see PLATE XLV)

1783 Upper half of a design for a Christmas(?) card, showing a man blowing a trumpet, standing on a horse-drawn sleigh in the snow.
The sheet and card have been cut off. There is no wording (LL Cat.)
The lower half is BP.1503; cat.1785.
W/c and pen-and-ink, mounted on card.
8.5 x 12
BP.540 S.21.F.B

1784 Design for a Christmas card, probably for Hildesheimer and Faulkner. Father Christmas being drawn along in a sleigh by two horses in the snow.
Inscribed (in pencil): Wishing you a merry Christmas. H.B.P.
W/c and pen-and-ink, mounted on card. 17 x 12
BP.539 S.21.F.B

1785 Lower half of a design for a Christmas(?) card, showing a dog running.
Inscribed (in pen): H.B.P.; and (in pencil): A Happy New Year to You.
The upper half has been cut off and is BP.540; cat.1783.
W/c, pen-and-ink and pencil, mounted on card. 8.5 x 12
BP.1503 S.21.F.B

1784

1786 Design for a Christmas card, probably for Hildesheimer and Faulkner. Back view of two rabbits walking in the snow.
W/c and pen-and-ink. 17.5 x 22.5 (unfolded)
Verso: Spray of rose-hips on front fold.
Pen-and-ink.
BP.543   S.21.F.B

1787 Design for a Christmas card in the form of a mouse's nest viewed from the outside.
See BP.442(b); cat.1782 for the inside of the nest.
Early design for a Hildesheimer and Faulkner Christmas card. The final design shows mice in a coconut (see BP.565; cat.1788).
W/c with pen-and-ink. 12 x 7
BP.442(a)   S.15.F.A   (see PLATE XLV)

1788 Christmas card; Hildesheimer and Faulkner.
Two mice in a coconut: the card is shaped in the form of a coconut, which opens up to show the mice inside.
Printed greeting: A happy New Year to you.
8 x 5
Another version, printed: A happy Christmas to you.
BP.565(a,b)   T.23.R

1789 Christmas card; Hildesheimer and Faulkner.
Two rabbits carrying a Christmas pudding.
Printed greeting: A happy New Year to you.
1f; card with gilt edges printed from a w/c. 11 x 8
BP.566   T.23.R

1790 Christmas card; Hildesheimer and Faulkner.
A rabbit on a box with a bag and an umbrella in his hand; a trunk is leaning against the box.
Printed greeting: A very happy Christmas to you.
1f; card with gilt edges printed from a w/c. 11 x 9
BP.568   T.23.R

1791 Christmas card; Hildesheimer and Faulkner.
A rabbit (Peter Rabbit) as a postman with a post-bag and letters.
Printed greeting: Wishing you a happy New Year.
1f; card with gilt edges printed from a w/c. 11 x 9
Another version, printed: A happy Christmas to you.
BP.569(a,b)   T.23.R

1792 Christmas card; Hildesheimer and Faulkner. Three guinea pigs dressed in blue, chasing a guinea pig holding a bowl of food.
Printed greeting: A bright and happy Christmas.
1f; card with gilt edges printed from a w/c. 8.5 x 13
BP.570   T.23.R

1793 Christmas card; Hildesheimer and Faulkner. Five guinea pigs sitting at a long table. The guinea pig at the head of the table is about to give them food from a bowl.
Printed greeting: A bright and happy New Year.
1f; card with gilt edges printed from a w/c. 9 x 13
BP.571   T.23.R

1794 Christmas card; Hildesheimer and Faulkner. Two rabbits walking in the snow under an umbrella (the Happy Pair).
Printed greeting: A happy New Year to you.
1f; card with gilt edges printed from a w/c. 11 x 8
BP.567   T.23.R

1795 Christmas card; ICAA 1927. Showing Peter Rabbit being dosed by his mother (*Peter Rabbit* frontispiece).
Pencil. 20 x 12.5
BP.535(a)   S.21.F.A

1796 Christmas card; ICAA 1925. Showing two rabbits under an umbrella, one holding a basket and the other a letter.
3 unused copies in original transparent wrappings.
1f; card with gilt edges printed from a w/c.
14.5 x 10.5
BP.854(i–iii)   T.9

Other copies:
BP.838; T.8. Inscribed: To A.B.M. from Beatrix Potter.
BP.852; T.9. Inscribed: From 'Beatrix Potter' to Margaret & John Hough.
BP.534(b); S.21.F.A. Inscribed: From 'Beatrix Potter' Christmas 1925.
BP.860; T.9. Late issue (1930s?) of 1925 card (LL Cat.) 2ff. 17 x 11

1797 Christmas card; ICAA 1925. Rough sketch showing two rabbits under an umbrella.
Pencil. 23 x 15
BP.534(a)   S.21.F.A

1798 Christmas card; ICAA 1927. Showing Peter Rabbit being dosed by his mother (*Peter Rabbit* frontispiece).
Unused copy in original transparent wrapping.
1f; card with gilt edges printed from a w/c. 14 x 10
BP.855   T.9

Other copies:
BP.840; T.8. Inscribed: Annie B. Moore with love from Beatrix Potter Christmas 1927.
BP.853; T.9. Inscribed: To Margaret Hough from Beatrix Potter Christmas 1927.
BP.535(b); S.21.F.A. Inscribed: With best wishes for Christmas & New Year to all at Crosby, from 'Beatrix Potter' Dec 1927.
Crosby, near Marypoint, was where J. Mackereth lived (LL Cat.)

1799 Christmas card; ICAA 1932. Showing BP's animal characters dancing around a Christmas tree.
Printed signature: Beatrix Potter.
See also BP.856(ii); cat.1812.
For original drawing, see BP.538(a); cat.1811.
2ff; card printed from a pen-and-ink sketch.
11.5 x 15
BP.856(i)   T.9

Another copy:
BP.841; T.8. Inscribed: From Beatrix Potter to Annie B. Moore, Christmas 1932. 12 x 17.5

1800 Christmas card; ICAA 1933. Showing Father Christmas in a sleigh, waving to rabbits.
Printed signature: Beatrix Potter 1933; also autographed signature: 'Beatrix Potter'.
Inscribed: From Beatrix Heelis to Annie B. Moore. Christmas 1933.
2ff; card printed from a pen-and-ink sketch.
16.5 x 12
BP.842   T.8

Other copies:
BP.847; T.9. Inscribed: From Mr and Mrs Heelis to Miss Hammond and Miss Mills Christmas 1933.
BP.850; T.9. Inscribed: 'Beatrix Potter'; and: From W. and H.B. Heelis to all at Crosby Dec. 20. '33.

1801 Christmas card; ICAA 1934. Rough pencil sketch showing Jemima talking to Peter Rabbit.
Printed: 'Will you come to dinner with me, Peter?' 'I would love to, Jemima, but will there be any cats?' 'No cats, no foxes, only me and you!' 'Mew, I'll come too,' said Tom Kitten.
Pen-and-ink and pencil. 17.5 x 11.5
BP.536(a)   S.21.F.A

1802 Christmas card; ICAA 1934. Sketch showing Jemima talking to Peter near a gate, with kittens looking over the wall and another kitten (in pencil) walking in the foreground.
See also BP.1260(a); cat.1803.
Pen-and-ink and pencil. 17.5 x 11
BP.1260(b)   P.C.41

1803 Christmas card; ICAA 1934. Sketch showing Jemima talking to Peter near a gate, with kittens looking over the wall.
See also BP.1260(b); cat.1802.
Pen-and-ink and pencil. 17.5 x 11
Two versions.
BP.1260(a) i,ii   P.C.41

1804 Christmas card; ICAA 1934. Showing Jemima talking to Peter Rabbit.
Printed signature: Beatrix Potter.
2ff; card printed from a pen-and-ink sketch.
16.5 x 12
BP.857(i)   T.9

Other copies:
BP.857(ii); T.9.
BP.843; T.8. Inscribed: From Beatrix Potter to Annie B. Moore Christmas 1934.
BP.536(b); S.21.F.A. Inscribed: From 'Beatrix Potter' to Jennie and Isabel. Christmas 1934.

1805 Christmas card; ICAA 1935. Two sketches showing a rabbit holding a letter(?) in his left hand and a bouquet(?) in his right hand. Above: a sketch of two squirrels in a tree, and a rough of a page layout showing a landscape(?)
See BP.863; cat. 1807 for final version as printed card.
Pencil. 16.5 x 20
BP.1257(b)   P.C.41

1806 Christmas card; ICAA 1935. Early design: faint sketch showing a rabbit holding a letter(?) in his left hand and a bouquet(?) in his right hand.
See BP.863; cat. 1807 for final version as printed card.
Pencil. 14.5 x 10.5
BP.1257(a)   P.C.41

1807 Christmas card; ICAA 1935.
Showing Peter Rabbit as a postman.
Printed signature: Beatrix Potter.
Printed, above an illustration of three rabbits: 'Here comes Peter with the Post-bag!' – 'Is this the right rabbit hole, please?'
2ff; card printed from a w/c. 15 x 10.5
BP.863   T.9

Other copies:
BP.844; T.8. Inscribed: From 'Beatrix Potter' to Annie B. Moore. A merry Christmas 1935 to all at 20 Baskerville Road.
BP.848; T.9. Inscribed: From Beatrix Potter to Miss Hammond and Miss Mills. With all good wishes for Christmas and New Year. Below: original sketch of a dog's head, inscribed: From Suzee to Yum!

1808 Christmas card; ICAA 1936. Showing Peter and Benjamin standing outside Hill Top porch.
Printed signature: Beatrix Potter.
Printed, below an illustration of a cat looking out of a window: 'Tom Kitten's Mother lives in that house; I hope she is not looking–'
2ff; card printed from a w/c. 15 x 11
BP.859(i)   T.9

Other copies:
BP.859(ii); T.9.
BP.845; T.8. Inscribed: From 'Beatrix Potter' to Annie B. Moore with good wishes for Christmas and for New Year 1937.
BP.849; T.9. Inscribed: From 'Beatrix Potter' to Daisy and Cecily. Christmas 1936.

1809 Christmas card; ICAA 1938. Preliminary sketch showing four rabbits opening their Christmas stocking, tied to the bed-end.
Pencil, on ruled paper. 17 x 11
BP.537(a)   S.21.F.A

1810 Christmas card; ICAA 1938. Showing rabbits opening their stockings.
Printed signature: Beatrix Potter.
Inscribed: Beatrix Potter; and (inside):
From Beatrix Heelis to Annie B. Moore.
Christmas 1938.
2ff; card printed from a w/c. 15 x 11.5
BP.846   T.8

Another copy:
BP.537(b); S.21.F.A. Inscribed: From 'Beatrix Potter' to Isabel Mackereth. Best wishes to all at Crosby. Christmas 1938.

1811 Christmas card; ICAA 1932 and 1941. Drawing showing BP's animal characters dancing around a Christmas tree.
(LL Cat.): The original drawing belongs to Warne's. This drawing was given by Capt Duke to the ICAA to sell for funds.
Pen-and-ink with pencil. 16 x 20
BP.538(a)   S.21.F.A   (*illustration overleaf*)

1812 Christmas card; ICAA 1941 (reprint of 1932 card). Showing BP's animal characters dancing around a Christmas tree.
See also BP.856(i); cat. 1799.
2ff; card printed in sepia. 11.5 x 15
BP.856(ii)   T.9

Other copies:
BP.856(iii); T.9.
BP.538(b); S.21.F.A. Inscribed (in unknown hand): 1941.

1813 Christmas card; ICAA. Year unknown. Showing rabbits digging in the snow.
Inside: a partial border including some rabbits.
Inscribed: With all good wishes from Peter Rabbit to Isabel.
2ff; card printed from a w/c. 13 x 10
BP.851   T.9

1811

1814 Christmas card; ICAA. Year unknown. Showing
Mrs Rabbit in a doorway looking at a robin.
Inside: rabbits reading a letter.
Printed signature: Beatrix Potter.
2ff; card printed from a w/c. 15 x 11.5
BP.858   T.9

1815 Christmas card; ICAA. Year unknown. Showing a
rabbit holding a trowel and basket, outside a
potting shed.
Printed signature: Beatrix Potter.
Printed: 'Here comes Peter with the Post-bag!' –
'Is this the right rabbit hole, please?'
2ff; card printed from a w/c. 15 x 11
BP.861   T.9

1816 Christmas card; ICAA. Year unknown. Showing a
rabbit under an umbrella, holding a basket, and
approaching a door in the snow.
Printed signature: Beatrix Potter.
Printed: 'Here comes Peter with the Post-bag!' –
'Is this the right rabbit hole, please?'
2ff; card printed from a w/c. 15 x 11
Two copies.
BP.862(i,ii)   T.9

1817 Christmas card; ICAA. Year unknown. Sketch
showing two rabbits under an umbrella, one
holding a basket and the other a letter.
See also BP.854; cat. 1796 for final version, and
The Art, 2nd ed., p. 372.
Pencil, on paper. W/m: /s' Linen Ledge/oke
Mass 1895. 19.5 x 21.5
BP.1261   P.C.41

1818 Christmas card; ICAA. Year unknown. Sketch
showing side view of a rabbit under an umbrella,
holding a basket and approaching a door; set in an
oval frame.
See also BP.862; cat. 1816.
Pen-and-ink and pencil. 20 x 10.5
BP.1258   P.C.41

1819 Design for a Christmas card: little pig sitting on
a chair.
Inscribed: Beatrix Potter Christmas 1925.
A similar pig is used for 'Gravy and Potatoes' in
Appley Dapply's Nursery Rhymes and the same idea
is represented in Cecily Parsley's Nursery Rhymes.
Possibly an unused design for one of the ICAA
cards (LL Cat.)
W/c and sepia ink. 25.5 x 18
BP.545   S.21.F.B

1820 Christmas card; The Pierpont Morgan Library [*c*.1960?]. Showing BP's sketch (in their possession) of a rabbit throwing snowballs. Sketch reproduced from letter to Noël Moore, given to the Library in 1959.
2ff; card printed from a pen-and-ink sketch.
11.5 X 15.5
BP.1492 T.9

1821 Christmas card; LL's personal card. Year unknown. Showing a mouse on a cotton reel.
Printed inside: From the original blocks used by Beatrix Potter in December 1902 for the Frontispiece of her privately printed edition of *The Tailor of Gloucester*.
2ff. 15.5 X 12
BP.1493 T.9

1822 Christmas card; ICAA 1935. Photograph of copy in the Free Library of Philadelphia.
Inscribed: From Mr. & Mrs. Heelis to Janie & Agnes Watt Brown. best wishes for Christmas 1935 and New Year 1936. all well!
20 X 21
BP.1501 Top Tray

1823 ICAA collecting card. Front: colour illustration of BP's animal characters reading a notice board.
Printed: 'Peter and his friends need your help!'
Inside: BP's letter to children requesting aid, spaces for postage stamps etc.
2ff. 16 X 23.5
Two copies.
BP.1269(a,b) Top Tray

1824 ICAA collecting card and envelope to which the *Peter Rabbit* frontispiece has been pasted.
Front: colour illustration of BP's animal characters reading a notice board.
Inside: conversation between BP's animals concerning aid for invalid children, spaces for postage stamps etc.
See also BP.1269; cat.1823.
2ff. 14.5 X 22
BP.1269(c) Top Tray

1824a Text of a letter from BP to a child who subscribed to the ICAA, 'from Peter Rabbit'.
1f; typed copy. 26 X 17
BP.1574 S.21.F.A

Dinner and menu cards

1825 Three unfinished dinner cards used at Melford Hall by Stephanie Duke, showing Peter Rabbit, Jemima Puddle-Duck, Mr Tod.
See also BP.1568; cat.2141.
Pencil. 9 x 6
BP.573(a–c) T.24.L

1826 Unused menu card with gilt border and colour illustration of a butterfly by BP. Card printed by Marion & Co.
W/c. 4.5 x 8.5
BP.1480 T.23.R

1827 Unused menu card with gilt border and colour illustration of a butterfly by BP. Card printed by Marion & Co.
W/c. 14 x 9.5
BP.1479 T.23.R

1828 Three unused menu cards for the Potter family, with gilt borders and the word 'menu' in gilt letters. The back of BP.572(b) contains an MS list by LL headed: Book manuscripts at Hill Top.
15 X 11
BP.572(a–c) T.23.R

1829 Unfinished design for a small card (place card?) with a delicate line drawing of ivy and an oval inset for further design.
Pen-and-ink, on card. 9 x 11.5
BP.1181 P.C.42

Horn Book Magazine drawings

1830 Peter by the door in the wall.
Inscribed: Aug 1927 Beatrix Potter.
One of the *Horn Book* drawings not sent for sale (LL Cat.)
W/c and sepia ink. 20 x 13.5
(BP's copy)
BP.546 S.21.F.C

1831 Peter runs from Mr McGregor.
Inscribed: Beatrix Potter. Aug 1927.
Not sent for sale.
W/c and pen-and-ink. W/m: Britannia.
19.5 x 10.5
BP.547 S.21.F.C

1832 Mrs Rabbit with her basket and umbrella.
Inscribed: Beatrix Potter, Sept 1927.
Not sent for sale.
W/c and sepia ink. 15 x 12
BP.548   S.21.F.C

1833 Peter squeezes under the gate.
W/c and sepia ink. 21 x 13.5
BP.549(a)   S.21.F.C

1834 Preliminary sketch for Peter squeezing under
the gate.
Inscribed: Beatrix Potter Aug 1927 [deleted].
Sepia ink and pencil. 19.5 x 12.5
BP.549(b)   S.21.F.C

1835 Rough sketch for Peter walking past a frame.
Inscribed: 'First Peter ate some beans & then he ate
some raddishes [sic] & lettuces and then he went to
look for some parsley –' Beatrix Potter.
Pencil. 21 x 13.5
BP.549(c)   S.21.F.C

1836 Rough sketch for Mrs Rabbit with her basket.
Pencil and pen-and-ink. W/m: /nson 60.
20 x 12.5
BP.550(a)   S.21.F.C

1837 Rough sketch for Mrs Rabbit with her basket.
Pencil. 14.5 x 14
BP.550(b)   S.21.F.C

1838 Unfinished sketch for Mrs Rabbit with her basket.
Inscribed: Beatrix Potter 1927.
Pencil and sepia ink, with touches of wash.
14 x 10.5
BP.550(c)   S.21.F.C

1839 Two sketches for Peter and Mr McGregor beside
the vegetable frame.
Pencil and sepia ink. W/m (d): Towgood's Fine.
W/m (e): Regina Note. 20 x 14(d); 18 x 11(e)
BP.550(d,e)   S.21.F.C

1840 Six sketches for Peter caught in the net.
Sepia ink (5) and black ink (1). W/m (f,h,j):
Britannia. W/m (k): Towgood Extra Fin/.
20 x 13(f); 20.5 x 11(g); 20.5 x 12.5(h);
20.5 x 13(i); 19.5 x 13(j); 19.5 x 13.5(k)
BP.550(f–k)   S.21.F.C

1841 Three sketches for Peter squeezing under the gate.
Sepia ink. W/m (l,m): Britannia. W/m (n): /ons'
Linen/lyoke Ma/. 19.5 x 14.5(l); 21 x 13(m,n)
BP.550(l–n)   S.21.F.C

1842 Rough sketch for Peter by the door in the wall and
Mr McGregor running after him.
Inscribed: v.
Pencil. W/m: Towgood's Fine. 16 x 20
BP.550(o)   S.21.F.C

1843 Sketch of Peter running.
Pencil. W/m: Victoria Regina [and Queen's head].
18 x 11
BP.550(p)   S.21.F.C

1844 Rough sketch for Peter by the door in the wall.
Pencil. 19 x 13.5
BP.550(q)   S.21.F.C

1845 Study of a rabbit going into its burrow.
Sepia ink with pencil. 21.5 x 11.5
BP.550(r)   S.21.F.C

Leaflets

1846 Election leaflet concerning land tax. Photostat
copy of a printed sheet. Printed by Martin, Hood
& Larkin, London WC.
Photographs of BP's poster inserted.
See also BP.1308; cat.2040.
25 x 18
BP.737   T.39.R

1847 Horse leaflet. Four-page folder on the shortage
of horses. Printed and published by Edmund
Evans Ltd.
2 black-and-white illustrations (on pp. 1 and 4).
19 x 12.5
BP.736   T.39.R

1848 Horse and foal by a hillside hut.
Inscribed: Sept 16. '04.
Inscribed (verso): H.B. Potter.
Redrawn and used for the Horse leaflet, p.1.
Later drawings are scaled-down versions.
Sepia ink with pencil. 19 x 22.5
BP.350   S.9.F.C

1848

1849 Three horses drawing a plough against a hilly landscape. The design is set within a rectangular black border.
Possibly a drawing for a leaflet.
Black ink and pencil. W/m:/en Ledge/ass 1895.
12 x 14.5
BP.351(a)   S.9.F.C

1850 A more finished version of BP.351(a); cat.1849.
Horses ploughing, within a black border.
Inscribed (verso): H.B. Potter.
Possibly a drawing for a leaflet.
Black ink and process white over pencil. 13.5 x 21
BP.351(b)   S.9.F.C

1851 Horse leaflet (as BP.736; cat.1847).
19 x 12.5
BP.352   S.9.F.C

1852 Final drawing for the haycart (p.4) of the Horse leaflet. Squared up for the printers.
Inscribed (verso, in blue crayon): 8144.
Original block maker's number (LL Cat.)
Black ink and process white over pencil.
10.5 x 18.5
BP.353(a)   S.9.F.C

1853 Preliminary drawing for the illustration of a horse and foal by a hillside hut (p.1) of the Horse leaflet.
Sepia ink with pencil. W/m: Edmeston. 20 x 25.5
BP.353(b)   S.9.F.C

1854 Preliminary drawing for the illustration of a horse and foal by a hillside hut (p.1) of the Horse leaflet.
Black ink and process white over pencil.
W/m: Aviemore. 16 x 21
BP.353(c)   S.9.F.C

1855 Sketch of a horse and cart: design for Horse leaflet.
Horse and haycart not used in final design.
Also rough pencil sketch of a man running
(Mr McGregor? LL Cat.)
Black ink and pencil. 12.5 x 19
BP.353(d)   S.9.F.C

1856 Printer's proof of Horse leaflet. Horse and foal outside hillside hut. 9 x 12.5
BP.353(e)   S.9.F.C

1857 Warne, F., & Co. Specially for the little ones: a selected list of books published by F.W. & Co. List issued prior to the publication of the Peter Rabbit Books. London and New York [1901–02?].
8ff. Coloured illustrations (1 on cover). 22 x 11.5
BP.825   T.6

1858 Warne, F., & Co. A list of new picture books for children. London, 15 Bedford Street, Strand, and New York, Season 1903–1904.
16ff. 25 illustrations (some coloured on cover).
16 x 12.5
BP.826   T.6

1859 Warne, F., & Co. The Peter Rabbit Books by Beatrix Potter. A list of the titles. Chandos House, Bedford Street, London WC2.
2ff. 13 x 9.5
BP.827(b)   T.6

1860 Warne, F., & Co. A selected list of Frederick Warne & Co.'s new gift and coloured picture books for children. London, 15 Bedford Street, Strand, and New York, Season 1904–1905.
Cover (designed by BP) includes a little girl, copied from Stephanie Hyde-Parker (LL Cat.)
4ff. Colour illustrations. 19 x 13
BP.827(a)   T.6

1861 Warne, F., & Co. The Peter Rabbit Books by Beatrix Potter. A list of the titles. 1–4 Bedford Court, Bedford Street, London WC2.
Folder with 4 illustrations. 12.5 x 9.5
BP.827(c)   T.6

1862 Certificate thanking children who had sent letters and stamps to the ICAA. Inscribed: Yours sincerely, Beatrix Potter. Back view of Peter Rabbit as a postman (top L). Rabbit looking inside a glove (bottom R).
1f. 40.5 x 25.5
BP.1268   Top Tray

1863 Draft for the certificate thanking children for sending stamps and letters to the ICAA.
1f; ink, with pen-and-ink sketches, on ruled exercise paper. 20 x 16
BP.1270(a)   Top Tray

1864 Draft for the certificate thanking children for sending stamps and letters to the ICAA.
1f; ink, on ruled exercise paper. 20 x 16
BP.1270(b)   Top Tray

1865 Preliminary sketches for ICAA certificate thanking children for aid (see BP.1268; cat.1862).
Pen-and-ink with pencil. W/m: Victoria Regina Note [and Queen's head]. 18 x 22.5
BP.1271(a)   Top Tray

1866 Preliminary sketches for ICAA certificate thanking children for aid (see BP.1268; cat.1862).
Pen-and-ink with pencil. 16 x 20
BP.1271(b)   Top Tray

Non-book material

1867 Wooden plaque, used as calendar-holder. Stained wood, with two holes at the top. A large transfer print(?) of Jemima Puddle-Duck on the right and the words 'Beatrix Potter' and 'Jemima Puddle-Duck' in yellow below.
18 x 18
BP.875   T.1

1868 Calendar for 1904. Captions and dates in English. Tokyo: T. Hasegawa [1903?].
22ff. Colour illustrations, including cover.
4.5 x 5.5
BP.868(a)   T.10

1869 Calendar for 1905. Dates in English. Tokyo: T. Hasegawa; London: Simpkin, Marshall, Hamilton, Kent & Co. [1904?].
12ff; in folder. Colour illustrations. 22.5 x 11.5
BP.868(b)   T.10

1870 Dried ferns collected by BP.
BP.734   T.39.R

1871 Modelling in clay: a plaque showing cat, jug and bowl, in low relief against dark grey background.
3 x 5.5
BP.864   T.10

1872 Modelling in clay: a plaque showing a woman carrying a water pitcher on her head, in low relief against dark grey background. Clay has been broken into six pieces.
9 x 3
BP.865   T.10

1873 Paint-brush (damaged), Winsor and Newton. Brown handle.
Given by Mrs Mary Duke (LL).
18.5
BP.869   T.10

1874 A brass reproduction of the Potter family crest of a sea horse.
The crest was taken off some old harness at the stables and presented to me by the late Mrs Storey (LL Cat.)
4 x 3
BP.575   T.24.L

1875 Set of eight square table mats with fringes. W/c illustrations of Peter Rabbit and Benjamin Bunny painted on to the silk.
From *The Tale of Peter Rabbit*:
1 Mrs Rabbit saying: You may go into the fields.
2 Now run along, and don't get into mischief.
3 Then, feeling rather sick.
4 Cover picture, with robin added.
From *The Tale of Benjamin Bunny*:
5 Peter sitting by himself.
6 Peter and Benjamin about to go for a walk.
7 Old Mr Bunny whipping Benjamin.
8 Peter on the grass with a robin in the foreground.
Ref: Christie's Book Sale. 2 Dec 1970. Lot 177.
13.5 x 13 (including fringe)
BP.872   T.1

PLATE XLIII Toy picture: dinner party in a mousehole (1730)

PLATE XLIV Christmas card design: 'A Happy Pair' (1767)

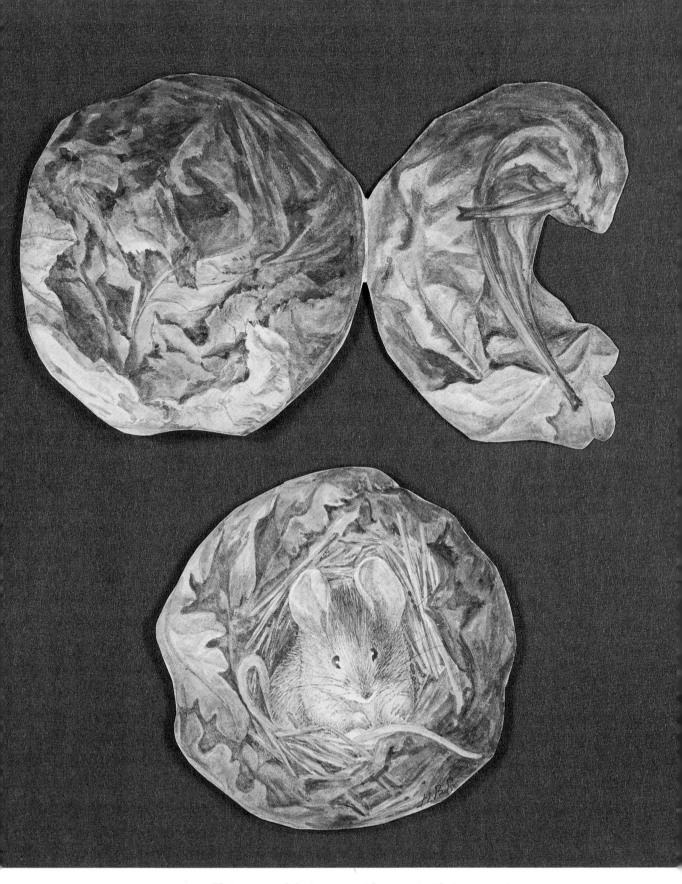

PLATE XLV Christmas card design: nest with mouse inside (1782, 1787)

PLATE XLVI *Jemima Puddle-Duck* table mat (**1877**)

1876 Set of six square table mats with fringes. W/c illustrations of Peter Rabbit and Two Bad Mice painted on to the silk.
From *The Tale of Peter Rabbit*:
1 Frontispiece.
2 Peter squeezes under gate.
3 Peter feels sick.
4 Mr McGregor chasing Peter.
5 Peter by gate in wall.
From *The Tale of Two Bad Mice*:
6 Frontispiece.
Ref: Christie's Book Sale. 16 Jul 1969. Lot 95.
19 x 19 (including fringe)
BP.873   T.1

1877 Set of twelve circular table mats with silk fringes. W/c illustrations painted on linen and with abridged text of *The Tale of Jemima Puddle-Duck* written in black ink beneath each picture.
1 Poultry being fed by Mrs Cannon.
2 Farm animals in a barn.
3 Jemima with Ralph Cannon in the rhubarb patch.
4 Jemima walking up the hill.
5 Jemima flying above the tree tops.
6 Mr Tod looking over his paper at Jemima.
7 Jemima talking to Mr Tod.
8 Mr Tod shutting Jemima in the shed.
9 Jemima coming out of the shed.
10 Mr Tod asks Jemima for herbs.
11 Jemima brings the herbs.
12 Jemima escorted home by the dogs.
Set of transcripts of text written out by LL.
Ref: Christie's Manuscripts Sale. 18 Dec 1968. Lot 39.
19.5 x 19.5 (including fringe)
BP.874   T.1   (*see* PLATE XLVI)

1878 Threads of cherry-coloured twist from Hill Top. Associated with *The Tailor of Gloucester* (LL Cat.)
17mm (length)
BP.866   T.10

1879 Wooden box with painted cut-outs of mice pasted on to the wood.
Given by BP to her mother and inscribed: A merry Christmas! Dec 99.
Found by BP when sorting through her mother's belongings after her death. Miss Margaret Hammond was with her at the time. BP threw it across the room to her, saying: You can have this (LL Cat.) Given to me (LL) by Miss Hammond.
10 x 3.5 x 2.5
BP.574   T.24.L

1880 Wool from sheep at Hill Top Farm, contained within a cardboard box; also a small pebble.
12.5 x 6.5 x 2 (size of box)
BP.867   T.10

Painting books

Peter Rabbit's Painting Book

1881 Grey-green stiff cover with white lettering and two colour illustrations, on back and front; transparent dust jacket. Title page: Peter Rabbit's Painting Book. London & New York, Frederick Warne & Co. Endpaper: Copyright 1911 by Frederick Warne & Co. Entered at Stationers Hall. In good condition. 1911 is first edition.
24ff; 10 colour illustrations, 10 sepia and white illustrations (identical with colour illustrations), 4 sepia illustrations on endpapers and title page.
21 x 18
BP.201

1882 Stiff cover. Title page and collation as BP.201; cat.1881. In worn condition.
Second edition, 1917 (LL).
Title page has mark of rubber stamp.
16ff; 8 pairs of illustrations, with variations from BP.201.
BP.203

1883 Limp cover with no dust jacket. Title page as BP.201; cat.1881. In fairly worn condition.
Second edition, 1917 (LL).
The cover has mark of rubber stamp.
16ff; 8 pairs of illustrations, with variations from BP.201.
BP.202

1884 American edition. Stiff boards. Title page: Peter Rabbit's Painting Book. New York, Frederick Warne & Co., 12 East 33rd. Street. London, Bedford Street, Strand. No wording opposite title page etc. Endpapers, back page and title page illustrations as BP.201; cat. 1881. In fair condition. 24ff; 12 pairs of illustrations. 20.5 x 18
BP.204

1885 Line study of Peter Rabbit running away, for the illustration of 'Mr McGregor chasing naughty Peter round the garden'.
Black ink and process white over pencil. 9 x 9
BP.1102   P.C.48   (*see front of case*)

1886 Design for endpaper. Showing Peter Rabbit preparing to paint, with four baby rabbits as spectators. The lines of type are indicated by rough pencil lines.
Black ink and process white over pencil. 25 x 19
BP.1103(i)   P.C.48

1887 Design for title page. Showing three rabbits behind a notice ('Peter Rabbit's Painting Book') with mice, box of paints etc.
Black ink over pencil. 19.5 x 25.5
BP.1103(iii)   P.C.48

1887

1888 Study for Peter Rabbit and Benjamin Bunny being whipped for visiting Mr McGregor's garden.
Pen-and-ink and pencil. W/m: Parsons' L/Holyoke. 21 x 26.5
BP.1105   P.C.48

1889 Set of twelve outlines of the coloured illustrations, in envelope. Printed (on front of envelope): London & New York, Frederick Warne & Co. For the little artist to colour as separate pictures. Price 4d net.
Sepia print on separate sheets. 21 x 18
Two copies.
BP.1117, 1118   P.C.54

1890 Printer's proof of first edition (?), 1911, hand-coloured by BP and showing designs for front and back cover: Peter in the watering can, Peter feeling ill, Peter in bed.
Sepia print and w/c. 28 x 19; 25 x 19 etc.
BP.1123(viii,x,xi,xiii,xiv)   P.C.56

1891 Printer's proof of first edition, 1911; eleven of the twelve illustrations, comprising:
   1 Peter running from Mr McGregor.
   2 Peter in the watering can.
   3 Peter in bed (coloured).
   4 Peter feeling ill.
   5 Tabitha Twitchit and kittens.
   6 Tom Kitten and Jemima Puddle-Duck (3 copies, 1 coloured).
   7 Jemima and the foxey-whiskered gentleman (3 copies, 1 coloured).
   8 Jemima with Ginger and Pickles (3 copies, 1 coloured).
   9 Mrs Tiggy-Winkle washing (4 copies, 1 coloured).
   10 Mr Brown and Squirrel Nutkin (2 copies, 1 coloured).
   11 Baby mice in a cradle.
Sepia print or colour. 25.5 x 19; 22 x 19 etc.
BP.1108–1115   P.C.55

1892 Printer's proof of first edition(?), 1911, hand-coloured by BP and with her comments on the sheets. Showing Mrs Tiggy-Winkle hanging out the washing, and Mr Brown with Squirrel Nutkin (two copies, one signed on verso).
Sepia print and w/c. 28 x 19.5
BP.1123(v,vi,vii)   P.C.56

1888

1893 Printer's proof of first edition, 1911. Showing Peter feeling ill and Tabitha Twitchit (both inscribed: B.M.); also Peter in bed and Jemima Puddle-Duck (both inscribed: H.M.).
File cover endorsed: LL.
Sent to Moore family and hand-coloured by Hilda (age 9) and Beatrix (18 months younger).
Sepia print and w/c. 20.5 x 18
BP.1123(i–iv)   P.C.56

1894 Printer's proof of second edition, 1911. The three new illustrations, showing Mrs Rabbit and the children, Mr McGregor and Peter (two copies), Peter being whipped.
Endorsed: LL.
Sepia print. 21.5 x 17
BP.1107(i–iv)   P.C.55

Jemima Puddle-duck's Painting Book

1895 Limp grey cover. Title page: Jemima Puddle-duck's Painting Book. London & New York, Frederick Warne & Co. Ltd. In very good condition.
First edition, 1925 (LL).
16ff; 8 pairs of illustrations.
BP.205

1896 Printer's proof of first edition, 1925. Four of the new drawings, showing the cover illustration, Jemima and the hens and chickens, Jemima flying over the tree tops, and Jemima entering the woodshed.
Endorsed (on cover): LL.
Printed in black. 21 x 14
BP.1116(i–iv)   P.C.55

1897 Printer's proof of first edition(?), showing hand-coloured designs by BP for the title page and of Jemima meeting the foxey-whiskered gentleman (both on same sheet); and of two lambs in 'another nest under the holly bush', inscribed (by BP): More blue, less green.
Printed in black, with w/c. 26.5 x 20; 25 x 17
BP.1123(ix,xii)   P.C.56

Tom Kitten's Painting Book

1898 Dark brown hard cover with two colour illustrations.
Title page: Tom Kitten's Painting Book. London & New York, Frederick Warne & Co., Ltd.
In good condition.
First edition, 1917 (LL).
16ff; 8 pairs of illustrations. 20.5 x 17.5
BP.206

1899 Design for endpaper. Showing three kittens crayoning.
Inscribed (top L corner): You can colour these pictures quite nicely with crayons.
Inscribed (bottom R): Painting . . . too messy for kitten[s]!
Black ink and pencil. 20 x 16
BP.1104   P.C.48   *(illustration overleaf)*

1900 Sketch for endpaper design. Showing two gentlemen mice in front of easels, and lady mouse from *The Tailor of Gloucester* posing with fan.
Pencil. 25.5 x 18.5
BP.1103(ii)   P.C.48

1901 Printer's proof for first edition, 1917. Showing Mrs Tiggy-Winkle hanging out the washing.
Endorsed: LL.
Light sepia print. 28 x 18
BP.1106   P.C.55

1899

Miscellaneous

1902 All painting books: back cover design. Showing roundel with the 'Peter Rabbit' characters looking at a sign (showing list of Peter Rabbit Books). Inscribed (verso): Design for list on back cover – H.B. Potter.
Black ink, process white and pencil. 21 x 16
BP.1103(iv)   P.C.48

1903 Captions for an unpublished painting book concerning farm animals at Hill Top, and eight very rough sketches of some of the proposed illustrations, including a cow being milked and Mrs Ribby. With accompanying cover of a green exercise book: The Educational Exercise Book.
2ff; pencil, on ruled exercise paper.
20.5 x 16
BP.691   T.36.L

Unpublished material for painting books

1904 Large-scale rough sketch of the fox inviting Jemima Puddle-Duck into the woodshed.
Pencil. 35.5 x 29
BP.1096(i)   P.C.57

1905 Two large-scale rough sketches of 'the gentleman with foxey whiskers'.
Pencil. 37 x 19
BP.1096(ii)   P.C.57

1906 Large-scale rough sketch (unfinished) for *The Tailor of Gloucester* of six mice sewing by candlelight on a table, with three more climbing up.
Pencil. 35.5 x 28
BP.1097(i)   P.C.57

1907 Large-scale rough sketch (unfinished) for *The Tailor of Gloucester* of seven mice sewing by candlelight on a table, with three more climbing up.
Pencil and black ink. 35.5 x 26.5
BP.1097(ii)   P.C.57

1908 Large-scale drawing for *The Tailor of Gloucester* of six mice sewing by candlelight on a table, with three more climbing up (one unfinished).
Pencil and black ink. 36.5 x 29.5
BP.1097(iii)   P.C.57

1909 Large-scale drawing of Anna Maria and Samuel Whiskers rolling out Tom Kitten.
Pencil and black ink. 36.5 x 28.5
BP.1098(i)   P.C.57

1910 Large-scale rough sketch (unfinished) of Jeremy Fisher seated on a waterlily leaf with a fishing line, and fish visible under the water.
Pencil and black ink. 35 x 27.5
BP.1099   P.C.57

1911 Large-scale rough sketch (unfinished) of Peter Rabbit and Benjamin Bunny with a lettuce.
Pencil and sepia ink. 35 x 28
BP.1100(i)   P.C.57

1912 Large-scale drawing of Peter Rabbit and Benjamin Bunny with a lettuce.
Pencil and black ink. 36.5 x 29.5
BP.1100(ii)   P.C.57

1913 Large-scale drawing of Ribby and Duchess at tea.
Pencil. 35 x 28
BP.1101   P.C.57

1914 Study for Samuel Whiskers with a wheelbarrow running away from 'Kep'. 1907(?).
Black ink and process white over pencil. 20 x 16
BP.1098(ii)   P.C.48

1908

Miscellaneous items

1915 Typed list of publication date announcements of BP titles, made by F. Warne & Co. 18 Mar 1968.
See letter sent with it (BP.1483(a); cat.1519).
4ff. 26 x 20.5
BP.1483(b)   T.5

1916 List of BP book sales written out by Warne's, annotated by LL.
6ff. 17 x 21 (folded)
BP.1486   T.6

1917 Xerox copy of 1895 map showing the situation of 2 Bolton Gardens.
See letter (BP.1487(a); cat.1530) in connection with the map.
1f. 32 x 22
BP.1487(b)   T.7

1918 Family tree (in pencil) of the Warne family made by Winifred Warne.
Sent with letter to LL (see BP.1481(a); cat.1524).
1f. 34 x 21.5
BP.1481(b)   T.4

1919 Xerox copy of documents relating to the sale of 2 Bolton Gardens.
4ff. 32 x 21.5
BP.1489   T.7

1920 Xerox copy of plan from lease of 2 Bolton Gardens.
1f. 32 x 21.5
BP.1489   T.7

1921 Copy of Helen Beatrix Potter's birth certificate made at Somerset House, 1966. Born 28 Jul 1866 2 Bolton Gardens to Rupert and Helen Potter.
1f. 15 x 33.5
BP.833   T.7

1922 Xerox copy of a typed will made by Helen Beatrix
Heelis, 31 Mar 1939. Also an office copy.
3ff. 45 x 20
BP.829(a,b)   T.7

1923 Xerox copy of a hand-written will made by William
Heelis, 20 Apr 1945.
2ff. 33 x 20
BP.830   T.7

1924 Xerox copy of Norman Warne's death certificate
made at Somerset House. Death: 25 Aug 1905,
8 Bedford Square.
1f. 20 x 33
BP.832   T.7

1925 Information concerning BP's books, mounted in a
booklet with a red cover; typed questionnaire, with
answers in pen-and-ink by BP.
Bound with it, a letter from BP to an unknown
correspondent, dated 27 Dec 1939 (see BP.834(b);
cat.1427).
25 x 20.5; 32 x 24.5 (mounted)
BP.834(a)   T.7

1926 Xerox copy of Warne's agreement with BP,
30 Jun 1902. Concerning royalties and copyright.
1f. 33 x 20
BP.831(a)   T.7

1927 Xerox copy of Warne's supplementary agreement
with BP, 2 Jul 1913. Concerning royalties.
1f. 33 x 20
BP.831(b)   T.7

1928 Xerox copy of a memorandum of Warne's
agreement with BP, 7 Jan 1917. Concerning
royalties.
1f. 33 x 20
BP.831(c)   T.7

1929 LL's receipt from Charles Rare Books for the sum of
£115 for a collection of 16 autograph letters.
1f. 17 x 20
BP.1498   T.39.R

1930 Holiday lists: Rupert Potter. A list of holidays,
1882–1907.
1f. 17.5 x 11.5
BP.801(ii)   T.42.R

1931 Holiday lists: Rupert Potter. A list of holidays,
1864–1902. With rubber stamp of Eeswyke,
Sawrey, Lancashire.
1f. 17.5 x 11.5
BP.801(i)   T.42.R

1932 Holiday lists: Mr Bright visited the Potters. A list
of visits from Sep 21, 1869–1885.
Verso: [numbers crossed out].
1f. 20.5 x 13
BP.801(iii)   T.42.R

1933 Torn-out page (p. 280) from an 18th century book:
sonnet from Petrarch.
1f. 19 x 13
BP.719(a)   T.38.R

1934 Brown wrapping paper. Inscribed: Microscopic
insects etc. very mildewed. Examined July 1940.
12 x 5.5
BP.735(a)   T.39.R

1935 Brown wrapping paper. Inscribed: Microsopic [sic]
drawings. HBH.
3 x 12
BP.735(b)   T.39.R

1936 Brown wrapping paper. Inscribed: 6 plates = 18
copper blocks. Tailor of Gloucester. 1st privately
printed edition.
19.5 x 7
BP.735(c)   T.39.R

1937 Brown wrapping paper. Inscribed: Zinc blocks of
Jeremy Fisher bought back, with copyright from
E. Nister & Co. for £3 or £5?
13 x 8.5
BP.735(d)   T.39.R

1938 Brown paper. Inscribed: Studies in a cottage, for
'Patty pan', not used. H.B. Potter.
10.5 x 19
BP.735(e)   T.39.R

1939 Leaf torn from cash book. Inscribed: Books to
be kept.
17.5 x 11
BP.735(f)   T.39.R

PHOTOGRAPHS

Both Beatrix Potter and her father, Rupert Potter, were keen photographers, and this section contains examples of work by each of them. Most of the photographs in the collection were taken by Rupert Potter, and many are signed and dated. Whenever a photograph is unsigned the photographer is recorded as 'unknown'; where the date is uncertain, this has been indicated by 'n.d.' (no date). Rupert Potter brought to his camera work an artist's eye as well as technical expertise. We know too that he sometimes supplied his friend Sir John Millais with photographs which the artist needed for his painting (see *Journal*, p.63 etc.). Beatrix Potter was a competent photographer and she too, like Millais, used photographs as an aid to her painting. A scene sketched during a summer holiday could be worked up during the winter from one of her photographs, so that we sometimes have both a photograph and a drawing of the same scene (see cat.464 and 1968). This collection is therefore more than just a record of people and places – it is yet another means of seeing the artist at work.

Volume 1

1940 Portrait of Rupert Potter. Mayson's of Keswick. *c.*1890.
BP.1528

1941 Salisbury Cathedral. R. Potter. Apr 1895.
BP.1354

1942 Fawe Park: path leading to garden gate. R. Potter. 22 Aug 1903.
BP.1355

1943 Derwentwater from Fawe Park. R. Potter. Sep 1903.
BP.1357

1944 Fawe Park: interior. R. Potter. 1903.
BP.1358

1945 Fawe Park: bedroom? R. Potter. 1903.
BP.1359

1946 Fawe Park: interior. R. Potter. Sep 1903.
BP.1360

1947 Three photographs of the Old Post Office, Sawrey, seen from Hill Top. R. Potter. Sep 1910.
BP.1361(a,b), 1362

1948 Sawrey: garden path (different view from BP.1363; cat.2090). R. Potter. 13 Jul 1912.
Two copies.
BP.1364(a,b)

1949 Portrait of Mrs Cannon(?) and 'Kep' at Hill Top. R. Potter. 9 Sep 1910.
BP.1365

1950 Hill Top, Sawrey: the carriage entrance. Unknown. 1906.
BP.1366

1951 Hill Top: garden (similar to view in BP.1363; cat.2090). R. Potter. Aug 1911.
BP.1367

1952 Hill Top: the carriage entrance in winter. Unknown. *c.*1906?
BP.1368

1953 Sheep at Hill Top. Unknown. n.d.
BP.1369

1954 Two variant portraits of Tom Thornley(?) taken outside the porch at Hill Top. Unknown. *c*. 1905?
BP. 1370, 1371

1955 Portrait of Mr T. Preston, farmer, Sawrey, in dog cart with son. Unknown. *c*. 1905?
BP. 1373

1956 Portrait of William Heelis in Hill Top porch. Unknown. 1913.
BP. 1374

1957 Portrait of William Heelis seated in Hill Top porch. Unknown. 1913.
BP. 1375

1958 Postcards showing sheep. Unknown. n.d. Two copies.
One copy inscribed (by LL): One of Mrs Heelis' prize sheep?
BP. 1372(a,b)

Volume II

Cat. 1959–1978 were taken at Melford Hall, Long Melford, Suffolk.

1959 Exterior, two children in the porch. BP. Apr 1903.
BP. 1376

1960 Exterior: showing roadway up to main entrance. BP. Apr 1903.
BP. 1377

1961 Exterior: from front lawn. Unknown. *c*. 1903?
BP. 1378

1962 Exterior: oblique view of rear. BP. Apr 1903.
BP. 1379

1963 Exterior: oblique view taken from rushes bordering lake. BP. Apr 1903.
BP. 1380

1964 Pathway along the side of the wall. BP? 1903?
BP. 1381

1965 Pathway leading to rear. BP? 1903?
BP. 1382

1966 Exterior: showing sundial at front. Unknown. 1903?
BP. 1383

1967 Exterior seen from lake: showing side of Hall. Unknown. 1903?
BP. 1384

1968 Boundary wall covered with blossom. BP. Apr 1903.
BP. 1385

1968

1969 Another view of boundary wall. BP. Apr 1903.
BP. 1386

1970 Drawing-room? BP. Apr 1903.
BP. 1387

1971 Interior: view through an open door. R. Potter. Apr 1903.
BP. 1388

1972 Fire-dog, 15th century? Unknown. *c*. 1900?
BP. 1389

1973 Garden house. Unknown. *c*. 1900?
BP. 1390

1974 Portrait of Stephanie Hyde-Parker seated on swing. Unknown. *c*.1900.
BP.1391

1975 Portrait of Amy Hyde-Parker(?) on swing. Unknown. *c*.1900.
BP.1392

1976 Stephanie and Amy(?) seated in front of swing. Unknown. *c*.1900.
BP.1393(a)

1977 Stephanie and Amy(?) seated in front of swing, different pose. Unknown. *c*.1900.
BP.1393(b)

1978 Ducks on a fishpond. Unknown. *c*.1900.
BP.1394

1979 Portrait of Millie Warne. W. Clark, Bristol. *c*.1900.
BP.1395

1980 Portrait of Millie Warne. T.C. Turner & Co. *c*.1900.
BP.1396

1981 Portrait of Millie Warne in garden. Unknown. *c*.1900.
BP.1397

1982 Group study of young man, child and old man, standing on the bank of a lake. Unknown. *c*.1900.
BP.1398

1983 Portrait of John Everett Millais (later Sir John) at Dalguise, seated reading *Punch*. R. Potter. 1873.
BP.1399

1984 Portrait of Lady (then Mrs) Millais posed with fan in hand. R. Potter? *c*.1875?
BP.1400

1985 Portrait of John Guille Millais (1865–1960), posed with flint-lock rifle. R. Potter. *c*.1880.
BP.1401

1986 Portrait of Mary and Caroline Millais (1860–1904, 1862–1936). R. Potter? *c*.1875.
BP.1402

1987 Portrait of John Bright (signed). R. Potter. 1871.
BP.1403

Volume III

1988 Portrait of Sir J.E. Millais seated, at Eastwood, nr. Dunkeld. R. Potter. 1879.
BP.1273(a)

1989 Portrait of Sir J.E. Millais seated, at Eastwood, nr. Dunkeld; different from cat.1988. R. Potter. 1879.
BP.1273(b)
(On same sheet as BP.1273(a); cat.1988)

1990 Portrait of Sir J.E. Millais and Effie Millais (daughter) and dog, Eastwood, nr. Dunkeld. R. Potter. 1879.
BP.1287

1991 Portrait of Sir J.E. Millais and Rupert Potter in garden at Dalguise. R. Potter? 28 Sep 1880.
BP.1517

1992 Group study of Sir J.E. Millais and daughters seated on front doorstep at Eastwood. R. Potter? Sep 1880.
BP.1274

1993 Portrait of Lady Millais at Dalguise, in front of Mercat Cross of Dunkeld. R. Potter. 1880s? See also BP.1284; cat.2007.
BP.1275

1994 Portrait of Sir John and Effie Millais holding tennis racquets. R. Potter. *c*.1885?
BP.1276

1995 Portrait of Sir J.E. Millais and Admiral de Koutzow in study at Dalguise. Unknown. Feb 1881.
BP.1277

1996 Portrait of Sir J.E. Millais and Mrs Lillie Langtry in garden at Eastwood. R. Potter. 1879?
BP.1278

1997 Portrait of Millais seated with gun, at Dalguise. R. Potter. 14 Sep 1880.
BP.1418

1998 Portrait of Millais standing with gun, at Dalguise. R. Potter. Sep 1880.
BP.1519
(On same sheet as another copy of BP.1418; cat.1997)

1999 Portrait of Millais and Mrs Lillie Langtry (wearing hat). R. Potter. 1879.
BP. 1518

2000 Portrait of Millais seated, front view. R. Potter. Sep 1880.
BP. 1279(a)

2001 Portrait of Millais seated, side view. R. Potter. Sep 1880.
BP. 1279(b)
(On same sheet as BP. 1279(a); cat.2000)

2002 Portrait of Millais seated, front view. R. Potter? 1880.
BP. 1280

2003 Portrait of Millais seated, profile. R. Potter. 29 Aug 1881.
Two copies.
BP. 1281(a,b)

2004 Portrait of Millais seated, front view. R. Potter. Sep 1880.
BP. 1282(a)

2005 Portrait of Millais, side view; similar to BP. 1279(b); cat.2001. R. Potter. 1880.
BP. 1282(b)

2006 Portrait of Millais and Albert Bray at Dalguise. R. Potter. 30 Sep 1880.
BP. 1283

2007 Portrait of Lady Millais at Dalguise, in front of Mercat Cross of Dunkeld. R. Potter. n.d.
See also drawing, BP.892; cat.75, and see also Index (Mercat Cross).
BP. 1284

2008 Portrait of Effie Millais seated; two different poses. R. Potter. n.d.
BP. 1285

2009 Portrait of Millais and Effie seated, at Dalguise. R. Potter. n.d.
BP. 1286(a)

2010 Portrait of Millais and Effie seated, at Dalguise; different pose from above. R. Potter? 1876.
BP. 1286(b)

2011 Portrait of Lady Millais, Effie and Caroline, at Dalguise. R. Potter? 1876?
BP. 1520

2012 Portrait of Millais seated and Effie standing, at Eastwood (missing).
BP. 1294?

2013 Portrait of Lady Millais. R. Potter. n.d.
BP. 1522

2014 Portrait of Caroline Millais (two prints superimposed). R. Potter. n.d.
BP. 1521

2015 Portrait of Effie Millais. Unknown. 5 Sep 1881.
BP. 1288

2016 Portrait of Effie Millais and child. Unknown. 5 Sep 1881.
BP. 1289

2007

2017 Portrait of Caroline Millais. R. Potter.
13 Oct 1881.
BP.1290(a)

2018 Portrait of Caroline Millais; different pose from
cat.2017. R. Potter? 13 Oct 1881.
BP.1290(b)

2019 Portrait of Millais and daughter (Mary?) seated.
R. Potter. Sep 1881.
BP.1291

2020 Portrait of Alice Millais and sister or friend.
R. Potter. n.d.
BP.1292

2021 Portrait of John Guille Millais at Dalguise.
R. Potter. n.d.
BP.1523

2022 Three portraits of Mary Millais(?) (two on one
sheet). Unknown. 13 Sep 1880.
BP.1293(a–c)

2023 Portrait of John Bright and daughter with Millais
and daughter (Mary?), at Dalguise. R. Potter?
5 Oct 1879.
BP.1295

2024 Portrait of Millais reading in his studio. R. Potter?
Jul 1886.
BP.1505

2025 Hill Top kitchen before alterations. BP. c.1908?
BP.1296

2026 Portrait of BP with Mr Gaskell. R. Potter? c.1874?
(modern print)
BP.1297

2024

2027

2027 BP in her pony carriage at Holehird. R. Potter. 1889.
BP. 1525

2028 View from 2 Bolton Gardens. R. Potter. Oct 1889.
BP. 1524

2029 Farmer Potatoes' barn where the rats hid the butter. Unknown. n.d. (modern print)
BP. 1526

2030 Hill Top kitchen after alterations. Unknown. n.d. (modern print)
BP. 1299(c)

2031 Portrait of Winifred Warne and doll's house. N. Warne. n.d. (modern print)
For original, see BP. 1408; cat. 2095.
Two copies.
BP. 1299(a,b)

2032 Portrait of Hilda Moore. Unknown. n.d.
BP. 1300

2033 Portrait of Beatrix Moore. Unknown. n.d.
BP. 1301

2034 Set of Beatrix Potter Christmas cards. Unknown. n.d. (modern print from an original in the Free Library of Philadelphia)
BP. 1302

2035 Portrait of BP aged 23. R. Potter? n.d. (modern print from an original in the Free Library of Philadelphia)
BP. 1303

2036 Portrait of BP with John Bright. R. Potter? n.d. (modern print from an original in the Free Library of Philadelphia)
BP. 1304

2037 Portrait of BP with her father and brother in the Potter garden. 12 Oct 1892. R. Potter? n.d. (modern print from an original in the Free Library of Philadelphia)
BP. 1305

2038 Portrait of Farmer Potatoes with his daughters Ruth and Mary Postlethwaite outside Buckle Yeat, Sawrey. Unknown. n.d. (modern print)
BP. 1306

2039 Farm ducks. Unknown. n.d. (modern print)
BP. 1307

2040 Hand-drawn poster, in protest against Free Trade. Unknown. c. 1910 (modern print)
For leaflet and extra photographs, see BP. 737; cat. 1846.
BP. 1308

2054

2041 BP's inscription from the back of the portrait, BP.1305; cat.2037: Oct 12 1892 (modern print from an original in the Free Library of Philadelphia)
BP.1309

2042 Three dogs begging, including 'Duchess' on chair. BP. Sep 1903.
BP.1310

2043 Two pages of an exercise book with a history essay (by BP?). Unknown. 1879 (modern prints)
BP.1311

Volume IV

2044 Painting by Bertram Potter, on easel in garden (at Lingholm?). R. Potter. 13 Sep 1904.
BP.1504

2045 Portrait of Millais. A. Ellis, London. Jun 1896.
BP.1312

2046 Portrait of Millais, side view. Mackenzie, Birnam. n.d.
BP.1313

2047 Portrait of Millais, front view. Mackenzie, Birnam. n.d.
BP.1314

2048 Portrait of Millais, standing. A. Ellis, London. 1896.
BP.1315

2049 Portrait of John Bright. R. Potter. n.d.
BP.1316

2050 Portrait of Bright and Millais at Dalguise. R. Potter. Sep 1881.
BP.1317

2051 Wray Castle with Beatrix and Bertram. R. Potter. Aug 1882.
BP.1318

2052 Wray Castle. R. Potter? 20 Aug 1899.
BP.1319

2053 Wray Castle. R. Potter? Sep 1882.
BP.1320(a)

2054 Wray Castle with Potter family and dog. R. Potter. 1882.
BP.1320(b)

2055 Dead stag. J. Millais. Nov 1886.
BP.1322

2056 Dead stag. J. Millais. Nov 1886.
BP.1506

2057 Ilfracombe (vignette). R. Potter. Apr 1883.
BP. 1507

2058 Holyhead harbour. R. Potter. 1889.
See also BP. 318; cat. 554.
BP. 1508

2059 Falmouth. R. Potter. 3 Apr 1894.
BP. 1324

2060 Gorse Hall, Stalybridge. Unknown. n.d.
BP. 1325

2061 Gorse Hall, Stalybridge. Unknown. n.d.
BP. 1326

2062 Grounds of Gorse Hall. Unknown. n.d.
BP. 1327

2063 Portrait of Edmund and Rupert Potter at Camfield
Place. R. Potter. 15 Aug 1883.
BP. 1328

2063

2069

2064 Lakefield, Sawrey. Unknown. Aug 1896.
BP.1329

2065 View over Esthwaite Water from Lakefield, Sawrey. Unknown. 26 Jul 1896.
BP.1509

2066 Holehird with ladies on croquet lawn. R. Potter. Aug 1889.
BP.1331

2067 Tenby. R. Potter. Apr 1900.
BP.1333

2068 Tenby. R. Potter. Apr 1900.
BP.1332

2069 Tenby. R. Potter. Apr 1900.
BP.1510

2070 Scottish(?) landscape. J. Millais. Nov 1886.
BP.1334

2071 Carved chair at Lennel. R. Potter. Sep 1894.
BP.1335

2072 Lennel: the grounds. R. Potter. Sep 1894.
BP.1336

2073 BP standing on a bridge at Bush Hall. R. Potter. Aug 1884.
Two copies.
BP.1511, 1512

2074 Bush Hall: Bertram and Beatrix Potter on lawn with dog. R. Potter. Sep 1884.
BP.1338

2075 Bush Hall: interior. R. Potter. Oct 1884.
BP.1513

2076 Fifteen photographs of various scenes around Eastwood, Dunkeld, on the River Tay. R. Potter. 1879; Sep 1893; Jul 1893; Aug 1893; Oct 1893.
BP.1340, 1341(a,b), 1342–51, 1515, 1419

2077 Portrait of BP aged 5 and Mr Gaskell at Dalguise. R. Potter? 1871.
BP.1516

2078 Rupert Potter at Dalguise. R. Potter? n.d.
BP.1352

2079 Gardens at Dalguise. R. Potter. n.d.
BP.1353

Volume v

2080 Portrait of Marjorie, Winifred, Norah and Joan Moore. R. Potter? 1900.
BP.836

2081 Portrait of Joan and Norah Moore with BP at Broad Leys, Windermere. R. Potter. 25 Aug 1912. With envelope addressed to Mrs Moore, dated [Sep] 6 1912.
BP.837

2082 Castle Cottage, Sawrey. R. Potter. 13 Jul 1912.
BP.838

2083 Portrait of BP, with dog 'Spot', at Dalguise. R. Potter? 1880.
BP.870

2083

2084 Unidentified country house. R. Potter.
18 Sep 1886.
BP.1531

2085 Unidentified country house, with gravestones.
R. Potter. 6 Sep 1886.
BP.1532

2086 Lingholm, Keswick. R. Potter. Sep 1885.
BP.1533

2087 Bertram's painting, held by Bertram, at Lingholm,
Keswick. R. Potter. Oct 1901.
BP.1534

2088 Twenty-one views of Lingholm, Keswick, Catbells
and Derwentwater. R. Potter. 1887–1907; the
majority, 1903.
BP.1535–49, 1550(a,b), 1551–54

2089 2 Bolton Gardens: two garden scenes and one view
from the house. R. Potter. Apr 1890; Jun 1891;
Jun 1907.
BP.1514(a–c)

Volume VI

2090 Sawrey: garden path (different from view in
BP.1364; cat.1948; similar to view in BP.1367;
cat.1951). R. Potter. 13 Jul 1912.
Two copies.
BP.1363(a,b)

2091 Doll's house: interior. N. Warne? n.d.
Inscribed: Mrs Boultbee, The Vicarage, Tolleshunt
Major, Maldon, Essex (LL).
BP.1404

2092 Doll's house: exterior. N. Warne? n.d.
Inscription as for BP.1404; cat.2091.
BP.1405

2093 Portrait of Caroline Hutton. Unknown. n.d.
BP.1406

2094 Portrait of BP with 'Kep'. Unknown. n.d.
(modern print?)
Used for *Journal*.
BP.1407

2104

2095 Portrait of Winifred Warne with her doll's house,
inscribed by her (original of BP.1299; cat.2031).
N. Warne. n.d.
Used for *Journal*.
BP.1408

2096 Portrait of BP when young. R. Potter? n.d.
Used for *Journal*.
BP.1409

2097 Portrait of Gladstone. R. Potter. 28 Jul 1884.
BP.1410

2098 Portrait of Millais seated, front view, at Dalguise.
R. Potter? 4 Sep 1881.
BP.1411

2099 Painting by Millais. R. Potter? Jan 1884.
BP.1412

2100 Painting by Millais: 'Sweetest eyes'. R. Potter?
1881.
BP.1413

2101 Painting by Millais: 'Cinderella'. R. Potter? 1881.
BP.1414

2102 Portrait of BP. R. Potter? n.d.
BP.1415

2103 Potter family with dog 'Spot'. R. Potter? n.d.
BP.1416

2104 Portrait of BP aged 26. A.F. Mackenzie,
Birnam. n.d.
BP.1417

2105 The Hill Farm, Westmorland (bridge and fields).
Walmsley Bros., Ambleside. n.d.
BP.1420

2106 Portrait of BP seated, aged 10. R. Potter? n.d.
Two copies.
BP.1421(a,b)

2107 Portrait of BP aged 8 with her parents
(at Dalguise?). R. Potter? n.d.
BP.1422

2108 Portrait of BP aged 9. R. Potter? n.d.
BP.1423

2109 BP with Rupert and Bertram Potter. R. Potter? n.d.
(modern print, original missing)
Two copies.
BP.1424(a,b)

2110 Portrait of BP aged 15, with dog 'Spot'
(at Dalguise?). R. Potter? n.d.
BP.1425

2111 Portrait of BP aged 12, with dog 'Sandy'.
R. Potter? n.d.
BP.1426

2112 Portrait of BP aged 10 (at Dalguise?).
R. Potter? n.d.
BP.1427

2113 Portrait of BP at Hill Top, with 'Kep'(?).
Unknown. c.1907.
BP.1428

2114 Portrait of BP in Hill Top doorway. Unknown.
c.1907.
BP.1429

2115 BP aged 17, with Rupert and Bertram Potter and
dog 'Spot'. R. Potter? n.d.
BP.1430

2116 Portrait of BP aged 26. R. Potter? n.d.
Used as frontispiece for *Journal*.
BP.1432

2117 BP aged 23, with Rupert and Bertram Potter and
dog ('Spot'?). R. Potter? n.d.
BP.1529

2118 Portrait of Millais and Mrs Lillie Langtry in garden
at Eastwood. R. Potter? n.d.
Mounted together with card signed by the subjects
and inscribed: A Jersey pair. Sep 1879.
BP.1530

2119 6 plate negatives: photographs taken and
developed by BP, Ringmore, Feb 1910 (LL Cat.)
Also photograph of buildings in snow, Jan. 1909
(Sawrey?).
BP.871(i–vi)   Photographs Safe

In 1983 Mrs Joan Duke gave the Victoria & Albert
Museum a collection of fifty photographs by Rupert
Potter. About forty of these are housed with the
Linder material; the rest are in the Photograph
Collection.

ADDENDA

Miniature letters

Bequeathed by Miss Enid Linder in 1980.

Letters to Drew Fayle, Kylemore, Co. Dublin

2120 Letter from T. Winkle.
1f. 62 x 32mm
BP.1569(a)

2121 Letter from Tiggy Winkle.
1f. 62 x 35mm
BP.1569(b)

2122 Letter from Sir Isaac Newton.
2ff. 52 x 34, 51 x 32mm
BP.1569(c)

2123 Letter from Jeremiah Fisher.
1f. 71 x 31mm
BP.1569(d)   (*illustration p. 166*)

2124 Letter from Alderman Pt. Tortoise.
1f. 66 x 35mm
BP.1569(e)

2125 Letter from Flopsy Bunny.
1f. 65 x 32mm
BP.1569(f)

2126 Letter from Mr J. Fisher, 22 Jan 1910 to Mrs
Tiggy-Winkle, Cat Bells.
1f. 62 x 34mm
BP.1569(g)

2127 Letter from Mr J. Fisher to Mrs Tiggy-Winkle,
Cat Bells.
1f. 64 x 32mm
BP.1569(h)

2128 Letter from Antony Rowley.
1f. 62 x 32mm
BP.1569(i)

2129 Letter from Tom Kitten.
1f. 64 x 33mm
BP.1569(j)

2130 Letter from Peter [Rabbit].
1f. 40 x 30mm
BP.1569(k)

2131 Letter from Tom Thumb and Hunca Munca.
1f. 48 x 30mm
BP.1569(l)

BP.1569(a-l)   T.25.R

Miscellaneous watercolours and drawings

Bequeathed by Miss Enid Linder in 1980.

2132 Black currant branch with fruit.
W/c and pen-and-ink. 24.5 x 18
BP.1559   T.25.R

2133 Hydrangea.
Inscribed: Aug 26. 13.
W/c and pen-and-ink. 19 x 23
BP.1560   T.25.R

2134 Rabbit jumping into watering can; pelargoniums in
pots in the background.
Pen-and-ink and pencil. 21 x 18
BP.1561   T.25.R

2135 Partly finished drawing of woman, child and cats in
doorway surrounded by flowers, within pencilled
frame: background sketch for 'The Veal and Ham
Pie' (see BP.502; cat.751).
Pen-and-ink and pencil. 22.5 x 29
BP.1562   S.18.F.C

2136 Studies of rabbits, mainly sitting.
Pencil. 16 x 25
BP.1563   T.25.R

2137 Studies of rabbits' heads.
Verso: Similar studies.
Pencil, slightly foxed. 23 x 15
BP.1564   T.25.R

2138 Studies of cows, hens, ducks, mouse etc.
Pencil. 16 x 25.5
Verso: Studies of cows, rabbits, hens, ducks,
peacock, pig etc.
Pencil, some pen-and-ink.
BP.1565   T.25.R

2139 Table mat with illustration of cottage.
Inscribed: Gt. Haseley, Oxon.
Inscribed (verso): 12.
W/c, with gold edges. 10 x 13.5
BP.1566   T.25.R

2134

2140 Unfinished Christmas card, *c.* 1897. On the outside, a spray of rose-hips; inside, an illustration from *Cecily Parsley* inscribed (in pencil): Gentlemen came every day.
Bought by LL at Sotheby's?
W/c and pen-and-ink. W/m: Embassy de la Rue & Co. 18 x 11
BP.1567   T.25.R

2141 Two dinner cards used at Melford Hall by Stephanie Duke (see *The Art*, p.365).
(a) Drawing of Peter Rabbit.
   Inscribed: "Hope I'm not late?"––
(b) Drawing of Jemima Puddle-Duck.
   Inscribed: "This is where I sit!"
Bought by LL at Sotheby's?
See also BP.573; cat.1825.
W/c and pen-and-ink. 9 x 6 (each card)
BP.1568(a,b)   T.25.R

Page designs

2142 Two unfinished page designs (for menu cards?): borders of squirrels and trees, the centre of each sheet left blank.
Pen-and-ink and pencil. W/m: Britannia.
20 x 16.5 (each sheet)
BP.1570(a,b)   T.24.L

Wood blocks

2143 Two blocks for *The Tale of Benjamin Bunny*.
(a) Peter Rabbit and Mr McGregor.
(b) Flopsy, Mopsy and Cottontail with basket of berries.
5 x 6 (each block)
BP.1434(a,b)   T.2

Microscopic spore studies etc

2144 Sixteen studies of fungal and lichen (*Pertusaria*) spores, some on two pieces of card joined at the back; most marked with scale diagram.

(a) 3 *Pertusaria* spores in different stages of growth. Inscribed: March 25. 97. April 8th. 97. Pencil, some pen-and-ink and wash. 21 x 27.5

(b) Ascospores (unidentified). Pencil, some pen-and-ink. 21.5 x 25

(c) Algal symbiont of *Pertusaria*. Inscribed: Pertusaria [gonidia] out of old plant; and: March 31st [etc.]. Inscribed (verso): Sent to John Clegg (LL). Pen-and-ink, pencil and wash. 21.5 x 28

(d) Unknown. Pencil and wash. 21.5 x 28

(e) Unfinished study of sporodochia of *Epicoccum purpurascens* on a yellow circle. Inscribed: Epicoccum argyrioides; and: June 25th. 98. Pen-and-ink, pencil and wash. 21.5 x 27.5

(f) Developing spores of fungus. Pen-and-ink, pencil and wash. 21.5 x 27.5

(g) 2 *Pertusaria* spores. Inscribed: April 1st. 98; and: Pertusaria, Woodcote, Horsley. Pen-and-ink, pencil and wash. 27.5 x 21.5

(h) Unknown fungus spores. Pencil, some pen-and-ink. 12 x 16.5

(i) Unknown. Pencil, some pen-and-ink. 10.5 x 17.5

(j) Unknown fungus spores (different magnifications). Pencil. 11 x 14

(k) *Pertusaria* spore. Pencil and pen-and-ink. 13 x 16.5

(l) *Pertusaria*. Pencil and wash. 10.5 x 18

(m) Unknown. Inscribed: March 29th 97. Verso: Table of the Peter Rabbit Books. Pencil, pen-and-ink and wash. 21.5 x 14

(n) Unknown. Pencil. 21.5 x 15

(o) Unknown (fragment). Inscribed: 19th. 97. on oak, also at Esthwaite. Pencil, pen-and-ink and wash. 16.5 x 22

(p) Sporodochia and one highly magnified spore of *Epicoccum purpurascens*. Inscribed: Epicoccum argyrioides [etc.]. Pen-and-ink, pencil and wash. 11 x 28

BP.961(a–p)   P.C.49

2145 Four studies, on card.

(a) Inscribed: Foxglove June 24th 97, and marked with scale diagram. Shows various stages of growth of pollen-tubes. Pencil. 24 x 30.5

(b) Unknown. Inscribed: 5.pm; and: July [9?]. Pencil. 24 x 30.5

(c) Red seaweed (*Plocamium coccineum*). Inscribed (verso) in ink: Nov. 86. from Eastbourne. Pink wash, pen-and-ink and pencil. 36.5 x 27

(d) Honey fungus (*Armillaria* sp.) on trunk of tree(?). W/c and pencil. 24 x 30.5

BP.962(a–d)   P.C.49

Portfolios

2146 Portfolios made by Beatrix Potter to hold her drawings, using materials from her grandfather's textile-printing works (including both dress and furnishing fabrics).
15 folders.
BP.1571(i–xv)   P.C.drawer 3

Manuscript catalogues

2147 Catalogue of fungi drawings by Beatrix Potter in the Armitt Library, transcribed by Leslie Linder. n.d.
BP.1555   Photographs Safe

2148 Letters of Beatrix Potter to Mr. Warne, etc. (including some to Millie Warne) transcribed by Enid Linder, with annotations by LL and frontispiece photograph of Beatrix Potter. 1953.
BP.1556   Photographs Safe

2149 Catalogue of Beatrix Potter drawings and books, by Leslie Linder (incomplete). 1971.
BP.1557   Photographs Safe

2150 Catalogue of Beatrix Potter manuscripts, letters, papers and other items, by Leslie Linder. 1971.
BP.1558   Photographs Safe

Appendix: Holiday Dates

Bibliography

General Index

APPENDIX: Holiday Dates
An aid to identification of the sketches

This section records both long stays and short visits between 1882 and October 1913, when Beatrix Potter married William Heelis and finally settled in Sawrey. The exact dates of each stay are not always known and some of the 'visits' may have lasted longer than a single day. Inevitably there are gaps, as for instance in the years 1889 to 1891. Evidence gleaned from the various sources (listed at the beginning of Part II) is often patchy and sometimes conflicting! The insertion of 'etc.' indicates that the stay must have begun or ended beyond the substantiated date; square brackets indicate a date deduced from the evidence, and square brackets with an added question-mark indicate a conjectural date. It is hoped that more accurate datings may emerge after further research into material in other collections.

PART I
By year

1870
Tulliemet, Perthshire (Summer)

1871–1881
Dalguise House, nr. Dunkeld (annual holiday)

1882
Camfield Place, Hatfield (20–6 January)
Tenby (February)
Ilfracombe (3 April for 2 weeks) with visits to Berrynarbor (5 April), Watermouth Harbour and Castle, West Down (6 April), Lee (7 April), Combe Martin (8 April)
Wray Castle, Windermere (21 July–31 October) with visits to Hawkshead (19 August; 21 September), Patterdale (6 September), Lakeside (16 September), Elterwater (6 October)

1883
Ilfracombe (2–16 April)
Woodfield, nr. Hatfield (26 July–12 October) with visits to Camfield Place (27 July; 15 August; 22 September), St. Albans (2 August), Hertford (9 August), Panshanger Park (29 August), Hatfield House (15 September), Bush Hall (September)

1884
Eastbourne (2 February, back by 8th?) with visit to Beachy Head (3 February)
Camfield Place (7–10 March)
Manchester (29 March–4 April) with visits to Fallowfield and Eccles (30, 31 March), Gorse Hall, Stalybridge (2 April)
Minehead (15–29 April) with visits to Dunster, Timberscombe, Cutcombe, Dunkery Beacon, Horner Woods and Cloutsham Hall (24 April)

Camfield Place (19 May)
Edinburgh (22 [–26] May)
Dunkeld (26 May etc.) with visit to Dalguise (27 May)
Oxford (2–25 June) with visit to Radley (9 June)
Bushey, The Hall (19–22 July)
Bush Hall, Hertfordshire (1 August–23 October) with visit to Camfield (21 October)
Eastbourne (8–10 November)
Portsmouth (10–12 November)
Camfield Place (8–13 December)

1885
Camfield Place (10–16 February)
Eastbourne (28 February–2 March) with visit to Pevensey Castle (1 March)
Ambleside (11–27 April) with visits to Wray Castle (13 April), Langdale Valley and Dungeon Ghyll (16 April)
Camfield Place (1 May)
Machynlleth (13 May)
Shrewsbury (14 May) returning via Birmingham, Warwick, Oxford (15 May)
Camfield Place (30 May)
Lingholm, Keswick (10 July–9 October) with visits to Carlisle (20 August), Buttermere (25 August)
Camfield Place (13 October; 26 October–3 November)
Eastbourne (14 November)
Camfield Place (27 November; 17–23 December)

1886
Camfield Place (25–6 January)
Pendleton, Manchester (19–25 February) with visits to Dukinfield and Stalybridge (20 February)
Camfield Place (14 April)
Low Wood Hotel, Ambleside (20 April etc.)
Camfield Place (mid-August–end of September for 6 weeks)
Eastbourne (3–11 November)
Scotland (November) [R. Potter and Millais only?]
Camfield Place (27 November–13 December; 23–8 December)

1887
Camfield Place (18–28 February)
Camfield Place (1 April)
Grange over Sands, Morecambe (19–25 April)
Ambleside (25 April–5 May)
Camfield Place (2 June)
Lingholm, Keswick (11 July–10 September etc.)

1888
Camfield Place (May)
Lingholm, Keswick (Summer by 14 August–October)

1889
Holyhead (May)
Holehird, Windermere (Summer including August)

1890

Coniston Bank [Summer including August and September]

1891

Bedwell Lodge, nr. Hatfield (Summer–4 October etc.)

1892

Falmouth (31 March–14 April) with visits to Plymouth (12 April), Exeter and Drake's Island (13 April)
Dunkeld (June)
Heath Park, Birnam, Perthshire (26 July–early November) with visits to Braan Valley (1, 15 August; 8, 23, 29, 30 September; 4 October), Ballinluig (4 August), Inver (5, 12 August; 6, 22, 28 October), Stenton, Caputh Bridge and Murthly Castle (9 August), Guay (16, 22 August; 10, 28 September; 3 October), Dalmarnock (29 August; 16 September), Loch of the Lowes (3, 12 September), Murthly (10 September), Perth (13 September), Caputh Bridge (17 September), Butterglen (26 September), Tullypowrie (3 October), Ballinloan (8 October), Butterstone (11 October), Dalguise (13 October)

1893

Torquay (14–17 March)
Falmouth (17 March–late April)
Eastwood, Dunkeld (July–8 October etc.) with visits to London (7 September etc.) and Braan (8 October)

1894

Hertfordshire (Winter, date unknown)
Falmouth (28 March–3 April etc.)
Harescombe Grange, Stroud (12 etc.–20 June)
Lennel, Coldstream (17 July–[11] October) with visits to Branxton (26 July; 8 August; 18 September; 3 October), Birgham (3 August), Carham (6, 20 August), Alnwick (7 August), Crookham (11 August), Kelso (13 August), The Hirsel (14, 17 August), Wark (23 August; 4, 26 September), Norham Castle (24 August), East Learmouth (25 August), Berwick (28 August; 10, 12, 21 September), Edlingham (29 August), Twizzell (3 September), Burnmouth (14 September), Dryburgh (17 September), Tweed Mill (19 September), Kilham (22 September), Smailholm (25 September)

1895

Weymouth (9–18 April) with visits to Portland Island (11 April), Chalbury Ring (12 April), Dorchester (13 April), Osmington (15 April), Abbotsbury (16 April)
Salisbury (18–22 April) with visit to Stonehenge (19 April)
Gwaynynog, Denbighshire (28 May–4 June)
Harescombe Grange, Stroud (8–17 June)
Holehird, Windermere (26 July–23 September) with visits to Wray Castle (31 July; 10 September), Coniston (8 August; 2 September), Troutbeck (10 August), Kirkstone (17 August), Grasmere (22 August), Ambleside

(24 August), Kentmere Hall (31 August), Skelwith Bridge (5, 16 September), Dungeon Ghyll (9 September), Claife Heights and Hawkshead (21 September)
Manchester (23–6 September)

1896

Woodcote, Horsley (21–3 March)
Swanage (13–25 April) with visits to Wareham and Corfe, and to Silchester (27, 30 April)
Ferry Hotel, Windermere [May–June, before 11th] with visit to Lakefield, Sawrey
Eeswyke (Lakefield), Sawrey (15 July–6 October) with visits to Claife Woods (14 August), Ambleside (15, 26 August), Skelwith Bridge (17 August), Hawkshead (29 August; 2 September), Holehird (4 September), Wray Castle (21 September)
Harescombe Grange, Stroud (2–11 November)

1897

Woodcote, Horsley (9 January)
Lingholm, Keswick (25 July etc.–3 October etc.)
Harescombe Grange, Stroud (3 November etc.)

1898

Woodcote, Horsley (1–16 etc. April) with visit to Sidbury Camp (16 April)
Lingholm, Keswick (by 30 July–Autumn) with tour, accompanied by Bertram (16–24 or 27 August), via Carlisle, Dumfries, Kirkcudbright, Stranraer, Belfast, Stranraer, Dumfries (23 August)
Hastings (up to 28 December)

1899

Hastings (by 13–16 January)
Sidmouth (March)
Lingholm, Keswick (by 1–20 August etc.) with visit to Kelbarrow and Grasmere (1 August), Wray Castle (20 August)
Kirkcudbright and Galloway (27 September etc.)

1900

Harescombe Grange, Stroud (Winter, date unknown)
Derwent Cottage, Winchelsea (24 January–5 February)
Tenby (6–26 April)
Eeswyke, Sawrey (16 August etc.–1 October etc.)

1901

Tenby (February)
Sidmouth (April)
Lingholm, Keswick (by 11 September–October)
Melford (26 October–November)

1902

'The country' (after 19 January for about a week) [Woodcote?]
Sidmouth (15 April etc.)

223

Kalemouth, Roxburghshire (1 May for 2 weeks)
Laund House, Bolton Abbey (2–8 July)
Eeswyke, Sawrey (16 July for 3 months including 6 October)
Melford Hall, Suffolk (22 etc.–24 November)
Woodcote, Horsley (Winter, date unknown) [this could
    refer to earlier in the year – see above]

1903
Gwaynynog, Denbighshire (6–16 February)
Melford Hall ([9]–13 April etc.)
Folkestone (Easter for 2 weeks–2 May)
Portinscale, Keswick (11–15 May)
Harescombe Grange, Stroud (late May–[1] June)
Fawe Park, Keswick (16 July–[23] September) with visits
    to London (9 August etc.)
Hastings (26 November–3 December)
Melford Hall (Christmas for 1 week after 15 December)

1904
Gwaynynog, Denbighshire (11–25 March)
Burley, Lyme Regis (7–20 April)
Melford Hall (20–9 June)
Lingholm, Keswick (20 July–[27?] September) with visit
    to Greta (19 September)
Sidmouth (19 September)?
Harescombe Grange, Stroud (2–9 October) with visit to
    Brookthorpe Farm
Lingholm, Keswick ([19?]–28 October)
Gwaynynog, Denbighshire (3–5 November)

1905
Pullycrochan Hotel, Colwyn Bay (28–31 March)
St. Asaph (31 March–[11] April)
Gwaynynog, Denbighshire (26–9 May)
Painswick, nr. Stroud ([10] July etc.)
Hafod-y-Bryn, Llanbedr, Merioneth (before [25?] July–
    [25] August)
Amersham (3 August)?
Bath (end of September)

1906
Bath (1–5 February etc.)
Hill Top, Sawrey ([4]–[10] April)
Brighton ([10] April etc.)
Hill Top, Sawrey (early May; 18 July etc.)
Lingholm, Keswick (3 August–12 October etc.) with visits
    to Windermere (end of August) and Sawrey (including
    5–8, 30 September; 4, 12 October)

1907
Croughton (7–10 January)
Hastings (4–14 February)
Croughton (16–19 March)
Lingholm, Keswick (31 July etc.–3 September etc.)
Gwaynynog, Denbighshire (23 September etc.)
Hill Top, Sawrey (1 October for 2 weeks)

1908
Windermere [near] (28 July etc.–7 August etc.)
Gwaynynog, Denbighshire (19–23 etc. September)
Hill Top, Sawrey ([12] October etc.; 1–[5] December etc.)

1909
Hill Top, Sawrey (January; 2–7 March)
Gwaynynog, Denbighshire (10 March etc.)
Teignmouth (21 August)?
Broad Leys, Windermere (9 September etc.)
Gwaynynog, Denbighshire (10 October etc.)
Hill Top, Sawrey (15–21 November etc.)

1910
Hill Top, Sawrey (11 January etc.)
Ringmore, Devon (February)
Woodcote, Horsley (early Spring)
Bowness, Windermere ([16] March etc.) with visit to
    Sawrey (18 March)
Sidmouth (Easter–[27] March, i.e. Easter Sunday)
Teignmouth (28 March–4 April etc.)
Gwaynynog, Denbighshire (4 etc.–7 May)
Hill Top, Sawrey (11 June etc.)
Helm Farm, Windermere (Summer by 13 August–14 or 15
    September) with visits to Sawrey (including 24–[26], 29
    August; 3, 9 September)
Hatfield (23 September)
Hill Top, Sawrey (9–[14] October; 17–23 or 24 November)

1911
Hill Top, Sawrey ([23] January–7 February)
Gwaynynog, Denbighshire (3 June etc.)
Melford Hall and Long Melford (11 June etc.)
Hill Top, Sawrey (16 June etc.)
Gwaynynog, Denbighshire (30 June–4 July)
Hill Top, Sawrey (22 August etc.–5 November etc.;
    12 December etc.) with visit to Lingholm (1 October)?

1912
Gwaynynog, Denbighshire (18 May etc.)
Hill Top, Sawrey (13 July etc.)
Broad Leys, Windermere (long stay including
    22–5 August and September) with visits to Sawrey
Hill Top, Sawrey (Autumn visits including 13 November
    for about a week) with visit to Lingholm (21 October)?

1913
Hill Top, Sawrey (11 January etc.; 7 April–17 May etc.
    with visits to parents in hotel)
Hill Top, Sawrey (4 June etc.)
Lindeth Howe, Windermere (with parents, 10 July etc.–
    [26?] September) with visits to Sawrey (including
    16 September)
Castle Cottage, Sawrey (soon after 15 October)

Unsubstantiated holiday dates

'Original reference untraced' usually indicates information provided by someone other than the compiler.

1881

Stay in 'Devonshire', 6 April (P) – possibly Rupert Potter only?

1893

Visit to London from Eastwood, Dunkeld (see H, p.14) seems doubtful

1897

Esthwaite visit in March (see Cat.2144): merely implies 'also at Esthwaite'?
Lingholm visit in December? (original reference untraced)

1899

Visit to London from Lingholm? (original reference untraced)

1902

Details of Woodcote visit not known

1903

Woodcote visit in Winter? (original reference untraced)
Gwaynynog visit in Summer? (original reference untraced)

1904

Visit to London from Lingholm in September? (original reference untraced)
Sidmouth visit (see Cat.829) does not tally with long stay at Lingholm

1905

Melford visit, April–May? (original reference untraced)
Amersham visit, 3 August (see NBL 13/B/1,2) does not tally with Merioneth visit (for which evidence is conflicting also). It is unlikely that NBL 15/A/6 represents a Hill Top field

1909

Teignmouth visit, 21 August (original reference untraced)

1911

Lingholm visit, 1 October (original reference untraced)

1912

Lingholm visit, 21 October (original reference untraced)

1913

Gwaynynog visit in May? (original reference untraced)

PART II

By place

References

The Art	*The Art of Beatrix Potter*, (rev. ed.) 1972
Cat.	This catalogue [nos.1940–2119 refer to photographs]
H	*A History of the Writings of Beatrix Potter*, Leslie Linder, 1971
HL	Holiday Lists (Cat.1930–1)
J	*The Journal of Beatrix Potter*, 1881–1897, 1966
MY	*The Magic Years of Beatrix Potter*, Margaret Lane, 1978
NBL	The Linder Collection, National Book League
P	Photographs (not in Linder Bequest)
W	Letters of Beatrix Potter to Mr Warne etc. (Cat.2148)

Some references to this catalogue have been omitted where they merely duplicate references in the *History*, *Journal* etc. All other references to place-names may be found in the index.

Ambleside

1885 11–27 April (J, pp.139–40)
1886 20 April etc. [Low Wood Hotel] (J, p.191)
1887 25 April–5 May (J, pp.194–5)
1895 24 August (visit) (J, p.388)
1896 15,26 August (visits) (J, p.419)
See also Windermere

Amersham

1905 3 August? (*The Art*, pp.82–3; NBL 13/B/1,2)

Bath

1905 end of September (MY, p.138)
1906 1–5 etc. February (W, p.307)

Bedwell Lodge, nr. Hatfield

1891 Summer–4 October etc. (*The Art*, pp.32, 45–7, 65, 190–1; Cat.430, 496; J, pp.70, 256, 267, plate opp. p.72; NBL 2/A/2,12/B/2,4)

Belfast

1898 mid-August (visit) (H, p.30)

Berwickshire *see* Lennel

Birnam, Perthshire
1892 26 July–early November [Heath Park] (*H*, pp. 155, 175; *J*, pp. 238–302)
See also Dunkeld

Bolton Abbey, Yorkshire
1902 2–8 July [Laund House] (*The Art*, pp. 58, 70–1; *H*, p. 114)

Bowness *see* Windermere

Brighton
1906 [10] April etc. (*W*, p. 315)

Broad Leys *see* Windermere

Brookthorpe Farm *see* Harescombe Grange

Burley *see* Lyme Regis

Bushey
1885 19–22 July [The Hall, a 'hydropathic'] (*J*, pp. 98–9)

Bush Hall, Hertfordshire (on the Lea)
1883 September (visit) (Cat. 128)
1884 1 August–23 October (*The Art*, pp. 33, 56, 60–4; *J*, pp. 101–6; Cat. 2073–5)

Camfield Place, Essendon, Hatfield
1882 20–6 January (*J*, p. 9)
1883 27 July, 15 August, 22 September (visits) (Cat. 2063; *J*, pp. 47, 52)
1884 7–10 March (*J*, p. 70), 19 May (*J*, p. 83), 21 October (visit) (*J*, p. 106), 8–13 December (*The Art*, p. 67; Cat. 530; *J*, p. 118)
1885 10–16 February (*J*, p. 125), 1 May (*J*, p. 140), 30 May (*J*, p. 144), 13 October (*J*, p. 152), 26 October–3 November (*J*, p. 152), 27 November (*J*, p. 157), 17–23 December (*J*, p. 161)
1886 25, 26 January (*J*, p. 166), 14 April (*J*, p. 191), mid-August–end of September for 6 weeks (*J*, pp. 192–3), 27 November–13 December (Cat. 158; *J*, p. 194), 23–8 December (*J*, p. 194)
1887 18–28 February (Cat. 159; *J*, p. 194), 1 April (NBL 7/B/2), 2 June (*J*, p. 196)
1888 May (*The Art*, p. 150; NBL 19/A/5)
[Also other unrecorded short visits]

Carlisle
1885 20 August (visit) (*J*, p. 149)
1898 mid-August (visit) (*H*, p. 30)

Castle Cottage *see* Sawrey

Coldstream *see* Lennel

Colwyn Bay
1905 28–31 March [Pullycrochan Hotel] (*W*, p. 219)

Coniston Bank
1890 [Summer including August and September] (HL; P)

Croughton
1907 7–10 January (Cat. 1100), 16–19 March (NBL 13/B/5)

Dalguise House, nr. Dunkeld
1871–81 (annual holiday) (*H*, p. 155)
1884 27 May (visit) (*J*, p. 86)
1892 13 October (visit) (*J*, p. 284)
See also Dunkeld

Derwent Cottage *see* Winchelsea

Dumfries
1898 mid-August including 23rd (visit) (Cat. 1464; *H*, p. 30)

Dunkeld
1884 26 May etc. (*J*, p. 86)
1892 June [Inver] (*The Art*, p. 88; NBL 14/B/4; P)
1893 July–8 October etc. [Eastwood] (*The Art*, pp. 140, 142, 144; Cat. 2076; *H*, pp. 7, 14, 92, 175; *J*, plate opp. p. 352; MY, p. 42)
See also Birnam, Dalguise House, Lennel

Eastbourne
1884 2 February (back by 8th?) (*J*, p. 64), 8–10 November (*J*, p. 108)
1885 28 February–2 March (*J*, p. 130), 14 November (*J*, p. 154)
1886 3–11 November (Cat. 2145; *J*, p. 193)

Eastwood, Dunkeld *see* Dunkeld

Edinburgh
1884 22[–26] May (*J*, pp. 84–6)

Eeswyke (Lakefield) *see* Sawrey

Esthwaite *see* Sawrey

Exeter *see* Falmouth

Falmouth
1892 31 March–14 April (and to Exeter) (*J*, pp. 211–38)
1893 17 March–late April (*J*, pp. 309–10)
1894 28 March–3 April etc. (Cat. 1463, 2059; *H*, p. 15)

Fawe Park, Keswick
1903 16 July–[23] September (*The Art*, pp.297, 301;
     Cat.474, 544, 801, 1095, 2088; *H*, p.120; NBL
     24/A/1–3; W, pp.94, 112)
See also Lingholm

Ferry Hotel *see* Windermere

Folkestone
1903 Easter for 2 weeks–2 May (*H*, p.119; W, pp.57, 73)

Galloway *see* Kirkcudbright

Gorse Hall *see* Stalybridge

Grange over Sands, Morecambe
1887 19–25 April (*J*, pp.194–5)

Grasmere *see* Lingholm, 1899

Gwaynynog, Denbighshire
1895 28 May–4 June (*J*, pp.376–9)
1903 6–16 February (*The Art*, p.37; Cat.931; *H*, p.136)
1904 11–25 March (*The Art*, p.36; NBL 12/A/3),
     3–5 November (NBL 27/A/4; W, pp.193, 196)
1905 26–9 May (*H*, p.170; W, pp.227–8 etc.)
1907 23 September etc. (Cat.938)
1908 19–23 etc. September (*The Art*, pp.31, 128; Cat.480)
1909 10 March etc. (Cat.934; *H*, p.195), 1 October etc.
     (Cat.547)
1910 4 etc.–7 May (Cat.481, 483)
1911 3 June etc. (Cat.549), 30 June–4 July (Cat.935)
1912 18 May etc. (Cat.548)

Hafod-y-Bryn *see* Merioneth

Harescombe Grange, Stroud
1894 12 etc.–20 June (*H*, p.111; *J*, pp.312–19)
1895 8–17 June etc. (*J*, pp.379–80)
1896 2–11 November (*J*, p.423)
1897 3 November etc. (*H*, p.134, plate opp. p.233)
1900 Winter (date unknown) (MY, p.103)
1903 late May–[1] June (Cat.789; *H*, p.119; W, p.82)
1904 2–9 October [and to Brookthorpe Farm] (*The Art*,
     p.84; Cat.598; NBL 13/A/6, 31/A/3)

Hastings
1898 up to 28 December (*H*, pp.34ff)
1899 by 13–16 January (*H*, pp.34ff; Cat.1462, 1465)
1903 26 November–3 December (*H*, pp.149, 293)
1907 4–14 February (Cat.1236; *H*, p.338)

Hatfield
1910 23 September (*The Art*, p.85; NBL 13/B/6)
See also Bedwell Lodge, Bush Hall, Camfield Place,
St. Albans, Woodfield

Hawkshead
1882 19 August, 21 September (visits) (*J*, pp.20, 22)
1895 21 September (visit) (*J*, p.394)
1896 29 August, 2 September (visits) (*J*, pp.419–20)

Heath Park *see* Birnam

Helm Farm *see* Windermere

'Hertfordshire'
1894 Winter (date unknown) (Cat.986)
See also Bedwell Lodge, etc.

Holehird *see* Windermere

Holyhead
1889 May (*The Art*, p.94; Cat.553, 2058)

Ilfracombe
1882 3 April for 2 weeks (*J*, pp.11–14)
1883 2–16 April (Cat.1355, 2057; *H*, p.256; *J*, p.35)

Kalemouth, Roxburghshire
1902 1 May for 2 weeks (*H*, p.102; MY, p.101)

Kelbarrow, Grasmere *see* Lingholm, 1899

Kelso *see* Lennel

Keswick *see* Fawe Park, Lingholm, Portinscale

Kirkcudbright and Galloway
1898 mid-August (visit) (*H*, p.30)
1899 27 September etc. (*The Art*, p.86; Cat.566;
     NBL 14/A/3, 15/B/5)

Lakefield (Eeswyke) *see* Sawrey

Laund House *see* Bolton Abbey

Lennel, Coldstream, Berwickshire
1894 17 July–[11] October (*The Art*, pp.141, 143;
     Cat.2071–2; *H*, pp.93, 350; *J*, pp.320–59)
See also Dunkeld

Lingholm, Keswick
1885 10 July–9 October (*J*, pp.147–51; Cat.2086)
1887 11 July–10 September etc. (Cat.2088; NBL 7/A/3,
     19/B/3)
1888 Summer by 14 August–October (Cat.2088; NBL
     16/B/1, 4)
1897 25 July etc.–3 October etc. (Cat.395, 2088;
     H, pp.26, 135, plate opp. p.310; *J*, plates opp.
     pp.321, 428; MY, p.43; P; NBL 6/A/2)
1898 by 30 July–Autumn (*The Art*, p.75; Cat.555, 2088;
     H, p.30)

1899 by 1 August–20 August etc. (*The Art*, p. 311; Cat. 865, 2052; *H*, p. 156; HL; NBL 25/B/1)

1901 by 11 September–October (Cat. 2087; *H*, pp. 54, 135; W, p. 1)

1904 20 July–[27?] September (Cat. 557ff; *H*, pp. 147, 156; MY, p. 131; W, pp. 178–9, 186, 190), [19?]–28 October (*H*, p. 227; W, pp. 187, 192–3)

1906 3 August–12 October etc. [with visits to Sawrey] (*H*, p. 186; W, pp. 317–22)

1907 31 July etc.–23 September etc. (Cat. 422, 2088; MY, p. 98)

1911 1 October (visit)? (NBL 14/B/2)

1912 21 October (visit)? (NBL 14/B/1)

Llanbedr *see* Merioneth

Low Wood Hotel *see* Ambleside

Lyme Regis
1904 7–20 April [Burley] (*The Art*, p. 58; *H*, pp. 144, 152, 399; W, p. 150)

Machynlleth
1885 13 May (*J*, p. 142)

Manchester
1884 29 March–4 April [and to Stalybridge] (*J*, pp. 76–8)
1886 19–25 February [Pendleton, and to Stalybridge] (*J*, pp. 176–80)
1895 23–6 September (*J*, pp. 395–6)
See also Stalybridge

Melford Hall, Suffolk
1901 26 October–November (Cat. 1024; *H*, pp. 155, 159)
1902 22 etc.–24 November (*H*, p. 136; W, p. 42)
1903 [9]–13 etc. April (Cat. 1959ff; *H*, pp. 118, 139; W, p. 66), Christmas, for 1 week after 15 December (*H*, p. 149; NBL 13/A/4; W, p. 127)
1904 20–9 June (*H*, p. 230; W, pp. 164, 169–70)
1911 11 June etc. [Long Melford] (Cat. 574)
[Also other unrecorded visits]

Merioneth, Wales
1905 by 25 July?–[25] August [Hafod-y-Bryn, Llanbedr] (Cat. 578; *H*, p. 171; MY, pp. 133, 136–8; W, pp. 251–6, 308)

Minehead
1884 15–29 April (Cat. 378; *J*, pp. 78–9)

Morecambe *see* Grange over Sands

Oxford
1884 2–25 June (*J*, pp. 89–91)
1885 15 May (visit) (*J*, p. 142)

Painswick, nr. Stroud
1905 [10] July etc. (W, p. 251)

Pendleton *see* Manchester

Perth
1892 13 September (visit) (*J*, p. 260)
See also Birnam

Plymouth
1892 12 April (visit) (*J*, pp. 234–5)

Portinscale, Keswick
1903 11–15 May (*H*, pp. 119, 140; W, pp. 77–9 etc.)

Portsmouth
1884 10–12 November (*J*, pp. 108–10)

Pullycrochan Hotel *see* Colwyn Bay

Ringmore, Devon
1910 February (Cat. 2119)

Roxburgh *see* Kalemouth

St. Albans
1883 2 August (visit) (*J*, p. 48)

St. Asaph
1905 31 March–[11] April (W, pp. 219, 223)

Salisbury
1895 18–22 April (*J*, pp. 371–4)

Sawrey
1896 late Spring [Lakefield] (visit) (MY, p. 86), 15 July–6 October [Eeswyke] (*H*, pp. 168, 185; *J*, pp. 416–22; MY, p. 94; P)
1900 16 August etc.–1 October etc. [Eeswyke] (Cat. 501; *H*, p. 168; P)
1902 16 July for 3 months incl. 6 October [Eeswyke] (*H*, pp. 107, 168, 225)
1906 [4]–10 April [Hill Top Farm and Belle Green] (*H*, p. 191; W, pp. 313, 315), early May (W, p. 316), 18 July etc. (*H*, p. 185; W, pp. 310–11), visits throughout Autumn including 5–8, 30 September, 4, 12 October (*H*, p. 191; W, pp. 320–31)
1907 1 October for 2 weeks (W, pp. 335–6)
1908 [12] October etc. (W, pp. 345–6), 1 etc.–[5] December (W, p. 305)
1909 January (Cat. 2119; W, p. 305), 2–7 March (*The Art*, 1955 ed., p. 134; Cat. 178, 669ff; MY, p. 202; NBL 15/A/3), 15–21 etc. November (Cat. 541–2, 594; *H*, p. 213; MY, p. 194; NBL 28/B/2; W, pp. 338, 341)

1910 11 January etc. (Cat. 1347), 18 March etc. (visit) (Cat. 1485), 11 June etc. (W, p. 349), visits throughout Summer and Autumn including 24 [–26], 29 August, 3, 9 September, 9[–14] October, 17–23 or 24 November (Cat. 183, 586, 596, 684, 1947, 1949; W, pp. 353, 355–6, 358–60)

1911 [23] January–7 February (W, pp. 361–2), 16 June etc. (MY, p. 94; NBL 15/A/4), 22 August etc.– 5 November etc. (Cat. 587, 1951; H, p. 376), 12 December etc. (Cat. 1426; W, pp. 364–5)

1912 13 July etc. (Cat. 1948, 2082, 2090), visits in August (W, p. 367), Autumn visits including 13 November for about a week (W, pp. 259–60)

1913 11 January etc. (The Art, pp. 90–1; Cat. 670), 7 April–17 May etc. (H, pp. 214–15; MY, p. 192; W, pp. 263–81), 4 June etc. (W, p. 285), visits including 16 September (W, p. 294 etc.), moved to Castle Cottage soon after 15 October (H, p. 217)

[Also other unrecorded visits]

Scotland
1886 November [R. Potter only?] (Cat. 2055–6)

Shrewsbury
1885 14 May (J, p. 142)

Sidmouth
1899 March (NBL 13/B/3)
1901 April (H, p. 256)
1902 15 April etc. (The Art, pp. 74, 110; Cat. 601)
1904 19 September? (Cat. 829)
1910 Easter [–27 March] (MY, p. 185)

Silchester see Swanage, 1896

Stalybridge [Gorse Hall]
1884 2 April (visit) (J, p. 77)
1886 20 February (visit) (J, p. 176)
[Also childhood visits]
See also Manchester

Stroud see Harescombe Grange, Painswick

Swanage
1896 13–25 April (Cat. 196; J, pp. 410–12; MY, p. 90)

Teignmouth
1909 21 August? (NBL 14/A/6)
1910 28 March–4 April etc. (Cat. 1487–9)

Tenby
1882 February (Cat. 19, 79)
1900 6–26 April (The Art, pp. 100, 173; Cat. 468, 1467; H, p. 46; MY, p. 90; NBL 3/B/4)
1901 February (The Art, p. 101; Cat. 468)

Torquay
1893 14–17 March (J, pp. 307–9)

Tulliemet, Perthshire
1870 Summer (J, p. 273)

Weymouth
1895 9–18 April (The Art, p. 149; J, pp. 365–71)

Winchelsea [Derwent Cottage, now Haskards]
1900 24 January–5 February (The Art, pp. 40–4, 124; H, pp. 38, 42ff; NBL 11/B/2, 3)

Windermere
1889 Summer including August [Holehird] (Cat. 2027, 2066; J, p. 382, plate opp. p. 297; MY, p. 8; P)
1895 26 July–23 September [Holehird] (J, pp. 382–95)
1896 [May–June, before 11th] [Ferry Hotel] (J, p. 415; MY, p. 86), 4 September [Holehird] (visit) (J, p. 420)
1906 end of August (W, p. 319)
1908 28 July etc.–17 August etc. (P)
1909 9 September etc. [Broad Leys] (P)
1910 [16] March etc. [Bowness] (Cat. 1485; MY, p. 185), Summer by 13 August–14 or 15 September [Helm Farm, with visits to Sawrey] (NBL 14/B/3; W, p. 352)
1912 Summer including 22–5 August and September [Broad Leys, with visits to Sawrey] (Cat. 2081; P; W, p. 367)
1913 10 July etc.–[26?] September [Lindeth Howe, with visits to Sawrey] (Cat. 1494; H, p. 216; W, pp. 284–94)
See also Ambleside, Wray Castle

Woodcote, Horsley
1896 21–3 March (J, pp. 409–10)
1897 9 January (J, p. 429)
1898 1–16 etc. April (Cat. 288, 2144)
1902 Winter (date unknown [January?]) (The Art, pp. 149, 178; Cat. 118; H, p. 101)
1910 early Spring (MY, p. 185)
[Also other unrecorded visits]

Woodfield, nr. Hatfield
1883 26 July–12 October (Cat. 90; J, pp. 47–53)

Wray Castle, Windermere
1882 21 July–31 October (J, pp. 19–23)
1885 13 April (visit) (J, p. 139)
1895 31 July, 10 September (visits) (J, pp. 383, 392)
1896 21 September (visit) (J, p. 421; MY, p. 94)
1899 20 August (visit) (Cat. 2052)

BIBLIOGRAPHY

Biographical studies

The Tale of Beatrix Potter: a biography, Margaret Lane, 1946; new ed. 1967

The Art of Beatrix Potter, 1955; 2 ed. 1972

The Journal of Beatrix Potter, 1881–1897, transcribed from her code-written manuscript by Leslie Linder, 1966

A History of the Writings of Beatrix Potter, Leslie Linder, 1971

Beatrix Potter: artist and author, Leslie Linder, 1977

The Magic Years of Beatrix Potter, Margaret Lane, 1978

Beatrix Potter in Scotland, Deborah Rolland, 1981

Cousin Beattie: a memoir, Ulla Hyde-Parker, 1981

Beatrix Potter's Americans, Jane Crowell Morse, *The Horn Book*, Boston, 1982

The Peter Rabbit books
Arranged in alphabetical order

Appley-Dapply's Nursery Rhymes, 1917

Cecily Parsley's Nursery Rhymes, 1922

Ginger and Pickles, 1909

The Pie and the Patty-Pan, 1905

The Roly-Poly Pudding (later renamed *The Tale of Samuel Whiskers*), 1908

The Story of a Fierce Bad Rabbit, 1906

The Story of Miss Moppet, 1906

The Tailor of Gloucester, privately printed ed. 1902; Warne's ed. 1903

The Tale of Benjamin Bunny, 1904

The Tale of Jemima Puddle-Duck, 1908

The Tale of Johnny Town-Mouse, 1918

The Tale of Little Pig Robinson, Philadelphia 1930; Warne's ed. 1930

The Tale of Mrs Tiggy-Winkle, 1905

The Tale of Mr Jeremy Fisher, 1906

The Tale of Mrs Tittlemouse, 1910

The Tale of Mr Tod, 1912

The Tale of Peter Rabbit, privately printed ed. 1901; Warne's ed. 1902

The Tale of Pigling Bland, 1913

The Tale of Squirrel Nutkin, 1903

The Tale of the Flopsy Bunnies, 1909

The Tale of Timmy Tiptoes, 1911

The Tale of Tom Kitten, 1907

The Tale of Two Bad Mice, 1904

The Peter Rabbit books: Appendix

Peter Rabbit's Almanac for 1929, 1928

Peter Rabbit's Painting Book, 1911

Tom Kitten's Painting Book, 1917

Jemima Puddle-Duck's Painting Book, 1925

The Tailor of Gloucester: facsimile of the original manuscript and illustrations, limited ed. Warne, New York 1968; English ed. 1969

The History of the Tale of Peter Rabbit (adapted from Leslie Linder's *A History of the Writings of Beatrix Potter*), 1976

Other works

The Fairy Caravan, privately printed ed. 1929; Philadelphia 1929; English ed. 1952

Sister Anne, Philadelphia 1932

Wag-by-Wall, limited ed. 1944; *The Horn Book*, Boston 1944

The Tale of the Faithful Dove, limited ed. 1955; New York 1956; with illustrations by Marie Angel, New York 1970; English ed. 1971

The Sly Old Cat, 1971

The Tale of Tuppenny, with illustrations by Marie Angel, New York 1973

Associated works

The Tale of the Tales, Rumer Godden, 1971

Beatrix Potter's Birthday Book, compiled by Enid Linder, 1974

Peter Rabbit's Natural Foods Cook Book, Arnold Dobrin, New York 1977

Children's Plays from Beatrix Potter, dramatized by Rona Laurie, 1980

Peter Rabbit's Cookery Book, Anne Emerson, 1980

The Beatrix Potter Country Cookery Book, Margaret Lane, 1981

The Peter Rabbit Diary (from *Peter Rabbit's Almanac for 1929*), 1982

Beatrix Potter's Address Book, 1982

Lakeland Walks from Beatrix Potter, Wynne Bartlett, 1982

The Complete Adventures of Peter Rabbit, 1982

The Peter Rabbit Pop-up Book, pictures redrawn by Colin Twinn, designed by Dick Dudley, paper mechanics by Keith Moseley, 1983

My First Year: a Beatrix Potter baby record book, devised by Judy Taylor, 1983

The Peter Rabbit Theatre, Colin Twinn, 1983

Peter Rabbit's Gardening Book, Sarah Garland, 1983

Yours affectionately, Peter Rabbit: a collection of the miniature letters, edited by Anne Emerson, 1983

Beatrix Potter's Sketchbook 1903 – A Facsimile, with Commentary by Joyce Irene Whalley and Wynne Bartlett, 1984

Beatrix Potter's Nursery Rhyme Book, 1984

The Complete Adventures of Tom Kitten, 1984

Peter Rabbit & His Friends Colouring Book, 1984

Tom Kitten & His Friends Colouring Book, 1984

Books printed in Braille
(The Royal Institute for the Blind)

Peter Rabbit; Mrs Tiggy-Winkle; Tom Kitten; Flopsy Bunnies; Pigling Bland; Johnny Town-Mouse, 1921
The Journal of Beatrix Potter has been tape-recorded by The British Talking Book Service for the Blind, 1970

Books printed in i.t.a.

Peter Rabbit; Benjamin Bunny; Two Bad Mice; Mrs Tiggy-Winkle; Mr Jeremy Fisher; Tom Kitten; Jemima Puddle-Duck; Flopsy Bunnies; Mrs Tittlemouse, 1965
Timmy Tiptoes, 1966

Books translated into other languages

Afrikaans

Die verhaal van Pieter Konyntjie (Peter Rabbit), 1929
Die verhaal van Bennie Blinkhaar (Benjamin Bunny), 1935
Die verhaal van die Flopsie-Familie (Flopsy Bunnies), 1935
Die verhaal van Mevrou Piekfyn (Mrs Tittlemouse), 1935

The following published under licence by Human & Rousseau Publishers (Pty.) Ltd., Cape Town:
Die verhaal van Diederik Dorpsmuis (Johnny Town-Mouse), 1970
Die verhaal van Gertjie Kat (Tom Kitten), 1970
Die verhaal van Tys Toontjies (Timmy Tiptoes), 1971
Die verhaal van Meraai Plassie-Eend (Jemima Puddle-Duck), 1971
Die verhaal van Doppertjie (Squirrel Nutkin), 1972
Die verhaal van Joachim Visser (Jeremy Fisher), 1972
Die verhaal van Ta' Pinkie-Winkie (Mrs Tiggy-Winkle), 1975
Die verhaal van die Twee Stout Muise (Two Bad Mice), 1975
Die verhaal van Frederik Haas (Peter Rabbit), 1975
Die verhaal van die Huppel-Hase (Flopsy Bunnies), 1975
Die verhaal van Kosie Konyn (Benjamin Bunny), 1975
Die verhaal van Mevrou Trippelmuis (Mrs Tittlemouse), 1975
Die Snyer en sy Kat (Tailor of Gloucester), 1977
Die verhaal van Meneer de Vos (Mr Tod), 1977
Die verhaal van Otjie Lietie (Pigling Bland), 1979
Die verhaal van Juffie Kiets (Miss Moppet), 1980
Die verhaal van die Stegte, Stout Haas (Fierce Bad Rabbit), 1980

Bulgarian

The following published under licence by Otechestvo:
Misis Mishimaus (Mrs Tittlemouse), 1979
Koteto Tom (Tom Kitten), 1979
Dzherŭmi Ribarya (Jeremy Fisher), 1979
Misis Tigi-Migŭl (Mrs Tiggy-Winkle), 1979
Zaicheto Pitŭr (Peter Rabbit), 1979

Danish

Tom Kitte (Tom Kitten), 1946

The following published under licence by Gyldendal Forlag, Copenhagen:
Historien om Peter Kanin (Peter Rabbit), 1971
Historien om Benjamin Langøre (Benjamin Bunny), 1972
Historien om de Små Langører (Flopsy Bunnies), 1972
Historien om Tom Kispus (Tom Kitten), 1972
Historien om To Uartige Mus (Two Bad Mice), 1974
Historien om hr. Joakim Fisker (Jeremy Fisher), 1974
Historien om fru Vimsemus (Mrs Tittlemouse), 1974
Historien om Johnny Bymus (Johnny Town-Mouse), 1974

Dutch

Het verhaal van Pieter Langoor (Peter Rabbit), 1912
Het verhaal van Kwakkel Waggel-Eend (Jemima Puddle-Duck), 1912

The following published under licence by Nijgh & van Ditmar's Uitgevers- Maatschappij, Rotterdam:
Benjamin Knabbel (Benjamin Bunny), 1946
Twee Stoute Muisjes (Two Bad Mice), 1946
Jeremias de Hengelaar (Mr Jeremy Fisher), 1946
Tom het Poesje (Tom Kitten), 1946
De Kleine Langoortjes (Flopsy Bunnies), 1946

The following published under licence by Uitgeverij Ploegsma, Amsterdam:
Het verhaal van Pieter Konijn (Peter Rabbit), 1968
Het verhaal van Jozefien Kwebbeleend (Jemima Puddle-Duck), 1968
Het verhaal van Timmie Tuimelaar (Timmy Tiptoes), 1968
Het verhaal van Eekhoorn Hakketak (Squirrel Nutkin), 1969
Het verhaal van Benjamin Wollepluis (Benjamin Bunny), 1969
Het verhaal van Twee Stoute Muizen (Two Bad Mice), 1969
Het verhaal van Vrouwtje Plooi (Mrs Tiggy-Winkle), 1969
Het verhaal van de Wollepluis-Konijntjes (Flopsy Bunnies), 1969
Het verhaal van Diederik Stadsmuis (Johnny Town-Mouse), 1969
Het verhaal van Jeremias Hengelaar (Jeremy Fisher), 1970
Het verhaal van Poekie Poes (Tom Kitten), 1970
Het verhaal van Minetje Miezemuis (Mrs Tittlemouse), 1970

Finnish

The following published under licence by Kustannusosakeyhtio Otava, Helsinki:
Petteri Kaniini (Peter Rabbit), 1967
Nokkela ja Vikkelä (Squirrel Nutkin), 1967
Rouva Siiri Sipinen (Mrs Tiggy-Winkle), 1967
Tarina räätälistä (Tailor of Gloucester), 1979

Penna Pupu (Benjamin Bunny), 1979
Kaksi Tuhmaa Hiirtä (Two Bad Mice), 1979
Hanna-Hiiren Kuokkavieraat (Mrs Tittlemouse), 1979
Pikku Salaattivarkaat (Flopsy Bunnies), 1979
Hemmo Harmaatassu (Timmy Tiptoes), 1979
Tommin Roimahousut (Tom Kitten), 1979
Jeremias Rimppakinttu (Jeremy Fisher), 1979
Joonas Kaupunkihiiri (Johnny Town-Mouse), 1979
Rosina Ankkanen Maailmalla (Jermima Puddle-Duck), 1980

French

Pierre Lapin (Peter Rabbit), 1921
Jeannot Lapin (Benjamin Bunny), 1921
Poupette-à-l'Épingle (Mrs Tiggy-Winkle), 1922
Sophie Canétang (Jemima Puddle-Duck), 1922
Noisy-Noisette (Squirrel Nutkin), 1931
La Famille Flopsaut (Flopsy Bunnies), 1931
Jérémie Pêche-à-la-Ligne (Jeremy Fisher), 1940
Toto le Minet (Tom Kitten), 1951
Le Tailleur de Gloucester (Tailor of Gloucester), 1967
Madame Trotte-Menu (Mrs Tittlemouse), 1975
Deux Vilaines Souris (Two Bad Mice), 1975
Petit-Jean des Villes (Johnny Town-Mouse), 1976
Mademoiselle Moppette (Miss Moppet), 1976
Méchant Petit Lapin Mal Élevé (Fierce Bad Rabbit), 1978
Tonton-le-Voltigeur (Timmy Tiptoes), 1978
Samuel le Moustachu (Samuel Whiskers), 1979

The following published under licence by Éditions
Gallimard, Paris:
Pierre Lapin (Peter Rabbit), 1980
Le Tailleur de Gloucester (Tailor of Gloucester), 1980
Deux Vilaines Souris (Two Bad Mice), 1980
Madame Piquedru la Blanchisseuse (Mrs Tiggy-Winkle), 1980
Le Méchant Petit Lapin (Fierce Bad Rabbit), 1980
La Famille Flopsaut (Flopsy Bunnies), 1980
Noisette l'Écureuil (Squirrel Nutkin), 1980
Jérémie Pêche-à-la-Ligne (Jeremy Fisher), 1980
Sophie Canétang (Jemima Puddle-Duck), 1980
Tom Chaton (Tom Kitten), 1980
Petit-Jean des Villes (Johnny Town-Mouse), 1982
Jeannot Lapin (Benjamin Bunny), 1982
Mademoiselle Mitoufle (Miss Moppet), 1982
Mademoiselle Trotte-Menu (Mrs Tittlemouse), 1982
Panache Petitgris (Timmy Tiptoes), 1982

German

Die Geschichte des Peterchen Hase (Peter Rabbit), 1934
   (style 1, English type; style 2, Gothic type)
Die Geschichte von den zwei bösen Mäuschen (Two Bad Mice),
   1939
Die Geschichte der Hasenfamilie Plumps (Flopsy Bunnies),
   1947
Die Geschichte von Frau Tiggy-Winkle (Mrs Tiggy-Winkle),
   1948

Die Geschichte von Samuel Hagezahn (Samuel Whiskers),
   1951
Die Geschichte von Herrn Reineke (Mr Tod), 1951

The following published under licence by Diogenes Verlag
AG, Zürich:
Die Geschichte von Peter Hase (Peter Rabbit), 1973
Die Geschichte von den beiden bösen Mäusen (Two Bad Mice),
   1973
Die Geschichte von Stoffel Kätzchen (Tom Kitten), 1973
Die Geschichte von Bernard Schnauzbart (Samuel Whiskers),
   1973
Die Geschichte von Herrn Gebissig (Mr Tod), 1973
Die Geschichte von Schweinchen Schwapp (Pigling Bland),
   1973
Die Geschichte von Eichhörnchen Nusper (Squirrel Nutkin),
   1978
Die Geschichte von Benjamin Kaninchen (Benjamin Bunny),
   1978
Die Geschichte von Emma Ententropf (Jemima Puddle-Duck),
   1978
Die Geschichte von den Flopsi Kaninchen (Flopsy Bunnies),
   1984
Die Geschichte von Frau Tupfelmaus (Mrs Tittlemouse), 1984

Icelandic

The following published under licence by Almenna
Bokafelagid:
Sagan um Pétur Kanínu (Peter Rabbit), 1983
Sagan um Tuma Kettling (Tom Kitten), 1983
Sagan um Jemínu Pollaönd (Jemima Puddle-Duck), 1983

Italian

Il Coniglio Pierino (Peter Rabbit), 1948

The following published under licence by Emme Edizione
S.p.A., Milan:
La favola di Ludovico Coniglio (Peter Rabbit), 1981
La favola di Tom Miciozzino (Tom Kitten), 1981
La favola della Signora Riccio Rotolò (Mrs Tiggy-Winkle),
   1981
La favola del Signor Geremia Pescatore (Jeremy Fisher), 1981
La favola dello Scoiattolo Nocciolina (Squirrel Nutkin), 1981
La favola di Costantino Coniglietto (Benjamin Bunny), 1981

Japanese

The following published under licence by Fukuinan-Shoten,
Tokyo (in Japanese):
The Tale of Peter Rabbit, 1971
The Tale of Benjamin Bunny, 1971
The Tale of the Flopsy Bunnies, 1971
The Tale of Tom Kitten, 1971
The Story of Miss Moppet, 1971
The Story of a Fierce Bad Rabbit, 1971
The Tale of Two Bad Mice, 1972

The Tale of Mrs Tittlemouse, 1972
The Tale of Johnny Town-Mouse, 1972
The Tale of Squirrel Nutkin, 1973
The Tale of Jemima Puddle-Duck, 1973
The Tale of Ginger and Pickles, 1973
The Tailor of Gloucester, 1974
The Tale of Mr Tod, 1974
The Tale of Samuel Whiskers or *The Roly-Poly Pudding*, 1974
The Tale of Mrs Tiggy-Winkle, 1983
The Tale of Mr Jeremy Fisher, 1983
The Tale of Timmy Tiptoes, 1983

Latin

Fabula de Petro Cuniculo (Peter Rabbit), 1962
Fabula de Jemima Anate-Aquatica (Jemima Puddle-Duck), 1965
Fabula de Domino Ieremia Piscatore (Jeremy Fisher), 1978

Norwegian

Fortellingen om Nina Pytt-And (Jemima Puddle-Duck), 1948

The following published under licence by Gyldendal Norsk Forlag, Oslo:
Eventyret om Petter Kanin (Peter Rabbit), 1972
Eventyret om Benjamin Kanin (Benjamin Bunny), 1972
Eventyret om Vipsen-Kaninene (Flopsy Bunnies), 1972
Eventyret om Tom Kattepus (Tom Kitten), 1972
Eventyret om To Slemme Mus (Two Bad Mice), 1974
Eventyret om Jeremias Fisker (Jeremy Fisher), 1974
Eventyret om Fure Tittenmus (Mrs Tittlemouse), 1974
Eventyret om Jon Bymus (Johnny Town-Mouse), 1974

Spanish

Pedrin el Conejo Travieso (Peter Rabbit), 1931

Swedish

Den Lillae Grisen Robinsons äventyr (Little Pig Robinson, no illustrations), 1938
Sagan om Pelle Kanin (Peter Rabbit), 1948
Sagan om Kurre Nötpigg (Squirrel Nutkin), 1954

The following published under licence by Bonniers Förlag, Stockholm:
Sagan om Pelle Kanin (Peter Rabbit), 1972
Sagan om Flopsijs Ungar (Flopsy Bunnies), 1972
Sagen om Tom Titten (Tom Kitten), 1972
Sagan om Två Busiga Möss (Two Bad Mice), 1972
Sagan om Moses Metare (Jeremy Fisher), 1974
Sagan om Fru Muslina (Mrs Tittlemouse), 1974
Sagan om Linus Lantmus och Stefan Stadsmus (Johnny Town-Mouse), 1974

Welsh

Hanes Dili Minllyn (Jemima Puddle-Duck), 1924
Hanes Pwtan y Wningen (Peter Rabbit), 1932
Hanes Meistres Tigi-Dwt (Mrs Tiggy-Winkle), 1932
Hanes Benda Bynni (Benjamin Bunny), 1948
Hanes Meistr Tod (Mr Tod), 1963

GENERAL INDEX

Compiled by Anne Stevenson Hobbs